C000156014

Cindi Myers is the author ~~...~~
novels. When she's not plotti~~ng...~~
she enjoys skiing, gardening, cooking, crafting and
daydreaming. A lover of small-town life, she lives with her
husband and two spoiled dogs in the Colorado mountains.

Lena Diaz was born in Kentucky and has also lived in
California, Louisiana and Florida, where she now resides
with her husband and two children. Before becoming a
romantic suspense author, she was a computer programmer.
A Romance Writers of America Golden Heart® Award
finalist, she has also won the prestigious Daphne du
Maurier Award for Excellence in Mystery/Suspense. To
get the latest news about Lena, please visit her website,
lenadiaz.com

Also by Cindi Myers

Eagle Mountain: Critical Response
Deception at Dixon Pass
Pursuit at Panther Point

Eagle Mountain Search and Rescue
Canyon Kidnapping
Mountain Terror
Close Call in Colorado

Eagle Mountain: Search for Suspects
Conspiracy in the Rockies
Missing at Full Moon Mine
Grizzly Creek Standoff

Also by Lena Diaz

A Tennessee Cold Case Story
Serial Slayer Cold Case
Shrouded in the Smokies

The Justice Seekers
Agent Under Siege
Killer Conspiracy
Deadly Double-Cross

The Mighty McKenzies
Smokies Special Agent
Conflicting Evidence
Undercover Rebel

Discover more at millsandboon.co.uk

KILLER ON KESTREL TRAIL

CINDI MYERS

THE SECRET SHE KEEPS

LENA DIAZ

MILLS & BOON

First Published in Great Britain 2023
by Mills & Boon, an imprint of HarperCollins*Publishers* Ltd
1 London Bridge Street, London, SE1 9GF

www.harpercollins.co.uk

HarperCollins*Publishers*
Macken House, 39/40 Mayor Street Upper,
Dublin 1, D01 C9W8, Ireland

Killer on Kestrel Trail © 2023 Cynthia Myers
The Secret She Keeps © 2023 Lena Diaz

ISBN: 978-0-263-30745-0

1023

This book is produced from independently certified FSC™ paper
to ensure responsible forest management.

For more information visit: www.harpercollins.co.uk/green

Printed and Bound in the UK using 100% Renewable Electricity at
CPI Group (UK) Ltd, Croydon, CR0 4YY

KILLER ON
KESTREL TRAIL

CINDI MYERS

For Gini.

Chapter One

Tony Meisner gritted his teeth against the pain in his leg and focused on getting down the trail. Hot sun beat down on the back of his neck; he wished he could stop and shed the blue Eagle Mountain Search and Rescue parka he was wearing. He had needed the coat on the shady side of the mountain, but here in the early-April sun, he was hot in spite of patches of snow on the ground. Carrying one corner of a stretcher with a one-hundred-eighty-pound man aboard was proving how out of shape he was after months off-duty.

But he was still mobile, he reminded himself—unlike the poor guy he was helping to carry on the litter. The hiker had fallen when a section of Kestrel Trail broke loose, and he sustained a closed fracture in his right leg. Thanks to Eagle Mountain Search and Rescue, he was on his way to a waiting medical helicopter. With time and therapy, he would hike again in a few months.

"And here's our relief," Danny Irwin called out as a quartet of SAR volunteers appeared over the next rise.

Tony tried not to groan as he lowered his corner of the litter and volunteers Eldon Ramsey, Ryan Welch, Carrie Andrews and Grace Whitlock moved in to carry their patient for the last leg to the helicopter-landing zone.

Tony pulled a bottle of water from his pack and eased onto a rock. "How are you doing?" Medical officer Hannah Richards, whose day job was a paramedic, sent him a concerned look.

"I'm fine," Tony said. He rubbed his hands down his thighs, both of which had sustained fractures in a climbing fall last year. The pain didn't matter, because he knew every day would be a little better. He could have waited a few more months to return to duty, but he had needed to be back with Search and Rescue where he belonged.

Caleb Garrison, a new volunteer with the group, settled beside Tony on the rock. "I understand you've been with SAR a long time," he said.

"Since I was seventeen, and I'm thirty-eight now," Tony said. He stowed his water bottle. Caleb was twenty-five. Tony was a SAR veteran at that age. He had a wealth of experience now, but he tried to stay open to the possibility of always learning more.

"You don't get burned-out?" Caleb gestured down the trail, in the direction the other volunteers had headed. "You must have seen some pretty intense stuff."

Tony nodded. He had responded to suicides, drownings, fatal falls and more than one mission that had gone from rescue to body recovery in a matter of minutes. "I guess this work is part of my DNA now," he said. "I missed it while I was out."

"Not many high school kids would be interested in doing this, I wouldn't think," Caleb said.

"We require all our volunteers to be eighteen now, but when I started, there wasn't an age limit," Tony said. He had been new in town, lost and lonely. Eagle Mountain Search and Rescue had welcomed him and given him a new family. He owed them more than he could ever repay.

He looked around and realized with a start that he and Caleb were sitting almost exactly where one of his first rescues had taken place. "I had only been with the group a few weeks when we found the body of a missing young woman right here," he said.

"No kidding?" Caleb said. "What happened to her?"

Tony shook his head. "We never found out. A teacher reported her missing a little over a week before. The medical examiner ruled she had been strangled, but I don't think the person who did it was ever found." He shrugged. "Thankfully, we don't get that kind of call very often. All of our missions don't have happy endings, but we usually have a good idea of exactly what happened." The *knowing* was a kind of closure. At the end of the day, a good mission might mean being confident they had done everything they could to help the person they'd been called to save.

"How many calls do you think you've been on all these years?" Caleb asked.

"A couple of thousand?" Tony guessed. In the early days, they might get one call a month. Now, with increased tourism and more people drawn to outdoor adventures, they might respond to half a dozen calls a month. Tony hadn't responded to all of them, but he had been part of the team for most and captain three different times.

"I'm amazed you remember a call that happened so long ago," Caleb said.

"You know what they say," Danny, who had been listening, chimed in. He winked and smirked at Tony. "You never forget your first."

"I remember them all," Tony said. Every mission was

seared on his memory—what the weather was like, who had participated, the challenges they had overcome, and whether or not their patient had survived.

"Did you ever think about not coming back to SAR after your accident?" Caleb asked.

"Never." Through the long days in the hospital and during his time in a rehabilitation facility—and the hours and hours of difficult and sometimes excruciating physical therapy—the prospect of returning to search and rescue work had sustained him and kept him going. Every time they responded to a call, SAR volunteers had the chance to make a difference—for the people whose lives they attempted to save and for their families. "We do this work for other people," Tony said. "But we do it for ourselves, too. Because it fills some space inside of us. At least, it does for me." Everyone wasn't as dedicated to Eagle Mountain SAR as he was. Maybe that meant they didn't need it to complete them the way he did.

Sometimes the memories of the rescues that hadn't ended well weighed on him, but most of the time he was proud to have made a difference. So little else in his life had.

KELSEY CHAPMAN HAD never been west of Mount Vernon, Iowa, when she steered her Honda Civic down the main street of Eagle Mountain, Colorado, on a bright Tuesday morning in early April. She slowed the car to a crawl and almost stopped in the middle of the street as she stared up at the snow-covered mountains surrounding the town. *This* was the place Liz had described as "the most beautiful spot in the world." Now Kelsey finally knew what her sister had meant.

She forced her gaze back to the street until she spotted

the sign ahead for the Alpiner Inn. Some of the tension went out of her shoulders as she pulled the car into an angled spot right in front of the inn. She had made the reservation online not knowing what to expect, but the place looked nice—a sort of Swiss Alps vibe, with fancy wood trim on the eaves and shutters, and window boxes awaiting flowers. She paused for a second on the sidewalk to gaze at the mountains again. Liz had been up there somewhere. All these years, Kelsey had wondered what had happened to her sister, and now she was finally going to find out. It hardly seemed real.

Her cell phone vibrated; she pulled it out of her pocket, glanced at the screen and then answered. "Hi, Mom. I just pulled up in front of my hotel here in Eagle Mountain."

"So you haven't found out anything yet?" Mary Chapman sounded out of breath, as she too often was these days.

"Are you using your oxygen, Mom?" Kelsey asked.

"I'm fine."

"The doctor said you needed to use it if you got short of breath."

"I don't like dragging that machine around. And I'm just excited, that's all. What is Eagle Mountain like?"

"It's very pretty." Looking down the street literally meant looking *down*, as the elevation fell from one end of the town to the other. "Lots of Victorian buildings, cute little shops and restaurants, and snow-covered mountains in the distance. Like a postcard."

"I'll never think of that place as anything but ugly," Mary said.

A little of Kelsey's excitement over being here drained away. "Now that I'm here, I understand a little better what Liz loved about it."

"Find out what happened to her," Mary said. "That's all I care about."

"I'll call you tomorrow," Kelsey said. "Maybe I'll know more by then, but it might take longer than a couple of days."

"Someone must know something," Mary said. "I tried to persuade your father to hire a private detective to go down there right after it happened, but he wouldn't hear of it."

"Dad wanted to pretend Liz never existed," Kelsey said.

"Don't be too hard on your father," Mary said. "Losing Liz broke his heart. He couldn't talk about her because it hurt too much. And he felt guilty, too. The two of them said some ugly things before she left."

"You would think he would want to know who killed his daughter," Kelsey said.

"I think he felt better not knowing," Mary said. "You don't understand that now, but someday, when you have children, you might."

They said goodbye, and Kelsey pulled her roller bag from the back of the Civic and trundled it inside the lobby. A blonde close to Kelsey's age looked up as she entered. "Hello," she said. "What can I do for you?"

"I'm Kelsey Chapman. I reserved a room for two weeks." She didn't know if that was enough time for what she needed to do, but she had to start somewhere.

"Welcome to Eagle Mountain. I'm Hannah, and my parents, Brit and Thad, own the inn. If you need anything while you're here, let one of us know."

Kelsey handed over her credit card and waited while Hannah processed the charge. The inn had what Kelsey imagined was Scandinavian decor—lots of pale wood and blue and white cushions, antique ice skates, and skis and sleds on the wall, in addition to many framed photos of the surrounding mountains. "Are you here on business or plea-sure?" Hannah asked as she returned Kelsey's credit card.

"Um, just vacationing," Kelsey said. Certainly no one was paying her to be here, but she couldn't consider her task a pleasurable one, either.

"There's lots to see and do around here," Hannah said. "Let me know if there's anything in particular you're inter-ested in. And definitely check with me before you go hik-ing. Some of the trails higher up still have too much snow on them to attempt just yet. I don't want to have to bring you back to town on a stretcher."

At Kelsey's alarmed look, Hannah laughed. "Sorry. I volunteer with Search and Rescue. Plus, my main job is as a paramedic. I've seen so many accidents I tend to want to warn everyone who is new around here."

Kelsey's heartbeat sped up. "How long have you been with Search and Rescue?" she asked.

"Six years."

Not long enough, Kelsey thought. "Do you have volun-teers who have been with the group longer?" she asked.

"Oh, sure. We've got one member who has been with the group almost twenty-one years."

"What's his—or her—name?" Kelsey asked.

Hannah looked amused. "Why are you so interested?"

Kelsey could have spilled the whole story then and there, but she was afraid people might dismiss her as a kook. "I'm always interested in people's stories," she said. "If I run into someone who's volunteered to save other people for twenty-one years, I want to know their name."

"It's Tony," Hannah said. "And you'll know when you see him because he's probably wearing a Search and Res-cue T-shirt or hoodie. I think that's his whole wardrobe."

She leaned closer, her tone confiding. "But seriously, don't let all this search and rescue talk make you think this is a dangerous place."

This is *a dangerous place*, Kelsey thought, but she only smiled as she accepted her room key from Hannah. *My sister died here*, she could have said. *And I'm trying to find out who killed her.*

TONY STAPLED THE last of the handouts for the training session he was teaching Tuesday evening on dealing with head injuries and added it to the stack at the end of the folding table. The power point equipment was hooked up and functioning. He had added a few new photographs from last week's rescue up on Kestrel Trail. The man they had rescued was at St. Joseph's in Junction and expected to make a full recovery.

A beep indicated a door had opened, and he turned to see a young woman with long dark brown hair leaning around the door. "Hello?" she called, tentative.

"Hello." Tony walked forward to meet her. He had been making more of an effort not to limp, and he thought the practice was paying off. His goal was to get back to his previous level of fitness, no matter how long it took. "What can I do for you?" he asked.

"I'm looking for Tony." She smiled, and he felt a tightness in his chest. She was beautiful, with straight hair almost to her waist; blue, blue eyes; and a slender yet decidedly feminine figure. She was also young—ten or even fifteen years younger than he was, which made him feel a little like a dirty old man.

"I'm Tony Meisner. What can I do for you?" Was she a

relative of someone they had previously rescued? Occasionally someone like that would stop by to say thank you.

"I'm Kelsey Chapman." She stared at him intently.

The name jolted him. "Elizabeth Chapman," he said without thinking.

The flash of pain in her eyes told him he had guessed right. "Yes," she said. "But everyone called her Liz." Her expression softened. "She was my sister. I didn't know if anyone would remember her after so much time."

"I remember," Tony said.

"You remember...finding her?" Kelsey said. "Someone told me you were with Search and Rescue back then. Were you there the day...the day they found her...her body?"

All these years, he had wondered if anyone would ever show up asking about Liz. She had come to town alone, and she had died alone, but he had never believed a person so full of sweetness hadn't had someone, somewhere, who loved her. The woman standing in front of him now looked enough like Liz that he could almost imagine they were standing together in the hallway at the high school, after class. "I was there," he said. "I knew Liz before she disappeared. And I was the one who found her."

Chapter Two

Wanting to make the most of her time in Eagle Mountain, Kelsey had stayed at the Alpiner only long enough to drop her luggage and freshen up. She had driven through town, trying to get a feel for the place and hoping to figure out where to begin her search. When she'd spotted the sign for Eagle Mountain Search and Rescue headquarters, she took a chance someone would be there who would know Tony Meisner or another veteran volunteer who could fill in some of the details about Liz's death. She hadn't expected to get this lucky.

When she thought about the Search and Rescue team who had located Liz's body and carried her down a mountain into town, she had pictured a bunch of buff, young guys. Lifeguards in ski jackets, maybe. But Tony Meisner had silver streaks in his thinning blond hair and even more gray in his neatly trimmed goatee. He had fine lines at the corners of his blue eyes, as if he had spent a lot of time squinting into the sun. The skin of his face was weathered, too, like someone who had lived a life outdoors. It was a nice face, though; one she liked looking at. Not movie-star handsome but attractive. And it was a kind face. One Liz would have liked.

Then the full impact of his words hit her. "You knew Liz?" she asked. "Before she died?" *Before she was murdered.* It was such a hard thing to say.

"She and I were the same age," Tony said. "We went to the same high school. Well, the only high school in Eagle Mountain." He raked a hand back through his hair. He had big hands, with long fingers, and a trio of colored rubber bracelets around his wrist. "She was one of the popular kids. One of the beautiful girls. I didn't have the nerve to speak to her." He half smiled, his expression rueful. "I just admired her from afar."

"You had a crush on her."

His cheeks burned. "I guess so."

"Lots of guys had crushes on Liz." Their home phone had rung constantly with calls from boys wanting to speak to Kelsey's pretty, older sister. After Liz had left, the silence made them that much more aware of her absence.

"You must have been pretty young when she went missing," Tony said.

"I was eight. But I remember sitting on the end of her bed, watching her at her dressing table while she got ready for a date. She had so many boyfriends, and I thought she was the most beautiful girl in the world." Her expression sobered. "If you knew her, you must have recognized her right away when you found her?"

AND NOW CAME the questions. He understood. People wanted to know what had happened to their loved ones, as if knowing all the details might help them understand the tragedy better, help them accept it more easily—though Tony didn't believe that was ever the case. He checked his watch. He still had an hour before the other volunteers were likely to start showing up. "Why don't you take your coat off and sit down," he said. "I'll get us some coffee and try to answer your questions."

He retreated to the tiny galley kitchen that had been installed when Search and Rescue had constructed these "new" headquarters ten years before. By the time he returned to the front of the building with two cups of coffee, Kelsey had shed her coat and settled into a folding chair near the front of the room.

Tony took the chair beside her and passed over one of the cups of coffee. He held out a handful of creamer and sugar packets. "Thanks." She plucked out a packet of sugar but didn't immediately add it to her drink. Instead, she studied him until he began to feel uncomfortable.

"What is it?" he asked.

"I'm trying to picture you at eighteen," Kelsey said. "That's really young to be working search and rescue, isn't it?"

"Actually, I was seventeen. Maybe too young, but nobody thought about that in the day," he said. No one had worried he would be scarred by the tragedies he had seen, and no one had tried to shield him from the sight of dead or mangled bodies. He thought he had handled things as well as could be expected but was aware not everyone would agree.

She sprinkled the sugar into her coffee and stirred. He sipped his own drink and sat back in the chair. "What do you want to know?" he asked.

He braced himself for the usual questions: How was she found? What did she look like? Did she suffer? What happened to her?

But that's not what Kelsey asked. "Do you think she was happy here? Before she was killed, I mean?"

An image popped into his head. Liz Chapman, in low-rise jeans and a pink tank top that rode up to show off a gold hoop in her navel, leaning back against the stone wall outside Rocky Top Ice Cream, laughing. The sun always seemed to shine on people like Liz, and others had gravitated to her. She had been popular but also genuinely nice. "I think she was happy," he said. "Or as happy as any teenager ever is."

Kelsey smiled. "I do remember the angst of high school." She rested her chin in her hand. "Did she ever talk about her home back in Iowa?" she asked. "About us?"

"I'm sorry," he said. "I didn't know her that well. I didn't even know until later that she wasn't living with her family here in town. I don't think I had ever met a high school student who was just...on her own."

"Not exactly on her own," Kelsey said. "She was living with a guy. Did you know him?"

He frowned. "I didn't know she was seeing anyone in particular." She had flirted with several guys at school, though he couldn't remember her dating anyone. Their senior class had been small—eighteen people. Everyone knew everything about everyone else, or so they had thought. After she died, they'd learned Liz had a lot of secrets.

Kelsey sipped her coffee. "Liz met a guy online. I don't know his name. The only thing my mom could remember was that he signed his emails 'Mountain Man.' He was supposedly twenty-one and lived in Eagle Mountain, Colorado. Liz said he had a good job and he wanted her to come live with him. She was eighteen, so my parents couldn't really stop her." She looked into her coffee. "I used to wonder sometimes how hard they tried. Does that sound awful?"

He shook his head. Then, because she still wasn't looking up at him, he said, "No. But some parents keep a tighter hold on their children than others." His own had kept almost no hold at all, happy to have him drift away from their responsibility.

Kelsey nodded but didn't seem inclined to continue the conversation. He wanted her to keep talking, so he picked up where she had left off. "I heard there was a guy the sheriff's department was looking for after she died," he said.

"Then why didn't they find him?" Her voice rose with agitation. "I looked online, and this is a small town—only about fifteen hundred people. And it was even smaller back then. How could someone not know this guy?"

"I don't think anyone at school knew she was living with a boyfriend," Tony said. "She was just another teenage girl, and she acted like one. She flirted with the popular guys and hung out with the other cool kids. I never saw her with an older guy."

Kelsey nodded. "That's what the police told my mother—that no one in town knew Liz was living with an older man. My mom said the cop who called practically accused her of making up the whole story. Or maybe there was no boyfriend and Liz lied to our parents about why she wanted to leave. But if that was true, how was she supporting herself? She didn't have any money saved up, and the cops said she didn't even have a part-time job after school. She had to be living somewhere and eating regular meals."

"Do they think the boyfriend killed her?"

"That seems the most likely thing, doesn't it?" Kelsey said. "Especially since he disappeared after she died. Mom said the police never even found Liz's belongings—just the items she had in her locker at school. She took two suitcases with her when she left home, and we don't have any idea what happened to them." She leaned toward him. "What did people in town say about her? Surely there was gossip."

"All I heard was that everyone was shocked that she was here on her own, without her family," he said. "People were worried some random serial killer had come to town. Things like this didn't happen in Eagle Mountain back then. Before Liz was killed, I don't think there had been a murder here in thirty years."

"Had Liz made any enemies while she was here?" Kelsey asked. "Were there any suspects at all?"

"I don't know," he said. "A few months after she was found, I graduated and left for a summer job with a white water raft company in Montana, and college after that, so I lost track of what happened." By the time he had moved back to town, no one was talking about Liz anymore.

"My dad was so angry after Liz left that he couldn't stand for anyone to even mention her name. My mom tried to stay in touch, but Liz didn't have a cell phone. Not many people did back then. I know Mom sent a few letters in the mail, but they came back unopened."

"That must have been hard." He thought about his own family, who hadn't really kept in touch with him, for different reasons. "Do your parents know you're here now?" he asked.

"My mom does. My dad died last year." She traced a finger around the rim of her coffee mug. "After he was gone, my mom started talking about Liz again. Mom has COPD and couldn't make this trip, but I think she's happy I decided to come." Her eyes met his, the blue of lake water, sad but not despairing. "We can't bring Liz back, but we'd still like to know what happened."

He nodded. "Of course you would. I would, too."

Kelsey pushed the half-full cup of coffee away. "I think I'm ready now," she said. "Tell me about when you found her."

Twenty years ago

TONY TOLD HIMSELF he would run all the way to the top of the trail, then allow himself to walk part of the way down. He had to get in better shape if he was going to keep up on search and rescue calls in the mountains. He was pretty tall—over six feet already, and he would probably add a couple more inches by the time he stopped growing. But he was too scrawny. His sweat-soaked T-shirt clung to his torso, showing the outline of his ribs. He had started lifting weights, but his brother had already complained Tony was eating him out of house and home. He tried to fill up at the restaurant where he worked after school, where one meal was included as part of his pay, but lately, he was always hungry.

He pushed himself to keep pounding up the trail, though he had a stitch in his side and his lungs hurt. He could do this. He wiped sweat from his eyes and squinted into the sun. Just a few more yards. One foot in front of the other.

Whomp! He fell hard, knees stinging when they hit the ground. He swore and rolled over, one hand shielding his eyes from the sun. He lay there panting, trying to catch his breath, then slowly sat up and looked around. At least no one else was around to see him. He leaned over and rubbed his left knee, which was bleeding a little. He felt his ankle. It seemed okay. With a grunt, he pushed himself up.

Then he looked around for whatever had tripped him. Something white lay in the middle of the trail. White and pink. At first he thought it was a deer bone. A leg, maybe.

He leaned over for a closer look, and something about the arrangement of bone and ligament sent a shudder through him. Heart pounding, he searched near the trail. To the right of the trail, up a small rise, something fluttered. Like a scarf floating in the breeze.

He hiked up toward it. Not a scarf. Hair, long and brown—a silk banner lifted by the wind.

He didn't recognize Liz Chapman right away. Death distorts the features, and animals had found her before he did. But something about the body was so familiar that he forced himself to look closer. He thought it might be Liz. Those same low-rise jeans, with the rip above the left knee. She had had this little gold chain with a heart pendant that she wore around her neck, but he didn't see it now. A pack rat or crow might have claimed such a treasure. He remembered those details from too many hours of watching Liz when she didn't know he was looking at her.

And everyone knew Liz was missing. There had been an article in the paper, and kids talked about it at school.

Tony closed his eyes, surprised to feel tears. Then he turned and began running again. Back down the trail and toward town.

"THEY TOLD US she had been strangled," Kelsey said, her voice bringing Tony back to the present and the quiet of the Search and Rescue building.

"I couldn't tell you anything about that," he said. He set his coffee cup aside and leaned forward, elbows on his knees. "When a body has been exposed to the elements, that takes a toll. And we have a lot of wild animals up here, too. I'm not trying to upset you—just trying to explain why it's hard to tell much just by looking."

She swallowed and nodded, but he knew she didn't really understand. He hadn't, until he had seen Liz. Later, there had been others: People ejected from motor vehicles. Fallen climbers. Skiers caught in avalanches. Fishermen who'd drowned. Every death horrible in its own way. The only comfort for him was knowing the person hadn't felt anything after their last breath. They didn't care what happened to their body after that.

"Was there anything about her body or the scene that struck you as unusual?" she asked.

"No." Not that death was ever ordinary, especially a violent death in the middle of nowhere. But he thought he knew what she meant. Had he seen anything that stood out, that might provide a clue as to what had happened to her? He shook his head. "There was nothing." The place where she had lain had been quiet and peaceful. "When I found her, I thought she must have fallen and hit her head," he said. "I was shocked to find out she had been murdered."

"I'd like to see where you found her," Kelsey said.

He nodded. "I can take you." Kestrel Trail was a pretty spot, one he had visited many times since—most recently when rescuing the fallen hiker. Liz had died there so long ago that there was nothing left to indicate her passing. Going there might help Kelsey find a little peace.

Chapter Three

Kelsey's friend Amber had suggested Kelsey begin her search at the Eagle Mountain newspaper. "Small town papers keep back issues," Amber, who had majored in journalism at the university where she and Kelsey had been roommates, had said. "You should be able to find the issues around the time your sister disappeared. And the local library probably has the high school yearbooks. You could check those for any pictures of her while she was there."

Part of Kelsey's mission here was to try to reconstruct what Liz's life had been like, in hopes of discovering how that had led to her murder, and to try to understand what was here that had led Liz to leave them all behind. On her second morning in Eagle Mountain, Kelsey went to the offices of the *Eagle Mountain Examiner.* A woman with a cascade of blonde corkscrew curls looked up from a desk as Kelsey entered. "May I help you?"

"I'm looking for some back issues of the paper," Kelsey said. "From twenty years ago."

The woman slid out of her chair and moved from behind the desk. "I'm Tammy Patterson," she said, and extended a hand.

"Kelsey Chapman." They shook, and Kelsey was sure

Tammy was taking in every detail, from her scuffed flats to her wind-blown hair.

"What dates of the paper are you looking for?" Tammy asked.

She gave her the information, anticipating just what Tammy would be able to unearth in the archives.

"Come through here to our morgue," Tammy said. "Let's see what we can find."

She led the way to a small room lined floor to ceiling with shelves that supported oversize scrapbooks full of past issues of the paper. Tammy pulled out a ladder, climbed it and started passing down volumes to Kelsey. "Each one of these books has six months of the paper," Tammy said. "We came out twice a week back then. Now we're just a weekly."

Kelsey deposited each volume on the table behind her before turning to accept the next. Tammy climbed down and dusted off her hands. "Is there something in particular you're looking for?" she asked.

"My sister disappeared from Eagle Mountain twenty years ago last May," she said. "Her body was found a little over a week later."

"I'm so sorry." Tammy rested a gentle hand on Kelsey's shoulder.

"Thanks. I just want to know as much as I can about what happened."

"Of course. Take as much time as you need. And if you want copies of anything, I can help you with that, too."

Left alone, Kelsey opened the first volume. She was two weeks into the month before she found the first story. "Local Woman Missing," declared the headline, with a photograph of Liz, one Kelsey hadn't seen before. She leaned closer, the musty odor of newsprint filling her nose as she studied the grainy image. Liz stood in a group of other girls, in what must have been a school gymnasium. She wore shorts and a T-shirt that read Lady Eagles on the front, and knee pads. What sport was she playing? Volleyball, maybe?

Liz's image had been singled out and enlarged, but her features were blurred. She was a pretty, young girl with a big smile, her hair pulled back in a ponytail. She looked younger than Kelsey remembered. Less glamorous when seen from Kelsey's adult perspective. Much too young to be on her own in the world.

Kelsey read the article, which reported that one of Liz's teachers had contacted the sheriff's department after being unable to reach Liz and finding that the address she had given on her school records was a vacant apartment. "Elizabeth Chapman, 18, moved to Eagle Mountain in late March of this year and enrolled in the local high school as a senior," the article continued. "When contacted in Ms. Chapman's hometown of Mount Vernon, Iowa, her father, Reginald Chapman, stated that his daughter had left home of her own accord shortly after her 18th birthday and the family had not been in contact with her since."

Kelsey turned the page, and glanced over ads for a video-rental place, a bowling alley and the local grocery store. The paper carried high school sports scores, horoscopes and an article about plans for the upcoming senior prom.

The next issue of the *Examiner* contained another article about Liz, this one without a picture. "Law enforcement officials are searching for information about a man Elizabeth Chapman may have been dating and possibly living with when she disappeared," the article reported. "Her family in Iowa know this man only as Mountain Man, from emails he sent to Elizabeth before she left Iowa. Students at Eagle

Mountain High who knew her say she never mentioned a male friend or talked about her living arrangements. 'We figured she lived with her parents, like the rest of us,' said Jessica Stringfellow, a teammate of Elizabeth's on the Lady Eagles volleyball team."

The third issue Kelsey opened contained papers from the first two weeks in May. Almost immediately, Liz's photo jumped out at Kelsey. Not the blurry school photograph but the professional shot taken at the beginning of Liz's senior year, before she left home. A coy smile on her lips, one hand tucked under her chin, Liz looked directly into the camera—a pretty, fresh-faced brunette, with a look of such confidence in her eyes it made Kelsey catch her breath. This picture had hung in the hallway of their home for several months after Liz left, until one day, Kelsey had come home from school to find it gone, along with every other photograph of her sister.

"Your father burned them all," her mother had told her shortly after her father's funeral. "He said it hurt too much to see them."

Kelsey would get a copy of this article and send it to her mom. At least she would have this one photo of her eldest daughter.

The article that accompanied the photo told of the discovery of remains near Kestrel Trail that were suspected to be those of Elizabeth Chapman, eighteen, who had disappeared approximately eight days before, after having run away from her home in Iowa to Eagle Mountain, supposedly to live with a man who had not been identified or located.

The article was continued on a second page, where Kelsey found a photograph of a young Tony Meisner, shaggy blond hair falling over his eyes, smooth faced and bony shouldered. His eyes were the same: pale hazel and sadder than anyone that young should be.

Two more articles after that reported that Liz appeared to have been strangled, probably very close to the time she disappeared. No one had come forward with information about Mountain Man, and her personal belongings, beyond the few items collected from her locker at the high school, had never been found.

Smaller articles over the coming weeks reported on the failure to locate the mysterious Mountain Man and the disappearance of Liz's personal belongings. Some students had organized a candlelight vigil for her at a local park. Kelsey studied the picture of the event—a cluster of girls and a few boys holding candles and looking solemn. Was one of the people in this photo the person who had killed her? Her gaze focused on a tall, skinny boy at the edge of the crowd, a mop of blond hair falling into his eyes, and she smiled. Tony looked so young and awkward in this photo, so different from the strong, capable man he appeared to be today. Yet this boy had the same light eyes, their expression shy and slightly troubled.

And then there was nothing else. No more updates or photos. Everyone had forgotten about Liz Chapman. Everyone except her family and Tony Meisner. Kelsey could tell from the way he had described finding Liz's body that he had never forgotten.

TONY HAD ARRANGED to pick up Kelsey from the Alpiner Inn Wednesday afternoon at five, after he got off work at Eagle Surveying. He had been in the field all day, and he came straight to the inn in his usual uniform of khaki hiking pants and an Eagle Mountain Search and Rescue T-shirt. "Hey, Tony," Hannah greeted him as he entered the lobby of the inn.

"Hello, Hannah."

Hannah's dad, Thad Richards, emerged from a back room. "Hi, Tony," he said. "You're looking fully recovered. Are you climbing again yet?"

"Starting to," he said. His doctors had cautioned him not to attempt much yet, but he was beginning with some easy ascents and descents.

"Did you need something from me?" Hannah asked.

"Actually, I'm here to see Kelsey."

Hannah didn't even try to hide her surprise. "Kelsey Chapman?"

"Hi, Tony. Sorry I kept you waiting." Kelsey came into the lobby and saved him from having to respond to Hannah—who apparently found the idea of a man like Tony with a woman like Kelsey incredulous.

Kelsey looked ready for a hike, in jeans and a long-sleeved T-shirt and hiking boots. She carried a day pack in one hand. "See you later," she said, and waved to Thad and Hannah.

"Are we in a hurry?" she called after Tony as he rushed across the parking lot.

He stopped and waited for her to catch up. "Sorry," he said. "I tend to walk fast." Really, he had just wanted to get away from Hannah's and Thad's stares.

He opened the passenger door of his truck, and Kelsey tossed in her pack, then climbed in after it. She was buckling her seat belt by the time he slid behind the wheel. "Thanks for doing this," she said.

"No problem. It's a beautiful day for a hike." He inserted the key and started the engine.

"I spent the morning at the newspaper office," she said. "I read some articles about Liz that were printed at the time of her disappearance. They talked about a place called Kestrel Trail?"

"That's where we're headed."

"Is it very far up in the mountains?" she asked.

"Not too far. A couple of miles."

"I'm just trying to figure out what Liz was doing up there. We don't have mountains—or really that much hiking—in Iowa."

"Hiking is really popular here," he said. "There are so many beautiful places to go."

"So her killer might have suggested they take a hike and then, when they were all alone, he strangled her?" She grimaced.

He thought about how to answer. "It could have happened that way," he said after a moment. "Even though the trails are popular, it's possible to spend a whole day hiking and never see anyone else. But I don't know if the sheriff's department believed she was killed where she was found. I never heard."

She swiveled toward him. "Do they think she was killed somewhere else and brought to that location?"

"I don't know." Liz had looked almost peaceful when he found her but also unreal—more like a mannequin than a once-living person. "You should talk to someone at the sheriff's department. Maybe they'll let you see their files." He glanced at her. "If you're sure you really want that much detail."

"I want detail." She faced forward again. "I want to find Mountain Man. Someone must have seen him or knows who he is, even if they never connected him to Liz."

"I'm sure local law enforcement looked hard for him," Tony said.

"I read a lot of other articles in the paper while I was looking for news about Liz," Kelsey said. "I found out that the Rayford County Sheriff's Department in 2002 had only three full-time deputies and the sheriff. And two of the officers and the sheriff were convicted of drug trafficking only two months after you found Liz's body. So I don't think they looked that hard for her killer at all."

He remembered hearing about that scandal now, though he had been away during that time. "The current sheriff isn't like that," he said. "Maybe he'll try to help you."

She turned toward him again. "You went away to school, but you came back here to live," she said. "How long were you away?"

"A little over two years." Long enough to get his associates degree and his license as a surveyor. He had landed a job with Eagle Surveying, signed back on with Search and Rescue, and hadn't left since.

"Do a lot of people do that? Come back here after they graduate?"

"Some do. Quite a few, I guess." He could name a dozen of his classmates who still lived in town. "There are a lot of people here who went to school with Liz, if that's what you're getting at."

"Could you introduce me to some of them?" she asked.

"I could do that." He wondered how much they would remember. Had Liz made as much of an impression on them as she had on him?

They reached the trail head and got out. Kelsey slipped on her pack, then turned in a slow circle, looking up at the surrounding mountain peaks. "This really is gorgeous," she said.

"In another month, most of the snow will be melted and the meadows will be carpeted with wildflowers," he said. "I'm sorry you'll miss it." She hadn't said how long she intended to stay in Eagle Mountain, but she probably had a job and family and friends to go back to.

"It's still beautiful," she said.

He led the way up the trail, careful to keep his steps slower. Behind him, he could hear her breathing hard. It always took a few weeks for people from other places to adjust to the altitude. "Tell me if I'm walking too fast," he said.

"You're fine." She moved in closer. "Have you lived in Eagle Mountain all your life?"

"No. I moved here the year before Liz." In a small town where most of the students had been together since preschool, he had been the "new kid" until Liz had shown up.

She didn't respond right away, but he could sense her waiting for him to elaborate. She was expecting to hear about his family moving to town for work or because they had vacationed here and loved it. "I came to live with my brother," he said. "He was sixteen years older than me."

"Oh." Another long pause. "Did something happen to your parents?"

Something *had* happened. "They got tired of raising me." He glanced at her, trying to read her expression behind her dark sunglasses but unable to do so. Still, she didn't make any noises that sounded like pity. "I was a surprise baby. Way later than my brother. My mom made no secret of the fact that she was horrified when she got the news that she was pregnant with me. The summer I turned sixteen, she sent me to stay with my brother. At the end of the summer, she informed me that she and Dad felt it would be better for everyone if I stayed here. Then they sold the house and moved to Arizona."

"Wow," Kelsey said. "How did your brother react?"

"He tried to be nice about it. He said he was happy to have me here, but who is really happy to take in a teenager? Especially an unhappy teenager?"

"I saw your picture in the paper. You were cute."

"I was a skinny, awkward kid—too shy to string two sentences together."

"How did you get involved with Search and Rescue?"

The tension in his shoulders eased. Here was something he was more comfortable talking about. "I saw a poster at school, about a program to be a junior SAR volunteer. The idea was to get young people interested in the work. Me and one other kid showed up to the first meeting. I was the only one who came back for the second. Rather than run a program for one person, they decided to treat me like any other volunteer, and I started training. Nobody there seemed to care that I was from someplace else or too quiet or awkward. They treated me like everyone else and made me feel like I wasn't a total loser. I could make a difference." He glanced at her again. "And now you know way more about me than you want to."

She hooked her thumbs beneath the straps of her pack. "You and I have more in common than I thought," she said.

"How is that?"

"My parents didn't move away or send me to live with a relative when I was in high school. But they might as well have. After Liz died, it was as if every bit of life went out of our house. They were so wrapped up in guilt and grief

I might not have even existed. They stopped caring about anything. It felt like they stopped caring about me."

He heard the pain in her voice and felt it in his chest—that pain of being abandoned. When he had first come to Eagle Mountain, his brand-new driver's license told him he was almost an adult. He ought to have been able to take care of himself. But inside, he'd felt like a little boy, wanting to cry out for his mother but not daring to do so. "I'm sorry," he said. "That's rough."

"I didn't just miss my parents," she said. "I missed Liz, too. She was ten years older than me, but she never acted like I was in the way. She liked hanging out with me and was always taking me with her and playing with me. If I got scared in the middle of the night, I would crawl into her bed, not my parents'." She paused, head down as she walked up the trail. Tony said nothing, knowing that sometimes silence offered the greatest comfort.

"The night before she left, she came to my room and gave me a present," Kelsey continued after a moment. "It was a little gold necklace with a heart. She had one just like it. She said she wasn't ever going to take off her necklace, because it reminded her of me. She had to go away for a little while, but she would come back to see me soon. She would bring Mountain Man with her so I could meet him, and she knew I would like him as much as she did.

"I cried and begged her not to leave me, but she said she had to." Her voice broke, and she cleared her throat. "She said when you loved someone, you wanted to be with them—and as much as she loved me, she needed to be with him right now."

"She called him 'Mountain Man' when she was talking to you?" Tony asked. "Not his name?"

"She said he had asked her not to use his real name."

"Do you think it's possible she didn't *know* his real name?" Tony asked.

"I don't know. I've thought about it a lot over the years, and I wondered if he wasn't some serial killer who lured young women over the internet, then murdered them. I used to go online and look for similar crimes, but I never found any."

"What did she tell you about him?" Tony asked. "I've been trying to think of all the men I knew in town then. Maybe I knew this guy and didn't even realize it."

"She said he was twenty-one, he was good-looking, and he had a good job and his own apartment in Eagle Mountain, Colorado."

"'Good-looking' how?"

"She didn't say. And I didn't ask. I mean, I was eight years old. I thought *good-looking* meant he looked like an actor on television."

He laughed in spite of himself, and she laughed too. The sound was like tension being released from a spring. "I'm hoping she confided more in someone here," she said. "Maybe a girlfriend she was close to."

"I'll find some people for you to meet," he said. "I want to help."

He stopped at the top of a rise and looked around, orienting himself. The air was still and hushed, with green grass showing between patches of melting snow and clouds scudding along in a cerulean sky. "Is this the place?" Kelsey asked, her voice quiet.

"This is where I found the first bone." He pointed to the trail beneath their feet. "The rest of her was up there, on that little ledge." He started out, picking his way around snow and across rock until he came to the place. For a moment, he imagined he saw her there, her long hair floating on the breeze; his mind was playing tricks on him.

Kelsey stared at the site for a long time, not saying anything, then looked up at him. "Were you afraid?" she asked.

He blinked. "No. I wasn't afraid. Just...sad."

"Sad because she was your friend?"

"Yes. And sad because I couldn't help her."

"It was too late for you to rescue her."

He nodded. He hadn't thought about it like that, but he supposed that was true.

"How far have we hiked up the trail?" Kelsey asked.

"A little over two miles."

"So you had a long way to run for help that day. And a long way to carry the body down after that."

"Not so far in search and rescue terms. Some days we travel a lot farther, and not on defined trails."

"It still seems such a remote place for Liz to come with her killer." She shook her head. "And I can't see someone hauling a dead body all the way up here."

"Is there anything else you'd like to see while we're here?" he asked.

"No. I'm ready to leave. Thank you for bringing me up here." She hooked her arm through his and leaned against him. "I wish you had known her better," she said. "I think she would have liked you."

He wasn't so sure about that. The Liz he had known was one of those girls who were aware of the power of their beauty. She hadn't been cruel, but she was oblivious to the feelings of those outside her immediate circle. She might have noticed Tony, but only to assess that he wasn't someone she needed to be concerned about. He'd moved outside of her orbit. It was probably the way he struck most people. He had a lot of friends in Eagle Mountain, but he wasn't really close to anyone. He didn't let that bother him. Some people were loners, and he was one of them.

Chapter Four

Kelsey had never been inside a police station before—or, in this case, a sheriff's department. She steeled herself to have to plead to see her sister's case file; she was determined to make the best argument possible to be allowed access. But instead of the brusque desk sergeant she had imagined—possibly from watching too many crime shows—at the Rayford County Sheriff's Department, she was greeted by a pleasant older woman with a cap of white hair, blue-rimmed glasses and earrings in the shape of dragonflies. "How can I help you?" the woman, whose name tag identified her as Adelaide, asked.

"My name is Kelsey Chapman, and my sister, Elizabeth, was murdered here over twenty years ago," she said. "The case was never solved, and I would like to see her case file."

Adelaide nodded. "Let me find someone to speak with you," she said, and disappeared through a door.

While she waited, Kelsey studied the photographs on the walls of the small waiting area. Men and women in khaki uniforms posed for the camera, in groups and alone. One prominent photo showed a very handsome dark-haired man looking into the camera lens with a solemn, determined expression.

"Sheriff Walker will see you now," Adelaide said. She led Kelsey down a short hallway to an office, and the man in the photo, who was even better looking in person.

"Travis Walker," he introduced himself with a firm handshake.

Kelsey sat across from him, and he lowered himself into his leather desk chair. "Your sister was Elizabeth Chapman?" he asked.

Kelsey nodded.

"You must have been very young when she left home."

"I was eight."

"Why are you looking into her death now?" he asked.

Kelsey told herself she should have anticipated this question. Her first instinct was to reply "Because she was my sister," but she expected the sheriff wanted more. "My parents refused to talk about what happened when I was growing up," she said. "After my father died, my mother opened up a little more, but she couldn't tell me much. I really think I need to know the details, to put together a picture of what happened here." She leaned forward, gripping the edge of the desk. "There was a big age difference between me and my sister, but I loved her very much. I believe she loved me."

"I've asked someone to retrieve the file for you," the sheriff said. "When I took over as sheriff, I reviewed all our cold case files, so I'm familiar with your sister's case. There are some things in there that would be difficult for most people to see. When Elizabeth's body was found, it had been exposed to the elements for a number of days."

"I'm aware." She wet her dry lips. "I've spoken with Tony Meisner."

"The photos are in a separate envelope within the file. You don't have to view them if you don't want to."

Kelsey didn't want to, but she felt she needed to. She nodded.

"No one on the force now was part of the sheriff's department back then," Travis said. "The force was much smaller at that time, and there were problems with corruption."

"I saw some articles in the paper," she said, "when I was researching Liz's murder."

Travis's mouth tightened. "I'm not making excuses for them. The case is still considered open—and if, after reviewing the file, you believe you have new information that can help locate her killer, I want to hear it."

"Of course."

"Also, if you have questions about anything in the file, I or one of my deputies will do our best to answer them. Sometimes the things we do in the course of an investigation don't make sense to civilians."

"Thank you." What else could she say? She hadn't expected it to be so easy to get the information they had collected about Liz's death.

A knock on the door interrupted them, and a big, blond deputy came in and set a trio of cardboard file boxes on the desk. Kelsey's eyes widened. "There's more than I expected," she said.

"This doesn't include the physical and DNA evidence," the sheriff said. "That's stored at a separate facility. But there are descriptions in the case files."

"You have DNA evidence?"

"Yes. We've run it through the state and national databases and attempted matches a couple of times but have never come up with anything."

"So if you had a good suspect, you could take a sample of his DNA, and if it matched, you would know you had the killer?"

"Yes," the sheriff said. "If you're aware of someone we should take a closer look at, be sure to let us know."

"I will." She had a lot of questions about Liz and what had happened to her, but she wanted to wait until after she read the file to see what information she could glean from there.

The sheriff stood, and she rose also. "Deputy Ellis will show you to a room where you can look through these. Take your time, and if you need anything, let us know."

The blond deputy picked up the file boxes again and led the way to a small, windowless gray room with a single table and chair. A box of tissues sat in the middle of the table. "The ladies' room is at the end of the hall on the right, and there's a watercooler right outside the door," he said as he set the boxes on the table. "Can I get you some coffee or anything else?"

"No thank you." She laid a hand on top of the boxes. "I appreciate your help."

He nodded. "I'm sorry for your loss." Then he left the room and closed the door behind him.

Kelsey settled in the chair. It wasn't particularly comfortable, but she wasn't here to be comfortable. She wondered if this was a room where they interviewed suspects. Overhead, the round eye of a camera was focused on the table. There was probably a microphone, too. Was she being recorded right now? If so, it was going to be a very boring tape.

She set her purse on the floor beside her chair and removed her jacket, then lifted the lid on the first box. Her initial impression was of many thin pieces of paper shoved into file folders. Most of the papers were forms, with many

lines of typed or handwritten narrative. It took a moment
to orientate herself. The first piece of paper was the initial
missing person report, filed by a woman named Deborah
Raymond, identified as an English Literature teacher at
Eagle Mountain High School. She had stated that Liz had
failed to attend classes for the past three days. None of her
friends had reported seeing her. Ms. Raymond had visited
the home address in Elizabeth's school records and found
a vacant apartment. She'd spoken with a neighbor, who had
told her no one had lived in the apartment for months. The
woman hadn't known Liz.

Subsequent papers included reports of interviews with
other teachers, Liz's friends and the owner of the empty
apartment, who reported the rental had been unoccupied
since the first of the year. Liz had never lived there.

She studied the names of the friends: Madison Gruenwald, Jessica Stringfellow, Marcus White, Ben Everett, Sally
d'Orio. None of them had known what had happened to Liz.
All of them had seemed surprised to learn that she didn't
live with her mother and father. School administrators had
reported that Liz had enrolled with all the proper paperwork, including transcripts from the school she had attended
in Iowa. None of the people questioned had ever met Liz's
parents, but since the enrollment forms had been properly
signed, administrators hadn't been alarmed.

Finally, there was a record of a telephone interview with
Kelsey's mother and father, who had only reported that Liz
left home after she'd turned eighteen; there was no mention
in this report of Mountain Man.

Fascinated, Kelsey kept reading and began to take notes,
writing down the names of everyone the sheriff's department had interviewed and any information she hadn't known

before. Two weeks after Liz was reported missing, Kelsey found the first mention of Mountain Man. A follow-up interview with Mr. and Mrs. Chapman, conducted by a sheriff's deputy in Iowa on behalf of the Rayford County Sheriff's Department, had revealed Liz's online relationship with someone who'd signed off on his emails as "Mountain Man." He and Liz had met on an internet chat board for the band Phish, then began a long correspondence.

Kelsey turned the page and stared at printouts of some of these conversations, apparently printed from the Chapman-family computer:

MountainMan MountainMan@hotmail.com
To: RealLiz@iowanet.com
Subject: Life Together

Parents always have a hard time letting their chicks leave the nest, but you're a grown woman and you know your own mind. It's one of the things I love about you. Can't wait to have you here with me. I want to show you the mountains. I want to be a real lover to you, not just on paper. Let me know when you're ready and I'll send you the bus tickets.

RealLiz RealLiz@iowanet.com
To: MountainMan@hotmail.com
Subject: Re: Life Together

I'm ready! Send the tickets. I am getting everything together here. I can't believe how easy it was to get everything I needed from school. I walked into the vice principal's office and told him I was moving to Colorado and needed my transcripts and stuff to enroll in school there and he printed out everything right then, no questions asked. I haven't told anyone else (except the parents, who are in denial. They're pretending I'm not going to go through with this, but I am!)

MountainMan MountainMan@hotmail.com
To: RealLiz@iowanet.com
Subject: Re: Life Together

I'm so proud of you, Babe. You are going to love it here. Look for the tickets in the mail ASAP. Remember what we talked about—don't give your folks any way to find us, in case they get it into their heads to try to keep you from doing what you've decided to do. After you're settled here you can send them your new address but for now, let's keep it a secret.

RealLiz RealLiz@iowanet.com
To: MountainMan@hotmail.com
Subject: Ready or Not, Here I Come

Got the tickets and my bags are packed. I am so ready. Big fight with the parents last night. I thought Pop was going to stroke out. But I'm 18 and he can't stop me. The hardest part is leaving little Kelsey behind. But we'll get her out for a visit as soon as we can—maybe this summer. She's a cool kid—I know you'll like her.

Three days and counting til I see you. Can't wait! Hugs and kisses, Liz.

Kelsey blinked back tears and reached for the tissue box. Hearing Liz describe her as a "cool kid" made a lump swell in her throat that threatened to overwhelm her. She got up and fetched water from the cooler in the hall. *Keep it together*, she told herself. She still had a long way to go.

She returned to the files. The next folder contained correspondence with Hotmail and Iowanet, trying to discover the identity of Mountain Man, but this led nowhere. Hotmail verified that the account originated in Eagle Mountain, Colorado, yet could not provide a name, address or any other information about the account holder. But a handwritten scrawl at the bottom of one page noted that the Mountain Man account had been closed on February 14—the day Liz arrived in Eagle Mountain.

There was a gap in the paperwork after that. For more than a month, nothing was added to the file. Then another flurry of reports, dated May 23. First up was Tony's statement about finding the body. It included everything he had told her—clearly the details hadn't faded with time. There were statements from the deputies who'd responded to the scene and the coroner's autopsy report.

Kelsey hesitated before reading this last, then plunged in. The clinical language was distancing, making it easier to absorb the information without really relating it to her sister. The victim had been a Caucasian female, aged seventeen to thirty; brown hair, blue eyes; five feet, seven inches tall; approximately 125 pounds. Her remains had been found by a hiker midmorning on May 23.

A detailed description of the physical examination and findings followed, but the salient points for Kelsey were that Liz had died of strangulation approximately two weeks before the remains were found. She had no other significant injuries, though broken fingernails and skin cells recovered from beneath her fingernails indicated she had struggled with her attacker. There was no evidence of sexual assault or recent sexual activity. No indication of illegal or prescription drug use was found. The skin cells underneath her fingernails had been collected for a possible DNA match to any suspects.

Kelsey closed her eyes and thought for a moment of her sister struggling with her killer. Liz had been young and fit. Maybe a woman could have overpowered her, but her killer was probably a man. She liked men and always had at least one trailing after her. She had come to Eagle Mountain to meet her Mountain Man. And with her last breath, she had fought with her killer, collecting the evidence beneath her fingernails that might one day be used to convict him.

It has to be Mountain Man, Kelsey thought. If he wasn't the killer, why hadn't he come forward to report that Liz was missing? If he had really loved her, he would have been frantic, wouldn't he?

But if he had killed her, he would want to make sure no one knew he existed.

Someone must know. Eagle Mountain was a small town. All she needed was to find one person who knew about Mountain Man. Then the sheriff could test for a DNA match.

The first file box was almost empty now. A thick brown envelope labeled Crime Scene Photos lay at the bottom. Kelsey fished it out and weighed it in her hand. Did she really want to see these?

She did not, but what if she—the person who knew her sister better than any of these dispassionate investigators—spotted something at the scene that could lead to the killer? It was probably a fantasy, thinking she would arrive and miraculously solve the crime, but she couldn't let go of the idea.

She took a deep breath and slid the stack of photos out from the file.

The first photo wasn't too shocking—a distant view taken from the trail of the area where the body lay. Various people stood around the area Kelsey recognized as the bench where she had stood with Tony.

Subsequent photos moved in closer, like a slow-motion movie. When she finally arrived at the body, it was so unlike the live Liz that at first it was like looking at a doll or some other inanimate object—limbs sprawled, hair trailing. Nothing about the image suggested the lively, loving girl Liz had been.

Next came a series of close-ups of the body. Kelsey skimmed these, rapidly shuffling through them. She wasn't going to see anything here except the stuff of nightmares.

She paused when she reached a series of photos of the scene. Apparently, these were items found on the ground near the body—a cigarette butt, a ruler laid beside it to show that the size was two centimeters long. A note on the back indicated the brand of cigarette. A tube of lip balm and a single gum wrapper received similar treatment.

Next came photos taken indoors: A pair of women's jeans, size four, a small rip above the left knee. A pink long-sleeved blouse, ruffles at the wrists. Three gold hoops—a pair of earrings and a navel ring.

Kelsey stilled and reached up to finger the necklace she was wearing. She had rarely taken off the small gold heart on a gold chain since Liz had given it to her over twenty years before. Liz had one just like it, and Kelsey couldn't remember seeing her sister without it since she had received it as a gift from their grandmother on her sixteenth birthday. She gripped the heart and stared at all that was left of her sister. "What happened to you?" she whispered.

THURSDAY AFTER WORK, Tony hit the gym. He did a few stretches to warm up, then grabbed a pair of twenty-pound dumbbells and set up for lunges. Left side. Right side. He concentrated on keeping the proper form, not leaning forward. His recently mended legs protested at the strain, and the surgery scars down both legs glowed white against his flushed skin. After ten reps, he rested, sweat beading on his forehead. Then he did another ten. And another.

He sat on the weight bench for bicep curls, muscles bulging. He was still tall and thin but no longer skinny. Hours of climbing had sculpted the muscles of his back, chest and arms. He didn't lift out of vanity—who was he going to impress? But strength might save his life one day, or the life of someone else.

"Hey, Tony."

He looked up and smiled as Ted Carruthers dropped his towel onto the bench next to Tony's. Ted was one of the founders of Eagle Mountain Search and Rescue. He had been captain the year Tony joined and had served as the younger man's mentor. Retired now in his midsixties, Ted still served as the group's historian and was writing a book about some of their most exciting rescues. "How's it going, Ted?"

"Days like this, I think I retired too soon," Ted said. He sat on the bench and began pulling on elastic knee braces. "I'm still in better shape than most guys half my age."

Tony said nothing. Ted had been pressured to retire from search and rescue work after a series of mistakes and bad choices that had endangered his fellow volunteers and the people they served. Ted was a good guy, but he let ego get in the way of good sense sometimes. Having him as historian—still available to consult, if necessary—was a better fit for the group these days. No one had a better understanding of local topography than Ted, who had lived and worked in the area for forty years.

"I heard everyone came down without a scratch off Mount Baker the other day," Ted said, referring to the rescue SAR had made of a skier who had been trapped in a couloir.

"Everything went smooth as butter," Tony agreed. He resumed curling the weight, moving slowly and deliberately.

"Anything new with SAR?" Ted selected a dumbbell and lay back for a series of chest presses.

"Do you remember that girl who went missing not long after I joined SAR—Elizabeth Chapman?"

Ted sat up. "What made you think of her?" he asked.

"Her sister is in town. Younger sister. She was only eight when Elizabeth—she calls her Liz—left home. She's trying to find out what happened and came to me because she heard I'd found the body. But you were captain then. You probably remember more than I do."

Ted lay back down again and resumed exercising. "Why would she want to bring all that up again after twenty years?" he asked.

"They never found out who killed her sister," Tony said. "I guess she just wants to know more of the story."

"Not much to tell," Ted said. "We found her body up on that mountainside. No clues. We'll probably never know what happened."

"Still, I think Kelsey would like to talk to you."

Ted grunted, thrusting the weights. He lowered them and turned his head to look at Tony. "What's the sister like?"

"She looks a lot like Liz." The Liz he remembered from high school.

"What does she do when she's not digging up the past?"

"I don't know. I didn't ask her."

Ted snorted. "I bet you don't know anything else about her, do you?"

He knew that she had felt abandoned by her family, the way he had. He knew she had loved her sister and felt close to her in spite of their age difference. He knew he felt comfortable with her, something he didn't feel with most people. "We talked about her sister," he said.

"It's just as well you're a bachelor," Ted said. "You would drive a woman up the wall."

"Says a man who's never been married himself."

"Never married, but I've had plenty of women in my life. You might not believe it now, but I was quite the stud in my day."

Tony bit the inside of his mouth to keep from laughing at the use of the word *stud*. He did have memories of the younger Ted escorting various women around town, several of them married to other people. He had long suspected the older man liked women he wouldn't have to commit to. "Will you talk to Kelsey Chapman?" he asked.

"Sure, I'll talk to her." He sat up again. "I can't tell her any more than you did. Probably less since I didn't know that girl while she was alive. But if she wants to know how Search and Rescue operated back in the day, I'm happy to bore her with all the details."

"Great. I'll tell her." It would give him an excuse to talk to Kelsey again. The thought was a nice distraction from the pain of working out.

Chapter Five

Kelsey had set aside the second file box and was preparing to start on the third when someone knocked on the door of the little room. She looked up to see Sheriff Walker. "How's it going?" he asked.

"I'm learning a lot," she said. She looked at the notes she had made. "I think the killer had to be Mountain Man."

Sheriff Walker leaned against the door frame, arms crossed. "What do you know about him?"

"Not much. Liz never used his real name. She told us he was in his early twenties, had his own place and a good job. She didn't say what kind of work he did. She never described him, except to say he was good-looking." She shook her head. "I can't believe no one who knew Liz had heard of him."

"He apparently wanted her to keep their relationship secret."

"Why?"

"Maybe he was married. Maybe he was older than he had told her. There could be a lot of reasons. She may have thought it was exciting or romantic, sneaking around."

"She might have. Mom always said Liz loved drama."

He nodded toward the file boxes. "Is there anything else in there that stood out for you?"

"Liz's necklace is missing." She pulled out her heart necklace again. "Like this. She had one like it, and she never took it off. But I didn't see it listed in the description of her clothing and jewelry."

He leaned forward to study the gold heart. "I'll double-check the evidence locker, but if she was wearing that when she was found, it would have been listed. There were problems with the department back then, but it looks as if they did a thorough investigation."

"Yes," she agreed. "They talked to everyone who knew Liz, even a little bit. But they still couldn't find out who killed her."

"There's no statute of limitations on murder," the sheriff said. "If we find any new information, we'll investigate it."

She nodded. "Thank you."

He straightened. "Take as much time as you like. If you have any more questions, come to my office or ask someone to find me."

"Thank you."

He left, and she prepared to examine the last box, which seemed to include follow-up interviews. She hadn't gotten far when another knock interrupted her. The door opened and Adelaide entered, a to-go cup in one hand, a paper bag in the other. "I brought you some lunch," she said. She set the bag and cup on the table, then took a chair from the corner and moved it across from Kelsey and sat. "And I thought I'd keep you company while you ate. Give you a break from all this." She nodded at the case files. "It can be pretty grim, reading cold case files."

"You've done it?" she asked. She popped the lid on the

cup and saw a tea bag floating in hot water. Not her favorite, but she wouldn't be picky. The sandwich was chicken, which *was* her favorite. "You didn't have to bring me lunch," she added.

"You need to eat," Adelaide said, and Kelsey smiled.

"To answer your question, yes, I've looked through case files before," Adelaide said. "My husband was a police officer, then a detective, in Cleveland for many years before we retired to Eagle Mountain. After he passed, I was bored silly. I applied for an opening for an office manager here at the sheriff's department, and I've been here ever since."

"Were you here when my sister disappeared?" Kelsey asked.

"No. But I know the stories you've probably heard about the sheriff's department back then." She met Kelsey's gaze, her expression stern. "I want you to know the men and women here now aren't like that. Sheriff Walker is a straight arrow. A good man, and every deputy he hires is the same. If they weren't, they wouldn't be here. If you find any information about your sister's killer, you can trust them with it. You can trust them to do the right thing."

Kelsey nodded and chewed a bite of sandwich. After she swallowed, she said, "I know the department didn't have the best reputation back then, but from what I'm reading, they did a pretty thorough investigation. They collected a lot of evidence, and they interviewed lots of people who knew Liz. There just isn't much to go on. Liz supposedly came to Eagle Mountain to be with a guy she called Mountain Man. No one here has heard of him, and I can't find anyone who knew his real name or who even saw him with Liz."

"Could she have made him up?"

Kelsey sipped her tea. "She could have. But I never knew

her to lie before. And there are lots of emails between her and this guy, and he sent her bus tickets to get from Iowa to Eagle Mountain. It would be a pretty elaborate ruse for her to go to the trouble to make all that up. And how would she have even heard of Eagle Mountain all the way back in Iowa?"

"So the guy was probably real, just very cagey," Adelaide said. "He probably told her not to tell anyone who he was. He would have made it sound mysterious and romantic. Some girls really like that sort of thing."

"Liz liked that sort of thing," Kelsey said. "My dad used to tease her, when they were still getting along, about being a drama queen."

Adelaide nodded. "You weren't the drama queen type, I'm thinking."

Kelsey looked down at the table. "I guess I figured my parents had suffered enough," she said. She had been a quiet kid—too quiet, really. She did well in school and went straight home afterward, the loss of her sister like a shield wrapped around her, keeping everyone else at bay. No one else could understand what she had been through, so why even try to make friends?

Later, in college, she had opened up a little more. She had joined several groups on campus, played tennis and started dating. But she had never gotten really close to anyone. She wasn't sure she ever could.

A phone rang and Adelaide pulled a handset from her pocket. "I'll leave you to your lunch," she said. "Remember, if it gets too overwhelming, you can always come back tomorrow. Those records have sat in those boxes twenty years. They can wait for you a day longer."

She left the room, the door closing softly behind her.

Kelsey rewrapped the rest of the sandwich and set it aside, then reached for the next folder in the next box. Liz had waited a long time for justice. Kelsey didn't want her to have to wait even one day more.

THE DAY AFTER his meeting with Kelsey, Tony came home from work to find an unfamiliar motorcycle occupying the space where he usually parked his truck. A young man with blond hair to his shoulders and ragged jeans moved out of the shade of the arbor at one end of the front deck as Tony walked up from the street. "Hey, Uncle Tony," he called. "Long time no see."

Tony stopped and stared. "Chris?" he asked, taking a closer look at his brother's youngest boy. Chris had been three when Tony moved out of his brother's home and left for college, and Tony had seen him only sporadically in the twenty years since.

"The one and only." Chris held his arms wide, then walked over to Tony and enveloped him in a rib-crushing hug. They were the same height and had the same thin frame, though Chris was less muscular and still had a bit of a baby face.

"What are you doing here?" Tony asked when Chris finally released him.

"I thought maybe I could stay with you for a while." Chris smiled, but Tony read doubt in his hazel eyes.

"So you just decided to come all the way from Denver for a visit?"

"Yeah, well... Mom and Dad sort of kicked me out."

Tony's stomach knotted. "What happened?"

Chris looked up at the sky. "I remember he took you in

when you were a little younger than me, so I figured you could return the favor."

"Why did your parents kick you out?" Tony asked again.

Chris stared at the ground and scratched the back of his neck. "I got in a little trouble—borrowed a friend's car and sort of wrecked it."

"'*Sort of* wrecked it'?"

"Yeah, well, I smashed it up pretty good. But it wasn't my fault. A deer ran out in front of me, and I swerved to avoid it and hit a tree."

Tony nodded. This sounded like exactly the sort of thing Chris—whom his brother had described more than once as "irresponsible"—would do. "I guess your friend was pretty upset."

"Yeah, especially since I hadn't exactly asked before I took the car. I thought I could have it back to his place before he even knew it was missing."

"Why aren't you in jail?"

"It was my first offense." Chris grinned. "Well, the first time I ever got caught. And I talked to the friend and pointed out his insurance would pay for the damage, so he agreed not to press charges if I would leave town for a while." He held his arms wide once more. "So I decided to come visit you."

Tony didn't know whether to be flattered or fearful of this declaration. "Did your mom and dad really kick you out, or not?" he asked.

"Well, they agreed I needed to leave town for a while, so when I suggested I come see you, they thought it was a good idea."

Tony had lived alone a long time, and the thought of

having a roommate held no appeal. "I only have one bed-room," he said.

"No problem. I'll crash on the couch. I took a peek in the window, and it looks pretty comfy."

Tony wanted to say no. He didn't need this kind of com-plication in his life. But he still had a memory of two-year-old Chris climbing into his lap and falling asleep—maybe the first person who had ever trusted him so completely. "You'll have to get a job," he said.

"Yeah, sure. This is a tourist town, right? I'll find work at a restaurant or something."

"And no more borrowing cars. Or my truck." He looked back at his truck, parked at the curb. "And you need to move your bike out of my parking space."

"Sure. No problem. So can I stay?"

"You can stay. But only for a few weeks."

That grin again. The little boy shining through the al-most-man. "Thanks!" He slapped Tony on the back. "We're going to have a great time. You'll see."

BY THE TIME Kelsey left the sheriff's department late Thurs-day afternoon, she felt as if her head was gripped in a vise and her shoulders ached with tension. Her mind was a jum-ble of visions and facts, from the images of Liz's body lying on that rocky mountainside to details about her last meal—a chicken sandwich and fries consumed five hours before she'd been killed. She knew more about her sister's life here in Eagle Mountain and subsequent death than she ever had before, but all the new information only blurred the pic-ture of what had happened to end Liz's life more than ever.

Back at the Alpiner, she lay back on the bed, eyes closed, and tried to clear her head. She must have drifted off, because the buzzing of her phone on the bedside table jolted her awake. She sat up and grabbed the phone, seeing her mother's number on the display.

"Hi, Mom," she said. "How are you?"

"Have you found out anything yet?" Mom asked. No *how are you* or *you sound tired* or anything like that. Mary always got straight to the point.

"I spent most of the day at the sheriff's department," Kelsey said. She lay back on the bed again, phone to her ear. "I read through the case file on Liz's murder."

"And?"

"It looks like they worked hard investigating the case," Kelsey said. "They talked to a lot of people and gathered a lot of evidence."

"But they didn't find Liz's killer, did they?"

"No," Kelsey admitted.

"Then they must have missed something. Did they even learn who Mountain Man was?"

"No. Apparently, Liz gave the school a fake address, and her friends all thought she lived with her parents."

"I thought everyone knew everything about everybody in small towns," her mother said. "Who were the primary suspects?"

"There weren't any," Kelsey said.

"That's ridiculous. They must have been suspicious of someone."

"There wasn't anyone, Mom."

"Then you need to find someone," her mother said. "That's why I paid for you to make this trip."

Kelsey winced. Her mother had paid for the room at the Alpiner for two weeks, her contribution to this fact-finding mission. Kelsey hadn't wanted to accept, knowing that her mother's gifts always came with strings. But she wouldn't have been able to afford to stay here without her mother's contribution, so she had kept silent. Now it was her turn to pay. "There's a lot to sort through," she said. "But I'm working hard to put everything together. I'm hoping I'll see or uncover something the investigators missed before."

"I hope so, too," her mother said. "Call me when you have news."

"Wait, Mom. How are you—" But Mary had already hung up.

Kelsey dropped the phone on the bed and closed her eyes again. A line from the report about the law enforcement interview with her parents came to mind: *Parents are upset but unable or unwilling to supply much information.*

That was her parents in a nutshell. Always holding back, afraid of giving away too much, whether it was facts or affection.

TONY WAITED UNTIL Chris had gone "to check out the town" to call his brother, Eddie—he went by Edward now. He answered on the second ring. "I figured I was going to hear from you soon," he said. "I take it Chris showed up in one piece?"

"Was it your idea for him to come stay with me?" Tony asked.

"He had to go somewhere," Eddie said. When Tony didn't respond right away, he sighed. "Look, he's not a bad kid, he just doesn't think. It doesn't help that his friends here are as clueless and unmotivated as he is. Paula and I figured it would do him good to get away for a while, make a fresh start. And he might listen to you more than he does us. Make him get a job, help out around your place, whatever you think will straighten him out."

"I don't know anything about raising a kid—much less one who's already twenty years old."

"At his age, you and I were men," Eddie said. "We had to be. Chris still has some growing up to do. And he doesn't need another parent. He just needs a good example."

Tony almost laughed. "You think I'm a good example?"

"You own your own home, are gainfully employed in a good profession and you're involved in that wilderness-rescue stuff. And Chris has always idolized you. The two of you are a lot alike, you know."

Warmth spread through Tony's chest. "He hardly knows me," he said. "How can he idolize me?"

"He talks about you all the time, and he reads about you online, in that little paper Eagle Mountain has—all your search and rescue exploits. You gave us all a scare when you were hurt last year."

Eddie had made the five-hour drive from Denver to visit Tony in the hospital after he was out of ICU, but Chris hadn't come with him. "He wanted to come see you in the hospital," Eddie said. "I wouldn't let him, because I thought it would be too upsetting to see you like that, all banged up."

"You spoil him," Tony said without thinking.

"I wanted him to have a better childhood than you or I had," Eddie said. "Maybe I went a little overboard sometimes, but I'm not apologizing."

"I never said you should," Tony said. "I'll try to look after him while he's here. I told him he needs to get a job, and he said he would."

"That's a great start," Eddie said. "And if you need any money or anything…"

"No," Tony said. "I'm good."

"Well...thanks. He's a good kid, really. Hopefully, he won't give you too much trouble."

"Is that what Mom and Dad told you when they sent me to live with you?" Tony asked.

Eddie laughed. "They didn't tell me anything—just dropped you off and said, 'You look after him now,' and drove off."

Tony nodded, stomach clenching. He had a memory of standing in front of his brother's house, a suitcase and a couple of boxes at his feet, watching as his parents' sedan disappeared down the road. He had been sixteen but felt about twelve, wanting to cry but determined not to. Eddie hadn't said anything, simply picked up the suitcase and led the way into the house, to a room that obviously belonged to one of his two boys. "The kids can bunk together," Eddie had said, and dropped the suitcase beside the bed, with its *Star Wars* comforter. Tony had slept under that comforter for the next two years. Nothing in that house had felt like his. Nothing in his life had felt like his.

"I'll do my best for Chris," Tony said.

"Call me if you need anything," Eddie said. "And thanks. I owe you one."

They ended the call, and Tony tucked his phone away again. Eddie didn't owe him. Until today, Tony hadn't thought about what a debt he owed his brother. Despite their sometimes-difficult relationship, Eddie had saved him when he had nowhere else to turn. He would try to do the same for Chris.

Chapter Six

"Liz was only with us a couple of months, but she was one of those students who make an impression." Deborah Raymond, the English literature teacher who had first reported Liz missing, sat across the desk from Kelsey in her office at Eagle Mountain High School. A woman in her midforties with a long bob of dark blonde hair and stylish glasses, she had invited Kelsey to meet her at the school during her conference period Friday afternoon.

"What kind of impression?" Kelsey asked.

"A good one." Ms. Raymond smiled, revealing a slight gap between her upper front teeth. "You have to understand that I was in my first year of teaching then, so I wasn't that much older than my students. And Liz seemed more mature than most of her classmates—more of an adult than a teenager."

"You felt a connection to her?" Kelsey guessed.

"Yes and no." Ms. Raymond tilted her head, thoughtful. "Liz was friendly. She was popular with the other students. They were intrigued by this newcomer. Most of them had been together all through school, and Liz was an exotic outsider. She dressed a little more fashionably and had a navel piercing and this really independent attitude. She was charismatic and they were drawn to her. I was, too. But she didn't let anyone get too close. She never revealed a lot about her personal life or her inner feelings. A lot of kids that age wear all their emotions on the outside. I can tell by now when things aren't going well at home or a student has broken up with a boyfriend or had a fight with their best friend. Liz wasn't like that—I never really knew what she was thinking."

"What did you think when she didn't show up for class?" Kelsey asked.

"I thought she was probably ill. She was a good student, and she seemed to like school. She had never missed a class before—but, again, she had only been enrolled here a couple of months. One day out didn't concern me. On the second day, I asked some of her friends if any of them had heard from her, but they said they hadn't. I checked with the school office and learned this was an unexcused absence. No one had answered the phone when the attendance secretary called."

Fine lines creased her forehead, and she laced her fingers together. "By day three, I was concerned. I still thought Liz was probably ill, so I decided to go see her. I had the address on file with the school, so I drove over there."

Kelsey read real grief in Ms. Raymond's expression. "What did you find?" she prompted.

"The apartment was empty. Not just of people—of furniture and pictures and everything. The windows were dusty, and there were construction materials piled in the front room. It was clear no one had lived there in a long time."

"What did you think?"

"Honestly, my first emotion was hurt that Liz had lied to us all. Then I wondered why she would have done that. I became frightened and decided I had to contact the sheriff."

"Did Liz ever mention a boyfriend?"

"The investigators asked me that back then, too. But no, I never heard of Liz dating anyone, and she never spoke about a boyfriend—or any man in her life, really. Kids, especially the girls, talked to me about that kind of thing back then. I was close enough to their age that they felt comfortable confiding in me."

"Did Liz ever confide in you about anything else?"

"No. She was very good at keeping secrets without appearing to do so." She leaned forward. "I told her once I wanted to meet her parents. I knew all the other students' families. Most of them, I ran into regularly in town. But I hadn't met Liz's family yet. She smiled and said she was sure I would meet them soon, then changed the subject."

"Did that strike you as odd?" Kelsey asked.

"Not really. Not every teenager wants to talk about their parents. And not every kid has the ideal home life. But Liz never gave off any signs of being abused or neglected, so I didn't push."

"Did you have Tony Meisner in your class?" Kelsey wasn't sure why she asked the question, except she had been thinking a lot about Tony since their hike together. She was curious about him and what he had been like when he knew Liz.

Ms. Raymond smiled again. "Oh, yes. Tony was another of those students who has stayed with me," she said. "Of course, I still see him around town all the time."

"He was friends with Liz."

"He knew her," Ms. Raymond said. "In a class of only eighteen seniors, they all knew each other. But Tony and Liz weren't close. Tony was also a relative newcomer. He had moved to town the year before. He was quiet. Not unfriendly but definitely more of a loner. Liz was very outgoing."

"He found Liz's body," Kelsey said.

"Yes." Ms. Raymond picked up a pen and turned it over and over in her hand. "I think the experience shook him badly, as it would anyone," she said. "I remember the other students wanted to talk about it, and he wouldn't say anything. I worried about him. He seemed so alone. It was a relief when he came back to town and settled down and I could see he was doing well."

"He told me he had a crush on Liz," Kelsey said.

Ms. Raymond laughed. "I'm sure he did. All the boys in school did."

"But you never heard any gossip about Liz and a man outside of school, possibly someone older?"

Ms. Raymond shook her head. "I never did. I'm sorry. I wish I knew something that would help you, but I don't." She glanced at the clock. "And I'm afraid my conference period is almost over."

Kelsey pushed back her chair and stood. "Thank you for talking with me," she said. "It helps, knowing Liz had friends here."

"She did. We didn't know her very long, but we were all very upset to lose her."

As Kelsey drove away from the school, she thought about the language people used when talking about death. *Losing* Liz seemed as apt a description as any, as if they had misplaced her sister and might someday recover her. Nothing Kelsey or anyone else did would bring Liz back to life. But in coming to Eagle Mountain, Kelsey did feel she was finding her sister again.

TONY SPENT THE hours after work on Friday at Search and Rescue headquarters, inspecting and repacking gear. Hannah Richards had volunteered to help, and the two of them unloaded the specially equipped Jeep they used to transport volunteers and equipment, and laid out the climbing ropes, harnesses, packs, litters and assortment of safety and first aid supplies the group had used in Tuesday's rescue of a quartet of hikers cliffed out on a rocky ridge. The rescue had involved stringing out what felt like half their gear across that mountain face, and they had even hauled out their new drone to help locate the quartet ahead of the searchers' arrival.

Though everything had been assembled and made ready-to-go in case of another immediate callout, Tony wanted to take a closer look at all the gear while they had the time. There had been a lot of mud up there on the cliff, and it was easier to remove it after it had dried.

"How do you know Kelsey Chapman?" Hannah asked as she sponged mud off a climbing helmet.

Tony looked at her. "Why are you so nosy?" He had known Hannah most of her life, so he wasn't afraid to give her a hard time. He and her dad, Thad, had climbed together for years.

"I was just wondering how, if she's just visiting in town, you two hit it off so quickly."

He laid aside the climbing harness he had been examining and picked up another. "Her sister was a part of a rescue I was involved in years ago," he said. "Kelsey came to me and asked me to tell her the story."

Hannah's face clouded. "Was her sister a fatality?"

"Yes." He didn't elaborate. It wasn't his story to tell.

"I'm sorry," she said. "I guess I jumped to the wrong conclusion."

"What conclusion was that?"

Hannah blushed. "I thought the two of you were dating." She laughed. "But I guess that was silly."

"Why was it silly?"

"She's a lot younger than you, isn't she?" She flushed. "Not that younger women don't date older men, but you don't really…" She set aside the helmet. "I'm going to need some stronger cleaner for this. I think there's some in the closet."

Tony went back to counting carabiners but, in his mind, completed the sentence Hannah had been about to say. He didn't really date. Search and Rescue was full of single men and women in their prime, and members coupled, broke up and recoupled over the years. Some married. Some divorced. Some lived together long-term, and some had a new partner every month. But Tony never participated in that particular dance.

It wasn't that he had never dated. But he had never had a relationship with a woman that lasted more than a few weeks. He had never connected with others, always holding himself back.

His phone rang, and when he pulled it from his pocket, he was surprised to see an Iowa number. He only knew one person from Iowa, and his heart beat a little faster at the thought. "Hello?"

"Hi, Tony. It's Kelsey. I hope I'm not interrupting anything."

"No. I'm good. How are you?" *Why are you calling me?* he wanted to ask. But even he knew that sounded rude.

"I spent most of yesterday at the sheriff's department," she said. "They let me see their file on Liz. It was pretty grim."

He winced. "I'm sorry."

"It's okay. It was good that I saw it. And this morning, I talked to one of Liz's teachers, Deborah Raymond."

Tony remembered Ms. Raymond. Pretty and young, she

had been a favorite with all of them. When Ms. Raymond spoke to him, he'd always had the impression she really cared.

"I have a lot more information about Liz's life here," Kelsey continued. "But I also have a lot more questions. I learned one good thing, though—the sheriff told me they have DNA evidence in storage, so if they ever find a suspect, they can test him. That makes me want to find Mountain Man even more."

"I found someone else for you to talk to," Tony said. "He was Search and Rescue captain when Liz was found. I don't think he can give you any information on Mountain Man, but maybe he can fill in some gaps about the scene that day."

"Oh, Tony, that is so wonderful. Thank you so much. So, what are you doing?"

"I'm at Search and Rescue headquarters, cleaning and packing gear. What are you doing?"

"I'm thinking about what I'm going to have for dinner."

"Yeah, I guess I'll be doing that soon, too."

"Want to have dinner with me?"

Was she asking him out? He opened his mouth to answer, but nothing came out.

"You don't have to if you're busy," she said. "I just didn't want to sit here by myself, all that stuff from Liz's case file in my head—"

"I'd love to have dinner with you," he blurted out. "Where?"

They settled on pizza at Mo's Pub at six thirty and ended the call.

Hannah returned as he was pocketing his phone. He began gathering up gear and returning it to the totes where it was stored. "Are we done already?" Hannah asked.

"I am," Tony said. "I need to go."

"What's the rush?"

He grinned. "I have a date."

It was worth saying the words just to see the surprise on her face.

TONY GOT TO Mo's ahead of Kelsey and snagged a booth at the back, where they would have more privacy. Even if all she wanted to do was talk about her sister, she would appreciate doing so without an audience. She slid into the booth across from him right at six thirty. She smelled fresh, like some kind of floral soap, and her hair was glossy. When she picked up the menu, he noticed her slender fingers and the half dozen silver rings she wore.

They made small talk, ordered pizza and beer; then she smiled across at him. "Let's talk about anything but murder," she said. "Tell me your best rescue story that has a happy ending."

"There are so many." He searched his memories for something to tell her. Something that wouldn't depress her. "If you do this work long enough, you learn how amazing people can be," he said. "Your fellow volunteers but also the people we rescue. You learn to never give up hope, because people can survive the most amazing things."

She leaned forward, rapt. "Such as?"

"We got a call one morning, a nice summer day. A family was hiking, and their ten-year-old daughter slipped and fell off the trail. A bad fall, at the base of a waterfall. When they described to the dispatcher where they were, we didn't see how the kid could survive. Ted Carruthers and I—he's the guy I said you need to talk to—packed a body bag, thinking we'd have to use it to bring her out. We ran up that mountain trail to get to her while the rest of the team followed. We ran for forty-five minutes. Ted was twenty years older than me and had a full pack, but I could barely keep up with him."

He stopped to sip his beer. "It must be harder, when it's kids who are injured," Kelsey said.

He nodded. "Her mom met us on the trail. It was a local family, so we all knew the names, even if we didn't know them personally. She said her husband had climbed down to the girl and covered her with all their jackets. This was a really high-up trail—almost ten thousand feet in elevation, and the girl had fallen three hundred feet or more. It was a real scramble getting down to her, but when we got there, she was still alive."

A server arrived to deliver their pizza, and Tony took a slice but didn't eat it right away. He was back at the base of that waterfall. "The falls were thundering, so we had to shout to hear each other. Within minutes, both of us and everything we had with us was wet. Snowmelt, so it was ice cold. The girl—her name was Susie—was really bad off. She had a closed head injury, a dislocated shoulder, a broken arm. She was having trouble breathing. Her dad was there, trying hard to keep it together, so we were trying to speak in a kind of code, not letting him know how bad off she was. On every scale we can use to measure medically, she was on the edge of dying."

He took a bite of pizza and chewed. He was surprised to see goose bumps on his forearm—visceral memory of how cold he had been that day.

"What happened next?" Kelsey asked after a pause.

He came back to the moment and the woman across from him. "The captain at the time, Mike Lawton, was trying to get a helicopter in to airlift the girl out of that canyon.

They radioed they were at least an hour out, so we decided we needed to carry her down the trail to a flat area where the helicopter could meet us. By that time, the rest of the team had shown up. One of them brought a canister of oxygen, so we able to get a mask on her and try to help her breathe. It took us an hour and a half to get her down that steep, narrow trail to the helicopter, but she was still alive when we got there."

"And she lived?" Kelsey asked.

"She did." He cleared his throat, surprised he was so emotional about this after so long. "Three months later we had a picnic, and Susie and her family showed up. She was running around like a regular kid." She had thrown her arms around him in a hug, eyes shining, and he had had to turn away to keep from breaking down crying. "Her doctors said they had never seen anyone make such a quick recovery. They thought the fact that she had fallen in that cold water and become hypothermic so quickly—plus her young age—had lessened the impact of her injuries."

"The fact that you all got to her so quickly must have made a difference, too," Kelsey said.

"I'm sure it did." He took another drink, feeling steadier. "Every time you go out on a call, you don't know what kind of impact you're going to have," he said. "I think that's why it never feels routine or boring."

"I think it's pretty amazing," she said.

She was smiling at him, her eyes full of such admiration that he began to feel self-conscious. "Enough about me," he said. "Tell me more about you. What kind of work do you do?"

"Nothing as exciting as search and rescue," she said. "I'm an accountant."

"In my day job, I'm a surveyor," he said. "That's not terribly exciting, either."

"But you get to be outside in this beautiful country."

"I get to be outside when it's raining and blowing snow, too," he said, and grinned.

"Go ahead and admit you love it," she teased.

And just like that, he was falling into an easy back-and-forth of conversation, laughing and maybe even flirting a little. Thirty-eight years old and he felt so far out of his depth, but gladly let her lead him along.

"Do you two need anything else?" Chris, wearing a black apron and with his blond hair pulled back in a ponytail, grinned at them. "Hey, Uncle Tony. I told you I'd get a job." He readjusted the bus tub on one hip.

Tony was aware of Kelsey looking at him expectantly. "Kelsey, this is my nephew, Chris. Chris, this is Kelsey Chapman."

"Nice to meet you." Chris nodded. "Sorry for interrupting, but they sent me over to clear this table." He lowered his voice. "It's almost closing time."

Kelsey pushed her chair back from the table. "I guess we should go."

"No rush." Chris picked up their plates and slid them into the bus tub. "But you'll have to leave soon anyway."

Tony frowned and Chris hurried to collect the remaining dishes and left.

"He's cute," Kelsey said. "He looks a lot like you did at that age. At least, judging from the pictures I've seen."

"He just moved in with me." Tony looked into his empty beer mug. "I've lived alone for so long it's been a bit of an adjustment, but he's a good kid."

"I bet he really looks up to you," she said.

"Yeah, well, I've never been a role model before. I'm not sure how I feel about it."

She laughed as if he had made a joke, but he liked the sound. It made him feel lighter somehow. He pulled out his wallet and reached for the check.

"No." She wrapped her fingers around his wrist. "This is my treat. I asked you out."

He started to argue, but she patted the back of his hand. "You can pay next time."

Next time. Next time they shared a meal. A date?

He pushed the thought aside. He had no idea how she felt about him. Maybe he was just a helpful older man she felt sorry for. He had always felt older than his real age, and she seemed so young and fresh. "You said you're ten years younger than Liz?" he asked as they exited the restaurant. "So, you're twenty-eight?"

"Yes. How old are you?"

"Thirty-eight."

She nodded but made no further comment as they walked back to the Alpiner Inn. The night was clear and not too cold, the stars sharp as broken glass overhead. Kelsey looked up at them. "This really is the most beautiful place," she said.

"Yes," he agreed, but he wasn't looking at the sky. He was taking advantage of her distraction to look at her—the elegant arc of her neck as she tilted her head back, the silken fall of her hair down her back.

They stopped outside the inn, and she took both his hands in hers. "Thank you for saving me from a depressing evening in my room," she said. "I'm feeling much better now."

"Thank *you*," he said. "It's not often I have such good

company." Did that sound too stilted? He never knew what to say.

"I'll see you soon," she said. She leaned forward and pressed her lips to his cheek, then released his hands and hurried inside, leaving him dazed and half believing he had dreamed the whole evening.

Chapter Seven

"Hi, Mom, how are you doing today?" Kelsey sat on the edge of the bed Saturday morning, picturing her mom in the living room of the home Kelsey had grown up in. She could hear the television playing in the background—some morning-news program, she guessed.

"I'm as well as can be expected," her mother said—her usual answer. "Thank you for the newspaper article about Liz. It was hard to read, but I appreciated the picture. It was one of my favorites of her."

Kelsey again felt a flash of anger at her father, who, in refusing to keep any reminders of Liz, had deprived the rest of them of so many precious memories. "Is the young man in the photo the one you talked to?" her mother asked.

"He is, but he's not so young now. He's thirty-eight."

"Liz would be thirty-eight." *Does everyone who has lost a loved one do this?* Kelsey wondered. *Automatically calculate the age the person would be right now if they had lived?*

"But he remembers Liz," her mother added.

"He remembers her. He's been very helpful." Tony had made some of the hardest parts of this journey not so hard. He was so quiet and calm. So capable. He looked like a college professor, until you noticed the corded muscles in his arms and felt his rock-hard biceps. Someone first meeting him might mistake him for meek until they learned he routinely did incredible things like run up mountain trails, descend cliffs on a rope or wade in ice-cold water in order to save the lives of strangers. No city gym rat could compete with that when it came to sexiness.

The thought jolted her a little, but the surprise quickly faded. Why shouldn't she think Tony was sexy? He was different from the men she usually dated—older, less polished. But different was good.

Besides, they weren't dating. He was her friend. Someone who was guiding her through a difficult time.

She realized her mother was talking to her. "I'm sorry, Mom, what did you say?"

"Have you found out anything else about Liz?"

"I spoke with the teacher who reported Liz missing. She said Liz was very popular."

"Of course she was," Mary said. "She was beautiful and bright. Everyone who knew her loved her."

Kelsey had always thought of her sister that way, but had Liz really been so perfect? Was her sister dead because of random circumstances or because of her own bad choices? "The teacher said Liz was popular but that she also didn't tell people details about her life. Everyone here thought she was living with her family."

"She would have been here with us if not for that man," Mary said. "Did the teacher say anything about him?"

Kelsey knew her mother meant Mountain Man. "She said Liz kept him a secret. No one here seems to have known about him. The sheriff's deputies interviewed everyone who knew Liz, and none of them had heard of any man in her life."

"He was a real person. You need to find him."

They both let that thought sink in, along with the question that hung over this whole expedition to Eagle Mountain: How do you find a man who had remained invisible for twenty years?

"What are you doing today?" her mother asked.

"I'm going to the library to look at the high school yearbook from when Liz was here," Kelsey said. "I'm hoping to make a list of names of classmates who knew her and find as many of them as possible to talk to while I'm here." Surely Liz would have told at least one girlfriend about the older man she was living with. At home in Iowa, Liz had annoyed them all, talking about Mountain Man incessantly, though she never used his name. Why had her parents not seen his insistence on anonymity as a warning sign? She couldn't ask her mother. Why contribute more to her guilt and pain?

"I'll let you go, then," her mother said, and ended the call.

That was Mom—not sentimental or concerned about manners. She had tried to get closer to Kelsey after her husband died, but Kelsey thought she was out of practice. Liz was the only thing they had real conversations about. If Kelsey tried to talk about her job or her apartment or a movie she had seen, Mom lost interest. Kelsey wanted to be there for her, to be a real daughter. But it was hard when her mother didn't feel like a real mother. Not the person concerned with the details of her life that her friends' mothers were. They complained of feeling stifled by love sometimes, but Kelsey wanted to tell them being stifled was better than being starved.

SATURDAY AFTERNOON, Tony scanned the listing of Search and Rescue donors until he found the name he wanted. Then he punched in the number for Jessica Stringfellow, now Jessica Macintosh. "Hello, Jessica? It's Tony Meisner."

"Hey, Tony," she said as if it had not been at least fifteen years since they had more than nodded on the street.

"This is going to seem out of the blue, but do you remember that girl who went to school with us who went missing? Liz Chapman?"

"Oh my goodness. Of course I remember Liz. That was terrible what happened to her. You're the one who found her body, weren't you?"

"I did. Her sister is in town, and she asked me if I knew any of Liz's friends who might talk to her, and I thought of you."

"She wants to talk to me about Liz? I don't know what I can tell her."

"She's just trying to come to terms with what happened, I think. She was a little kid when Liz left home, and she wants to hear what Liz was like, that kind of thing."

"Well, sure, I can talk to her."

"Do you know anyone else I can ask? People who knew Liz and might have been close to her?"

"There were lots of us who knew her, but she was kind of an odd duck, you know? Lots of fun to be around and really nice, but she didn't let people get too close. It was like she had secrets she was keeping. And I guess it turned out she was. I mean, we were all shocked when we found out she had moved here on her own, without her parents, and that she may have been involved with some mysterious older man. It was like something out of a movie."

"Who else can I call who would talk to her?" he asked again.

"Let me call," Jessica said. "I can think of a few people

who are still around. I'll get back to you about when we can meet. It's really sweet of you to help the sister."

He couldn't remember anyone ever calling him *sweet*. "I couldn't turn down someone who asked for help," he said.

"Some people would, you know."

He ended the call, and after only a moment's hesitation, he called Kelsey.

"Hello?"

"Is everything okay?" he asked. "You sound out of breath."

"I'm just walking around the park. Trying to get some exercise, but the altitude has me puffing a little."

"If you stick around long enough, you'll get used to it." Why had he said that? When she had all the answers she could find here, she would leave and go back to Iowa. Back to accounting and her mom and whatever man she was seeing—though she hadn't mentioned a relationship, had she?

"I spent this morning at the library, looking at her class yearbook," she said. "I found some good pictures of her. Apparently, she really dove right into high school life—volleyball team, yearbook committee, Spanish club."

"It's like that in a small school," he said. "There were only eighteen students in our graduating class."

"That must have made relationships awkward. And prom."

He laughed. "Relationships *are* awkward. Especially when you're a teen. But a lot of kids dated kids from nearby towns, and we had a joint prom with Delta."

"There was a photo of you in there, too, in your search and rescue gear. Hubba, hubba."

He laughed again. "I doubt many girls were swooning over the SAR geek."

"Oh, I think you're wrong there. You had that shy-guy demeanor that some women find very sexy. And there's the whole *risking your life for others* mystique. I bet you Search and Rescue guys even have groupies."

He had heard stories—though if any women had ever hit on him after a rescue, he had been oblivious. "If any of the high school girls were admiring me from afar, I was too awkward to notice," he said.

"You were too busy crushing on my sister."

"Who didn't know I was alive."

"Liz took it for granted that men admired her," Kelsey said. "I don't think she was arrogant about it—she just knew she was beautiful."

"You look a lot like her, you know."

"People have told me that, but I don't see it. I mean, we have the same hair, but I think part of beauty is attitude. Liz had it but I don't."

"There are all kinds of attitude and all kinds of beauty," he said, then winced, sure he sounded impossibly cringe-worthy. Time to change the subject. "I talked to one of Liz's friends. She's going to contact some others and arrange a meeting so you can talk to them all."

"And the former SAR commander you mentioned, too. How can I get in touch with him?"

"I'll run him to ground," Tony said. "Maybe the three of us can get together for a drink later today."

"That would be great. And remember—this time, you're paying." She was still laughing when she ended the call. She didn't laugh like Liz. Kelsey's mirth was warmer and softer, a little more restrained. As if she wasn't ready to give everything away just yet.

Chris shuffled into the room, shirtless and toweling his

hair, the smell of herbal shampoo heralding his arrival. "Was that Kelsey on the phone?" he asked.

"Nosy," Tony said.

"Hey, don't get all up in my face about it. I liked her." He gave Tony a thumbs-up. "You're doing all right for yourself, with the hot younger girlfriend and all."

"Kelsey isn't my girlfriend."

"But you want her to be." Chris laughed. "Don't lie. You should have seen the expression on your face while you were talking to her."

Tony glared, but that only made Chris laugh more. "For what it's worth, I think she was pretty into you, too," Chris said.

"Since when are you an expert?"

"I've been doing mostly restaurant work for a few years now. A good server has to be able to read body language, know when someone is in a good mood or upset about something. The secret to good tips is knowing how to read people."

"You're not a server," Tony said. "You're a busboy."

"I'm a busboy now, but I'm going to get promoted. It's just a matter of time."

"Is that what you want to do for the rest of your life? Wait tables?"

Chris shrugged. "Probably not, but it's good for now."

"But what about the future?" Tony asked.

"What about it?" He tossed the towel back toward the bathroom and missed. It landed in a wet heap on the hall floor. "Nice talking to you, but I have to get going."

Tony stared after him, a feeling he couldn't identify surging through him. With a start, he realized the emotion was jealousy. Did he envy Chris more for his youth or his confidence? A little of both, probably.

Had Chris been right—that Kelsey was into Tony? If his own attraction to her was so obvious to his nephew, he needed to be more careful not to let other people see it. Having all your teenage friends know that you were crushing on the girl they all wanted, too, was very different from a grown man infatuated with a newcomer who was ten years younger. He didn't want anyone—especially Kelsey—to get the wrong idea.

TED CARRUTHERS LOOKED pretty much as Kelsey had pictured him when Tony had described Ted as "an old cowboy and search and rescue veteran." When she walked into Mo's at seven that evening, she spotted the silver-haired man in the Western shirt and boots in the booth before she even saw Tony across from him. He had the leathered skin of men in Charlie Russell paintings, a drooping mustache and tinted aviator glasses.

Tony stood as Kelsey approached the table, and Ted shoved to his feet as well. "Kelsey, this is Ted Carruthers. Ted, Kelsey Chapman."

Ted shook her hand. "It's nice to meet you," he said. "Though I don't know how much help I can be to you. I didn't know your sister."

Kelsey slid into the booth across from Ted, who had a large glass of beer in front of him. Beside her, Tony sipped from a glass of what looked like iced tea. "Just tell me about the day Search and Rescue retrieved her body," she said.

"Tony here made the call, you know." Ted nodded at his friend. "He was just a kid, and I don't know if he'd ever seen a dead body before."

"I hadn't," Tony said.

Ted grimaced. "It's worse when it's someone you know. Of course, that happens a lot when you work search and rescue in a small remote town. Eventually, you know a lot of the people you help. And some who die."

"What was the weather like that day?" Kelsey asked.

Ted frowned. "The weather? What difference does the weather make?"

"I'm trying to picture in my mind what it was like."

Ted shook his head. "Suit yourself." He tilted his head back. "Let's see. It was sunny. A little breeze. Good conditions for a rescue, and right near a pretty easy trail. The biggest hassle was waiting around until the sheriff's deputies finished collecting all their evidence." He smirked. "Not that it took that long. There were only three deputies back then, and the sheriff. He and one of the deputies showed up at the scene initially. Then he called in the third. They crawled around in the grass and rocks for the better part of an hour and came up with a gum wrapper and some other trash that could have been left by who knows who. I wouldn't call it *evidence*."

"Was anyone else there who shouldn't have been?" Kelsey asked. "Any hikers or tourists or anything?"

Ted took a long swallow of beer before he answered. "Nobody else," he said. "We didn't have the crowds of tourists in town back then that we do now." He rubbed his chin. "Tony was there, of course. And Mel Wheeler. Do you remember him?" he asked Tony.

"Mel lives in Phoenix now," Tony said.

"That's right. Let's see. Peggy Pendleton was there, and that fellow from—where was it, Mexico?"

"Peru. Alejandro Garcia."

"Right. That was it." He shrugged. "We didn't need many people for that kind of mission. It was just a matter of loading everything on the litter and carrying it down."

Kelsey kept her face expressionless, refusing to let him see her react to his reference to Liz as "everything." "Tell me about the other volunteers," she said. "What was Alejandro like?" The name sounded sexy.

"He was a professional climber out of South America," Ted said. "He worked as a local guide for a couple of years, and he could climb anything." He chuckled. "I was around forty then and in the best shape of my life. But Alejandro, at fifty-two, could climb rings around any of us." He jerked his head in Tony's direction once more. "He was even better than this kid."

"Alejandro was married and had five children," Tony said.

So, unlikely to have either appealed to Liz or to be able to hide her existence from his wife and many children. "What about Mel Wheeler?"

"Thirtysomething carpenter from Paradise," Ted said.

"He was only with us for the one year," Tony said.

"And he's in Phoenix now?" she asked.

"Last I heard," Tony said.

Kelsey made a mental note to check into Mel Wheeler. Maybe he was Mountain Man and had left town to avoid detection after Liz had died.

Ted drained the last of his beer and set the empty glass down with a thunk. "Anything else you want to know?"

She had intended to ask him the same questions she had asked Tony: What had Liz looked like when they found her? Had he noticed anything unusual? But he didn't have Tony's sensitivity or the attention to detail she had found in the sheriff's deputy's reports. There was no sense asking him to repeat what she had already gleaned elsewhere. "Did you know Liz?" she asked. "Before she died?"

He shook his head. "No reason I would. Like I said, I was forty. She was a kid."

A kid who never got to grow up, Kelsey thought. "Thank you for talking with me," she said.

"I don't see how I've helped." He stood. "Thanks for the beer," he said to Tony, and left.

"TED CAN BE a crotchety old guy," Tony said when Ted was gone.

"He's given me a couple of names to look into," she said. "Alejandro and Mel."

"I don't think either of them killed Liz," Tony said. "I could be wrong, but I was there that day and they didn't show a flicker of recognition."

"Maybe a sociopath wouldn't."

"I don't think all killers are sociopaths."

"I'm no expert, but I think a man who would lure a young woman away from her family only to kill her a few weeks later has something wired wrong in them."

"You're right. And I guess that kind of thing doesn't always show on the outside."

She turned to look at him. The booth was small, forcing them to sit close together, their thighs almost touching. "Thanks for listening to me and for trying to help. You must have a lot of other things you could be doing with your time."

"Not really. And you've made me curious now. I want to see how all this works out."

"Have you heard any more from Liz's friends?"

He nodded. "Jessica MacIntosh—she used to be Jessica Stringfellow—has invited a few of Liz's classmates to her house tomorrow night. She says you can come and meet them, and they'll tell you what they know."

"And you waited to tell me this?" She swatted his arm—more of a brush of her fingers against his bicep.

"I knew Ted wouldn't be an easy interview, so I saved the good news for last."

"He wasn't that bad."

"He can be a little insensitive."

"Not everyone is as thoughtful as you."

She was looking at him again, eyes lingering in a way that made him feel as if she was trying to peel back the layers. He faced forward once more. "Do you want to order dinner?"

"Do you?"

"Could you stand to eat with me two nights in a row?"

"I think I could manage." She reached past him and plucked a menu from behind the salt and pepper shakers. The side of her breast brushed his shoulder, and sensation shuddered through him. "Besides," she said, "you owe me a meal."

"Then I had better pay up," he said, keeping his tone light. Inside, he was thinking he was too old to be this foolish. Thirty-eight-year-old men didn't have crushes on women who were out of their reach.

Chapter Eight

Jessica and Andrew MacIntosh lived in a cedar-sided cabin in a heavily treed neighborhood up Carolina Gulch, on the south side of Eagle Mountain. As Tony guided his Toyota up the dozen switchbacks leading to the MacIntosh home Saturday evening, Kelsey gaped out the window at the spectacular vistas and sheer drop-offs, icy waterfalls, snow-capped peaks and evergreen-choked drainages. It was the kind of scenery that either frightened people into never coming back or made them return again and again, leading many to up and move from wherever they had called home before.

"What do people do for a living around here?" she asked.

"A lot of them work online," he said. "Andy MacIntosh is a pilot, and Jessica builds websites, I think. I'm not a techie, so I'm not exactly sure."

The driveway was full of cars by the time they arrived, so Tony parked on the street, and he and Kelsey walked up to the house. The home had plenty of windows to take advantage of the view and decks on three sides for relaxing outdoors. Jessica, barefoot and in wide-legged black pants and a multicolored tunic, greeted them at the door. She wore her hair shorter than in high school, and she wasn't as slender, but she had the same smile that had stood out in every photo of the Eagle Mountain cheer squad. "Come in, come in." She ushered them inside. "Tony, it's so good to see you. I see your picture in the paper all the time, on those amazing rescues."

"Jessica, this is Kelsey Chapman," he said.

"It's nice to meet you, Kelsey," Jessica said. "You can hang your coats in that closet. Then come on through to the living room, and I'll introduce you to everyone else."

Tony was surprised to find six people besides Jessica and her husband seated on sofas and chairs in the expansive great room of the MacIntosh home. Jessica introduced Marcus White, who had sat on the bench at basketball games with Tony; Madison Gruenwald, who had been a plump, vivacious redhead and now was a thin, still-vivacious woman with dyed purple hair. Veronica Olivares was another volleyball player, whose dark hair had been cut short but was otherwise looking remarkably as she had in their senior year. Taylor Redmond, Sarah Fish and Darla Cash rounded out the six. Taylor and Sarah had also played volleyball, while Darla had worked with Liz on the yearbook committee.

"Let me get you a glass of wine," Jessica said. "And help yourself to snacks." She indicated the platters of hors d'oeuvres set out on the large coffee table in the center of the seating area.

While Jessica went around the room with wine bottles, everyone made small talk with Kelsey. Where did she live? What kind of work did she do? How did she know Tony?

Half-involved in a conversation with Marcus, Tony strained his ears to hear Kelsey's answer to the last question. "Tony was with the Search and Rescue team that retrieved Liz's body," she said. "He's been helping me find out as much as I can about what happened to her."

"That was so terrible," Veronica said. "We were all just in shock when we found out."

"They never found whoever did it, did they?" Andy asked. He was a few years older than the rest of them and from Houston, but Jessica must have told him Liz's story.

"They never did," Marcus said. "I think they decided it was some kind of random killer, you know? Like Ted Bundy."

"What questions did you have for us?" Jessica asked, bringing the conversation back to the point of the get-together.

"What did you know about Liz?" Kelsey asked. "What did she tell you about herself—her history?"

The other people in the room exchanged looks as if waiting for someone else to go first. "Liz didn't really talk about herself much," Madison finally said. "I think I knew she had moved here from Iowa or Ohio or somewhere in the Midwest."

The others nodded in agreement. "She was pretty and popular, and we didn't really care where she was from," Marcus said.

"What did she say about her family or her living situation?" Kelsey asked.

"We never talked about that stuff," Madison said.

"I asked her once why she never talked about her mom and dad," Veronica said. "She said they were good people— they just didn't understand her. Which was all of our parents, right?" She rolled her eyes. "My kids are only seven and nine, and already I'm dreading those teenage years. No matter what I do as a mom, it won't be right. That's just how it is."

More agreement and some chuckles from the others.

"What about guys?" Kelsey asked. "Did she go out with anyone at school? Or with anyone else? Did you ever see her with a guy or hear her talk about a boyfriend?"

"No boyfriend," Darla said. "I asked her once, and she said relationships were too complicated and she just wanted to have fun. Which I thought was wild because she had all these boys who were wild about her, and it was all I could do to get Bobby Preston to ask me to prom."

More laughter. "There was always Ben Everett," someone—Tony didn't see who—said.

"Yes, Ben!" Taylor said. "I know he asked her to the prom that year, though I don't know if she accepted or not."

"He asked her out more than that," Marcus said. "Maybe four or five times. He really had it bad for her." He cast a sideways glance at Tony. "We all crushed on her a little. I mean, she was the new girl, and so pretty and friendly and everything. But Ben had it really bad."

"What about that one night at the ice-cream parlor?" Madison asked. "You remember? A bunch of us were there, and Liz said she was meeting someone. But she wouldn't say who it was."

"Oh my gosh, I forgot all about that!" Jessica said. "But I remember. Liz was all mysterious, and I got the impression she wanted us to think this guy was an older guy—a real man and not just some boy from school."

"She said that? That he was older?" Kelsey asked.

"She didn't really say it," Taylor said. "But we were all trying to find out who it was, and she said something like, 'Oh, it's not a *boy* from school.' Like that, with the emphasis on *boy*."

"I don't think it was Ben," Sarah said. "Because I dated him for a while after Liz died, and if he had ever gone out with her, I'm sure he would have said something. Before him, I didn't know boys could talk so much."

The other women laughed. The men looked uncomfortable. "Did anyone see this guy?" Kelsey asked. "The one she was meeting that night at the ice-cream parlor?"

Everyone shook their heads. "I told Madison I was going to follow Liz and get a look at the guy," Jessica said. "But I had to go to the bathroom, and when I came out, Liz was already gone. Then someone asked me about a play I had made in the last game we had had against Delta, and I forgot all about Liz's mystery man."

"Did you tell the sheriff's department about this guy?" Kelsey asked.

Jessica frowned. "There wasn't really anything to tell, was there? She could even have been making the whole thing up. I mean, there was so much she didn't tell us. Maybe she wanted us all to believe she was dating some glamorous older man, when really she was just walking home alone."

"So, no one saw Liz with any man?" she asked.

Veronica looked thoughtful. "You know, I came in right before Liz left. Ted Carruthers was standing a few doors down from the ice-cream parlor, smoking a cigarette. You might ask him if he saw anything."

Kelsey glanced at Tony. "We talked to Ted yesterday, but I'll ask him about that night." She glanced at the notes she had been making. "Do you have any idea how I can get in touch with Ben?"

Again, they exchanged glances. "I don't think I've seen or heard from him since graduation," Jessica said.

"Didn't he go out of state for college?" Sarah asked. "Tennessee or Michigan or something?"

"I know the sheriff questioned him at the time," Veronica said.

"Oh, he talked about that," Madison said. "He said two big officers backed him into a corner and accused him of strangling Liz. They said he did it because she wouldn't go out with him. He said he was terrified, and I believe it. He was shaking when he told me."

"I think I heard they took his DNA and it didn't match up with the evidence they found," Marcus said.

"I'd still like to talk to him," Kelsey said. "If he was always watching Liz, maybe he saw her with another man some time."

"All of us talked to the police after Liz went missing," Madison said. "And again after they found her body. We thought we knew her—that she was our friend. But then we found out there was so much we didn't know."

"We thought she was like us," Taylor said. "A kid living with her parents. Not a girl with this secret life none of us knew about."

"Is there anyone else the police interviewed?" Kelsey asked.

Jessica laughed. "Well, there was Tony."

All eyes focused on him. "That's right!" Madison said. "For a while there, Tony was the number one suspect." She leaned toward him. "I guess because you found the body but also because you were always mooning after her."

"Don't blush," Jessica said as his face heated. "All the guys in school had a crush on Liz. And all the girls were jealous of her, but none of us killed her."

The conversation shifted then to more-general high school reminiscences. As they fell into recollections of games and dances and pranks, Tony felt more and more distanced. Kelsey touched his elbow and leaned over to whisper, "I think we can go now."

They thanked Jessica and said goodbye to everyone else. Tony didn't say anything else until they were halfway down the long series of switchbacks. The air between them was as brittle as a skim of ice. "I didn't kill your sister," he said finally. "I didn't have anything to do with her death."

She shifted toward him, her features barely discernible in the darkness. "Did the sheriff really suspect you?" she asked.

"The sheriff talked to me. One of his deputies accused me of killing her, then waiting to find the body so I could be a hero." He gripped the steering wheel more tightly, remembering the hot, claustrophobic room where they had questioned him; the smell of his own fear-sweat, metallic in the air. "They tested my DNA and cleared me."

She nodded. "I wasn't going to ask."

"I wanted you to know."

"I never thought you killed her." The leather of the car seat creaked as she shifted position again. "What about Ben Everett? Did you know him?"

"As well as I knew anyone. He was smart. Class salutatorian. His dad was a doctor in the ER in Junction, and he had three or four older sisters. He was the only one who had the nerve to ask Liz out, but I don't think he would kill her. And anyway, they tested his DNA, too."

She sighed, a weary sound. "I'd still like to talk to him. And I'll talk to Ted again, too. What do you think he was doing there that night?"

Tony thought back to the location of the ice-cream parlor. There was a T-shirt shop there now. "There was a bar two doors down from there," he said. "The White Elephant

Tavern. It was a place where cowboys hung out. Ted was probably there and had stepped out for a smoke."

She nodded. "I need to talk to him again."

"There's a meeting at SAR headquarters tomorrow morning," Tony said. "You could talk to Ted then."

"I thought he was retired from search and rescue work?"

"He doesn't go on calls anymore, but he still comes to meetings. And he's our historian."

"What does a SAR historian do?"

"He writes up a narrative about each call—who was there, what the call involved, the outcome. It's a good record of all the calls over the years."

"Is there a write-up about Liz's call?"

"We'll ask him. I don't know who was keeping records back then, but Ted will know."

"Maybe he saw this man Liz was supposedly meeting that night at the ice-cream parlor."

"If there *was* a man," Tony said.

"There had to be someone," Kelsey said. "We don't know much, but we know for sure Liz didn't kill herself."

Chapter Nine

Kelsey slept poorly that night, her sleep interrupted by snatches of the conversation with Liz's friends. They had painted a picture of the same Liz whom Kelsey had known—pretty, popular and outgoing, with a large circle of friends. Yet there had been a shadow side of her, living a second life she let no one else see. The mood in the room hadn't been unfriendly, but there had been an underlying current of—not animosity but distrust. They felt betrayed by the things Liz hadn't told them.

Kelsey felt that betrayal, too. Why had Liz kept so many secrets? Why had she lied about so much, from the real name of the man she was seeing to her address on school records? Kelsey didn't even understand how her sister had managed to enroll in school, but maybe because she was eighteen, she had enrolled herself and the authorities believed what she had told them.

Was she secretive because Mountain Man had told her to be—forced her to be? Or had she been indulging her sense of drama, enjoying being a woman of mystery, with a secret affair no one knew about?

Someone must know something. Eagle Mountain was a small town. People paid attention, especially to a pretty, new girl. How was it that no one knew anything to help identify Liz's Mountain Man?

She recalled the stricken look on Tony's face when Madison had mentioned that he had been a suspect in Liz's murder. She never would have believed he would kill anyone, but she was grateful for the DNA test to remove all doubt. She would have hated to have that between them, even if only in the form of him worrying about her doubting him.

Odd that she had met him such a short time ago yet felt she knew him so well. She had imagined having to do all her investigating of Liz's death on her own. Instead, she had him to bounce ideas off of and help arrange meetings with people who might help her, like Liz's friends, and Ted Carruthers. She had never expected to be so lucky.

The next morning, she tried to cover the dark shadows beneath her eyes with makeup and drove up the steep county road to Search and Rescue headquarters. The lot was full of cars, and she wondered if an emergency had summoned all the volunteers. As she was walking up to the building, Hannah Richards hailed her. "Hey, Kelsey."

Hannah was with a handsome brown-haired man she introduced as her fiancé, Jake Gwynne. "Are you thinking of joining Eagle Mountain Search and Rescue?" Hannah asked.

"No, I just needed to talk to Ted Carruthers for a minute," Kelsey said. "I understand he was the captain of Search and Rescue when Liz's body was found. I'll leave before the meeting."

"I'm sure Ted is around here somewhere," Hannah said.

More than a dozen people milled about inside the cavernous space of the building's main room. Kelsey looked around for Tony but spotted Ted first. He looked surprised to see her. "Couldn't get enough of us, could you?" he asked.

"I had a couple more questions for you." She looked around the crowded room. "Can we go somewhere to talk for a minute?"

He frowned and she thought he was going to say no. Instead, he jerked his head toward the back of the room. "This way."

She followed him through a plain metal door to a narrow dirt lot behind the building. Wind whipped around the corner, sending snow spiraling about their knees. Ted leaned against the metal siding of the building, arms folded over his chest. Though his face showed the weathered lines of a man in his sixties, the muscles of his arms bulged with the strength of a younger man. "What do you want to know?" he asked.

"I talked to some of Liz's friends last night," she said. "I'm trying to find out about the man Liz was supposedly dating. She called him Mountain Man whenever she mentioned him to my mom and dad. No one seems to have heard of him or to have ever seen her with anyone in particular."

"How am I supposed to know anything about that?" he asked.

"Her friends remembered one night when they were gathered at an ice-cream parlor in town. Liz told them she was meeting someone, an older man she was dating—or at least, not a high school boy. None of them saw the guy when Liz went out to meet him, but one of them remembered seeing you on the sidewalk near the ice-cream parlor, smoking a cigarette. I wondered if you saw the guy—maybe when Liz came out to meet him?"

Ted stared at her, annoyance twisting his mouth. "You expect me to remember something that happened one random night over twenty years ago, to a girl I didn't even know?"

"Think about it," she said. "Maybe you remember."

He shook his head. "I'm sorry you lost your sister, but this is ridiculous. I was forty years old back then. I had my own busy life. I wouldn't have paid much attention to a bunch of kids."

Kelsey fought disappointment. "It may seem foolish to you, but you might have remembered," she said. "I had to take the chance and ask. I'm sorry I bothered you."

She turned to leave, but his hand on her shoulder stopped her. "Hey," he said.

She turned to look at him, and he dropped his hand. "I'm sorry I went off on you," he said. "I'm just a grouchy old guy. I wish I could help you, but I just can't."

She nodded. "Thanks."

"Look," he said. "You didn't ask my advice, but I'm going to give it to you anyway because I'm a lot older than you, and you don't get old without learning a few things." He went on, not waiting for her to reply. "I know you came here with some idea that you were going to bring this all out in the open and find out what really happened to your sister, but think what you're asking. It's been over twenty years, and in all that time, no one has found one shred of evidence to point to your sister's killer. If there was anything out there, they would have found it by now. If someone knew something, they would have spoken up. This is a small town. There are no secrets here. How are you—someone who isn't a trained investigator or even a law enforcement officer—going to find what other people haven't found before you?"

"I don't have to solve the crime," she said. "All I have to do is find a credible suspect. Someone whose DNA can be compared to the evidence on file at the sheriff's department."

"What kind of evidence?" Ted asked.

"Skin cells under Liz's fingernails, where she fought with her killer. If I find anyone who might be the man who lured her to Eagle Mountain, he can be tested. If he's a match, then they'll have Liz's killer."

"And if they don't?"

"Then I'll have to keep looking." She pushed open the door and went back inside. Saying those words out loud made the task ahead of her almost overwhelming, despite her bravado. The truth was, while reading the files and talking to people made Kelsey feel closer to Liz, she had discovered nothing to help her find out who had ended her sister's life.

THOUGH MANY OF the calls Search and Rescue responded to involved vacationers or travelers on the mountain highway, it wasn't unusual for volunteers to know the people they were called to assist. But Tony didn't recognize the description of the Jeep that had rolled at what was locally known as Dead Man's Curve on the drive down from Dixon Pass. "Driver and passenger both responsive but trapped in the vehicle," Sheri said when the team assembled on Sunday afternoon on the roadside above where the Jeep had gone over. "Eldon and Jake, you go down to the vehicle," she directed. "Caleb and Danny, you go with them. Tony, you help with the ropes up here."

Tony nodded. This time last year, he would have been the one leading the climb down, but since his accident, he'd been relegated to helping with the gear. He told himself that was okay. He was here to contribute in whatever way he could. But a small part of him acknowledged wanting to be climbing down that rope, more directly involved in the rescue instead of waiting for someone to need him up here.

Within twenty minutes, Eldon and the others had reached the vehicle, stabilized it and deployed the Jaws of Life to free the two occupants. Tony's shoulder-mounted radio crackled; Danny's voice came over the speaker. "Hey, Tony. The passenger says he's related to you. Some kid named Chris."

Tony's chest constricted, and he almost dropped the brake-bar rack he was holding. "Chris Meisner is my nephew," he said. "Is he okay?"

"He's going to be sore for a while, but so far it doesn't look like anything serious," Danny said. "I didn't think you had any family in town."

"He hasn't been here long," Tony said. "You're sure he's okay?"

"He's good, but you can check him out yourself. We're going to send him up in a few minutes."

Apparently, Chris had been deemed fit enough to make the climb out of the canyon under his own power, assisted by Caleb. Tony waited as the two of them climbed up over the rim, then hurried to help his nephew out of the harness and helmet. "What happened?" he asked, one hand on Chris's arm.

"Blake and I were talking, and the next thing I know, we're sailing out into nothing." Chris grinned, but his face was paper white beneath his tan, and his laughter sounded forced. "I guess we missed the curve."

"Come over here and sit down." Tony led him to the Search and Rescue vehicle, known as the Beast, and sat him on the back bumper. "Who is Blake?"

"A guy I work with at Mo's."

Tony handed the young man a bottle of water.

"Thanks." But Chris's hands shook so badly Tony had to open the water for him. "That was wild," Chris said, then chugged the water.

"You're sure you're okay?" Tony bent to look in Chris's eyes. "Did you hit your head? How does your back feel?"

"I don't think I hit my head." He ran a hand through his hair. "No bumps or blood. I banged my knee on the dash." He rubbed his left kneecap, then massaged the back of his neck. "Danny said I might have a neck strain, but honestly, I'm okay." He looked around. "How's Blake?"

Tony looked over his shoulder to where others were hauling the litter with the Jeep's driver on board. He should really be over there helping, but he couldn't bring himself to leave Chris. "I'll check on him in a bit," he said. "Was he conscious when you left him?"

Chris laughed again, sounding more relaxed this time. "He was swearing a blue streak and pounding on the steering wheel, furious that he'd torn up his Jeep. He's only had it a few months." His expression sobered. "I think Danny said something about a broken bone? And he had some cuts from the windshield glass." He stared out toward the canyon. "It's wild, isn't it? I can't believe we both walked away from something like that. Well, Blake isn't *walking*, but he will be soon."

Tony clapped him on the back, his throat tight. "I'm glad you're okay," he managed to say. "I'm going to go check on your friend."

Blake was sitting up, being examined by one of the paramedics. Tony pulled Danny aside. "Is he going to be okay?"

"Probable fracture of the distal radius, though he'll need x-rays to confirm," Danny said. "And he's got one cut that might need a few stitches." He looked back toward Chris.

"Your nephew got off with hardly a scratch. So, how long has he been in town?"

"He moved in three days ago."

"I never heard you mention it," Danny said.

"It didn't come up." Tony didn't talk about his personal life much. Before, when he'd lived alone, there wasn't much to say. Chris moving in hadn't really changed that.

"Go be with him," Danny said. "The rest of us can clean up here."

Tony started to argue but thought better of it and returned to Chris, who stood at his approach. Chris drained the rest of the water and crushed the plastic bottle. "So, this is what you do, huh?" He looked around at the ambulance crew and the volunteers gathering up supplies. "Go out and rescue hapless strangers?"

"Some of them not so hapless. And some of them not strangers. Yeah."

Chris nodded. "Cool." He looked toward the drop-off, then away. "I don't think I could do that. I mean, the climbing and stuff would be cool, but dealing with bleeding people…" He shook his head. "I think I'm too empathetic, you know?"

And I'm not empathetic enough, Tony thought. But it wasn't that he didn't care about people. He just kept those feelings to himself. It felt safer that way.

By Monday, Kelsey realized she had run out of people to interview. She had read all the police reports and made copies of some, which she had highlighted and underlined. She had compiled a database in her computer, with a list of everyone she had talked to and everything they had told her. She had created a rough timeline of Liz's life between the time she'd left Iowa and the time she had disappeared. The only information she had gathered that wasn't already in the police reports was that Liz had said she was meeting someone outside the ice cream parlor a few weeks before she went missing. But no one had seen the man or the meeting.

Kelsey decided to go back to the newspaper office. This time, she was looking for news items in the year before Liz's arrival in town—any stories about young women, newly arrived in town, who'd been assaulted or had fights with a boyfriend. She knew there had been no murders reported in the county in the decades prior to Liz's death—a fact that had been stated both in an article in the paper about Liz's murder and in one of the reports in her file.

It was a very long shot, but Kelsey was betting that the man who had killed Liz might have tried with someone else before. Maybe Liz wasn't the first young woman he had lured to town, but that woman had gotten away.

Yet hours of paging through the heavy volumes of back issues yielded only a pounding head and ink-stained fingers.

The door to the morgue opened, and Tammy Patterson stepped in. Her curly hair was in a messy bun today, a pen stuck through the topknot. "How's it going?" she asked.

"Not that well," Kelsey admitted. She closed the volume she'd had open before her. "The truth is, I've read everything you have here, and I'm not finding what I need. I don't know where to look."

Tammy sat in the chair across from Kelsey. "You're looking for information about your sister's murder, right? Elizabeth Chapman?"

Kelsey nodded. "Are you familiar with the story?"

"I looked it up after you were here the first time. Such a tragedy."

"There are so many things I don't know," Kelsey said. "I was hoping by coming here, I could fill in at least a few of the blanks."

"What if I wrote a story about your search?"

"You mean, a newspaper story?"

"It's what I do. And I think it's interesting." She swept her hand in front of her at eye level as if underlining a headline. "'A Sister's Search for Justice.'" She grinned. "That sounds good, doesn't it?"

"I don't know," Kelsey said. Being written about in the paper felt so...exposed.

"It would be a great way to get the case back in the public eye again," Tammy said. "Someone might come forward with new evidence. If there are any specific things you want to know, we could ask people to contact you. Someone might have seen something and not even know its significance. For all the newcomers we have in town, there are still a lot of people who live here now who were living in Eagle Mountain back then."

Tammy's enthusiasm was infectious, and hope flared in Kelsey again. "All right," she said. "When do you want to interview me?"

"How about right now?" Tammy pulled a notebook from her pocket. "We've got space in the next issue."

Chapter Ten

Tony was surprised to get a call from Jessica MacIntosh Monday morning. He was surveying a utility right-of-way and moved into the shade of a pinyon tree to answer his phone. "Hey, Tony," Jessica said. "Is your friend still in town—Liz's sister?"

"Kelsey is still here." At least, he assumed she was. She hadn't contacted him to say goodbye, and she struck him as the type who would.

"Talking with her got Andy and me thinking about Liz and what happened to her."

Tony removed his straw hat and wiped the sweat from his brow. Even on a cool spring day like this, the sun was intense. "Did you remember something?" he asked.

"No, but I did some digging, and I found Ben Everett."

"The guy who wanted to date Liz?"

"Yeah. He's living in Junction now—can you believe it? He just moved back to the area. I told him about Kelsey, and he wants to talk to her."

"That's great."

"Let me give you his number and you can pass it on to Kelsey, okay?"

"Sure. Let me get something to write with." He found a

pen and jotted down the number on the back of a gas receipt he found in his pocket. "Thanks a lot, Jessica."

"I don't know if it will help, but at least it's something, right?"

"At least it's something," he repeated as he tucked away his phone once more. Ben probably didn't know any more than anyone else, but the more people Tony found for Kelsey to talk to, the longer she would stay in town. He knew she would leave eventually, but while she was around, his life felt better.

KELSEY WALKED BACK to the Alpiner Inn Monday afternoon after her interview with Tammy Patterson and was surprised to find Tony waiting for her. "Tony, it's so good to see you," she said, and impulsively embraced him. It was like hugging a stone statue, until he relaxed a little and returned the embrace.

"It's good to see you, too," he said.

"I was just interviewed for the paper," she said. "Tammy Patterson is going to write an article about my search for Mountain Man and information about Liz's life here. We're hoping someone who remembers something will read the article and contact me. Isn't that a good idea?"

"I guess so."

"You guess so?" She frowned. "Do you think it was a bad idea?"

"It's a good idea," he said. "As long as the killer doesn't see it and decide to come after you."

She stared at him, a little light-headed at the thought. He grabbed her elbow. "I shouldn't have said that. I'm sorry. I'm sure it will be fine. Just...promise you'll be careful."

His genuine concern touched her. How long had it been

since anyone had cared about her that much? Her mother was trying, but long years of indifference had carved deep grooves in their lives that were hard to steer out of.

"I promise I'll be careful," she said. "So, what brings you my way this afternoon?"

"I have Ben Everett's contact information. He wants to talk to you about Liz."

Some of her tension eased. "That's wonderful! Where is he? How did you find him?"

"I can't take credit. Jessica found him. He's in Junction."

"And that's near here?" she asked, unsure.

"It's about an hour from here."

"And he wants to talk to me. That's fantastic." She grabbed his arm. "Will you go with me to see him? I know you're really busy, but I would love to have you with me."

"I'll go with you. As long as I don't get a callout from Search and Rescue." It was probably the first time in his life he had wished for no calls at all on that date.

"When can you go?" she asked.

"Why don't you call him and set something up?" he said. "As long as it's after five or on a weekend, I should be available." He handed her the piece of paper with Ben's number.

"I'm going to call him right now." She pulled out her phone and punched in the number. She listened to a message telling her that Ben Everett was unable to come to the phone, then said, "This is Kelsey Chapman. I'm looking for information about my sister, Liz, and I understand you knew her in high school. Please call me so we can set up a time for me to come to Junction and we can talk." She left her number and ended the call.

"What are you going to do now?" Tony asked.

"Are you tired of having dinner with me?"

He shook his head. "No."

She took his hand again. He had rough hands, calloused and strong. She liked the feel of them against her skin. "I was hoping you'd say that," she said.

KELSEY AND TONY stayed late at the restaurant, talking about their college experiences—neither of them was a big joiner, but they had branched out a little and made friends. "I felt more normal in college," she said. "Though I was still aware that I was different from my classmates. They had parents who visited the campus and families they looked forward to seeing at the holidays."

"I only attended school for two more years after high school," Tony said. "That's all I needed to get my surveyor's license, and I wanted to come back to Eagle Mountain and work search and rescue."

"Is your brother still here?" she asked.

"He moved while I was away at school." He smiled, a rueful look. "It didn't matter. I'd already decided I wasn't going to live with him when I got back."

"Do you still see him?"

"Sometimes. He's in Denver. Our lives are so different."

She nodded. She had spent much of her life trying to figure out how to get past the differences that separated her from other people. "But your nephew is still here, right? Chris?"

Tony nodded. "He just showed up on my doorstep a few days ago and asked if he could stay." He sat back, one leg stretched out in front of him, as if he was trying to get comfortable. "He pointed out that since his dad had taken me in when I was a teenager, the least I could do was return the favor. I couldn't argue with that."

"How old is Chris?"

"He's twenty-three. Probably almost twenty-four."

"And he just decided to move back to his old home town?" She sensed Tony wasn't going to offer any details if she didn't ask.

Tony let out a long sigh, and she wondered if she had pushed too far. She was about to say it was really none of her business when he said, "He got in a little trouble back in Denver and needed somewhere to make a fresh start."

"That was good of you to take him in. How's the arrangement working out?" From what she had seen, Tony's house was small, and he struck her as a very private person. Adding a roommate couldn't have been easy.

"It's okay." Tony shook his head. "He's a lot different from me at his age. He got the job at Mo's right away, but he doesn't seem to have any idea what he wants to do with his life."

"You had a plan for your life right out of high school," she said. "It took me forever to figure out what I wanted to do."

"You didn't always want to be an accountant?" Now his smile was genuine—teasing, with a little heat behind it.

"I didn't even like math in school." She laughed. "But it's a good job. I don't dislike it."

"And when you're not working?" he asked. "What do you like to do?"

She thought for a moment. She didn't have any real hobbies, like painting or knitting. She didn't play any sports. "I like to read," she said. "And I like walking. Taking long walks in parks or through towns. I've enjoyed the walks I've taken here."

"If you like hiking, this is the place to be," he said. "There are hundreds of miles of trails in the mountains."

"It would be fun to explore them. With the right guide." She met his gaze and felt the tension between them. The wanting. She sensed he was like her—someone who had spent so many years craving an intimacy that had been denied them. Only now, with him, that kind of closeness felt almost within reach.

He was the first to look away. "How long are you staying in town?" he asked.

"I don't know." She had the room for another week, but would it be so bad to stay longer? To explore those trails and wait for the wildflowers to bloom? To get to know Tony better?

The clatter of glasses startled her out of her reverie. Who was she kidding? If anyone was a confirmed loner, it was Tony. She was pretty sure he was attracted to her, too, but when she went back to Iowa, he would probably settle back into his regular life without a ripple of concern.

"What's your favorite hike in the area?" she asked, steering the conversation into safer territory. Sharing her deepest thoughts and emotions with him had felt liberating, but it also made her vulnerable. She wanted to drop her guard and trust him, but doing so with other people had burned her badly before.

They talked until closing time yet again, then he walked her back to the inn. Eagle Mountain was dark and silent; every business was closed, and no cars were on the street. They walked close together, not touching, but she could feel the warmth of his body. She'd just opened her mouth to say something about how beautiful the night was when the screech of tires jolted a cry from her.

She turned, only to be bombarded by bright headlights. Tony grabbed her arm and jerked her off her feet, pulling her with him as the vehicle raced past, veering onto the sidewalk before roaring into the night.

She clung to Tony, and the two of them huddled against the cold brick of a closed art gallery, hearts pounding painfully. She could hear the drumbeat of his pulse against her ear— her head pressed to his neck, both his arms wrapped tightly around her. She closed her eyes and listened to that steady rhythm, willing herself to breathe evenly, to calm down.

"What was wrong with that guy?" she asked after a while. "Was he drunk or something?"

"I don't know." He loosened his hold on her and pulled away enough to look at her. The streetlight on the corner cast long shadows across his face, hiding his eyes, but she heard the concern in his voice. "Are you okay?"

"I'm fine." She pushed herself upright but kept her hands on his chest. "How could he not see us? We were almost under the streetlight."

"Maybe he did see us," Tony said.

A few seconds passed before the meaning behind his words hit her. "You think he ran us down on purpose?" She was having trouble breathing again, panic rising.

"I don't know." He tightened his hold once more.

She looked in the direction the car had disappeared. "Could you tell what kind of car it was?" she asked. "The engine was so loud. It sounded big."

"I think it might have been a truck. But he had his lights on bright. I couldn't really see anything." His voice shook with emotion. "I'm just glad you're all right."

"I'm all right." She slid one hand up to the back of his neck. "I'm all right because I'm with you." Then she stood on tiptoe and pressed her lips to his, kissing him as if this was the last chance for a kiss she would ever have.

He returned the kiss with the same fervor; his lips warm, assured. His beard was soft against her cheek, and he smelled like soap and pine and something indefinable she could only identify as *him*. As reserved as he might be at times, he held nothing back with this kiss. He was ardent yet tender. This wasn't the sloppy, demanding kisses of her college hookups or the hard, almost-mechanical passion of the men who assumed she wanted the quick release they sought. Tony's kisses made her feel cherished. Desired not for what she could give but for herself. Maybe he didn't have words to express how he felt, but he was showing her now. He slid his hands beneath her coat and caressed her hips. She arched to him, his hard arousal pressed against her sending a rush of heat through her. She wanted to wrap her legs around him, oblivious to their surroundings. "Tony!" she gasped when he finally released her mouth.

He pulled back as if scorched. "Did I hurt you?" he asked.

"No!" She cupped his face and stared into his eyes. "You could never hurt me," she said.

She wanted him to kiss her again—to keep kissing her for the rest of the night—but he turned away. "It's cold," he said. "I'd better get you back to the inn."

But he kept hold of her hand as they walked, fingers entwined, and when she raised his knuckles to her lips, he didn't protest. They stopped outside the inn, and she wanted to ask him in. He must have sensed what she was thinking because he said, "It would be awkward if the Richardses found me here in the morning."

She nodded. This was still a small town. These people were his friends, and she was a stranger. An outsider. Again. "Good night," she said, and stood on tiptoe to kiss him once more. Tenderly, a brush of her mouth to his that still left her trembling as she turned and walked away from him.

Chapter Eleven

Tony left the inn, but he didn't go home. Instead, he retraced their route, then drove in the direction the vehicle that had almost hit them had taken. He didn't know what he expected to find, but he was too restless to settle for the night. His heart raced with desire and anxiety and the knowledge of how close he had come to losing Kelsey. The memory of those headlights bearing down on them left him shaking.

He spotted a vehicle pulled over to the side of the road up ahead—a Rayford County Sheriff's Department SUV. He flashed his lights, then pulled over in front of the vehicle and cut the engine. Deputy Jake Gwynn got out and met him between the vehicles. "What are you doing out so late, Tony?" Jake asked.

Jake's schedule at the sheriff's department limited his availability for callouts. "How long have you been sitting here?" Tony asked.

"About half an hour," Jake said. "It's a good place to catch drunk drivers on their way out of town and catch up on paperwork."

"You stop anybody while you've been here?"

"No. It's been a quiet night. Why are you asking?"

"Kelsey Chapman and I were walking from the Cakewalk

Café to the Alpiner tonight, and someone almost ran us over. The vehicle came up on the sidewalk and must have been doing forty, at least. I don't know how we weren't killed." His heart raced again at the memory.

"What kind of vehicle?" Jake asked. "Did you get a plate number? Or a look at the driver?"

Tony shook his head. "He had his brights on. And he raced away so fast we couldn't see anything."

"Are you okay?"

Tony nodded. "Shook up but okay."

"A few people have driven by me but none of them speeding or driving erratically," Jake said. "Do you want to file a report?"

Tony shoved his hands into his jacket pockets. The wind had picked up, and he was cold. Probably the adrenaline draining off. "What would be the point? I was just hoping you'd seen someone."

"Sorry I couldn't help." Jake assumed a more casual stance, leaning against the front fender of his SUV. "So, you and Kelsey Chapman," he said. "She seems really nice."

"She is." He braced himself for some comment about Kelsey being so much younger than him, or her being from out of town, or even the observation that he didn't usually date.

Instead, Jake said, "Do you think what happened tonight had anything to do with all the questions she's been asking about her sister's murder?"

Tony nodded. "I wondered. If the killer is still around, he probably heard about her and isn't too happy. He's gotten away with murder for twenty years."

"Has anything else like this happened?" Jake asked. "Any threats or unexplained accidents?"

"Not that she's mentioned." But she might not. Tony was learning she could be as reserved as he was.

"Let me know if anything else happens," Jake said.

"I will." He walked back to his Toyota and turned it around, heading back toward his house. Jake had given voice to the suspicions he had been trying to ignore—that a killer had targeted Kelsey.

The idea panicked him, but panic wasn't going to solve anything. He gripped the steering wheel more tightly and focused instead on the sensation of Kelsey's body against his, the scent of her surrounding him, the heat of her warming places that had been cold for so long. Leaving her just now had been one of the hardest things he had ever done, but he'd had to go. Mistakes happened when he acted without thinking. Some people thrived on spontaneity and following their desires, but those were the people he pulled off ledges or rescued from the wilderness when they were lost. Logic and planning didn't solve every problem, but it prevented a lot of them.

There was nothing logical about his feelings for Kelsey, though. She was young and beautiful, and she never looked at him as if he was odd or awkward or all the things he knew others saw. She had *wanted* him tonight, and that in itself was a gift. But what would happen if he took that gift? She was going to leave, probably sooner rather than later. All his life, people had been leaving him, and strong as he tried to be, he didn't think he could take having Kelsey, only to lose her, too.

TUESDAY MORNING, Kelsey woke gasping for breath, heart pounding painfully. She put a hand to her chest and stared at the sun streaming in the window, the memory of the dream that had wakened her slow to recede. Her eyes burned from the glare of headlights coming toward her, the roar of an engine blocking all other sound. She focused on breathing deeply, reminding herself that she was okay. She was alive. She was safe.

She shifted her thoughts to the aftermath of those frightening moments on the sidewalk—she and Tony kissing, finally giving vent to the passion that had simmered between them for days. If he had stayed with her last night, she was sure she wouldn't have dreamed of that racing vehicle.

She thought about calling him but resisted the urge. He struck her as a man who needed space. She didn't want to push him away by being too clingy.

She didn't want to ask for more than he was ready to give. He hadn't been faking his feelings for her last night—she was sure. She would be patient and allow things to develop between them naturally.

Gradually, her heartbeat calmed and she was able to breathe normally. She sat up and checked the clock. It was almost seven o'clock. She would shower, get dressed, go down to breakfast and decide how to spend the rest of the day. Ben Everett should call her back today. If he didn't, she would call him.

She set about these tasks, but she couldn't completely shake the dream—which had, after all, only been a replay of terrifying reality. She tried to tell herself it had been a careless driver, maybe someone looking at their cell phone instead of paying attention to the road.

But the memory of that growling engine, the vehicle accelerating as it came up onto the sidewalk, sent a shudder through her. A distracted driver would have looked up the moment his tire hit the curb, and every instinct would have been to brake. This driver hadn't braked.

But who would want to deliberately hurt them?

Liz's killer. The thought ought to have frightened her, but perversely, a thrill raced through her. If that driver was the person who had murdered Liz, that meant he was here in Eagle Mountain. And she was close enough to identifying him to make him worried.

Maybe he was trying to scare her off, but he only made her more determined to keep digging. Every bit of new information she gathered brought her closer to discovering his identity and finding justice for Liz—and a little peace for her family.

TONY WOKE EARLY TUESDAY, his first thoughts of Liz and everything that had happened last night. Was she all right? He wanted to urge her again to be careful, that he didn't think that vehicle almost hitting them had been an accident. All those questions she had been asking about Liz's murder must be making someone uncomfortable. He knew she wanted to find Liz's killer, and he believed Liz deserved that justice. Her murderer should be punished.

But not if it meant Kelsey getting hurt. He reached for his phone on the nightstand, then pulled back. He had no claim on Kelsey. No right to suggest she act one way or another. If he called her, she might think he was going too far—pressuring her, even.

He set the phone aside, pulled on pants and headed for the kitchen to start coffee. As he passed through the living room, he looked toward the sofa, relieved to see the familiar lump of blankets, one pale foot uncovered. So Chris had made it home last night.

He turned toward the kitchen and almost collided with a woman with a mop of dark curls, long bare legs showing beneath the hem of the T-shirt that appeared to be the only thing she was wearing. He stumbled back and made some incoherent noise.

She smiled. "Hi. You must be Uncle Tony. I'm Amy."

Tony glanced over his shoulder toward the sofa. It was either that or continue staring at her. "You're a, um, friend of Chris's?" he asked.

"Yeah. I went ahead and started coffee. I hope you don't mind. It should be ready in a few."

"No. I mean, thanks. I'll, uh, just get dressed." He retreated to the bedroom to put on the rest of his clothes and hoped she would take the hint to do the same.

When he emerged from the bathroom after a quick shower ten minutes later, he found Chris and Amy, both dressed in jeans and T-shirts, giggling over coffee at the kitchen table while Chris dropped frozen waffles into the toaster. "Hey, Tony," Chris said. "Amy says you two met."

"We did." He filled a mug from the coffee carafe, noting there was just enough left for one cup.

"Chris told me how you were part of the Search and Rescue crew that hauled him up out of the canyon when Blake Russell's Jeep went over the edge Sunday," Amy said.

Tony nodded.

"Blake said the car is trashed," Chris said. "He's hoping the insurance pays enough to get a new one. He's thinking a truck this time."

"I'd get the exact same model of car," Amy said. "After all, that one survived the crash, and both of you lived to tell the tale."

"It was a wild ride," Chris said. "I wish now I'd taken the time to appreciate it."

"Did your life flash before your eyes like they say happens?" Amy asked.

"Nah. All I could think was that I sure wasn't going to ask Blake for a ride again."

They were still laughing as Tony left for work.

He was unlocking his truck when Chris ran up to him. "Hey," he said, stopping beside Tony.

"Hey, yourself." Tony opened the door of his truck.

"You're not upset about Amy, are you? About me bringing her back here last night?"

"I'm not upset." It was unsettling, having yet another person—a stranger—in the home that had been his alone for so long, but he remembered what it was like to be Chris's age. Or at least, he remembered what it had been like for him. "I want you to feel like this is your home. But it might have been a little awkward if I had walked in on you two last night."

Chris shoved his hands into the front pockets of his knit joggers. "Yeah, well, she still lives with her parents, so that's not an option." He grinned. "Maybe we should work out some kind of signal or something, like a rag tied to the doorknob or a window shade pulled down halfway—in case you have a lady friend over sometime and need privacy."

Tony started to say that wasn't going to happen, but he stopped himself. He had come close to asking Kelsey to come back here with him last night. The thought of possibly encountering Chris had kept him from extending the invitation, but obviously, his nephew wasn't a naive kid anymore. "We'll think of something," he said. "Though something tied to the doorknob or a window shade isn't going to do any good if you come home after I'm in bed alone."

"We obviously didn't wake you," Chris said. "And anyway, I knew you were sound asleep. You snore like a grizzly bear. We could hear you all the way in the living room."

Laughing, he turned away. Tony smiled and slid into the truck. He liked that after all that had happened in his young life, Chris could still laugh so easily.

BEN EVERETT RETURNED Kelsey's call midday on Tuesday, and they arranged to meet at six thirty that evening at his home in Junction. As soon as she ended the call with him, she phoned Tony. "Hey," he said. "I'm driving to a job site, so you're on the speaker in the car. My helper, Brad, is with me."

"Hello," a male voice said.

Kelsey had intended to say something flirtatious and maybe even a little risqué but thought better of it. "Ben can meet us this evening at six thirty at his house," she said. "Will that work for you?"

"I'll pick you up at five thirty," he said.

"Great. See you then."

She started to end the call, but he asked, "What are you doing today?"

"I'm going to review all my notes, maybe make some calls related to work," she said. "And I need to think about what I want to ask Ben."

"That's good," he said. "If you go out, be careful."

The concern she heard behind the words touched her. "I will," she said.

"See you at five thirty," he said, and ended the call.

She lay back on the bed and stared at the ceiling, the

memory of kissing him last night coming back to her, every sensation so vivid it was almost as if he were still touching her. The intensity of her feelings frightened her. She wasn't like this. When other people panicked, she was calm. It wasn't that she didn't feel things, but she didn't let those emotions show. She didn't want to be that vulnerable.

But Tony had stripped away every pretense. Every nerve felt exposed to him, and it was both painful and exhilarating. And none of it made sense. She had come here to learn about her sister. Not to discover this hidden side of herself.

BEN EVERETT LIVED in a very modern steel-and-glass home perched on the side of a canyon in a neighborhood full of similar modern homes on the west side of Junction. Tony pulled his Toyota into the driveway as the sun was setting and turning the expansive windows the deep oranges and pinks of saltwater taffy. Ben came to the door as they walked up a stone path—a slender man with swept-back blond hair, dressed in running shoes, gray slacks and a white polo. "Ben Everett," he said, and offered a firm handshake.

Kelsey introduced herself, then turned to Tony. "I remember you," Ben said, clapping Tony on the shoulder. "It's good to see you again."

"It's good to see you, too," Tony said. Ben's claim to remember him seemed sincere, but it surprised him. Though their high school class had been small, the two of them hadn't moved in the same circles, and Tony, having been new to the group, had always been on the edges of any activity, on the outside looking in. Ben had been handsome, athletic and popular—the one boy with enough confidence to pursue Liz Chapman.

Ben led them into a great room with soaring ceilings and

a wall of glass that looked out into the canyon, the dying sun bathing its sides in watercolor shades. Whatever he did for a living now, he had obviously done well financially. "Can I get you a drink or anything to eat?" he asked.

"No, thank you," Kelsey said, and settled onto a long brown suede sofa. Tony sat beside her and had the sensation of sinking into a marshmallow. Kelsey brushed her hand against his thigh and smiled as if grateful to have him near.

"My wife took the kids to soccer, so we have the place to ourselves for a couple of hours," Ben said, sinking into the chair across from them. He studied Kelsey a moment. "I can see the resemblance to your sister."

It was true that Kelsey and Liz had the same coloring and the same dimple on the left side of the mouth. But Tony saw all the ways she was different from her sister. Kelsey had none of the boldness that had made Liz both fascinating and forbidding. Kelsey was quieter and more contemplative. More introverted. More like him.

"Did you know Liz well?" she asked Ben.

"If you had asked me that back in high school, I would have said yes." He laced his fingers together over one knee. "She and I were friends. I wanted more, but she made it clear that wasn't possible."

Kelsey leaned forward, hope written so clearly in her expression. "When you say *friends*, do you mean she confided in you?"

"She did and she didn't." He tilted his head. "I'm sure you've already talked to enough people to know that after she disappeared, we found out a lot of things she hadn't told us. I had no idea she wasn't living with her parents. She said she had moved to Eagle Mountain from Iowa, and I just assumed she meant her whole family had moved."

"Did she ever mention a boyfriend?" Kelsey asked.

"Yes."

Kelsey fumbled her pen. "She did? Did she tell you his name?"

"She did not." He cracked his knuckles. "Why don't I start at the beginning, tell you what I know and you can ask questions to fill in the blanks. Though there are a lot of things I don't know."

"Yes, please." Kelsey laid down her pen and sat back, though Tony could feel the slight tremble that ran through her. He reached over and took her hand; she didn't pull away. "Tell me everything," she said.

Chapter Twelve

Twenty years ago

"Liz, I know you like me. Why won't you go to the prom with me?" Ben leaned against the locker next to Liz's and watched her rummage through the chaos inside, searching for who knew what. Liz was smart and beautiful and sharp as a razor—but organized, she was not.

"I can't go with you, Ben," she said. "But it's really sweet of you to ask."

Sweet was for little girls and puppy dogs. He didn't want Liz to think of him as sweet. "Are you going with someone else?" he asked. "You can tell me. I promise I won't get angry." Jealous as hell, but that was nothing new. Every guy in school lusted after Liz; it was a known fact.

"I'm not going with anyone else." She closed the locker and turned to face him. "I'm not going to prom."

"But why not?" He straightened. "It's the last big party before graduation. The prom committee goes all out to make it special."

She shook her head. "I'm not going."

"It won't be the same without you." He leaned closer, his voice low. "Is it a money thing? Because I could help you with the dress and stuff." Ben's parents had money, and they were generous with him and his sister.

She touched his shoulder, and his knees almost buckled. "That's so sweet, but no, it's not because of money." She moved past him, heading toward the exit doors. He lengthened his stride to catch up with her.

"I'm not going to leave you alone until you tell me why you can't go," he said.

She looked around them, as if checking for anyone who might be listening. They exited the doors, and she pulled him to one side, into an alcove behind what was supposed to be a native-plant garden but was mostly a circle of dirt with some rocks. "You have to swear to never tell a soul," she said.

"I swear," he said, excited by the prospect of sharing a secret with her.

She looked into his eyes, hers so blue—and a little sad. "I mean it. Not a word to anyone."

He nodded. "Okay."

She took a deep breath and let it out. "I can't go with you because I'm already seeing someone," she said.

"You're kidding." It wasn't the mature, reasonable response he wanted to make, but the words burst out before he could take them back.

"I'm not kidding." She smoothed her hands down her arms. "He's older, and he's really jealous."

"I've never seen you in town with anyone else," he said. Was she trying to spare his feelings or shake him off by making up this older guy?

"We have to keep our relationship secret," she said.

"Why? That's messed up."

She smiled, but her eyes still held that sad look.

"Who is this guy?" he asked. "How did you meet him?"

"I met him online," she said. "And you don't need to know his name."

He knotted his fists, beyond frustrated with this mystery game she insisted on playing. "Why do you want to hang out with some older guy?" he asked. He knew it was a pointless question. Girls always wanted older guys. Older guys had cool cars and money and experience with sex. He drove a Toyota, had an allowance and had slept with one girl, someone he had met over Christmas break on vacation in Vail. She had been nice, but they hadn't even talked since.

Liz put her hand on his arm again. She must have thought she was being kind; she didn't realize she was torturing him. "If I was going to go to prom, I would go with you," she said. "I have to go now. But remember—you swore not to tell anyone my secret."

"I won't tell." She left and he told himself he wasn't going to turn around and watch her like some lovesick fool. But he could only stare at the ground for a few seconds before he did turn and look after her. Her long brown hair swayed in counterpoint to her hips as she walked, graceful and almost not real.

"WHY DIDN'T YOU tell the sheriff about this older boyfriend?" Kelsey asked when Ben had finished his story. He had confirmed what she already believed—that Liz had moved to Eagle Mountain to be with Mountain Man. But if he had told the sheriff about this jealous boyfriend, they might have done more to try to find him right away.

"I had promised her I wouldn't say anything." Ben blew out a breath. "And the cops didn't ask. If they had, I probably would have caved and told them everything. I was scared spitless when they hauled me into the station. They accused me of killing her. They said I was angry because she wouldn't go out with me. I would have told them anything they wanted to know, but they didn't ask." He shook his head. "I thought I was being honorable, keeping her secret. I was just a kid. I know better now."

"You must have been watching her after that," Tony said. "Did you ever see her with anyone?"

Kelsey nodded, grateful he had thought to ask this question.

"Yeah, I watched her. You did, too. I saw you. I saw how all the guys looked at her, and it made me feel kind of hopeless. I was so gone over her, and I know to her, I was just a nice boy." He said the word *boy* as if it was a curse. "I never saw her with anyone but friends at school. Girlfriends. I even tried following her home one day, but she saw me and told me to leave her alone. She acted so hurt I had to go. I didn't want her to think I was some kind of creep." He turned back to Kelsey. "Do you think this boyfriend is the one who killed her?"

"I don't know," Kelsey said. "But if I could find him, the sheriff could compare his DNA to the evidence he still has."

"They took my DNA," Ben said. "I had nightmares afterwards that I had somehow left DNA on her clothes when I brushed against her or something, but it turned out I wasn't a match. What kind of evidence do they have? I never heard."

"They have skin cells from under the fingernails," Kelsey said. "They think she fought with her attacker."

"I hope she scarred him for life," he said. He stood and began to pace. "I was wrecked when I found out she was dead. I felt guilty, as if I could have saved her. That was foolish, too, but that's how kids are sometimes. Everything is all about you at that age." He stopped in front of Kelsey. "Do you know anything about this guy—the boyfriend?"

"She told you the truth when she said she met him online. There are copies of some of the emails they exchanged in the case file. He signed his messages Mountain Man, and that's how she referred to him with us. She refused to tell us his name. She told my parents she was going to Colorado to be with him, and then she left."

"Your parents must have been worried sick," Ben said.

"They were," Kelsey agreed. "But she was eighteen. My dad said if she wanted to leave, there wasn't anything he could do to stop her. He was sure she would come home after a few weeks."

Ben sat once more and leaned forward, elbows on his knees, head bowed. She pictured him as a good-looking yet awkward teen—almost a man but still a boy, too. In love with her sister, whom everyone seemed to adore.

Everyone but her killer.

"When they found her body, it broke something in me," Ben continued. He looked up, face anguished. "It broke something in all of us. I mean, none of us were old enough to have experienced real tragedy. And we thought we knew Liz. She was our friend. But then we found out how much we didn't know about her."

"Is there anything else you remember about Liz?" Kelsey asked. "Anything at all that might help?"

"I've thought and thought, but I really can't. When she first disappeared, I thought maybe she had moved and just not told all of us. Maybe her dad got transferred or something. Then one of her teachers asked me if I knew where she was. That's when I got really worried. That's when I first realized how much she hadn't told me about herself. I didn't know her parents' names or where she lived or anything. Then, when they found her body like that…" He shook his head. "At first, we all thought she must have fallen hiking and hit her head. It would still have been terrible, but those kinds of accidents happen. The first time I heard she had been murdered was when the sheriff's deputies brought me in for questioning and accused me of having killed her." He looked at Tony. "Did you know when you found her? Did you know she had been murdered?"

"No," Tony said. "I thought it was an accident, too." He cleared his throat. "The deputies tried to get me to confess to killing her, too."

Ben nodded. "I guess they were desperate to find the murderer, and since the evidence wasn't pointing to anyone in particular, they decided to try to pressure a confession out of every guy who'd ever been near her."

"Who else did they accuse?" Kelsey asked. "Do you know?"

Ben and Tony exchanged glances, then Ben shook his head. "I don't know who else they accused. I just know they never found the person who did that to her."

They sat in silence with this thought, then Kelsey gathered her notebook and purse and stood. "Thank you for talking with me," she said. "You're the first person to confirm there actually was a boyfriend, and I appreciate that."

"I hope it helps." He walked with them to the door. "I guess the boyfriend is the most likely suspect, but what if it wasn't him? What if it was just some random killer?"

"If that's the case, we'll probably never know," she said.

"Will you let me know if you find out anything?"

"I will."

They said goodbye and left. "That was intense," Tony said as he started the car.

"Yes." She blew out a breath. "But it was good to hear someone confirm that Mountain Man existed. If he was real, we ought to be able to find him."

"If anything happens to me, I hope I have someone like you on my side," he said. "You never give up."

"Neither do you." She angled her body toward him. "Think how many people would have died in these mountains if you and the rest of the Search and Rescue volunteers had given up."

"That was a matter of life or death," he said.

"This feels like that, too."

He nodded. "I guess it does." He smoothed his hands along the steering wheel. "So what next?"

"Let's go back to your place."

"You want to see where I live?"

"I want to finish what we started last night."

To his credit, he didn't falter, though she thought he turned a shade paler. "Are you sure that's a good idea?" he asked.

She leaned over and put a hand on his thigh. "I think it's a very good idea."

He cleared his throat. "If you're leaving town—"

"Shh. I know you're not afraid of risks. You risk everything every time you go out on a search and rescue call. Don't be afraid to take a chance on me. On us."

Chapter Thirteen

Tony knew all about being afraid and moving forward anyway. He wasn't afraid of Kelsey, of course—only of making a mistake. But he wasn't going to let that fear stop him from savoring this moment. He pulled into the driveway of his home and stopped the car. A quick glance showed no sign of Chris's motorcycle. It was only a few minutes after nine, and he seldom made it in before ten.

"Is your nephew home?" Kelsey asked, as if reading his mind.

"I'm pretty sure he's out." He gestured toward the front of the garage, where a security light cast a warm circle of light on the front of the house. "He parks his motorcycle there."

He got out of the car and wondered if he should walk around to open her door, but she slid out and met him at the front of the vehicle. They were halfway up the walk to the front door when she stopped and looked up at the house. "I like it," she said. "It looks like you."

"You've lost me there. How am I like a house? Or how is my house like me?"

"You're both simple yet handsome, strong and unpretentious. And you look like you belong in the mountains."

He laughed. "I'm not handsome."

She slid her arm around him. "You are to me."

He was half-afraid she was trying to flatter him, but he reminded himself she wasn't like that. He unlocked the door and let her in. He had brought women to this place before, but it had been a long time. And he had never wanted to impress them the way he wanted to impress Kelsey. "Welcome," he said, and tossed his keys onto the table by the door.

"It's beautiful," she said.

He knew her words were true because, unlike him, the house *was* beautiful. He had worked hard to make it so, replacing the old, narrow casements with larger picture windows, refinishing all the woodwork to a warm cherry hue, installing a tiled woodburning stove and sanding the wide pine floors to restore them to their original patina. The furniture was simple, mostly leather and wood. Comfortable.

"Chris, are you here?" he called. The bike hadn't been in the driveway, but there was always the chance that it had broken down and Chris had gotten a ride home from a friend.

No answer. Good. They were alone.

He watched Kelsey while she examined the house. She walked around the room, studying the books on the shelves; examining a coaster made of a wood round cut from a length of firewood; admiring the prints on the wall, most of them by local artists, purchased at fundraising events for the Search and Rescue team. He was still standing there when she turned and walked into his arms. "Thank you for bringing me here," she said. "For letting me invade your sanctuary."

"I'm happy to have you here." He kissed her. Not the desperate flood of passion like last night but a more deliberate caress, enjoying the sensation of her satin lips, her tongue sending sparks of desire through him as it tangled with his.

She slid her hands underneath his shirt and moaned. "You don't know how much I've wanted to do this," she whispered, her mouth against his neck.

"I think I have an idea." He put his hand over hers, stopping the tantalizing progress of her fingers up his body. "Give me a sec, okay?"

"Okay." Looking amused, she watched as he glanced around the room until he spotted a dish towel on the corner of the bar. He grabbed it, then returned to the front door and knotted the towel around the doorknob, where it would be clearly visible to anyone approaching. By the time he returned to her, she was trying to stifle a giggle. "Was that a...a signal?" she asked, laughter escaping from behind the hand that covered her mouth.

"I don't want any interruptions," he said. "Do you?"

She shook her head. He grabbed the hem of his T-shirt, pulled it off over his head and tossed it across the room. The soft look in her eyes made him feel unsteady on his feet, and when she reached out and traced her fingers along the knotted muscles of his shoulders, he suppressed a groan.

She stopped at the thick ridge of scar tissue across the top of his left shoulder. "What is this?" she asked, voice full of concern.

"I had an accident last winter," he said.

"What happened?"

He took her hand and led her toward the bedroom. "Come in here and I'll show you." She might as well know what she was getting into before they went too far. His body had a story to tell, and it wasn't always pretty.

The bedroom was a smaller space at the back of the

house, with an antique bed, a nightstand and a single chair where he dumped his clothes before they made it into the hamper. He stood beside the chair now and began to undress as she watched from the doorway. He wasn't embarrassed or self-conscious. Months of surgeries and hospital stays and grueling rehab had erased any remnants of modesty he might once have possessed.

He only cringed when he heard her small gasp. He knew the scars were ugly—white and recessed or red and raised. They were fading and would fade more as time passed, but they marked him and reminded him of how close he had walked to death.

He didn't hear her cross the room, but suddenly, she was beside him, reaching out to touch each scar, then bending to kiss the one on his chest, where they had inserted a tube to reinflate his collapsed lung. She bent lower, to the place where doctors had repaired his broken pelvis with metal screws and plates. Down farther, to the crisscross of scars on his right leg, broken in three places by the fall. Her hot breath against his skin made him shiver, and his erection was almost painful in its intensity.

He touched her shoulder and urged her to her feet again. "Come here," he said, and she moved closer.

She didn't make a move to remove her clothes but let him undress her. Unlike him, she was perfect, her skin creamy and unblemished, small round breasts tipped with pink nipples, a gentle curve of waist to hips and thighs poets would probably write odes to. All he could do was run his hands over her and curse the roughness of the calluses built up from many years of climbing.

She slipped her hand into his and kissed his shoulder. "Take me to bed, and tell me your story," she said.

There was no point asking if she still wanted him now that she had seen him. Clearly, she did. And he had never wanted anything as badly as he wanted her. But he forced himself to wait a little longer. Long enough to tell her. "I was descending into a canyon during a search and rescue training exercise," he said. "My ropes gave way and I fell."

She made a choking sound and pressed a hand to his chest. He covered her hand with his own, then lifted it to his mouth and kissed her fingers. "One of the other volunteers had burned the ropes with acid so that they broke when I was halfway down."

"He hated you that much?" she asked.

"He didn't hate me specifically. His fiancée had died in an accident in the mountains two years before. He blamed Search and Rescue for not saving her life. I was captain of the team at the time."

"You must have been hurt very badly," she said.

"I was. But the medical personnel and my fellow SAR members saved my life. They put me back together, but I'll always have these scars."

"Then each one is like a photograph," she said. "A reminder that you were strong enough to live." She moved over him, sliding her body onto his, covering his imperfections with her perfection. He closed his eyes and welcomed her kisses, tracing his hands and his mouth over her with growing excitement.

He was kissing his way across her stomach when sense returned, and he stilled. He looked up at her.

"What's wrong?" she asked, and brushed his hair out of his eyes.

"I don't have a condom," he said. "I haven't been, um, sexually active in a while."

"Neither have I." She smiled. "It's okay. I'm on birth control. For other reasons. I think it's safe to say we're both healthy."

He slid up to kiss her on the lips again, then she was shifting beneath him, opening to him, urging him inside her. She wasn't shy about telling him what she wanted, and he was happy to comply. And when she began to move beneath him, he had no trouble following her lead. He slipped one hand beneath her hips to bring her closer and caressed her with the other until she was panting and moaning, and he knew any moment he would be gone.

She tensed around him, arching, and her release reverberated through him, triggering his own climax. He cried out. He might have said her name. He was past sensible thought, reacting with old instincts when he pulled her close and buried his face against her neck, chest heaving. She wiggled out from under him; he moved over to make room for her, and she lay, one thigh draped across his, curled against his side. "Was it worth the risk?" she whispered.

Still dazed, it took him a moment to realize what she was referring to. He hugged her closer. "Yes," he said, and closed his eyes.

THEY MADE LOVE again in the early morning, the first rays of sunlight streaming through the bedroom's one window, and Kelsey discovered a playful side to Tony. "I'm beginning to wonder about your fascination with my scars," he said as she kissed her way along the path a surgeon's scalpel had made to repair his injured left femur.

"Maybe I've always had fantasies about being with a bionic man," she said.

"There's one part of me that's never been injured and is

one hundred percent original," he said, and pulled her up his body, his erection thrust against her.

"Are you sure you're ready to go again, old man?" she teased.

He let out a whoop and flipped her over on her back. "I'll show you *old*," he said, grinning, then proceeded to prove his vitality, much to her satisfaction.

The sun was up by the time they were both sated, the sheets a tangle. "Do you think Chris heard that?" she asked, then giggled.

"From what I've seen, he could sleep through an earthquake." Tony kissed her shoulder. "I'm going to make some coffee," he said, unwrapping himself from the covers and heading for the kitchen, giving her a lovely view of his naked backside and the corded muscles of his back. There wasn't an ounce of fat on the man, which was a little intimidating—and pretty impressive, too, despite his protestations that he wasn't handsome.

"I'm going to take a shower!" she called after him, half hoping he would join her.

When she emerged from the bathroom some ten minutes later, she found her way to the kitchen, where Chris grinned up at her from the kitchen table. "Good morning," he said around a mouthful of cold cereal. He finished chewing and wiped his mouth. "I saw the rag on the doorknob and figured we had company, so I made sure to get dressed before I wandered in here."

She laughed, even as her cheeks heated. She turned to pour a cup of coffee. "Where's Tony?"

"He got a call and went to take it outside." He turned back to his cereal.

She took her coffee to the table and sat across from him.

"Are you always up this early?" she asked. Tony had said he usually came home late.

"Nope." He pushed the empty cereal bowl away. "But I have to be somewhere this morning. If it pans out, I might have to change my night owl ways."

"Oh?" She arched one eyebrow in question, but he merely shook his head.

"Can't tell you," he said. He glanced over his shoulder. "I especially can't tell Tony. Not yet."

Before she could question him further, he waved and left the room. Moments later, the motorcycle roared to life. Tony came through the back door. "Where's Chris off to so early?" he asked. "Did he say?"

She shook her head. She was surprised to find him already dressed in black tactical pants and a long-sleeved Eagle Mountain Search and Rescue tee. He held up his phone. "I got a call from Search and Rescue," he said. "A hiker is injured up on Kestrel Trail."

"The trail where you found Liz," she said. Just the name of the place made her heart beat faster.

He nodded. "It doesn't sound serious, but I need to go. We're shorthanded, with some of our most reliable volunteers out of town. I'll drop you by the inn on the way to SAR headquarters."

"Of course." She hurried to gather her purse and shoes, conscious that someone's life depended on her haste. She was shaking with nerves by the time they hustled to the car. "Are you really as calm as you look?" she asked as she buckled her seat belt.

"I'm going over in my mind everything we need to get together and what we'll have to do when we get there," he said. He glanced at her. "I'm not in good-enough shape yet to do much climbing, so I'll probably assist up top with rigging the ropes or wherever I'm needed."

"Is that hard, letting other people do what you've done before?" she asked.

"This work isn't about ego," he said. "It's about protecting each other and the patient."

He pulled in front of the Alpiner a few minutes later, and she opened the door. "Call me when you get back so I'll know you're safe," she said.

He leaned over and kissed her, a hard press of her lips to his. "Go," he said, and she went.

He was out of sight by the time she reached the front door. Hannah exited before she came in. "Was that Tony?" she asked.

Kelsey nodded. She hadn't planned on keeping her relationship with Tony secret, but arriving at the Alpiner with him at this time of morning was tantamount to an announcement that they had spent the night together.

To Hannah's credit, she didn't comment. "If I had known, I would have asked him for a ride," she said. "But Jake is coming to get me."

Kelsey went inside and up to her room. She lay on the bed, exhausted by the flood of emotion from these past days and hours. Could she do this? Could she be with a man who left at a moment's notice to put his life on the line? This was who Tony was, and she couldn't ask him to give it up. But could she really be that strong?

THE WORST SEARCH and rescue calls, the ones that stuck in people's memories and got written up in the paper, involved dangerous ascents of mountains, treacherous drops into canyons, treks over rough terrain in snow or fording icy rivers.

Volunteers flirted with death as they battled the elements—
and sometimes the injured persons themselves—to bring
everyone to safety.

Then there were the calls like the one Eagle Mountain
Search and Rescue responded to Wednesday morning. Good
weather. A relatively minor injury on a marked trail. To the
hiker who had slipped on loose rock and broken an ankle,
the arrival of rescue volunteers was probably just as mem-
orable as those other, more risky missions. But to Tony,
Danny, Anna and Eldon, this save was a chance to be out
in beautiful weather and lend a helping hand.

Carla Simmons was a fifty-five-year-old mother of three
from Sacramento who had the bad luck to land the wrong
way when she fell while hiking Kestrel Trail, ending up with
a simple fracture of her right ankle. "You win a free ride
down the mountain," Danny announced after examining her.

She looked up at them, pale and growing foggy-eyed from
the pain medication Danny had administered. "Thank you,"
she said. "I'm sorry to be so much trouble."

"No trouble," Tony said. "It's a beautiful day to be on
the mountain."

"I thought so, too, until I fell," she said.

They made quick work of splinting the fracture and making Carla as comfortable as possible on the litter. They were
strapping her in for the trip down the trail when a voice
hailed them. Tony looked up and was startled to see Ted
striding toward them.

"What are you doing here, old man?" Danny asked.

"I was hiking and heard the call go out," Ted said. "Since
I was nearby, I thought I'd see if you needed any help."

"We've got it all covered, thanks," Tony said.

Ted nodded and moved on. Tony turned back to their patient. "Funny coincidence, him being out here this morning," Danny said. Like Tony, he had been a member of SAR long enough to know Ted well.

"I think he gets bored sometimes," Tony said. "He misses SAR. It was such a big part of his life for so long." He thought sometimes about how he would cope if he had to leave the group.

Danny looked up the trail, in the direction Ted had walked. "Go get him and tell him he can give us a hand with this litter. He could probably use the exercise, and I trust him not to slack off."

Tony jogged up the trail. He hadn't gone far before he spotted Ted, off to the side, on the rocky bench where Liz's body had lain. "I keep thinking about that girl," Ted said as Tony approached.

Tony stepped up beside him. "Yeah. I find myself on a rescue sometimes, and I'll remember another mission at that same place. You would think they would all blur together after a while—but for me, they don't."

"They don't for me, either," Ted said. "I keep wondering if there's something—some evidence—up here the cops didn't find." Ted kicked at the rock at their feet. "They were a bunch of bozos back then. None of them had any training in investigation. It's a wonder people didn't get away with murder every day."

"Sometimes law enforcement is able to solve cases a long time after the crime was committed," Tony said. "But I don't think it happens all that often."

"That girl, Kelsey, came to see me Sunday morning before the meeting," Ted said. "She thinks she's going to solve this thing, you know?"

"I know."

"She said the sheriff has DNA evidence and all she has to do is find a suspect for him to test. I told her if it was that easy, the cops would have done it a long time ago, but you know how kids are. They think they can do anything."

"Twenty-eight isn't exactly a *kid*," Tony said.

Ted grunted.

"Come on," Tony said. "We need you to help with this litter."

Ted straightened. "You do, do you?"

"We couldn't do it without you."

Ted nodded. "Then let's get to it." He set out ahead of Tony down the trail, back straight, head up. Looking younger than his sixty-two years.

Chapter Fourteen

Kelsey called the sheriff's department Wednesday afternoon. "I need an appointment with the sheriff," she said when Adelaide answered the phone. "I want to share with him everything I've found out about Liz's last days and ask him some questions."

She braced herself for a lecture about how the sheriff was a busy man, but all Adelaide said was, "He's here now, and I think this would be a good time if you can come on over."

Fifteen minutes later, she was seated across from the handsome sheriff, though Travis Walker looked a bit less pressed and polished than he had during their previous interview. His tie was loosened and his hair was a little mussed. He was staring at something in his hand when she entered the office, a look of deep concern on his face.

She waited for him to say something, but when he continued to stare at the square of paper in his hand, she cleared her throat. "Sheriff?" she asked.

He looked up and blinked, then straightened. "Hello, Ms. Chapman," he said. "I'm sorry, I'm a little distracted." He held out the piece of paper. "I just came from an ultrasound appointment with my wife. We're having twins, and they're due in six weeks. It's starting to seem very real."

His look of helplessness was so endearing she couldn't help but smile. "Congratulations," she said, and admired the image of two tiny infants curled around each other in their mother's womb. "That's a lot to take in, isn't it?" she asked.

He nodded, then opened the desk drawer and slid the photo inside. He smoothed his hand through his hair, then straightened his tie. When he addressed her again, he was all business. "Adelaide said you had some information about your sister?"

"I spoke with a former classmate of hers, Ben Everett," she said. "He lives in Junction now. He told me he asked Liz to be his date for the senior prom, but she turned him down. She said it was because she had an older boyfriend who was very jealous."

"Ben was interviewed at the time of Liz's death, and there's nothing about that in the case file."

"He didn't say anything because he had promised Liz he wouldn't. He thought he was being honorable."

Travis took a stack of files from the corner of his desk. As he opened the top one, she recognized notes from the murder investigation. "Did he know who this older boyfriend was?" he asked.

"No. He tried to find out. He even followed Liz from school one day. But she saw him and ordered him to leave her alone."

"Do you think he's telling the truth?"

"I do. He said deputies interviewed him after Liz's body was found, and they accused him of killing her. He was frightened, and I believe if he had known anything that would throw suspicion on someone else, he would have done so."

Travis nodded and flipped through the pages in the file. "Have you learned anything else?"

She consulted the notes she had compiled from her interviews. "Some classmates of Liz's remember one night at the ice-cream parlor. She said she had to leave soon, that she was meeting someone. She wouldn't tell them who, and after she left, no one saw who she met."

"No one?" Travis asked. "Weren't they curious?"

"They say they didn't see anyone. But Veronica Olivares remembered that Ted Carruthers was standing on the sidewalk outside of a bar near the ice-cream parlor when Liz left. They thought he might have seen something. I asked him, but he says he doesn't remember. He didn't know Liz, and he had probably just stepped out to smoke a cigarette."

Travis nodded. "Anything else?"

"Nothing that you don't already know," she said. "Were there any suspects other than Ben and Tony? Were there any older men in town that they considered as her boyfriend?"

"I was in middle school when your sister was killed," he said. "I remember that it was a popular topic of conversation around town, and people were shocked when her body was discovered. But everything I know about the investigation is in these files." He tapped the stack of folders in front of him. "The same ones you saw."

"What about Mel Wheeler?" she asked.

Travis frowned. "Who is Mel Wheeler?"

"I was reviewing my notes this morning and came across his name," she said. "He was one of the Search and Rescue volunteers who helped retrieve Liz's body. He moved to Phoenix the year after her death."

"And you think he had something to do with your sister's murder?"

She flushed. "Probably not, but he was a man living in town at the time—so shouldn't you check him out?"

Travis grabbed a pen and made some notes on a yellow legal pad. "I'll see what I can find out."

She nodded. "Is there anyone in town who was on the force then?" she asked.

"No." The fine lines at the corners of his eyes tightened. "Some of them are in jail, and others moved away. The department started over with a clean slate."

"I feel like we're so close to figuring out the identity of Mountain Man," she said. "I can't believe, in a town this small, that someone didn't see Liz with him. She was the type of woman other people noticed."

"I heard someone attempted to run down you and Tony Meisner Monday night," he said.

The fact that he knew this jolted her. "Who told you that?" she asked.

"Tony mentioned it to Jake Gwynn. Tell me what happened."

"A car or truck ran up on the sidewalk and might have hit us both if we hadn't dived out of the way," she said.

"Did you see the car or driver?" the sheriff asked.

"No. The headlights were too bright. Tony said he thought it was a truck, though."

"Have you had any other threats? Anyone behaving suspiciously?"

"No. If that was someone who was upset about me digging into Liz's death, they've kept quiet since."

Travis closed the file. "If anything else happens that feels threatening, let us know. I can't stop you from talking to people about your sister, but consider that you could be endangering yourself."

"I'll be careful," she said, and stood to leave. She wasn't going to stop trying to find out information. Not when she felt she was so close to finding Liz's killer.

THE CALLOUT TO Kestrel Trail meant Tony reported late for work Wednesday, which meant getting off late also. When he finally got back to the house, he was surprised—but not displeased—to find Kelsey's car parked there. He went inside and followed the sound of voices to the back deck. She sat in a plastic chair across from the grill, where Chris was turning burgers. "Hey, you're just in time for the party," Chris said. "The food's almost ready." He waved a spatula in the direction of a cooler next to Kelsey's chair. "Help yourself to a beer."

She planted her hand on the top of the cooler as he approached. "You have to pay the toll," she said.

"And what's the toll?"

"A kiss."

Aware of Chris's laughter behind him, he leaned in and gave her a kiss—a good, long one that had Chris making gagging noises.

They broke apart, laughing. Tony helped himself to a beer and settled into the chair next to Kelsey's. "Is there some special occasion?" he asked. "Or did you just feel like cooking?"

"Aren't you going to ask me why I'm not at Mo's, working?" Chris asked.

Tony frowned. "This isn't your night off?"

"I'm not at Mo's because I quit," Chris said.

Tony gripped his beer bottle tighter but forced himself not to shout. "Did something happen?" he asked.

Chris, spatula held aloft like a scepter, turned to face

him once more. "Something happened," he said. "I got a new job."

Beside him, Kelsey's grin matched Chris's. The two of them were watching him, gleeful. Tony took a long sip of beer before he responded. "Where's the new job?"

"Eagle Surveying," Chris said. "I blew them away in my interview this morning, and they hired me on the spot."

Tony set his beer down carefully to avoid spilling it. "Eagle Surveying is where I work," he said carefully.

Chris's grin broadened. "Isn't it great?" He dragged over a chair and plopped down in front of them. "I'm going to be kind of a general gofer to start, but I'm thinking this fall, I can enroll in some online courses to work toward my degree and eventually get my license."

"What made you decide on surveying?" he asked.

"I passed you one day out on the highway," Chris said. "You were out there in the woods on a beautiful day, just you and one other guy in a truck—no office, no one looking over your shoulder. I did a little research into it, and it sounded like something I would like."

"It's not all beautiful days and being on your own," Tony said. "Some days you're out in pouring rain or broiling heat. And you still have bosses and customers to answer to."

"Yeah, yeah, I know all that," Chris said. "But I still think this is the career for me. I start tomorrow. Some guy named Curtis is going to train me, but it probably won't be long before I'm working with you." He stood. "Who's ready for burgers?"

Kelsey leaned toward Tony. "He's so excited about this," she said. "He wants to be just like you."

Tony snorted and picked up his beer. "I don't know why he'd want that."

"He really does look up to you," she said. She leaned closer still and whispered, "Tell him you're proud of him."

He didn't say anything.

She sat back. "I'm sorry," she said. "It really isn't any of my business."

"No." He took her hand. "I'm glad you care so much. We just don't talk about that kind of stuff."

She patted his hand. "Then maybe you should."

"Here you go." Chris handed them plates full of burgers and potato chips.

"Thanks." Tony accepted the plate, then raised his beer. "To another surveyor in the family."

"To Chris," Kelsey said, and they clinked bottles while Chris beamed.

Tony had a flash of memory, of a seven-year-old Chris astride a new bike, on one of Tony's infrequent visits. "Watch me, Uncle Tony!" he called, and popped a wheelie in the family driveway.

"Way to go!" Tony shouted and pumped his fist, and Chris had pumped his own fist in imitation and sped away, shouting at the top of his lungs, "Way to goooooo!"

They had both come so far in that time...but maybe not that far after all.

ON KELSEY'S SECOND morning of returning to the Alpiner at dawn in Tony's truck, she was greeted at the door by Brit Richards, Hannah's mother. "Good morning," Brit said cheerily. "Aren't you the early bird."

Kelsey tried to fake looking like someone who had risen early and not been out all night, but she realized she wasn't fooling anyone when Brit said, "Next time, invite Tony in for a cup of coffee. We always enjoy seeing him."

Kelsey nodded and scurried up to her room, vowing to herself that next time, she would insist on going back to the Alpiner to spend the night, no matter how hard it was to leave Tony's bed. Between Chris's smirks and teasing over the breakfast table and Brit's knowing looks, she felt too many people were far too interested in what went on in Tony's bedroom. Better to let them guess.

After a nap and a shower, Kelsey left the inn to walk around town. She tried to think of someone else to talk to or someplace to go. Maybe she should find out the address of the place Liz had listed as her residence and visit there. Deborah Raymond had told her Liz had never lived there, but maybe she had lived nearby. Kelsey might see a neighboring house or apartment and realize it was exactly the kind of place Liz would have liked.

But that was a fantasy. Wherever Liz had lived, Mountain Man had been there, and Kelsey had no idea what her sister's mysterious suitor had been like. Instead, she walked through a neighborhood two blocks off Main and tried to imagine Liz here, in her low-cut jeans and cropped shirt, strolling these same streets, exploring her new home.

She had walked about a block when she suddenly had the sensation of being watched. Goose bumps prickled on her arms, and she whipped around, trying to spot whoever was spying on her. But she saw no one. She kept walking, faster now, turning her head from side to side to try to see who might be looking at her. Was someone really watching, or was she imagining this sensation?

"Hey, Kelsey!"

Tammy Patterson hailed Kelsey from across the street, then hurried to catch up with her. "I'm glad I ran into you," Tammy said. "I was going to call and tell you the story is going to run in the next issue—unless some big news pushes it out, but things like that seldom happen around here. So look for it Tuesday."

"Thanks so much for writing the story," Kelsey said.

"I hope it helps you find out more about what happened to your sister." Tammy squeezed her arm and hurried away.

Kelsey turned to head back toward the inn and almost collided with Ted Carruthers. "Whoa, there!" he said, steadying her. He looked past her. "Is that reporter bugging you?"

"No." She stepped back, out of his grasp. "She's great. Tammy wrote an article about my search for my sister's killer."

Ted frowned, bushy white eyebrows drawing together. "You really think that's a good idea?" he asked.

"Why wouldn't it be a good idea?"

"You might upset the wrong person."

"I hope I *do* upset the man who killed Liz."

"How do you know it was a man?"

"Fine. The *person* who killed Liz. I hope they read that article and know they aren't going to get away with murder."

"Finding out who killed her isn't going to bring your sister back," he said.

The comment enraged her. "I know that." What did he know about Liz or her family's grief? "The person who killed Liz deserves to pay for what he did," she said. "And yes, I think it was probably a man—the man she moved to Eagle Mountain to be with. He doesn't deserve to walk around free when she'll never have that chance again." Her voice broke on the words, and she turned and fled, not wanting to deal with him anymore. Not wanting him to see how much she felt the loss of a sister she hadn't spoken to in twenty years. Nothing she could do would bring Liz back, but her sister would always be part of her. The killer would never be able to take that away.

TONY AND CHRIS fell into the habit of having breakfast together in the morning, then leaving for work—Chris on his motorcycle to shadow Curtis Lefsen, who was training him on his duties as a surveyor's assistant; and Tony in his truck, to either the job site or the office to pick up Brad or another assistant. Often, Chris got home earlier than Tony and had dinner ready by the time Tony came in. Over spaghetti or tacos or whatever Chris had made, they would talk about work and Chris's plans to study for his surveyor's license. "I always liked math in school," Chris said during one of these conversations. "This is putting all those abstract principles in algebra and trigonometry and stuff to work in the real world."

"I thought you didn't like school," Tony said. He remembered Eddie complaining that his youngest never applied himself.

"I hated school," Chris said. "But that's because teachers made the classes so boring. Surveying is really interesting."

"I'm pretty sure to get your degree, you have to take English and history and everything else," Tony said.

Chris shrugged. "I can do it. I never had trouble learning stuff. I just didn't see the point. Now I do."

Tony did the dishes while Chris texted with friends or watched TV. He had thought having someone else in the house all the time, making noise and moving things around, would annoy him, but now he missed his nephew when he was out with friends. No more young women had appeared on the couch, though Chris had mentioned going out with

Amy again. Maybe they had found somewhere else for their assignations.

He was musing over this on the Wednesday after Chris had started work at Eagle Surveying when his text alert sounded. His first thought was that it was Kelsey, letting him know she was on the way over. She had gotten into the habit of coming over after dinner most nights. She had extended her stay at the Alpiner and hadn't said anything about when she might leave town. Tony wasn't going to ask.

But the text was from Sheri: Injured skier on Mount Baker, Raven Couloir. Report to HQ ASAP.

Tony dropped the dish towel and headed toward his bedroom to change. "I got a call and have to go out," he said as he passed through the living room.

Chris looked up from the television. "Someone's hurt?"

Tony didn't answer, but Chris followed him into his bedroom. "Who's hurt?" Chris asked.

"A skier. On Mount Baker."

"What was he doing up there?" Chris asked.

"Probably skiing down." Tony shucked off his sweatpants and pulled on a pair of insulated climbing pants. It would be cold up on the mountain at night. "This time of year, you can climb up and ski down in one day." He had done it himself several years before. The trip had been exhilarating, especially the final descent through the snow-filled couloir, the kind of expedition that tested every skill and made a person feel that much more accomplished and alive.

"Is there anything I can do to help?" Chris asked.

"You can finish the dishes," Tony said. He pulled on a thermal layer, then a heavy fleece.

"When will you be back?"

"When the job is done." He grabbed his parka, his radio

and his keys and headed toward the door. His pack and climbing gear were already in the truck. The familiar adrenaline surged through him, making him move faster and think more clearly. Someone needed him and he was ready.

CHRIS ANSWERED KELSEY'S knock on Tony's door. He stared at her, a confused look on his face. "Hey, Kelsey," he said after a bit. "Um, Tony's not here."

She glanced over her shoulder and realized Tony's truck wasn't in the driveway. "Where is he?" she asked.

"He got a call out from Search and Rescue. Something about an injured skier on Mount Baker. He didn't call you?"

"I haven't talked to him since early this morning." They had talked then about her coming over after supper to hang out.

"He was probably too focused on the call." Chris held the door open wider. "You want to come in and wait with me?"

She started to say no, she'd go back to the hotel, but changed her mind when she saw the pleading look in Chris's eyes. "Sure," she said, moving past him. "It will be good to have company."

"I don't know why I'm freaked out," Chris said. "Tony does this stuff all the time. I guess this is the first time it really hit me how dangerous it is. I don't like thinking about him on some mountain in the dark."

Kelsey shivered. She had thought about search and rescue work only in terms of the end results—people found or saved, their injuries tended. She had avoided contemplating the danger to the rescuers themselves. "I'm sure he'll be okay," she said. "Tony has done this lots of times."

"You know he was hurt really badly last year, don't you?" Chris said.

She settled onto the sofa. "But he's better now."

"He likes people to think so, but you haven't seen him. By the end of some days, he's in so much pain he can hardly move. I hear him up at night, pacing around."

She shook her head. "He's always fine when he's with me."

"He doesn't want you to know. He doesn't want anyone to know. But I figure it takes a lot longer than a year to recover from something like that."

"I'm sure he'll be fine," she said, and hugged a pillow to her stomach. And when he was back, she'd ask a few more questions. Was he really in pain every day? She would make it clear he didn't have to hide something like that from her.

Chris's smile struck her as forced. "So, how are things with you?" he asked. "How's the sleuthing going?"

"I keep running into dead ends," she admitted. "I heard from the sheriff today about a man I'd asked him to check out, and he probably wasn't the killer."

"Who was that?" Chris asked.

"Mel Wheeler. He was with Search and Rescue, part of the team that retrieved Liz's body from Kestrel Trail. He moved to Phoenix a year after Liz died, but Sheriff Walker was able to track him down. Or rather, he tracked down Mel's widow. She says she and Mel were vacationing in Cancun around the time Liz disappeared, and she sent him pictures to prove it. It was her birthday, and the hotel presented her with a cake with the date written on it." She blew out a breath. "It was a long shot anyway."

"I'm glad it wasn't him," Chris said. "I mean, that would be freaky, wouldn't it—someone who went out of his way to help strangers turning out to be a killer?"

"I don't know," she mused. "Isn't it almost a cliché for a

murderer's neighbors and friends to talk about what a nice guy he was? And Liz obviously trusted him enough to leave her family to be with him. There had to have been a good side to him for that to happen."

"He had a twisted view of love if he ended up killing her," Chris said.

"He did." Love was complicated for everyone to navigate, but at least most people didn't have to worry about the person they loved killing them.

That is, if her sister's killer really was Mountain Man. What if she was on the wrong track and a random hiker she'd met on the trail murdered Liz? She had been so sure that hard work and a fresh look at the evidence would lead her to the right suspect—but she had to admit, if only to herself, that she might never find the right person. Whoever had killed Liz, he might never be punished. And Kelsey and her mom would never know what really happened all those years ago. The idea left a hollow feeling in the center of her chest. She had lived all these years without knowing, but it felt worse, somehow, to be here where Liz had lived, to talk to the people who knew her and know that she might leave with no more answers than when she had arrived, only more questions.

Chapter Fifteen

As was often the case in a small community, Tony knew the people involved in this callout. Nick Teague and Tyler Hanran had decided to take advantage of the good spring snow on Mount Baker to ski down the central couloir to a forest service road where they could leave a car for the drive back to town.

"Everything was going great," Tyler told the assembled volunteers at Search and Rescue headquarters. "Until about a third of the way down. We hadn't accounted for the warmer temperatures yesterday and all the sun that was hitting that face. The snow got really crusty and icy. Nick was ahead of me, feeling out the route. It looked like he was doing great and then he just…slid." Tyler spread his hands wide in a gesture of helplessness. "I thought he was going to be okay and self-correct, but his ski must have caught an edge or something, and he started to cartwheel." He wiped a hand across his face. "It was terrible. I thought for sure he was dead. I stood there a long time, looking at him lying there, so still. Then I saw movement. I shouted down to him, and he kind of groaned. I was afraid if I tried to go down the same way he had, I would fall, too. And if I tried to climb down the rock directly above him, I could send a boulder down on him. So I moved way over to the left of him, took off my skis and climbed down this gnarly pitch to a point below him, then climbed up to him."

"Do you know exactly where he landed?" Captain Sheri Stevens asked.

"He's on this scree ledge about a third of the way into the col." Tyler pulled out his phone. "I've got GPS coordinates."

Tony imagined the collective sigh of relief from the assembled volunteers. For most of his time with Search and Rescue, finding someone on a mountain meant making an educated guess as to where they lay and relying on sharp vision and luck. Technology allowed them to zero in on the person needing help much more quickly and accurately.

"What's his condition?" Hannah asked.

Tyler grimaced. "He's pretty banged up. His left leg is facing backwards, and he was in a lot of pain. I was afraid to move him. Oh, and he's got two broken fingers and maybe broken ribs. He said it hurt a lot to breathe. I taped the fingers together and piled all the spare clothes we had in our packs on him. I gave him all our water, too. I hated to leave him, but I had to get help."

"It sounds like you did all the right things," Hannah said.

"How did you get down?" Tony asked. That might be a good route up to the patient.

"I inched my way along this narrow ledge to the summer hiking trail and hiked down," Tyler said. "It's really steep and icy, but I was so worried about Nick I just gutted it out."

"There's a lot of snow on the ledges above that trail," Ryan said. "With the warmer weather today, it's an avalanche risk."

"Jake, contact the avalanche center for a report," Sheri

said. "And I need a weather report for tomorrow. We can't risk sending people up that trail in the dark."

"There's a full moon tonight," Tony said. "And the colder temperatures will mean more stable snow. Still a risk, but we could do it."

"Better for Nick than spending the night waiting," Carrie said.

Sheri considered this. "Night-climbing isn't my favorite thing, but I've done it."

"The moon on the snow can make it pretty bright," Ryan said. "Almost as good as daylight."

"Then let's do it." Sheri moved to the map of the area pinned to the wall. "I want a team headed up the north side to the couloir," she said, indicating the route. "We'll send a south team up as far as it's deemed safe and see if there's another route they can take."

Tony, Sheri, Ryan and Caleb, a rookie volunteer who had skied the same route Nick and Tyler had taken only the week before, gathered around a map of Mount Baker to plot strategy while others assembled equipment. Lieutenant Carrie Andrews started making phone calls, trying to find a helicopter and flight crew that could lift Nick off the mountain.

Tony was part of the south-approach team, with Jake, Grace and Caleb. Sheri, Ryan, Eldon and Danny, the team's best mountaineers, made up the north team, which was expected to have the best chance of reaching the ledge in the couloir where Nick lay. Tyler wanted to go back up with them, but they persuaded him he was too exhausted and would only slow them down.

"I've got a chopper coming in from Durango at first light," Carrie reported. "But whether they can make the lift is at their discretion." As always, the flight crew had the final say as to whether the rescue was safe enough for them to attempt.

The teams were heading for the parking lot when Ted pulled up in his truck. "I heard the call was all hands on deck," he said. "What can I do?"

"Come with me," Carrie said. She was incident commander for this mission. "You can run resupply back and forth from town."

Tony volunteered to carry one of the oxygen canisters. "You're just a glutton for punishment, aren't you?" Jake said as he helped strap the heavy canister onto Tony's pack.

"If I get tired, I'll give it to you," Tony said. Jake might be younger, but he wasn't in the shape Tony was in, and he and Jake both knew it.

Ted joined them with two thermoses of coffee. "You'll appreciate these when you get up there," he said. He handed one to Jake and tucked the other into Tony's pack. "Heard anything from Kelsey lately?" he asked.

"Kelsey is fine," Tony said. Why was Ted asking about Kelsey now?

"I thought maybe she had left town by now."

"Not yet," Tony said. She would probably leave soon. He was trying to accept that while also not thinking about it.

They headed out and, twenty minutes later, started up the trail. The first mile was almost pleasant, the snow having receded to reveal a dry, packed trail. The moon was bright enough they didn't need their headlamps. But as soon as they hit the tree line, the conditions began to deteriorate—patches of frozen mud and loose rock, then slippery ice. The mud built up in the treads of their hiking boots, which made finding purchase on the ice difficult. They continually had to stop to scrape their boots on rocks. They tried jogging up the trail, but that proved almost impossible.

By the time they reached the exposed west-facing section of the trail, they were already flagging, and Tony's repaired legs and shoulder throbbed with every step. He thought about handing the oxygen canister off to Jake but fought against the idea.

They paused at a small bench that gave them a good view of the slopes above—rocky ridges frosted with heavy snow like dollops of frosting on a cake. Tony radioed to Carrie. "This place looks like an avalanche waiting to happen," he said.

"Can you cut over up the gulley to the west?" she asked. "Caleb says there's a ledge there that's protected and will take you across most of the way to the spot where Nick is."

"Ten-four," Tony said. "We'll head that way."

The cut-across was slow going. They all wanted to rush but knew they couldn't. Endangering themselves and the others with them wouldn't help save Nick. They had just reached the ledge when the radio crackled again. "Stand down," Carrie said. "Sheri and her team have reached Nick. We need you all back down here to ferry supplies to them."

So they turned around and went back down. The descent was faster, though they slid more than once in the slick mud. Back at the trailhead, they jogged over to Grace's Subaru, stored their gear and raced to the north staging area, where Carrie sent them up that route laden with the oxygen canister, food and another set of radios for talking with the helicopter pilots.

Though they all would have liked to stay to see the rest of the rescue, the avalanche danger was too high to risk it, so they left Nick with Danny and Ryan. Pale golden light was showing over the mountains by the time they reached the staging area once more, where they listened to the distant bass throb of the Chinook helicopter arriving, twin rotors cutting through the air with a sound like a heartbeat.

Tony, Carrie and Jake climbed a hundred feet up the trail to a ledge that gave them a view of the helicopter hovering above the couloir. They passed a pair of binoculars back and forth and watched as a long line with what looked like a hook on the end lowered toward the snow field. Moments later, the line retreated back toward the belly of the aircraft, a bundle that resembled a burrito swinging beneath it. They all cheered when the litter was safely pulled into the chopper. Nick Teague was safe.

Then the tension wound tight again as the hook descended a second time, much faster. It ascended faster, too, but Tony could just make out two figures clinging to it. They were almost to the belly of the chopper when the snow field gave way, a wave of white rippling down the couloir, powder billowing into the air like steam. The line jerked into the chopper, and it rose up with another jerk and swept away.

Sheri keyed the radio. "Ryan, what's your status?"

"Everyone is okay," he radioed back. "Nick is stable. Danny is monitoring him."

"We saw the avalanche," Sheri said.

"Yeah. We got out of there just in time."

KELSEY WOKE, groggy and with a stiff neck. She had fallen asleep on the sofa. Chris was slumped in the chair across from her, head back, snoring softly. She grabbed her phone from the coffee table and stared at the digital display. 5:35 a.m. And Tony still wasn't back?

She was trying to decide whom she might call to find

out if he was all right when the phone buzzed in her hand. She answered the unfamiliar number, and Brit Richards's cheery voice greeted her. "Kelsey, we're getting ready to take some food to Search and Rescue headquarters," Brit said. "Do you want to come with us?"

"Are they back?" Kelsey asked. "Is everyone okay?"

"I just spoke to Hannah, and she said the rescue went well," Brit said. "Everyone safe and sound, including the young man they were sent to help. But everyone is going to be exhausted and hungry. Thad and I are picking up food from Mo's to take to them."

"Of course I'll help." She looked across at Chris, who had sat up and was rubbing his face with his hands. "Chris and I will both help."

"Then hurry and meet us at Mo's."

Kelsey pocketed her phone and stood. "Come on," she told Chris. "We have to get to Mo's and help take food to Search and Rescue headquarters."

"They're back?" He looked around. "What time is it?"

"After five thirty. Come on. Brit is waiting."

At Mo's, she and Chris loaded into the car with Thad and Brit and what looked like three dozen to-go boxes of pizza, wings and nachos. The parking lot at Search and Rescue headquarters was filled with cars. "It looks like a party," Kelsey said as she helped unload the food.

"It is," Brit said. "Some of these people are family of the volunteers, and some of them are just neighbors who want to congratulate them or hear about the mission."

They trooped into the building, boxes piled up to their noses, and were relieved of their burden as soon as they entered. "Food!" someone bellowed, and a crowd of men and women surged forward. Kelsey spotted Tony with a slice of pizza in one hand and a chicken wing in the other and worked her way through the scrum toward him.

"Kelsey!" He popped the last of the pizza into his mouth, then pulled her close in a hug. "I'm sorry I couldn't see you last night, but Chris told you what was going on, right?"

"He did." She slapped his chest. "I was a little worried about you, though."

"Oh, I'm fine." He hugged her tighter. "Let's sit down." He pulled her to the end of a long table and gingerly lowered himself into a folding chair. Someone slid a pizza box toward him, and he snagged another slice. "Do you want something to eat?" he asked between mouthfuls.

She shook her head. "Are you okay?"

"I'm fine." He grimaced. "Sore. Stiff. Tired. And starving. But that's normal after a mission."

He looked good—sun-burnt and wind-blown but elated. "I take it the rescue went well?"

He nodded. "Everybody worked together to pull it off. Exactly like it's supposed to work."

Chris set a box of wings on the table in front of them. "How's it going?" he asked.

"I'm okay." Tony grabbed his hand. "Thanks for coming out." He looked around them. "Do you all know my nephew, Chris?" He introduced the young man to the volunteers around them. Kelsey heard the pride in his voice, and Chris was smiling so widely his face probably hurt.

Cheers rose from the crowd as two men moved through the crowd. They settled into chairs across from Tony and Kelsey and were immediately handed plates piled high with pizza and wings. "This is Ryan and Tyler," Tony said, pointing to each. "This is Kelsey."

They nodded to her and continued eating. "How is Nick?" someone asked.

"His right leg is a mess, but the surgeons will put him back together," Danny said. "Fractured ribs, broken finger. He's lucky Tyler was with him and got to us as soon as he could."

"If that slab had fractured while he was lying there in the couloir, he'd have been wiped out," Ryan said.

"I heard you got a free ride in a helicopter." A blonde with green eyes slipped in behind Ryan and wrapped her arms around him.

He smiled up at her. "Riding that hook up might have been a kick if I'd had time to enjoy it," he said.

"The pilot was yelling at us to hurry, hurry, he could see the snow started to fracture," Danny said. "I barely had time to grab hold before he starting hauling the line up. I almost wet my pants I was so terrified."

"Then I'm really glad you were hanging on below me," Ryan said.

The others laughed, and Danny reached for another slice of pizza. Tony slid his arm around Kelsey. "I was almost as happy to see you as I was to see this food," he said.

"'Almost'?"

He took a bite of pizza. "I must have hiked ten miles today with a heavy pack," he said. "I was starving."

"You get used to it," the blonde with Ryan addressed Kelsey. She held out her hand. "I'm Deni Traynor, by the way."

"Sorry." Tony set aside his slice of pizza. "Deni, this is Kelsey Chapman. Deni is Ryan's fiancée."

"Nice to meet you." Deni ruffled Ryan's hair. "He'll come home and sleep for twenty hours, get up and eat half the refrigerator, then be fine until the next hard call." She kissed his cheek. "My hero."

Ryan grimaced. "You know I hate that. It's a team effort. Nobody is a hero. Everybody is just working together to do a good job."

Danny and Tony murmured agreement. Ryan's girlfriend sent Kelsey a knowing look.

When Kelsey looked away, she found Tony watching her. She leaned closer. "It's like a big family, isn't it?" she said. Because she was with Tony, everyone around him accepted her. She had never experienced anything like it.

He squeezed her knee under the table. "I guess it can be a little overwhelming."

She shook her head. "No. It's really nice."

Ted carried a chair over to their table. "Move over," he said, and nudged Danny's shoulder.

Danny pushed his chair back. "I'm going to go find Carrie," he said before he left.

Ted set his chair against the wall and took the seat vacated by Danny. "Hello, Kelsey," he said.

"Hello, Ted."

"How's your detective work going?" he asked. "Have you found your suspect?"

"No."

"I've been thinking a lot about this," Ted said. "There was a guy in town back then—Ray somebody or other. He worked as a janitor at the high school, then they found out he'd been charged with rape back in Colorado Springs but let go on a technicality. He would have known your sister since he worked at the high school. Did the sheriff's department ever take a look at him?"

"Ray Jackman," Kelsey said. "The sheriff questioned

him. But he was out of town during the time Liz would have been killed, at a hearing back in Colorado Springs. And his DNA wasn't a match."

"Well, who's to say that DNA was even from the killer?" Ted said. "It could have been from anyone."

"I don't think Liz would have fought with anyone else that day," Tony said.

"Why didn't the cops just look for a guy with a scratched-up face?" Ted asked. "I don't remember anyone like that at the time."

"I don't know." Kelsey was aware of everyone around them watching her. She had been feeling so good, and Ted had spoiled the mood. "I don't want to talk about that now," she said. "I want to hear more about what happened last night."

They began talking about the rescue again, and she settled back against Tony. He had stopped eating and laced his hand with hers. She didn't understand half of what the rescuers were saying as they discussed the technical aspects of the mission, but it didn't matter. She let the words wash over her, the tension of the night giving way to a contentment she didn't think she had ever known before.

KELSEY RETURNED TO the Alpiner with Brit and Thad later that morning. As much as she would have liked to stay with Tony, she could see he was exhausted and in pain. He didn't protest when she suggested he go home and recover, and his parting kiss was as warm as ever.

Back at the inn, she called her mother. "Oh, hello, Kelsey." The volume of the television in the background lowered. "Are you home yet?"

"I'm still in Eagle Mountain," Kelsey said. "I'm still trying to find out what happened to Liz."

"Have you learned anything?" her mother asked.

"Not yet. But I'm still researching."

Canned laughter from the television. "If you haven't found out anything after all this time, I don't think you will," her mother said. "Maybe your father was right. We should forget all about this. None of it is going to bring Liz back. None of it is going to make things right."

What was *right* to her mother? Liz never having left? That was probably part of it. "Don't you want to know what happened?" Kelsey asked.

"I don't know any more what I want. We've lived all these years not knowing. I buried my daughter once. Why should I want to dig her up again? I've lived more of my life without Liz than with her. If she had stayed, maybe things would have been worse. She was always such a headstrong child. If she had lived, she might have still been a disappointment."

"Am I a disappointment?" Kelsey knew as soon as the words were out that she shouldn't have asked. There was no right answer to that. A long silence, so long she wondered if her mother had hung up. "Mom?"

"You couldn't be a disappointment to me," her mother said. "I never expected anything from you. With Liz gone, I didn't have it in me."

The truth, unvarnished and as painful as raw wood, full of splinters. "I'm thinking of staying in Eagle Mountain," Kelsey blurted out. She hadn't even considered this until now, but as soon as she said it, she realized it was what she wanted. Maybe what she needed.

Her mother sighed. "So you're going to abandon me, too."

You abandoned me a long time ago, Kelsey thought. *You*

and Dad both. But she didn't say it. "I'd still visit and call," she said.

"You do what you want to do," her mother said. "It doesn't matter to me."

It ought to matter, Kelsey thought after she ended the call. But Liz ought to have lived. Her killer ought to have been caught. Life was full of things that ought to be and didn't happen.

Chapter Sixteen

The next morning Tony woke to stabbing pain in his legs and a deep ache in his arms and shoulders. For a moment of disorientation, he thought he was back in the hospital, shortly after the accident, and his recovery had been merely a dream. But after another moment, full awareness returned, along with the memory of the previous day's rescue.

He had hiked miles over rough terrain yesterday, lugging heavy equipment. He remembered hurting then, too, but the pain had been tempered by the adrenaline and the urgency of the mission. Today, even getting out of bed was agony. He struggled to get to the bathroom and stared into the mirror, at the dark circles under his eyes. He looked almost as bad as he felt.

He brushed his teeth with shaking hands, then found his phone and dialed the number for his doctor. "It's possible you reinjured something," the nurse practitioner said. "Let's get you in this morning and make sure."

He texted his boss that he wouldn't be in to work that day. Bruce would have heard about yesterday's rescue by now and was used to Tony coming in late or not at all after a particularly complicated mission. Tony always made up the work and rarely took time off for any other reason.

He sat on the edge of the bed for a long time, gathering strength for the task of getting dressed. After a while, Chris knocked on the door. "You okay in there?" he asked.

"I'm fine," Tony said. "I already talked to Bruce. I'm not going in today."

The door opened and Chris leaned in. "What's wrong?" he asked. "Did you get hurt on that rescue and didn't tell anyone?"

"I'm fine." He shifted on the side of the bed. "I'm just a little stiff. I'm going to the doctor to make sure everything is okay."

"I could stay home and drive you," Chris said. "Or get Kelsey to go with you."

"No!" He didn't want Kelsey to see him like this. He shoved to his feet, trying not to grimace as he did so. "Go on. I'll be fine."

When Chris had left, he sank onto the bed again. What had he done? All those months of rehab thrown out the window for what? Because he wanted to be a hero? Because he craved the rush of being so needed? He grimaced, knowing how close to the truth that really was.

His phone rang and he glanced at the screen. Kelsey. He groaned. He couldn't talk to her right now. He wouldn't be able to hide how terrible he felt, and he didn't want her to know him like this. She deserved better.

Who was he kidding? She was going to leave anyway. Her home was in Iowa—her family and friends, her job. This thing between them was never going to be permanent, and he needed to accept that.

He gritted his teeth and pulled on pants and a shirt, forced his feet into shoes, then grabbed his keys and hobbled to his truck. By the time he hauled himself into the driver's seat, he was sweating and gasping for air like an eighty-year-old. Ha! He knew eighty-year-olds who were in better shape than he was right now.

He shoved the key into the ignition and started the engine. Driving itself wasn't too bad. At the doctor's office, he managed to slide out of the driver's seat and walk gingerly into the orthopedic office.

An hour and a half and a series of X-rays and a painful physical examination later, his doctor announced—with far more cheer than Tony appreciated—that there was no permanent damage. "You just overdid it," the doctor said. "You have to remember you're not in the shape you used to be. You need to take it a little easier. Dial it back a notch."

Except Tony didn't know how to do anything but go at the work full-tilt.

He left with a prescription for more physical therapy, some heavy-duty anti-inflammatories and instructions to "take it a little easier."

He collapsed onto the sofa as soon as he made it home, the doctor's words on repeat in his head. If he took it easy, that meant other team members had to pick up the slack. That wasn't acceptable, at least not to him. He had told himself he could live with pain and discomfort—a little suffering was part of rescue work in all weather conditions on usually rough terrain. But he was used to bouncing back quickly. What did it mean that he was in such bad shape right now?

His phone rang again, and he pulled it out, only to see Kelsey's name. What would happen if he didn't answer? Would she keep calling, or would she be angry he blew her off? "Hello?" he answered.

"Hi, Tony. I'm not interrupting you, am I?"

"Not really."

"How are you doing after yesterday? You must be exhausted."

"I'm a little tired."

"Do you want me to bring dinner over? We could chill and watch TV or something."

"No. I think I'm going to make it an early night. Don't come over."

"Oh." Was he imagining the disappointment in that single syllable? "If you're sure?"

"I'm sure. And I have to go now." He ended the call before she could say more, then tossed the phone onto the coffee table and fell back on the sofa. Wanting to see Kelsey was an ache almost worse than the pain in his legs, but he couldn't let her see him like this. When she went back to Iowa, he didn't want this image of him, broken, to be the one she took with her.

KELSEY TRIED NOT to be hurt that Tony hadn't wanted to see her. Maybe he had a routine after a tough rescue like this and he didn't want her interfering with whatever it was. She should respect that and not react as if he was rejecting her. But believing this and actually controlling her emotions were two different things. He had been so abrupt on the phone, as if he couldn't wait to hang up on her. All the warmth and closeness they had developed had vanished. When he ended the call, it was like having a door slammed in her face.

She kept herself busy the rest of the day. She went through her notes yet again and tried to watch TV, forcing herself not to contact Tony. But the fact that he didn't call her weighed on her and made sleep elusive.

When she came down for breakfast Friday morning, she was feeling grumpier than usual, though she tried to hide it when Hannah breezed into the breakfast room and headed for her table. "Hey, Kelsey," Hannah said. She paused, one hand on the back of the empty chair at the table across from Kelsey.

"Hey, Hannah." Kelsey sat up straighter and forced a smile. "How are you this morning?"

"I'm good. I was just wondering if you've talked to Tony last night or this morning?"

"I talked to him for a little bit yesterday afternoon."

"Is he okay?"

"He said he was tired and was going to turn in early."

Hannah frowned. "I bet he overdid it on that rescue Wednesday," she said. "I could see he was in pain, though he was trying to hide it. Did he say if he had talked to his doctor?"

"He didn't mention that." They hadn't really had much of a conversation.

"I'm just worried because he didn't show up for the SAR meeting last night," Hannah said. "I've never known him to miss a meeting before."

"I was thinking I'd go over to his house and check on him this morning," Kelsey said. "See if he needs anything."

She had been thinking no such thing until this moment, but now she could hardly wait to get to him.

"That would be great," Hannah said. "Let me know if there's anything I can do."

Kelsey finished her coffee, then grabbed her car keys from the room and headed out toward Tony's house. If he was upset that she was coming over unannounced, she would make him understand it was because she cared about him. If he was hurting, she wanted to help.

She rang the bell, then waited a long time for him to answer. She couldn't hear anything inside the house, but Tony's truck sat in the driveway. She rang again. What if he had passed out or something? Or fallen and broken a bone? Could she break in and find him? She reached for the door to see if it was unlocked, just as the door swung open.

Tony stared down at her. "You look terrible!" she said, then covered her mouth, as if she could take back the words. But it was true—he was hunched and pale, his beard untrimmed, hair uncombed.

"You need to leave," he said, and tried to close the door, but she pushed past him.

"Hannah told me she thought you overdid it on that rescue, and it looks like she was right," she said. She moved to his side and took his arm. "Have you talked to your doctor?"

He pulled his arm away. "I'm all right. I just need some rest."

The sharpness of his words stung. Fair enough. He didn't like being fussed over, so how about a little tough love? "You can't blow me off the way you did yesterday and not expect me to worry," she said.

"You don't need to worry about me." He turned away, and she followed as he lurched back to the sofa. She surreptitiously looked for signs that he had been self-medicating with liquor or pills but saw no indications of that—just a water bottle and a half-eaten sandwich on the coffee table.

She sat next to the sandwich, facing him where he half sprawled on the sofa. "I know we haven't known each other very long," she said. "But I care about you. It hurts me to see you hurting."

A look of confusion passed through his eyes before he turned away. "You can't do anything about the pain."

"Maybe not the physical pain," she said. "But you must be hurting inside, too, if you're pushing me away." Was that too much? she wondered. Did she sound like an amateur psychologist, trying to diagnose him?

"I'm going to be fine," he grumbled.

She moved from the coffee table to the sofa and sat with her hip and thigh touching his. "Do you want to be miserable by yourself, or maybe a little less miserable with me here, too?"

He made a choking sound, and she wondered if he was sobbing, then he turned his head toward her, and she realized he was laughing. She smiled, and he pulled her to him. Then they were kissing, wild hungry kisses that made her heart race, a little out of control.

He pulled her onto his lap, and soon they were undressing each other, moving a little awkwardly to accommodate his legs, which apparently hurt him a great deal, and his shoulder, also tender. But she didn't mind. She liked sitting on top of him like this, urging him to lie back while she worked her way down his body, aware of him watching her with a hungry look. And when they came together, she watched passion ease some of the tension from his body and drain the anger from his eyes. When he reached out to caress her, she smiled and told herself everything would be all right. The two of them were too good together for this not to work.

SOMETIME DURING THE NIGHT, they did make it to bed. She woke, ravenous, only to find Tony had risen before her. When she made her way to the kitchen, she found him dressed and standing in front of the coffee press. He had showered and shaved and looked more like his old self, less bent and drawn. She moved in behind him and wrapped her arms around him. "You're looking better this morning," she said.

"I'm fine." He filled a mug from the press, then pulled a second mug from a hook beneath the cabinet, filled it and handed it to her. "When are you going back to Iowa?" he asked.

The suddenness of the question startled her. She sipped her coffee and studied him over the rim of the mug, trying to gauge his mood. He stared down into his own cup, his expression sullen. "You sound like you're anxious for me to go," she said.

"You're not finding out anything about your sister here," he said. "I know you have a job and a home and friends there."

She set her unfinished coffee on the counter. "Do you want me to leave?"

He shrugged. "If you're going to go anyway, you might as well leave now."

Last night he had clung to her as if he never wanted to let go. Now he was practically pushing her out the door. "I don't understand you," she said. "I thought you liked me. I thought we were good together." She almost said she was thinking about staying in Eagle Mountain. Because of him. But she had too much pride to let him know how much he was hurting her.

"I don't do long relationships." He looked at her then, his expression bleak. "That's just how I am."

"Who says?"

"I say."

He didn't do long relationships—with her. That was all

she heard, the words making pain bloom somewhere mid-sternum. No wonder people who knew nothing about anat-omy talked about heartache as a physical illness.

But as much as she was hurting, she was also furious. How dare he make her care so much, then toss her away. She wanted to tell him as much—to scream that he was a horrible person for treating her this way. But when she opened her mouth, all that came out was an anguished cry. Tears flooding her eyes, she turned and ran from the house.

She started the car and, shaking all over, sped out of To-ny's driveway. When she reached the turn onto the road, she stopped and forced herself to calm down. The last thing she wanted was to wreck her car. She half laughed, half sobbed at the idea. She would be hurt in a ditch, and the call would go out to SAR and Tony would have to come and rescue her.

She kept her speed down and forced herself to pay at-tention as she drove. Focusing on driving was a good way to keep her emotions under control, though she had a knot of tears in the back of her throat, waiting to burst forth as soon as she was alone.

She turned onto the main highway leading to town and was starting to relax a little more when a blaring horn sent a jolt of panic through her. She stomped on the brakes and looked around, in time to see a pickup truck come up on her right, so close her car shook as it roared past, horn blasting. She tried to see who was driving but could make out noth-ing through the tinted windows. Before she could remember to note the license plate, the vehicle was gone.

Shaking, she pulled her car to the shoulder and sat, grip-ping the steering wheel so tightly her fingers ached. Her fantasy of having Tony come to rescue her didn't seem so far-fetched now. What was up with that driver? Was he just a jerk, or had he been trying to frighten her?

After a few minutes, she felt calm enough to proceed and drove the rest of the way to the inn. She managed to get to her room without being seen and sank onto her bed. But she didn't collapse, sobbing. She thought about Tony and about the reckless driver who had frightened her. And she thought about Liz and her failure to find anything that pointed to her sister's killer.

Maybe Tony was right. Maybe it was time for her to give up and go home.

good for me, being here," she says. "I feel like I understand what Liz loved about this place, and I've met people who remember her and what she was like then. It's made me feel closer to her, but nothing would be as good as knowing what really happened to her. I would really like that kind of closure."

Tony hurled the paper across the room. Of course, he had known Kelsey would leave soon, but seeing it confirmed in black and white made the pain worse. He ground the base of his palms into his eyes, then straightened and retrieved the paper. He smoothed it out and folded it so that Kelsey's picture was faceup. She smiled back at him. One more thing he wanted and couldn't have.

The text message alert from his phone pulled him from his misery, and he thumbed to a message from Search and Rescue. A semitruck had gone off the side of Dixon Pass. Driver alive and responsive, the message read.

Tony was relieved to have something to focus on besides himself. He arrived at SAR headquarters to find a full contingent of volunteers assembled, including Ted. "I was here reading through the archives for my book when the call came in," Ted said. "That driver is one lucky son of a gun. That area where he went off is a deadly sharp curve."

Sheri decided that she, Ryan and Danny would climb down to the driver, who had been able to shout a response to the tourist who had first noticed the fresh skid marks headed into the canyon. The tourist had seen the headlights of the big truck shining up from below and called in the incident. "Tony, I want you as incident commander up top," Sheri instructed.

"Happy to do it," Tony said. There was a time he would

have been one of the primary climbers on a descent like this, but he knew he wasn't up to that today. Sheri probably knew it, too, but didn't feel the need to point it out. He could still be useful managing the mission. He moved to help Ryan and Eldon collect the gear they would need. Ted joined them.

"I saw the article in the paper about Kelsey," Ted said.

Tony didn't reply. He didn't want to talk about Kelsey.

"Sounds like she'll be going back to Iowa soon," Ted said.

"I guess so." Tony grabbed another climbing helmet and shoved it into a duffel.

"It's just as well," Ted said. "She was just stirring up everybody. Whoever killed that girl is long gone."

"What do you know about it, Ted?" Ryan asked.

A red flush darkened Ted's neck and cheeks. "I don't know anything," he barked. "I didn't even know the girl. I'm just saying that stuff like that article in the paper upsets people for no reason. They start thinking this is a dangerous place and looking at guys like they might be murderers or something."

"Her sister was murdered," Tony said. "She has a right to try to find out who did it." He slung the duffel over his shoulder and headed for the Beast. It was either that or punch Ted. Usually, he tolerated the older man's pontificating, but he didn't have the patience for it today.

The sheriff's department had closed the road up the pass to one lane of traffic a quarter mile before the place where the 18-wheeler had gone off the side. Flashing lights from several sheriff's department SUVs and an ambulance that had gotten to the scene ahead of Search and Rescue were visible a mile up the canyon. "Looks like he took the curve here too sharp and the back wheels of the trailer went off the edge," Deputy Wes Landry said as the volunteers gathered around him for a status report. "The cargo in the trailer may have shifted and pulled him right down."

"That's a seventy-foot drop, easy," Tony said. "And straight down."

"You're sure the driver's alive?" Sheri asked.

"He shouted up that he's okay, just trapped in the driver's compartment."

Sheri took out a battery-operated hailer and went to the edge of the canyon. The others ranged along the rim, looking down at a truck, which more closely resembled a wad of tinfoil. Shredded cardboard littered the canyon like confetti, and miscellaneous bits of metal that might have been part of the cargo hung from tree limbs and draped across boulders. "This is Eagle Mountain Search and Rescue," Sheri called. "We're coming down to get you."

"Great!" came the clear response. "Be careful. I'm not going anywhere."

"He must be in pretty good shape," Ryan said. "He's kept his sense of humor."

Within minutes, the team had established anchors and begun the descent. Tony monitored the situation from above while the EMTs sat on the bumper of the ambulance and waited. The day was crisp but sunny, warm enough that Tony soon shed his jacket.

"How are you doing, Tony?" Hannah, on duty as a paramedic with the ambulance crew, came to stand beside him.

"I'm okay," he said. He focused on the climbers descending to the truck, but he could feel Hannah watching him.

"I was a little worried when you weren't at the meeting Friday night," she said. "Ted said he thought you were pretty banged up after that call on Mount Baker."

Ted always had an opinion, whether it was backed by fact or not. "I'm fine," Tony said again.

"That was a good article in the paper about Kelsey and her sister," Hannah said. "I hope it brings some new leads in the case."

"She hasn't had any luck turning up any new information so far," Tony said.

"Still, there are a lot of people in town who were here back when Liz was killed," Hannah said. "Someone must have seen or heard something, even if they didn't think it was important at the time. I asked Ted about it, and he said he never even heard of Liz Chapman until he responded to the call about her body."

"Ted was a lot older than Liz," Tony said. "No reason he would know her."

"She was really pretty," Hannah said. "I thought he might have remembered her for that reason alone. He can be a bit of a flirt, you know."

Tony stared at her. "Are we talking about the same Ted?"

Hannah laughed. "I know. But I remember when I first joined SAR, he went out of his way to be friendly to me. It wasn't sleazy or anything, but it was definitely flirty." She shrugged. "I just figured he was one of those older guys who thinks he's irresistible to all women."

Tony's radio crackled and Sheri said, "We're here and the truck is a wreck, but the driver's compartment somehow survived pretty much intact. As soon as we pry open the passenger door, we'll have him out. He says he's got a banged-up shoulder and a bump on his head, but he swears there's no blood and he sounds coherent and calm."

"Good news," Tony said. "Do you need the Jaws?" The hydraulic extractor, otherwise known as the Jaws of Life, could open up vehicles to allow access to an injured person inside.

"Ryan thinks he can pop the door with a pry bar," Sheri said. "I'll let you know if we need anything else."

Hannah returned to the ambulance, and Tony monitored the situation with Sheri. Ten minutes later, the driver was out of the cab of the truck, standing upright and telling everyone he could walk up under his own power. Danny examined him, said he should probably get his head injury checked out—just to be safe—then persuaded him to allow Search and Rescue to haul him up the cliff in a litter. When the driver balked, Sheri pointed out the only alternative was to climb straight up under his own power. With no previous climbing experience and an admitted fear of heights, the driver opted to be strapped onto the litter and hauled up with a volunteer on either side to steady his ascent.

Cheers rose from the gathered emergency personnel when the litter tipped over the edge of the canyon and volunteers rushed forward to free the driver, who stood shakily and thanked everyone in sight. Hannah escorted him to the ambulance for a ride to the hospital while the others gathered their gear and prepared to return to headquarters.

It wasn't until they were unloading at headquarters that Tony remembered Hannah's words. "Sheri, what did you think of Ted when you first joined Search and Rescue?" he asked.

"Everyone said he was the most experienced volunteer," she said. "Someone who had served in every capacity, and who knew the terrain around here better than anyone."

"Right. But what did you think of him personally?"

Sheri frowned at him. "Why are you asking?"

"Hannah said Ted flirted with her a lot when she first

joined," Tony said. "I wondered if he did that with all the women."

Sheri nodded. "Oh, yeah. Ted thinks he's quite the ladies' man." She shrugged. "I thought he was harmless. Way too old for me."

"Huh. I never noticed."

"Well, you wouldn't! He wouldn't have flirted with you, and he wasn't annoying about it. I told him flat-out I wasn't interested, and he backed off." She stowed a splint in a plastic bin and snapped on the lid, then turned to him. "Has someone complained about Ted? Said he was harassing them?"

Tony shook his head. "Nothing like that."

"Good. Because I never saw anything like that. He's just one of those men who flirt with women—especially younger women. To tell you the truth, I thought he was probably just lonely." She picked up the bin and carried it to the closet.

Tony felt a twinge of sympathy for Ted. Despite his bragging about being a ladies' man, Ted hadn't had a steady relationship that Tony knew about in all the time they had known each other. Neither had Tony, so he knew a few things about loneliness. And he had always looked up to Ted, who had taken the younger man under his wing and taught Tony most of what he knew about search and rescue work. He had sympathized with Ted's loss of physical prowess as he aged, which had forced his retirement from SAR, and had been happy that his mentor had found a new role with the organization as the group's historian.

But knowing Ted had hit on younger women was a little unsettling. If he was so interested in younger women, how had he failed to notice Liz Chapman—a new young woman in a small town where newcomers stood out? Was Ted telling the truth when he said he didn't know Liz, or was he lying to avoid having others look at him with suspicion, the way they had looked at Tony?

Tony knew there were still people who suspected him of having been involved in Liz's death. He had known her. He was known to have a crush on her. And he was the person who found her body. He supposed all of that looked suspicious.

But Kelsey had believed he was innocent.

Hadn't she?

KELSEY THOUGHT ABOUT sending the article from the *Eagle Mountain Examiner* to her mother, but why bother? Apparently, Mary had changed her mind about wanting to know anything about her elder daughter. She didn't want to "dig Liz up again." But Kelsey had never buried her sister. Liz lived on as the smiling, pretty teen who had snuggled with her and laughed with her and promised to see her again soon.

"Kelsey!" Brit flagged her down when she returned to the inn Wednesday afternoon, after another day searching the newspaper archives for any previous mention she might have missed that could related to Liz's case. Kelsey waited for Brit to catch up with her. "That was a good article in the paper yesterday," Brit said. "I hope it yields some results for the investigation."

"I hope so, too," Kelsey said. So far, no one had contacted her, but maybe the sheriff's department had heard something.

"Do you want to extend your stay again?" Brit asked. "We have you booked through Friday, and I'm not trying to run you off. We'd love to have you continue to stay with us. But I need to know sooner rather than later. It's getting to be our busy season and we have lots of calls for bookings."

Last week, she had been certain she would stay in Eagle Mountain, even relocate here. But that had been when she thought she and Tony had a future together. "I plan to leave, unless something turns up," she said. "I promise I'll let you know as soon as possible if I do end up staying, and I understand if you don't have anything available."

Brit patted Kelsey's arm. "We really would love to have you stay. It's been wonderful getting to know you."

Kelsey swallowed past a knot in her throat. Brit was so cheerful and kind—the way she remembered her own mother being before Liz had left them.

Brit turned to go, then turned back. "I almost forgot. I have a note for you at the front desk."

Kelsey's heart sped up. "Who is the note from?" Would Tony send a note? Why wouldn't he text or call or just stop by? She followed Brit to the front desk.

"I don't know." Brit retrieved an envelope from a drawer. "Someone dropped it through the mail slot. It was here when I came down this morning." She handed the envelope to Kelsey.

Kelsey studied her name on the front of the message. This wasn't Tony's precise script. And she didn't recognize the writing as belonging to anyone else she knew. She took the stairs to her room and waited until she was inside before she teased up the flap of the envelope. The message was typed on a half sheet of white paper: "I know some things I never told the cops about your sister because I was too afraid. But I want to tell you," she read. "Please meet me at six p.m. Wednesday at the trailhead for Kestrel Trail. There's something I need to show you."

She read the message over again. Was this for real or some cruel prank? If this had happened a few days ago, she would have asked Tony to go with her, but she couldn't do that now.

Should she tell the sheriff? Or would he think she was wasting his time? She punched in the number for the sheriff's department. Adelaide Kinkaid would know what she should do.

But instead of Adelaide, a different woman answered the phone. "Rayford County Sheriff," she said, her voice brisk.

"Is Adelaide there?" Kelsey asked.

"Ms. Kinkaid is away from the office today. How may I help you?"

"May I speak to the sheriff?"

"Sheriff Walker isn't available at the moment. What does this concern?"

Kelsey hung up. She didn't want to have to recap her whole story to a stranger. She read the note again. It was already after five. While the trail itself was fairly isolated, the trailhead was on a major road, and there were several trails branching off from it. Someone else would probably be there. And she had to find out who had written the note and what that person wanted to tell—and show—her about her sister.

She grabbed her backpack and keys and headed back downstairs. "Goodbye!" Brit called as Kelsey passed.

Kelsey waved but kept moving. She would have to hurry or she would be late. She didn't want to miss this opportunity.

Chapter Eighteen

"Set the stake right there, Ben." While his assistant hammered in the numbered stake marking the right-of-way for the new road project, Tony recorded the GPS coordinates and prepared to pack up his equipment.

"I hear that nephew of yours is doing a good job," Ben said when he had the stake in. He straightened and came to stand beside Tony. "Curtis says he'll be ready to go out in the field on his own next week, so you might be getting a new assistant."

"I don't know if I want to live *and* work with him," Tony said.

"Hey, it's a great excuse for you to boss him around," Ben said. "And really, he's a good kid. We had a beer after work the other day, and he sure thinks the world of you."

"Yeah, well, I think the world of him, too." Chris knew that, didn't he?

The growl of a pickup truck engine made him look up in time to see Ted race by in his battered vehicle. Tony lifted a hand in a wave but Ted, hunched over the steering wheel, never looked up.

"Sounds like Ted has an exhaust leak in his truck," Ben

said as he approached, tripod over one shoulder. "He ought to have that looked at."

Tony nodded, something else about the way the truck sounded in the back of his mind, but he couldn't quite retrieve the thought. He and Ben finished loading their gear and were just climbing into Tony's truck when his phone message alert went off. Tony checked the screen. "Is it a search and rescue call?" Ben asked.

Tony nodded. "Lost fisherman up at Crystal Lake."

Ben made a sucking sound with his teeth. "Bet he went through the ice. This time of year, there's always somebody who thinks it will hold. The county ought to just post signs telling people to stay off the ice after April 1. It might look solid, but there's just too much warm weather these days, even in the high country."

Tony nodded absently, not really listening as Ben continued with a story about a friend of his who went through the ice crossing a pond somewhere south of town. His attention was divided between thoughts of what they needed to prepare for the rescue—and possible body retrieval—of the fisherman and wondering where Ted had been going in such a hurry.

He dropped Ben at his truck at the surveying office, then headed to SAR headquarters. Most of the other volunteers were assembled, loading the Beast with the equipment they might need, from supplemental oxygen to waders and an inflatable rubber raft.

"We're waiting on Anna and Jacquie," Sheri said when Tony approached. "Jacquie hasn't been certified for water searches yet, but Anna has been training her and I think she's our best chance of finding this guy if he went in."

"You think we're searching for a body?" Tony asked.

Sheri nodded. "His brother and his son were with him and they searched for an hour before they called us."

She looked around at the crowd of volunteers. "Have you seen Ted?" she asked.

"I saw him right before I left to come here," Tony said. "He was in his truck, racing somewhere. After I got the call, I thought he might have been headed here."

Sheri shook her head. "No, and I'm more annoyed with him than usual. He was supposed to meet me here an hour ago to help with a grant application I'm working on. He has all the statistics on the number of rescues we've done in the past two years, miles logged and things like that I need for the application. Which direction was he headed?"

"South," Tony said. Not toward SAR headquarters, come to think of it.

"Crystal Lake is east, so he wasn't headed there." She shrugged. "Maybe he forgot."

Danny joined them in time to hear this last statement. "Are you talking about Ted?" he asked.

"Yes," Sheri said. "He flaked out on helping me with the grant application this afternoon."

"He's been acting strange lately," Danny said.

"Stranger than usual?" Sheri asked.

"He's always been a grouch, but yesterday he flew off the handle when I asked him if he'd seen the new issue of the *Examiner*," Danny said. "There was an ad in there for some Rossignol powder skis, and I knew he used to have that model and I wanted to know what he thought of them. But I never got around to asking him because he went on this rant about how he didn't have time to sit around reading the paper and all they printed was garbage anyway."

"Sometimes behavior changes like that are linked to

something physical," Sheri said. "Maybe it's time someone suggested he see a doctor." She turned to Tony. "You've known him longer than any of us. Maybe you could bring it up."

"I can try," Tony said. "But I doubt he'll take the suggestion well." Something was definitely up with Ted lately. He struck Tony as someone with a lot on his mind—but what had him so upset?

KELSEY SLOWED TO turn into the parking lot for the starting point for Kestrel Trail but hesitated when she saw that the only other vehicle there was an older model pickup truck. She flashed back to the headlights from the vehicle that had almost run her and Tony down the other night. Tony had said he thought that had been a truck. And a truck had come up behind her the other day, blaring its horn. But as she debated turning around and leaving, a familiar figure emerged from the vehicle and waved.

She relaxed as she recognized Ted, and then her heart began to beat faster—not with fear but with excitement. He had lived here when Liz was killed. He had been standing outside the ice-cream parlor the night her friends said she was meeting someone. Had he remembered the one thing that would help her find Liz's murderer?

She pulled in next to Ted and got out of her car. "Thanks for meeting me out here," he said. "I wanted someplace where we could talk privately, without worrying about anyone overhearing."

"Your note said you knew something about Liz," she said. "What is it?"

"I did see her with someone outside the ice-cream shop that night." He shoved both hands in the pockets of his jeans.

"I kept quiet because the person I saw is a good friend of mine," he said. "I couldn't believe he would do anything to hurt your sister, but now I think maybe I was wrong."

Kelsey curled her hands into fists, trying to keep them from shaking. She had waited for this so long. "Who did you see with Liz that night?" she asked, fighting to keep her voice steady.

He stared at the ground between them for a long moment. She fought the urge to shake him. To demand he tell her the truth he had been hiding all these years. But she forced herself to wait. When Ted finally looked up at her, his expression was mournful. "It was Tony," he said. "I know you don't want to hear this, but I think he's the one who killed your sister."

THE SEARCH AND Rescue team waited on the shores of Crystal Lake while Anna Trent and her search dog, a black standard poodle named Jacquie, trailed around the shoreline. Jacquie snuffled through the tall rushes around the dam inlet, then hurried down to the water, pulling Anna after her. The fisherman, Mike Munro, had come to the lake with his brother and son, who waited on a rise above the rescuers, with other friends and family members who had come to offer what support they could. A long half hour into the search, Anna raised her hand and called out, "I see something under the ice."

While Jacquie stood at attention on the shore, focused on the flash of red beneath the shelf of ice, Eldon, Tony and Danny took turns chopping at the frozen surface with an ax until they had cleared a space large enough to reach in with a grappling hook and snag Mike Munro's red fleece jacket. Mike's brother moved forward to confirm the identification, and they solemnly slid the body into an opaque black bag and carried it to the waiting ambulance, which would transport it to the morgue in the basement of the hospital.

A subdued group returned to Search and Rescue headquarters. Everything had gone off smoothly, exactly as it should have. The fisherman had probably died within minutes of going into the cold water, and there was nothing the group could have done to save him, but coming back without a live body never felt good.

The rescue over, Tony's thoughts shifted back to Ted. Too many things about the way his friend had been acting lately bothered him. Why was Ted so interested in Kelsey, constantly asking about her, yet disparaging her search for her sister?

The need to talk to Kelsey overwhelmed him. Why had he been so standoffish, staying away from her? He needed to apologize for being such a fool. Even if she hated him for treating her the way he had, he needed to make sure she was all right.

He left SAR headquarters and drove to the Alpiner. Brit looked up from behind the front desk when he entered. "Is Kelsey here?" he asked before Brit could even say hello.

"I'm sorry, Tony, she isn't. She left a couple of hours ago."

He grabbed hold of the front desk to steady himself and silently swore. He was too late. Kelsey had gone back to Iowa. She hadn't even bothered to say goodbye. But why should she? He hadn't given her any reason to think he was still her friend. Her lover. Though he wanted to be that, and so much more.

Maybe it wasn't too late. "Do you have an address for her in Iowa?" he asked.

Brit frowned. "I might have. But why do you need her address in Iowa?"

"If she's gone back there, I thought I might write her." Did that sound pathetic? Did people even write letters anymore?

Brit was still staring at him, confusion on her face. "Never mind," he said. "I'll call her." That's what he should do. He had her number.

"Oh my goodness, I just realized what you're thinking," Brit said. "Kelsey hasn't gone back to Iowa. Not yet, anyway. She just went out."

"Where did she go?" Maybe he could find her and try to explain himself in person.

"I think she might have gone hiking. She had her day pack with her."

"Hiking where?"

Brit shook her head. "I don't know. She didn't say."

He remembered again seeing Ted, driving out of town. Away from SAR headquarters. Away from Crystal Lake.

Toward the trailhead for Kestrel Trail. Suddenly, he was certain that was where Ted had been going. Where Kelsey had headed, as well. He might be wrong, but he couldn't ignore this instinct that told him he was right.

Hand shaking, he pulled out his phone and punched in Kelsey's number. It rang and rang before going to voice mail. "This is Tony. I'm sorry I've been so foolish. Please call me. I need to know you're okay."

Fear clawing at his chest, he called Ted. No answer. He didn't bother leaving a message. Instead, he thought about the sound of Ted's truck. Ben thought the truck had an exhaust leak. It was the same sound the truck that had tried to run them down weeks ago made.

Ted had denied knowing Liz, but how could he have not at least been aware of her? She was an attractive newcomer, at a time when newcomers were rare enough to draw a lot of attention. Ted had been standing on the sidewalk near the ice-cream parlor on the night she had told her friends she was meeting someone. He said he stepped out for a smoke, but back then, people still smoked in bars. There was no reason for Ted to stand outside that night unless he was waiting for someone.

Unless he was waiting for Liz.

Tony called the sheriff. Not the emergency number, but Travis's personal cell. "Is something wrong, Tony?" Travis asked by way of greeting.

"I'm not positive, but I think Kelsey Chapman is in trouble," he said. "I think she's with Ted Carruthers, and I think he might intend to hurt her."

He waited for Travis to ask him what proof he had to back his suspicions, but the sheriff did not. "Where are they now?" he asked.

"I'm not positive, but my best guess is that they're at Kestrel Trail." It was where Liz had died. Would Ted think there was some kind of symmetry in ending up there again after all these years?

"I'll send someone to check it out," Travis said.

Tony ended the call, grateful the sheriff was a man of few words. But Tony wasn't going to wait for a deputy to show up. Kelsey had been gone at least two hours now. More than enough time for Ted to harm her, if that was what he intended. Long years in rescue work had taught Tony that even a few minutes could make a difference when it came to saving someone. He had to hurry, before it was too late.

KELSEY STARED, sure she had heard Ted incorrectly. "Tony?" she gasped.

Expression still glum, Ted nodded. "I'm sorry," he said. "All these years, I've tried to put it out of my mind, to tell myself what I saw was innocent. But the other day I was up on this trail, near where Liz died." He pointed to the trail head. "And I saw something there that proved to me that Tony was the only one who could have killed your sister."

"I don't understand." She shook her head. Not Tony. Not the man who had been such a friend to her. Such a gentle lover. "Why would Tony have killed Liz?"

"Tony had a crush on Liz. A crush she didn't reciprocate. I think he invited her to go hiking with him that day and when they got to that rocky bench with the great view, he told her how he felt about her. Maybe she said something to hurt his feelings. Maybe she laughed. You women don't understand what something like that can do to a guy. There he was, pouring out his heart to her, and she acted like it didn't mean anything. That kind of rejection really messes with a man's head. It can make him do things he wouldn't ordinarily do."

Was Ted still talking about Tony? "Tony isn't like that," she said.

"Anyone could have done what he did, in that position," Ted said. "He snapped and killed her. Then he ran away. But his conscience wouldn't let him just leave her there, so when no one found her after a week, he played the hero and 'found' her body himself."

"I can't believe it." The words came out just above a whisper, though inside, Kelsey was shouting. *Not Tony!*

"It makes sense if you think about it," Ted said. "Tony has always been a little odd. Standoffish. He doesn't make friends easily, isn't one to socialize a lot. He's the kind of man who probably has a lot of secrets."

Those things don't make a person a killer, Kelsey wanted to say, but she couldn't force the words past the knot of fear in her throat. Tony had admitted to having a crush on Liz. And he had been the one to find her body. The sheriff's department had even suspected him of having killed her. "His DNA doesn't match what the sheriff's department collected from underneath Liz's fingernails," she said. "They tested Tony at the time."

"Maybe they made a mistake when they collected it," Ted said. "Or maybe that DNA is from someone who shook hands with her earlier in the day. We all know that so-called evidence can lie."

But could DNA evidence lie? She stared at Ted. "I'm having a hard time digesting all this."

He nodded. "It's a lot to take in. And I might have kept quiet longer. After all, Tony is like a son to me in some ways. I've been watching him, and I don't think he's ever hurt anyone else. Telling everyone about this won't bring your sister back."

"But you can't let a murderer go free!"

"I guess that's true." He stared off to the side, as if seeing something she couldn't see. "There's another reason I decided I had to tell you," he said. His gaze met hers again—mournful eyes set in a weathered face. "I saw how close Tony was getting to you—how much time the two of you were spending together. I knew you had to go back to Iowa soon and I worried that he might not take it well. He might do to you the same thing he did to your sister. You and Liz are a lot alike, you know. At least, from the pictures I've seen."

Kelsey put a hand to her head, as if to quell the dizziness his words sent washing over her. She couldn't believe Tony would ever hurt her. Would he?

"Hike up the trail with me a little ways, and I'll show you what I found," Ted said. "You'll want to show the sheriff. It pretty much proves Tony is the one who killed Liz." He motioned that she should go ahead of him.

Numb, she started up the trail, Ted close behind her. He didn't say anything, and she was grateful that he didn't try to engage her in further conversation. Thoughts tumbled in her head like gravel in a rushing stream. Was she such a poor judge of character that she had fallen for her sister's killer? She hugged her arms across her stomach, cold all over.

She walked slowly, as if her feet were reluctant to reach this supposed proof that the man she trusted—a man she had fallen in love with—was a murderer. Every step was an effort, but she forced herself to keep moving. After an hour they were at the place in the trail where Tony had taken her when they hiked together—the location where he said he had found Liz's body. She stared at the gray rock and bunches of green grass and short yellow wildflowers sprouting up around it. "If Tony killed Liz because she rejected him, who was Mountain Man?" she asked. "Who was the older man who persuaded her to come live with him in Eagle Mountain?"

Ted frowned. "Liz must have made him up."

"But she didn't," Kelsey said. "The sheriff has printouts between Liz and Mountain Man, and his messages originated in Eagle Mountain. And he sent her a bus ticket to come here. Liz never could have done that on her own."

"It sounds to me as if she could have done anything she put her mind to," he said. "She was that sure of herself, coming here by herself and even fooling the school the way she did."

Liz was stubborn. Impulsive. Strong-willed. But Kelsey had found no evidence that she was a liar. "What is it you wanted to show me?" she asked, impatient to be away from here. Alone, where she could think.

"It's right over here." He stepped up on the largest rock and held his hand out for her. "Come up and I'll show you."

She rejected his offer to help and hopped up on the rock beside him. "Where is it?"

"It's just behind there." He pointed toward the ground beside another boulder. "Do you see?"

She bent and stared at the ground. "I don't see anything. What—"

But she never finished the sentence. Piercing pain exploded in the back of her head, and everything went black.

TONY BROKE EVERY speed limit on the drive to the trailhead, praying as he gripped the steering wheel and kept his foot on the gas pedal that his instincts were wrong. But he spotted Ted's truck when he was still fifty yards from the parking area, and as he turned in, he caught sight of Kelsey's car parked beside it. He skidded to a stop, cut the engine and leapt out, racing up the steep trail. He ran, not as if his own life depended on speed but as if the life of the one person who mattered most to him was on the line.

His legs usually hurt when he tried to run, but today he felt nothing but the icy fear in the pit of his stomach as he pounded up the trail. With no pack or oxygen tank or awkward medical gear to carry, he covered ground quickly. As he topped each rise he stared ahead, expecting to see Ted, or Kelsey or—worst of all—both of them together. But only wildflowers and rocks and blue sky met his gaze.

Then he spotted movement far ahead. Two figures on the rocks. He picked up his pace, every part of him aching now, sharp pains in his legs, dull throbbing in his chest, a prickly sensation across his palms. He clenched and unclenched his fingers. Why hadn't he thought to bring a weapon? And what would he have brought? A kitchen knife? A scalpel?

"Stop right there, Tony!"

Ted's voice boomed out across the empty landscape. Tony stumbled in mid-stride, and had to pull back to catch himself. He stared up the slope, at Ted, who held Kelsey's limp body in his arms. "What did you do to her?" he shouted, his voice breaking with rage.

"I told her the truth." Ted shook his head. "Or a version of it. I told her how you murdered her sister because she didn't love you the way you loved her."

"But you murdered Liz," Tony said.

"She was supposed to stay with me for the rest of her life," Ted said. "That's why I sent her the bus ticket. Why I helped her lie to the school district. But she changed her mind. She told me she wanted to go home. She wanted to leave me. Do you know what it feels like to have someone you love abandon you that way?"

Tony stared, not at Ted but at Kelsey. She lay back in Ted's arms, head limp, eyes half-closed, mouth partly open.

"I couldn't let her leave me," Ted said. "She was all I ever wanted. I was good to her. Why wasn't that enough?"

Tony shifted his gaze back to his longtime friend and mentor. Ted didn't look good. His skin was gray, his face deeply lined. "And you killed her for that?" Tony asked.

Ted looked down at Kelsey, and Tony wondered if he was

seeing Liz there instead. "It was an accident," Ted said, his voice gentle. "I tried to move in closer, to kiss her and tell her we would find a way to work things out. She pushed me, so I pushed her back." He shook his head. "I only meant to grab her, to make her listen to sense, but she struggled so much. The more she struggled, the tighter I held her. And then she just…died. So in the end, she left me anyway."

"Why didn't you call for help?" Tony asked.

"It was too late. No one could have saved her."

"The medical examiner said she was strangled," Tony said.

Ted jerked his head up. "He's a liar," he said, his voice a harsh growl. "They're all liars." He shaped his hand to Kelsey's throat. His fingers wrapped around it easily. Dizziness and fear rocked Tony back on his heels. He took three steps forward while Ted was so focused on Kelsey. "You have to be very careful with people's necks," Ted said. "They're very delicate."

A chill shuddered through Tony as he remembered how Ted had said those very words in the CPR classes he taught every spring and fall at the fire house. They had never sounded so sinister before. He swallowed and tried to keep his voice calm. "You're right," he said. "Necks are very sensitive. Why don't you lay Kelsey down and I'll check hers for you?"

Ted jerked his gaze away from Kelsey again. "Don't move," he ordered.

Kelsey moaned, and they both stared. She rolled her head from side to side, grimacing. "Now look what you did," Ted said. "You woke her." He hefted her higher, though he had to move his hand away from her throat to do so.

Tony searched the ground for a weapon. Rocks were a

natural choice, but any with the size and heft to do damage were too far away to be of any use to him. All he had were words, and he had never been good with those. But he had to try. "The sheriff is on his way," he said. "I told him I suspected you killed Liz and that you might try to hurt Kelsey."

The lines on Ted's forehead and around his eyes deepened. "You shouldn't have done that," he said. He looked out past Tony's shoulder. "But it doesn't matter. They won't get here in time."

In time for what? Tony wanted to ask but didn't. Instead, he asked, "What are you going to do?"

"I'm going to kill Kelsey, then kill you," Ted said, in a voice someone might use to describe their morning workout. "When the sheriff does arrive, I'll tell him how I found you both—a murder-suicide I was too late to stop."

"Travis isn't a fool," Tony said. "He won't take your word for it. He'll want proof."

Ted shrugged. "Maybe I'll scrape Liz's hand across your face and collect some DNA for them to find," he said. "That should make them happy."

He had said Liz, not Kelsey. Did Ted even know where he was and who he was with right now? Or was he twenty years in the past, with another young woman who had rejected him? Tony didn't have any more time for questions like that one. He had to act. Ted's hand tightened around Kelsey's throat, and she groaned louder.

Tony ran—not away but straight toward Ted and Kelsey. He hit with all the force he could muster, trying to aim the brunt of the impact at Ted but unable to avoid Kelsey, who was crushed between them. The two men each struggled to hold on to her. Though Ted was older, he was still strong and refused to let go. Furious and frustrated, Tony leaned down and bit the older man, hard, on the wrist.

With a wounded yowl, Ted released his hold. Kelsey tumbled to the ground and Tony punched Ted in the jaw, knocking him backward, but Ted grabbed Tony's ankle and brought him down, too. The two men rolled and grappled, sharp rocks digging into Tony's back and shoulders. How close were they to the edge? The slope was steep enough here they would roll for a while if they tumbled over the edge of the bench.

Ted had him on his back now, trying to wrap his hands around Tony's throat as Tony grasped his wrists and tried to push him away. A rock with a knife edge dug into his back and his recently-knitted muscles and bones protested at this strain. He tried to shift beneath the older man, but Ted had him firmly pinned. Where was the deputy the sheriff had promised to send?

Maybe the deputy wasn't coming. Kelsey wasn't going to suddenly regain consciousness and pick up a rock and hurl it at Ted, either. Tony was on his own. He ought to be used to that by now.

With a howl of rage, he shoved up against Ted and rolled to his left, reversing their positions so that now he was on top and Ted on bottom. Then he brought his knee up and planted it firmly in Ted's stomach. He found the rock that had been digging into his back moments before and brought it down on Ted's forehead. Ted groaned, then fell silent, and Tony shoved to his feet, blood and tears dripping down his face.

He wiped his eyes to clear his vision, then staggered over to Kelsey. He knelt beside her, and gently touched her cheek. He ought to assess her, as he would any person in need he was called to rescue, but all he could do was stare. "Please wake up," he said, his voice choked with tears. "Please, please wake up."

Her eyes fluttered, and she looked up at him. "Tony," she whispered, before she closed her eyes again.

Tony tried to stand, but toppled to one side instead. He was trying again to get to his feet when Deputy Jake Gwynn and Sheriff Travis Walker came striding up the trail toward them. Travis stood over them. "What happened to you?" he asked.

"Ted killed Liz Chapman," Tony said. "And he tried to kill Kelsey. Then he was going to kill me and tell you I was the murderer."

"When I saw Ted's truck, I radioed for an ambulance," Travis said. "Just in case."

Tony nodded, then rested his forehead on his upraised knees, too exhausted to say anything else. But he kept one hand on Kelsey, her pulse steady beneath his fingers. She was alive, and right now that was all he needed.

KELSEY'S HEAD HURT, and when she opened her eyes, the light made the pain worse. She closed her eyes again, but someone was shaking her. "Kelsey. Kelsey, you need to wake up."

She shook her head, but the voice persisted, telling her she had to wake up. She forced her eyes open again and stared up at a man she didn't recognize. "Who are you?" she asked. Except her throat was so dry the words came out as more moaning.

"I'm Dr. Harrison," the man said. "Do you remember what happened to you?"

She closed her eyes again, some of the fog lifting as she remembered Ted telling her those awful things about Tony.

"Kelsey, don't go away from us again. Open your eyes for me, please."

She opened her eyes. "I think Ted hit me," she said, the words clearer now. "Can I have some water?"

The doctor disappeared from view, but moments later returned and slipped a straw between her lips. She could only manage a couple of weak sips before he took it away. "You've sustained a concussion," he said. "You're in St. Joseph's Hospital in Junction. There's someone here who insists on seeing you."

The doctor left again, and was replaced by another, more welcome face. "Tony!" she said, and tried to smile, but the movement hurt too much.

"How are you feeling?" he asked.

"I've been better." She stared, taking in his bruised face. "What happened to you?"

He touched his bruised cheek and winced. "I was in a bit of a fight."

"Where's Ted?" she asked. "He told me some terrible things. He tried to say you...you..." She couldn't get the words out. They were too horrible.

"He lied," Tony said. "He lied to me and to everyone else. He killed Liz. He was Mountain Man. I'm sorry. I'm sorry about all of this. Mostly, I'm sorry I was so awful. I should have been a lot smarter. About Ted, but especially about you."

The doctor reappeared. "The sheriff is here," he said. "I told him he could have two minutes, then everyone has to leave this woman in peace."

Sheriff Walker loomed over her now. "Do you remember what happened?" he asked.

She nodded. "Ted asked me to meet him to tell me something he knew about Liz's killer. Then he hit me in the head." She winced. "I guess he tried to kill me, too." She didn't bother mentioning everything Ted had told her about Tony. That had to be all lies.

"We have Ted in custody," Travis said. "As soon as we're able we'll collect his DNA and compare it to the evidence we have from your sister, but we searched his home and we found this." He held out a small plastic bag with a white label stamped Evidence.

Kelsey put a hand to her throat and felt the small gold heart necklace there. The necklace's twin was in that bag. "That's Liz's," she said. "She gave me one just like it." She tugged at the chain until the heart was freed from the top of her hospital gown.

"We found a photo of your sister and some other things that point to Ted's involvement with her," Travis said. He tucked the bag with the necklace back into his pocket. "I'll get a full statement from you as soon as the doctor agrees."

"Time's up," the doctor said.

"We'll talk more later," Travis said, then left.

"Please, can I see Tony again?" Kelsey asked.

The doctor frowned and shook his head, but moments later, Tony was back in place. "I didn't believe him," she said before Tony could speak. "I didn't believe Ted when he told me you murdered Liz. I knew you wouldn't do something like that."

He took her hand in his and kissed her knuckles. "A lot of people would have believed him," he said.

"I'm not a lot of people." She took a deep breath. "And

I'm in love with you. I have enough faith in myself to believe I wouldn't fall in love with a murderer."

He stilled, his hand still clutching her fingers. He stared into her eyes. "I love you, too," he said. "So much it scared me into pushing you away. Can you forgive me for that?"

"Yes. But don't let it happen again."

His smile was the warm, shy one that had made her catch her breath the very first time they met. As if even then her heart knew what her brain wasn't yet ready to accept. That all those other failed relationships and difficulties getting close to other people hadn't meant that she was too damaged to connect. She had only needed the right person to connect to. A man who understood what it was like to be alone from a young age. Someone like Tony, who was as afraid of pain as she was, but willing to take a risk. "Don't go back to Iowa," he said. "Stay here and give me a chance. Give us a chance."

She nodded. "I have to go back to settle things there, but I promise I'll come back here."

He patted her hand. "We'll find a way to make this work," he said, then left. She closed her eyes and drifted off. They would find a way, she was sure. They were two people who had made a habit now of doing the impossible.

Epilogue

Kelsey Chapman had never lived west of Mount Vernon, Iowa, when she steered her Honda Civic down the main street of Eagle Mountain, Colorado. She slowed the car to a crawl and almost stopped in the middle of the street as she stared up at the snow-covered mountains surrounding the town. She would always think of this place as the most beautiful spot in the world. Because of these mountains and that impossibly blue sky, and because of the friendships she had made here. The love she had found.

She drove on, through town to the A-frame cabin in the woods. She had barely turned into the drive when Tony emerged from the house and came to meet her. She shut off the engine and stepped out of the car and into his welcoming arms. "How was your trip?" he asked.

"Fine." They had talked every night while she was away, so he already knew she had quit her job and given up her lease on her apartment.

The door to the house opened and Chris emerged—as tall and lanky as his uncle, his hair a darker shade of blond, his face clean-shaven. He grinned at Kelsey. "Don't worry," he said. "I'm only here to help with the heavy lifting." He nodded toward the rental trailer she towed behind her car.

"I've got my own place now, so I won't be on the couch, cramping your style."

"It's a big change," Tony said, still watching her with concern.

"It's a good change." She patted his chest. "The Alpiner Inn has already hired me to do their accounts, and I'm sure I'll have other clients soon. Apparently, there's a real need for someone with my skills."

The worry left his eyes, replaced by warmth. "I have a real need for you," he said.

"Save it for later," Chris said. "Let's get this trailer unloaded."

They were bringing in the last of the boxes when a Rayford County Sheriff's Department SUV pulled into the drive. Sheriff Travis Walker stepped out and studied the trailer, then the trio in front of the house. "Hello, Kelsey," he said. "I heard you were arriving today."

"Hello, Sheriff," she said, wary.

Travis didn't keep them waiting long. "We got the DNA results back today," he said. "Ted is a match for what we collected from your sister."

Her shoulders sagged—with relief and sadness and so many emotions she couldn't untangle right now. Tony slipped his arm around her.

"Did you find any more of Liz's things?" she asked.

"Ted admitted he burned everything except the necklace," Travis said.

"Why did he insist on keeping their relationship secret?" Kelsey asked.

"Apparently, he had this fear that some other man would steal her away from him," Travis said. "He lied about his age in his emails because he worried she would hold that against him. Then, when she finally got to Eagle Mountain, he realized how many young, single men were in town compared to the number of single women. He was determined not to lose her."

"He was obsessed," she said.

Travis nodded. "For what it's worth, we don't think he killed anyone else. What happened with Liz apparently shook him enough he didn't risk it again—until you came along."

She shuddered, remembering those horrible moments beside Kestrel Trail. She still had headaches and dizzy spells from the concussion she had sustained, though her doctors assured her that would get better with time.

"The prosecutor will be in touch about the trial," Travis said. "In the meantime, welcome back." He nodded and returned to his vehicle.

Chris carried the last box into the house, then emerged, keys in hand. "I have to go," he said. "Good seeing you, Kelsey." He pulled on a helmet, then went to a motorcycle that had been parked beside the house.

Tony pulled her close again. "How did your mother take your leaving?"

Kelsey sighed. "She didn't have much of a reaction. She said, 'If that's what you really want to do,' then said she needed to go, she had a women's club meeting to attend. I think she spent so many years trying not to feel that she can't anymore."

"I almost made that mistake, until you came along," he said.

She stared into his eyes, so full of love and concern— and the doubts she shared. "Do you think we can do this?" she asked. "With our histories?"

He nodded. "We can do this. We both know how to do hard things. Good things." He kissed her, and the kiss made her believe him. She brought her hand up to cover the gold heart she wore around her neck. She was going to be happy here. The kind of happiness Liz would have wanted for her. The happiness she deserved.

* * * * *

THE SECRET
SHE KEEPS

LENA DIAZ

To Lisa and Laura, the sisters I would have chosen even if we weren't related. Together we will survive, overcome and learn how to navigate our new normal. Love will get us through. Laughter is just around the corner. Fake it until you make it. Love you. Always. Forever.

Chapter One

In a Smoky Mountains parking lot high above Gatlinburg, Tennessee, Raine Quintero watched for her prey through the windshield. Clutched in her hands was the unregistered nine-millimeter pistol she'd bought in the back room of a sleazy bar a week earlier.

As plans went, hers wasn't exactly inspired. The chance of success was probably fifty-fifty, at best. But everything else she'd tried had failed. She was out of options, desperate and almost out of time. Desperation, like grief, had stages. Reaching this final stage had taken fifteen agonizing years. Now she was prepared to do anything, cross any line, pay any price to save her brother's life.

Even if it meant threatening someone else's.

An inconvenient twinge of decency and shame had the pistol shaking in her hands. Like a thousand jagged knives, her conscience slashed through her carefully constructed excuses for what she was about to do. She rocked back and forth in her seat, a roller coaster of emotions twisting inside her. When a hot tear rolled down her cheek and dripped onto her hand, she swore and shoved the pistol inside the glove box.

Apparently, Callum Wright would get one last chance.

He could act, or refuse to act. His fate would be decided by his choice.

Unlike her brother, who'd never been given a choice.

Clenching her now empty hands together, she drew deep, even breaths until the shaking subsided. The guilt was still there. But she'd managed to force it back into its little box to be dealt with later. This didn't change her overall plan. She hadn't come here on a whim. Everything had led to this one crucial moment. Sometimes the end really did justify the means.

Or so she kept telling herself.

Blowing out another deep breath, she checked the time on the fitness tracker on her wrist. If this morning was like the last few, the man who held her brother's fate in his hands would be here in just a few more minutes.

Sure enough, at precisely seven thirty, Callum's black Lexus all-wheel-drive SUV turned into the parking lot of the company where he worked, Unfinished Business. It always took her aback when she saw him driving that type of vehicle. Although nice, it didn't cost anywhere near what he could afford.

From what she'd gleaned about UB, the company paid its investigators extremely well. It's how the billionaire owner had attracted top detectives around the country to give up their government jobs and switch to the private sector. It helped explain why Callum had traded life near his family in Athens, Georgia, to live in the Smoky Mountains of Gatlinburg, Tennessee. Although, surprisingly, none of her internet searches had ever revealed his exact address, either when he'd lived in Georgia or after he'd moved here.

His Lexus certainly didn't compare to her red Porsche Panamera sports car back home. Of course, that wasn't tion. "Good morning. My apologies, but I don't recall your name." He held out his hand.

She shook it, encouraged that he was talking to her. "We haven't met before. I'm Raine Quintero." She waited for a sign of recognition. Sadly, her last name didn't even trigger a flicker of reaction.

"How can I help you, Ms. Quintero?"

"I've been trying to reach you about investigating a case for me. But your office manager is a bit of a bulldog about putting me through on the phone. I'm guessing since you haven't returned any of my calls that she hasn't given you my messages."

He grimaced. "Sorry about that. We recently hired more administrative staff out of necessity. Our company's success has resulted in a flood of calls and visits off the street that were interfering with our ability to focus on our investigations. I'm guessing she told you we partner with law enforcement to try to solve the cold cases that they don't have the resources to work."

"She did. And I understand your company's charter. I've read the disclaimers on their website. But this is different, critically important. My brother was sent to prison thirteen years ago for a crime he didn't commit. It's urgent that I—"

He held up his hand to stop her. "Ms. Quintero, my sympathies about your brother, truly. But we can't help you. Our contracts are with the various law enforcement agencies of east Tennessee, including TBI—the Tennessee Bureau of Investigation. We don't hire out to private individuals."

"Your company just finished a case for a civilian, a nurse, Skylar Montgomery. I saw a story about it on the news. If you made an exception for her, you can make one for me.

I want to hire *you*. Money isn't an issue. I can afford whatever fees you charge."

He shook his head. "It's not about money. Ms. Montgomery's situation was unique, a one-off. I'm not sure why you're singling me out, specifically. But it doesn't change anything."

"I would hope my brother being on death row would change *everything*. I really need your help."

His jaw tightened. "If he's on death row, you need an attorney who specializes in capital punishment cases. Again, I'm sorry." He started past her again.

"Joey Quintero. Ring a bell?"

He stopped and turned around, his expression beginning to mirror impatience. "No, but I'm guessing you think it should."

She hurried to him, craning her neck back to meet his dark blue gaze. "You worked on his case when you were a police detective in Athens, Georgia. *That's* why I singled you out."

His expression turned thoughtful. "Thirteen years ago?"

"Fifteen when the case began. He was accused of strangling a young woman in her home, when her parents were out of town. Capital murder, death row, Quintero. You honestly don't remember?"

He stared off into space as if accessing off-site storage in his mental memory banks. The flash of recognition she'd been hoping to see finally happened. But the frown that accompanied it told her she wasn't going to like what he was about to say.

"My recollection is spotty on that case. As you said, it was a long time ago. And I wouldn't have been a lead detective back then."

"Farley was."

He slowly nodded. "Farley. Haven't heard that name in a while."

His flat tone suggested that he and Farley hadn't exactly been friends. That was encouraging.

"He passed away a few years ago," she told him. "Massive heart attack. But I did get to speak to him before that. Or, I tried. Several times. He told me to go to hell."

"Sounds like Farley."

"And now you're telling me to do the same."

"No. I've been politely explaining why I can't hire out to investigate for you. For one thing, the company I work for only handles cases for the eastern Tennessee region, not Georgia. That's part of our contract with the various counties we support. But even if I wanted to work independently, outside of my company, I don't have any unique insight into what happened that could help with an appeal. I was a brand-new detective, more of a gopher than a true investigator. Farley didn't involve me in the guts of any of the cases he was working. He had me do research on case law, minor witness interviews, follow up on calls to our crime tip line. Your brother confessed, didn't he? Seems like I remember that much."

"It was coerced, a false confession."

"That's hard to believe, considering that our interrogations were supposed to be recorded to protect against that sort of thing. Did his attorney review the recording and argue that his confession should be thrown out?"

"His defense attorney was an idiot."

"I'll take that as a no. Look, I'm sorry that you and your family are suffering—"

"What family, Mr. Wright? My parents died in a car

wreck four years ago. My brother's all I have and he's going to be executed in a matter of weeks unless I can find someone who can provide some kind of evidence, some kind of doubt, that could be used for a grant of clemency. I'm truly out of options or I wouldn't be here talking to one of the people responsible for sending an innocent man to prison in the first place."

He sighed deeply. "Ms. Quintero, if you knew me at all, you'd know that I'm a man who values honesty, integrity and justice over winning percentages. I live by the judicial system's golden rule, that everyone's innocent *unless* proven guilty. From what I'm starting to remember of the Quintero case, it was solid. Didn't the jury deliberate for just a few hours before returning with a guilty verdict?"

"Only because his attorney was incompetent. He put up a pathetic defense. My brother didn't hurt anyone."

His gaze hardened. "Tell that to the victim's family."

She grabbed his arm when he would have turned to leave. "Please, all I'm asking is for a meeting with you. An hour of your time to review—"

He gently but firmly pushed her hand away. "I don't get guilty people out of prison. That's what lawyers are for."

She sucked in a sharp breath at his insult to her profession. But before she could gather her composure to try again, he was rapidly striding away. His shiny boots flashed in the morning sun as he jogged up the front steps of UB headquarters and disappeared inside the glass-and-steel building.

Raine swore beneath her breath and hopped in her car. She glanced longingly at the glove box, then started the engine. Callum Wright had made his choice. He'd judged her brother guilty. But it was Callum who was guilty—of not caring that he'd helped send an innocent man to death row.

If she didn't do everything she could to correct that travesty, she'd be just as responsible for her brother's plight as Callum and Farley.

Her inconvenient conscience wasn't bothering her now. If anything, she was more determined than ever to follow through with her plan. Callum hadn't stopped her. He'd only delayed her.

Raine forced herself to slowly drive out of the parking lot even though she wanted to stomp the accelerator. As soon as she was out of sight of the building and reached the first cut-out area designed for sightseers or someone with car trouble, she pulled over.

All around her the infamous mist that gave the Smokies their name rose in white puffs like ancient smoke signals. But it did little to obscure the brilliant reds and golds that dressed the mountains in their spectacular autumn glory. At any other time, she'd have been awestruck by such beauty. But she wasn't here to enjoy the view. Grabbing her black backpack from the rear seat, she stowed her gun inside then got out.

A few moments later she'd made her way through the woods to the edge of the parking lot of Unfinished Business. When she reached the trees directly behind Callum's SUV, she located a bush that provided good cover along with a decent view through some gaps in the branches. In addition to his Lexus, she could see straight down the aisle to the front doors of UB headquarters. She pulled out her gun and used her backpack as a rather uncomfortable chair. But it beat sitting directly on the cold ground.

After assuming she'd be waiting most of the day for Callum to leave the building again, she was pleasantly surprised to see him heading toward her just a few hours later. A navy blue backpack was slung over one shoulder, the modern equivalent of the briefcases that executives carried decades earlier.

Was he on his way to meet someone? Or planning to take home some files to review in private instead of in the office? She hoped it was the latter. That would give her more time to do what she had to do before anyone realized he was missing.

Hefting the pistol in her left hand, she crept as close to the SUV's bumper as she dared. As soon as he slid into the driver's seat, she rushed to the open doorway, aiming her gun at him while she desperately tried not to shake too noticeably.

His blue eyes darkened with anger as he looked at the gun, then at her. "Ms. Quintero. Mind telling me what the hell you're doing?"

"We're about to have that meeting I requested. Very slowly, no sudden moves, take your gun out using only two fingers and pitch it onto the passenger floorboard."

"What makes you think I have a gun?"

"Don't play games. I've been watching you for a while. I've figured out you have a holster under that suit jacket. Toss it."

His eyes narrowed dangerously, but he did as she asked. "Now what?"

His hard expression and clipped tone had her hands shaking even harder. She pushed one of the buttons on his door, unlocking the rest of the doors.

"If you honk the horn, flash your lights or do anything else to attract attention, you'll earn a bullet. And anyone you alert will get shot too. Understood?"

His jaw tightened. "Understood."

She yanked open the door behind him and hopped inside. "Close your door."

As he pulled it closed, she quickly fastened her seat belt then brought up her gun again. A bead of sweat ran down the side of her face in spite of the chilly interior of his SUV. She pressed the bore of the pistol hard against his seat. "Feel that?"

"I assume that's your gun pushing against my back."

"You assume correctly. Start the engine."

The SUV roared to life. As he reached for his seat belt, she shoved the pistol harder against his chair.

"No seat belt."

His angry gaze met hers in the rearview mirror. "Why?"

"If you don't have your seat belt on, you'll think twice about pulling some stunt, like purposely wrecking to try to get away. Pull out of the parking lot, slowly. Don't draw any attention."

He hesitated.

She swallowed hard, wincing as she moved the gun to the back of his head.

He swore and slowly pulled out of the parking space.

Chapter Two

Callum took a quick glance at his rearview mirror as he maneuvered his SUV down the narrow two-lane road that wound around Prescott Mountain. Had there been another car back there at the last curve? Had someone been in the parking lot and saw what was happening? Or was it just the sun casting shadows through the trees?

"Slow down," Quintero warned.

Her pistol was still pushing against his seat. Barely enough to feel the pressure against his back, but enough to remind him it was there.

"If we end up in a ditch, I swear I'll shoot you." Her voice was as shaky as her hands had been on her gun earlier.

She probably *would* shoot him if he wrecked, whether she meant to or not. She didn't have the sense to keep her finger on the gun's frame instead of the trigger to avoid accidentally firing the pistol. That was the first thing he'd noticed when she'd stood in his open door. It was the only reason he hadn't immediately tackled her.

"I mean it." She jabbed the pistol harder. "Be careful."

"I'll slow down when you quit digging your gun into my back. And while we're at it, unless you plan on shooting me while I'm driving, move your finger from the trigger to the gun frame. It's safer that way. For both of us."

In the rearview mirror he caught her look of surprise. She glanced down, presumably at her gun. The pressure on his back eased. He hoped that meant she'd moved her finger off the trigger too. She was obviously a novice around guns, which only made her more dangerous.

As they passed the turnoff he'd have taken to go home, he eased his foot off the accelerator, slowing down as she'd requested. It wasn't necessary. He knew every curve of this mountain and how fast he could safely go without skidding into a guardrail. Wherever she lived there must not be any mountains, as skittish as she seemed.

"Better?" He gentled his voice, wanting her to feel less threatened, less anxious, even though he intended to take that gun away from her at the first viable opportunity.

She wiped some sweat from her brow. "Better." Her striking green eyes met his in the rearview mirror. "Thank you," she added grudgingly, as if she couldn't help herself.

He nodded, noting that her hand had still been shaking when she'd wiped her brow. Abducting people wasn't something she was comfortable with. He wished he'd researched her after their brief discussion earlier this morning. If he had, he'd at least have some background information. Maybe he could have used that to his advantage. But he'd forgotten about her when he'd stepped inside and fellow investigator Asher Whitfield had pulled him into a meeting about the serial killer cold case they were working together.

Given her brother's history, it was surprising that there was nothing about Raine that screamed criminal. In his experience, when one sibling was a murderer, the other was often intimately familiar with the wrong side of the law as well. And yet, he was willing to bet the most serious offense on her record before today was speeding.

In spite of his anger over her putting him in this situation, he couldn't help admiring her loyalty to her family and her willingness to risk everything to try to save her brother. Too bad for her that saving him was probably impossible.

Thirteen years on death row meant he'd likely exhausted most, if not all, of his appeals. His last resort would be a grant of clemency from the governor—assuming the governor of Georgia had that authority. Callum wasn't familiar with Georgia's laws regarding overturning convictions or granting stays of execution. As a cop, his focus had always been on putting the bad guys away, not getting them out.

That's what lawyers did.

He didn't know why she believed he might be able to even speak to anyone with authority over her brother's situation. Politicians weren't part of his social circle. And he didn't know the governor of *any* state.

His friend Noah Reid might have some pull with the governor of Georgia. He held an executive position in their Department of Corrections. But was Reid in a position to influence the fate of a death row inmate? Callum rather doubted it.

His boss, Grayson Prescott, had a handful of governors on speed dial and no doubt held considerable sway. But any hope that he'd speak on Raine's brother's behalf had ended the second she'd pulled a gun on one of his investigators.

Regret gnawed at Callum as he glanced at her in the mirror. Her shoulder-length dark hair accentuated her pale complexion. She was obviously scared, even though she was the one with the gun. She must have felt like she had no choice after he'd refused to give her one hour of his time. That's all she'd requested. And he'd been too busy to bother. Maybe this was his wake-up call to pay more attention to the pain of those around him instead of immersing himself in his work. Too bad it had come too late to save Raine Quintero from the consequences of her rather drastic actions.

They were getting close to the bottom of the mountain. Soon, the road would end and he'd have to turn. Left, toward town, where the tourists were no doubt clogging River Road, frequenting the little shops and restaurants. Or they could turn right toward the more rural part of the area without the kinds of attractions that drew hordes of out-of-towners.

To Callum's thinking, the rural part was the most beautiful and worth seeing. But if that's where she wanted to go, it meant driving farther away from the possibility of someone noticing them and realizing he was in trouble.

Unless the shadow on the road earlier wasn't a shadow.

He checked the rearview mirror again. No one behind them. Raine's reflection showed her frowning, then glancing over her shoulder.

"What are you looking at?" she asked.

"You. We're going to come to a stop sign soon. It would be easier for me to drive if I know where to go."

Her frown eased. "West. Turn right at the sign."

He nodded, unsurprised but disappointed. Without the sights and sounds of traffic and people around, it would be harder to catch her off guard. Then again, it also meant less risk to innocent bystanders, so it was probably for the best. He'd bide his time, do what he could to keep her calm and thinking she was completely in control of the situation.

Then he'd take her gun.

His cell phone beeped in his pocket.

She sat up straighter. "What's that?"

He sighed and pulled out the phone. "Someone's calling from the office. If I don't answer, they'll get suspicious."

She chewed her bottom lip, then pressed the gun into the back of the seat again. "Remember what I said. Your life, and the life of anyone you try to warn, is at risk. Put the call on speaker and get off as quickly as possible, without pulling any stunts."

Being on speaker would make it difficult to alert anyone. He'd have to wing it and see if there was anything he could do to let them know he was in trouble and where he was. He pressed the speaker button on the phone and held it up in the air beside him.

"Callum. You're on speaker."

"Hey, it's Thomas. Everything okay? I thought we were going to review those files at your house, but you're either not home or ignoring the doorbell."

He glanced at Raine before answering. "Sorry, forgot I had another appointment out of town."

The gun shoved harder against the seat at his *out of town* reference. She was smart. He'd have to remember that.

"I won't be back for a while," he said. "You might as well head to your house and start without me." Which would take him in the same direction that she'd just told Callum to go.

"Do you have an ETA on when I can expect you?" Thomas asked.

Raine shook her head, her hair bouncing on her shoulders.

"Hard to say. I really couldn't guess," Callum answered.

She made a rolling motion with her right hand, letting him know to hurry. They'd just reached the stop sign so he braked and made sure no one was coming before pulling out.

"I've got to go, Thomas. Again, sorry for the mix-up. Talk

to you later." He pressed a button on the side of the phone and set it in the console, facedown.

She let out a deep breath, an expression of relief on her face.

"Where to now, Ms. Quintero? Or should I call you Raine? If you're trusting me to help your brother, we should be on a first-name basis."

"We're not friends. Ms. Quintero is fine." She motioned toward the road. "Just keep going straight. I'll let you know when to turn again."

"Can you at least give me a guesstimate on mileage? I've got less than a quarter tank of gas."

She leaned over, peering at the dash. "What kind of miles-per-gallon does this thing get?"

"I've probably got enough fuel to go about seventy miles, give or take. Half that if this is a round trip. Less if we climb up into the mountains."

"We should be okay. We've only got about twelve more miles to go and we're staying in the valley."

When she sat back, he glanced toward his phone to double-check that the screen wasn't visible. He didn't want her to realize that all he'd done was press the button to silence the ringer. He hadn't ended the call.

And he didn't work with anyone named Thomas.

Chapter Three

The closer they got to the turnoff, the more Raine began to think she'd made a terrible mistake. Not in getting him to meet with her. She needed to show him the evidence she had, tell him her hopes for freeing Joey. But even though *how* she was carrying out this plan had made sense on paper, the reality felt entirely different.

For one thing, Callum was much more intimidating up close than she'd expected. He made her nervous. Not just because he was so much taller than her, and so obviously stronger. The real problem was that she liked him. He'd made her angry when he'd refused to meet with her. But aside from that, he'd been polite, even kind. He wasn't trying to scare her. And aside from initially pretending he didn't have a gun—which was understandable—he hadn't pulled any tricks even though she knew she would have in his situation.

If she hadn't known he'd been involved in sending her brother to death row, she'd have thought he was a decent guy. Heck, she'd have been all over him. He was the epitome of tall, dark and handsome. Exactly her type.

That was a problem.

She needed to focus. But seeing him as a *man*, and as a

surprisingly decent person, was making it difficult to continue to treat him so deplorably. Her actions seemed…evil, even though her goal—saving a life—was anything but evil. Still, she'd gone too far down this path to stop now. Being awful to Callum was something she'd have to learn to forgive herself for, eventually. But if Joey died, and she hadn't done everything she could to prevent his death, she'd *never* forgive herself for that.

A flash of color through the windshield had her shaking herself from her thoughts. "See that yellow sign up there? The one with the squiggles on it?"

He smiled in the rearview mirror. "The one warning that the road ahead has lots of tight curves?"

Her face heated. "The turn is just before it, on the left. It's a private driveway. The brush is overgrown, which makes it hard to find. You'll have to slow down."

"I see it."

He turned into the narrow dirt-and-gravel driveway. Raine winced as the tree branches on either side made sickening metallic scraping sounds whenever they came into contact with the sides of his vehicle. Regardless of today's outcome, she owed him a paint job.

About fifty yards later the driveway ended in front of a small, one-story clapboard house. The flaking yellowed paint had probably been white at one time. Gingerbread millwork beneath the sagging porch roof proclaimed that someone had loved this home once, long before it had been abandoned and left to rot.

"Cut the engine," she told him.

"We're actually going inside that thing?"

"It's not as bad as you think. I cleaned out the animal droppings and squirrel nests. At least I think they were squirrels."

"Wonderful."

She hopped out and yanked open his door just in time to see him grabbing his cell phone.

"Toss the phone on the floorboard," she ordered, quickly backing out of his reach.

He sighed and pitched it beside his discarded pistol. "You know, it's really not necessary to keep pointing your gun at me."

"I wish I could believe that." She moved farther away, both hands on the pistol grip. "Into the house, please."

He stepped down from the SUV. "I'll listen to whatever you have to say. Put the gun down first."

"Inside. Then we'll talk."

She needed him in the house to give her an advantage. Out here, the trees offered too many hiding places if he made a run for it. Inside the dilapidated structure she had better control over what happened. She just needed to keep her pistol pointed at him and stay out of his reach. He looked like he wanted to pounce on her. Not in a good way.

He paused at the bottom of the steps, testing one with his foot as if worried that it might not support his weight.

"It's safe," she assured him. "I checked the beams underneath. The boards are weathered but solid."

He nodded his thanks and headed up the stairs. She winced as he pushed the front door open and it creaked like something in an old horror movie. Behind him, she set her backpack on the wooden floor and closed the door. He stopped halfway into the room and looked around.

There wasn't much to see.

It was small and nearly empty. The grimy windows had no coverings, so the sunlight filtering through the trees overhead illuminated the place well enough. If he'd smelled it before she'd cleaned it, he'd have fallen over. She was pretty sure feral cats had taken up residence. Even now, essence of wild animals was still detectable. But it was bearable.

The kitchen, with its sagging cabinets and lack of appliances, was visible through a doorway on the left. There were two small bedrooms down the middle hallway, not that he would know that since the doors were closed. What mattered was what was sitting in the middle of the main room—a wooden chair she'd dragged in from the back porch. A pair of handcuffs dangled from each of the arms.

"Take a seat," she said behind him, careful to keep her distance.

He slowly walked to the chair. But when he reached it, he turned to face her. "You're not handcuffing me."

"You're right. I'm not. You are." She raised the pistol, proud of herself for not shaking this time. And she kept her finger on the frame as he'd cautioned earlier, to make him less worried. "I don't want to hurt you. I truly don't. But I won't mourn your loss if you force me to shoot. After all, if it wasn't for you and Farley, my brother wouldn't be on death row."

He stared at her a long moment as if weighing her resolve. Then he sat.

She let out a relieved breath. Almost there. "Left-or right-handed?" she asked.

"Left."

Figuring he was lying, she said, "Fasten the cuff on your right wrist."

He chuckled. "Don't believe me, huh?"

"Nope."

He pulled the cuff that was open and dangling from the chair arm and fastened it on his wrist.

She slowly moved forward, the pistol never wavering. But instead of getting in front of him, she moved behind him and peered over his right shoulder. He raised his arm and shook the chain, proving it was fastened securely.

"Pull the other one up and work your left wrist inside the cuff."

"Kind of hard to do with only one free hand."

"Put the cuff on your thigh for leverage. The chain's long enough. Once it's around your wrist, press against your thigh to ratchet it."

He tried to look at her over his shoulder but she'd stepped back again. "You put a lot of thought into this."

"I always do when something's important." She'd actually cuffed herself to the chair, only one arm at a time, of course, trying it out. She'd been able to do it and had no doubt he could too.

He sighed and did as she asked.

Again, she leaned slightly over his shoulder to make sure he'd truly fastened the cuff. When she saw that he had, the tension in her shoulders eased. Now she was safe and she had a captive audience—literally. He had no choice but to listen to her.

"Now we can talk. I'll grab my folder."

She shoved her pistol in the waistband of her jeans, then retrieved a two-inch-thick folder from her backpack. It was the only one she'd brought with her on this little escapade. Just enough information to whet his appetite. If he agreed to her terms, she'd give him four more folders thicker than this one, with a lot more detail.

As she hurried toward him, she couldn't help smiling. For the first time in a long time, she had hope for the future. For Joey's future.

"I've been working on this for over a year," she said. "Nights, weekends, vacations. Even hired a few private investigators for some of it." She grimaced. "Can't say I'd recommend them. They'd fail miserably at your company. Not at all the caliber that UB hires, from what I've heard." She pulled out one of the summary sheets. "Regardless of how you feel about my brother, I guarantee you'll want to see this." She set it on his lap.

He suddenly grabbed the arms of the chair and swept out his right leg. She squeaked in surprise as his foot hooked behind her knees, dumping her backward onto the hard wood floor. Her head made a sickening crack and everything went blurry. She winced at the awful, throbbing pain in her skull and desperately tried to focus. When she did, Callum was standing a few feet away holding the chair up in the air.

She screamed and covered her head, certain her life was about to end with a brutally violent blow. Instead, the chair crashed against the floor a few feet away in an explosion of sound. Pieces of wood pinged off the walls and floor. Sawdust and papers rained down like dirty snowflakes.

She was alive. He hadn't hurt her, even though her throbbing head disagreed. Just as it occurred to her to reach for her gun, he was on top of her, pinning her wrists above her head. She stared up at him, her muddled mind still struggling to understand what had happened.

"Next time you abduct someone," he told her, his tone matter-of-fact as if he wasn't practically crushing her, "secure their legs too."

The door flew open and slammed against the wall. Raine jerked against him, her body trembling as half a dozen people ran inside. As one, they surrounded the two of them and aimed their pistols at her head.

Callum grinned at the man standing to his right. "Took you long enough."

"Yeah, well. Your directions were lousy."

Callum laughed as he looked down again. "Raine Quintero, meet *Thomas*. Except his real name is Asher Whitfield. All of these men and women are investigators at Unfinished Business. We have each other's backs. Always. Consider yourself under citizen's arrest until we get the cops here."

To her horror, tears started coursing down her cheeks. She drew a shaky breath and tried to reason with him. "Please, Callum. If you send me to jail, you might as well execute my brother yourself."

His smile faded and he stood, pulling her to standing. She winced and grabbed her head. It felt as if someone was hammering it from inside her skull. There was a tug at her waistband and she realized that he'd taken her pistol. He handed it to one of his teammates.

"Handcuff key." He held out his hand toward her, the remaining pieces of a chair arm dangling from the chain around his wrist.

Trying desperately to ignore the crushing pain in her head, she pulled the key out of her front jeans pocket and gave it to him. As he stepped back to unlock the cuffs, two of his teammates grabbed her arms. Not that it mattered. She could barely stand, let alone run away. The room kept tilting at crazy angles. No doubt she had a concussion, maybe worse. If she threw up, she hoped she was fortunate enough to do it on Callum's shoes.

"This isn't even loaded." The teammate who'd taken her gun from Callum held up the magazine. "Empty. And there's nothing in the chamber."

Callum stared at her incredulously. "You abducted me

with an unloaded gun? What were you thinking? I could have killed you."

"It was my choice to risk my own life. But it wouldn't have been right to risk anyone else's."

"You bluffed. Knowing I likely had a loaded gun." He couldn't seem to get past that fact.

She nodded, then winced at the pounding in her head.

He swore.

"Hey, Callum." Asher stood with some of her papers that he'd scooped off the floor. "These aren't documents about her brother that I heard you mention on the phone." His expression mirrored his surprise. "They're about the serial killer you and I have been investigating for the past few months. And this…" He held up one of the pages. "This is about a murder we've never even connected to the others, one that she attributes to the same killer. It says she's figured out a viable suspect for the murders. His name's right here. Except that it's written in some kind of code."

The room fell silent and everyone stared at her.

Callum's expression was a mixture of shock and admiration. "Is that true? You know the killer's identity? The one who's murdered five people in east Tennessee over the past decade?"

"Eight. Not five." In spite of the sickening way the room kept pitching back and forth, she forced her chin up a notch. "That was my bargaining chip. I was going to share my research with you to try to make a deal so you'd help me save my brother. But it's too late now. The cops are on their way."

He stared at her a long moment, then glanced questioningly at a young blonde woman. "Faith?"

"I called 911 as soon as we had the room secured." She

chuckled. "Or, rather, as soon as *you* had it secured. You didn't end up needing the cavalry after all."

He smiled, but his smile faded when he looked down at Raine again. Instead, his brow furrowed with worry. "Faith. Call an ambulance. She doesn't look so good."

He motioned to the people holding her arms and they slowly lowered her to sit on the floor. The room wasn't spinning quite as badly now. She aimed a look of gratitude at him, not willing to risk something as painful as nodding. "I don't suppose you could have Faith cancel the police request when she asks for that ambulance."

He crouched and reached for her. She ducked to avoid his hand, sucking in a sharp breath when it made her head throb anew.

Swearing, he said, "Be still. I'm not going to hurt you."

She froze and allowed him to feel along the back of her head. His touch was incredibly careful, gentle. But the moment his fingers brushed where she'd cracked her skull against the floor, pain lanced through her. She winced and ducked away.

"I'm sorry, Raine. I didn't mean to cause you more pain."

His contrite tone and the concerned look on his face told her he genuinely meant what he'd said. Which made her even more confused. She'd been awful to him. And here he was concerned about her. That guilt that she'd thought she'd locked away was roaring back now, making her face heat with embarrassment. "I know. Thanks. I'm okay."

"You're definitely not okay. You've got quite a lump there. Probably a concussion. No blood though. Your scalp isn't lacerated. No need for stitches."

"Thank God for small favors I suppose."

He glanced at the blonde woman again, Faith. She gave

him a small nod, as if to assure him the ambulance was on the way.

Just when Raine thought maybe he was rethinking the whole cop thing and having her arrested, his gaze met hers again. The look of concern had been replaced with one of determination.

"You wanted to meet with me," he said. "Here's your chance. The only reason I'm giving it to you is because your gun wasn't loaded. Start talking."

She bristled at his command. "I don't see the point in pleading my case. The police are going to throw me in jail when they get here."

"Not if I don't press charges."

She hesitated. Was this a trick? "Why would you change your mind now?"

The man named Asher nodded in agreement. "Good question. She abducted you, Callum. Held you at gunpoint and handcuffed you to a chair. Whether the gun was loaded or not is irrelevant."

"What she did was reprehensible," Callum agreed. "But I wasn't hurt. And we both have something each other needs. I want the name of that killer. She wants my help to save her brother. Faith, how long before the police arrive?"

"I'd guess ten minutes, give or take."

"The clock's ticking, Raine. I need a name and enough background to convince me your information is legit. If I believe you, I'll make all of this go away and I'll help with your brother's case."

Asher stared at him as if he'd lost his mind. "You can't promise to save her brother. No one can."

"I'm not saying that I can keep him from being executed. What I'm committing to is doing everything I can to dig into his case and, if I believe he could possibly be innocent as she claims, I'll *try* to prevent his execution."

"That's a lot of ifs," she grumbled.

"I'm not done yet. Everything I just said, I'll only do it if you can convince me that you're not playing some kind of twisted game, that your information is worth the paper it's printed on, before the police get here."

She looked around, panic making her heart pound faster, her head throb even worse. "I've been researching those murders for a long time. I can't possibly explain enough in ten minutes to—"

"Convince me, or go to jail."

Chapter Four

Callum looked up from his phone's screen as Faith and Asher entered the emergency room waiting area. Faith was pulling a small black duffel bag on wheels behind her. He waved to catch their attention and they hurried over.

There was only one empty seat on his side of the long, crowded room, right beside Callum. Asher waved Faith to the chair and leaned against a post a few feet away.

She nodded her thanks and set the bag beside her chair. "How's our unarmed abductor doing?"

Callum shook his head. "I still can't believe she pulled that stunt with an empty gun."

"She's lucky to be alive," Asher said. "That's for sure."

"Which brings me back to my question." Faith arched a brow at Callum. "How is she? Since she wouldn't let go of your hand at that ramshackle cottage and you rode in the ambulance with her, you must have some juicy details to share."

He rolled his eyes. "She grabbed my hand when the police arrived because she was afraid I'd change my mind and have them arrest her. There's nothing juicy to share."

"If you say so."

Asher laughed, then coughed when Callum narrowed his eyes at him.

"Is she going to be okay?" Faith pressed. "Why aren't you in the emergency room with her?"

"Because I'm not her family." He didn't volunteer the fact that she had no family, no one outside of prison anyway. His guilt over hurting her had only been compounded when she told the triage nurse that she didn't have *anyone* to call to be with her. "She did sign a form, though, giving the doctor permission to provide me with updates once he's completed his examination."

He gestured toward the volunteer desk at the other end of the room where a middle-aged woman sat with an old-fashioned clipboard. "The last update I received confirmed she has a concussion but her vital signs are normal. When the CT scan comes back, if it looks good and she doesn't exhibit any neurological symptoms, aside from the headache, the doctor may let her leave rather than admit her."

Faith flipped her long hair over her shoulder. "Even if they release her today, she'll have to be checked every few hours to make sure she doesn't get worse or slip into a coma. That's what the doctor ordered for my sister when she had a concussion."

"Daphne had a concussion?" Asher asked. "She never told me that."

"She was ten, fell off her bicycle and wasn't wearing a helmet. And if my sister ever gets chummy enough with you to share details about her childhood, you're spending way too much time with her."

Asher grinned. "Thou shalt not date Faith's baby sister. Got it."

"Dang straight." She gave him a warning look, which only made him laugh.

Callum shook his head at them. "If the doctor releases her and wants her checked on throughout the night, we'll have to arrange for a home health-care nurse."

"No need," Faith said. "I don't mind watching over her. The cabin she's renting isn't far from my place."

He frowned. "Why would you do that?"

"Why wouldn't I? She needs our help. Besides." She waved toward the duffel bag. "She delivered on her end of the deal you two made. All of the files were in the cabin right where she told us they'd be. The ones for her brother's case are in that bag. The others we put in Asher's car to take back to the office."

Asher cleared his throat, the look on his face immediately making Callum wary. "We may have stumbled on a little surprise while gathering all those folders. Did Raine happen to tell you that she's a lawyer?"

Callum groaned.

"She's not a *defense* attorney," Asher clarified, as Faith glanced back and forth between the two of them, clearly puzzled. "Not quite the lowest species on the legal food chain. She's employed by a firm near where you used to work, in Athens, Georgia. They specialize in business law. Seems like a catchall for everything from mergers and acquisitions to human resource violations."

"That explains why she didn't seem knowledgeable about criminal law and death penalty cases. How did you find out about her firm? I wouldn't have thought you had time to research that deeply yet."

"I'd like to claim that I'm just that good, but instead I'll admit that her business card was stapled to the front of one of the folders she told us to get."

"Have you ascertained whether or not the information in those folders is worth me not pressing criminal charges and having to work with a lawyer on her brother's case?"

Faith held up her hands. "Hold it. Catch me up here. You have a problem with lawyers?"

Asher chuckled. "Massive understatement."

She frowned at him before looking at Callum again. "All of us, including you, respect and like the lawyers our company keeps on retainer. They've helped us countless times when we need legal muscle for our cases. And if I remember right, your friend in Athens, Brandon, is a prosecutor, isn't he?"

He shrugged, unwilling to concede the point.

"Come on, Callum. It's insulting that Asher knows this about you and I don't. Clue me in. Why are you so against an entire profession?"

"It's not a huge secret or anything. I've just… I had several bad experiences with lawyers when I was a police detective. I still bear the scars from my last major case at court. The defense attorney was unscrupulous and twisted everything around to confuse the jury. Because of him, a murderer was set free."

"Major ouch. But automatically assuming Raine is a bad person because she's in the same profession as your nemesis isn't fair."

Callum stared at her in amazement. "Is it fair to assume she's a bad person because she held me at gunpoint and handcuffed me to a chair?"

Asher chuckled. "He's got you there, Faith."

"No. He doesn't. The gun wasn't loaded. She didn't actually hurt Callum. And she only threatened him because she loves her brother, believes he's innocent and is desperate to save his life. Love and family loyalty drove her to do what she did. Otherwise, she'd never have crossed that line."

"Which line?" Asher asked. "The one where she kidnapped someone or the one where she tied them up?"

"Shut up, Asher."

He grinned.

"Back to Raine's research for our serial killer case. What did you find?" Callum asked.

Asher sobered. "An impressive amount of information, amazingly indexed and detailed. When she said she'd been investigating, she didn't mean as a hobby. She poured herself into it. I'd be hard-pressed to find a better documented case in my own archives."

"But will it help with our current investigation?"

He shrugged. "Until I review it more in-depth and corroborate her findings, I can't say for sure. But from what I've seen so far, if it pans out, yeah. It'll help. A lot. She may very well have found the key we need. As to the suspect she's zeroed in on, Pete Scoggin, Lance is already on his way to Athens, Georgia, to start surveillance on him while we build our own dossier. But even if Raine's wrong about the killer's identity, it looks promising that she's found several other murders that bear remarkable similarities to the murders we've already attributed to the serial killer we're trying to find."

"Meaning," Callum said, "if her information is reliable, then worst case, she's given us a lot more evidence to work with. Best case, she's solved a string of murders and all we have to do is tie up the loose ends."

"Pretty much."

Callum swore.

Faith lightly shoved him. "Stop being such a pessimist. This is good news."

"It's horrible news. It means I have to follow through on my part of the deal and work with her."

She shook her head in exasperation. "You never know. You may actually become friends."

"Not in this lifetime."

"You're impossible. When you come to her cabin to work on her brother's case, I may have to stick around so she at least has one person there who's friendly and supportive."

"You really plan on watching over her?"

"As long as she needs me, yes."

"If you want to spend your time getting chummy with her, feel free. Meanwhile, I'll be focusing on her brother's death row situation so I can resolve this as fast as possible and move on to my next cold case for UB."

The person sitting on Callum's right gave him an odd look, then got up and left the waiting room.

Asher chuckled and took the vacated seat. "If we raise our voices and talk more murder and mayhem, we could probably clear the whole waiting room."

Faith gave him an admonishing look. "This isn't a laughing matter. Poor Raine. Can you imagine a sister being under that kind of pressure, knowing she's the only hope her brother has at not being executed? Be nice to her, Callum. She's going through a lot." She held up her hands. "And don't lecture me again about what she put you through. You've survived far worse. And that was truly horrible that you counted down the minutes out loud until the police arrived, making her scramble to convince you about the information she had even though her head was hurting so much. You owe her an apology."

Asher's mouth dropped open in shock as he stared at her.

"Please tell me that was a joke," Callum said.

"Men." She crossed her arms. "In addition to the folders Asher and I have, we've got Raine's laptop. She gave me her password right before the EMTs loaded her into the ambulance, said she has more information on her brother's case on her computer. We'll take a look and see what we can find and print it out for you."

"Leave the laptop with me so I don't have to wait for printouts. Speed is the name of the game with the clock ticking on her brother's case."

She arched a brow. "You sure you want to tackle her computer? You know how you are with electronics."

"Oh, good grief. Dumb luck and a few missteps here and there doesn't make me technologically challenged. And I'm not the only one who has problems using our ridiculously complicated videoconferencing system at the office."

Asher's eyes widened. "What about that time you managed to erase a suspect's confession while you were playing it back?"

Callum narrowed his eyes.

Asher laughed.

Faith shook her head at both of them. "I'll text you the password, Callum."

"I appreciate it. Asher, you said Lance is going to watch our potential suspect. I'm almost afraid to ask, but if we have a name and address, and as much information as you alluded to, can I assume that Raine performed physical surveillance on our would-be killer?"

Asher sobered. "No question. There are logs she kept that speak to his routine."

Callum fisted his hands on his knees. "I can see a lawyer, with no police background, performing surveillance on me by sitting in her car in the parking lot. I wouldn't have had a reason to notice her. But a murderer, a serial killer, is always on the hunt for his next victim. And on the watch for police who may be on to him. We need to consider that he may have noticed her at some point. For all we know, he could have decided to add her to his future victim list."

Faith turned pale. "He could be following her right now."

He nodded. "It's certainly possible. As soon as either of you hear back from Lance, give me an update. I'd feel a lot better about her security if our team locates him and we know he's nowhere near this place, or Raine's cabin she rented here."

"I'll let you know the minute Lance reports in," Asher told him.

"Thanks."

Faith motioned to Asher. "Go ahead and get Raine's laptop. It's under my book bag on the left side of your trunk."

"A please would be nice."

"Asher—"

"Okay, okay." He aimed a long-suffering look at Callum. "I'm not only Faith's chauffeur today, I'm her gopher."

Callum glanced back and forth between them. "Is there something I should know about the two of you? Something *juicy* the rest of our team might want to hear about?"

Horrified didn't begin to describe the expressions on their faces.

"My car's in the shop. I needed a ride." Faith managed to

sound defensive and insulted at the same time. "And, please, seriously? Asher? And me? Not a chance, ever."

Asher frowned. "Hold on a minute. What's so bad about me?"

She arched a brow. "How much time do you have?"

Callum laughed and held up his hands. "All right, children. Continue your argument elsewhere." He motioned toward the volunteer working the desk, who was waving at him. "Looks like I'm being summoned." He stood and extended the duffel bag's handle so he could roll it behind him.

Asher frowned at Faith before heading toward the exit with long, angry strides.

She chuckled. "Be nice to Raine, Callum. Keep me updated on her medical status and let me know when to head over to her cabin."

"I'm always nice. And I'll keep you updated on Ms. Quintero as long as you keep me updated on your and Asher's budding relationship." He laughed when she made a rude gesture and hurried after Asher.

At the volunteer desk, he smiled at the bright red–haired woman in charge of updating visitors about their loved ones. "You have an update about Ms. Quintero?"

She added a check to one of the boxes on her clipboard and stood. "Doctor Bagnoli will meet you in privacy room three, just around the corner. I'll show you the way."

Callum had just settled into one of the plastic chairs in the windowless closet-like room when the doctor rapped on the door and stepped inside. Less than a minute later, Dr. Bagnoli was gone. And just like that, Callum was responsible for the health and well-being of a woman he barely knew. A woman he'd met under bizarre circumstances that had him wavering between wanting to help her and wanting to send her on her way.

Of course, that decision had already been made. A deal had been struck between them seconds before the police had arrived at the run-down cottage in the woods. As a result, he'd lied to the police. Something vague about misunderstandings. It was obvious they hadn't bought his fabrication. But Gatlinburg PD's excellent relationship and history with UB had smoothed the way for them to pretend they believed him and leave. Callum changing his mind wasn't an option now. There was no going back.

A few moments later, a nurse brought him into the busy part of the emergency room where patients were being treated and medical staff were scurrying around like ants in a thunderstorm. She pointed toward the curtained alcove where Raine was and hurried off to another patient.

When Callum was just a few feet away, he stopped, stunned and riddled with guilt again at how pitiful she looked. She was lying on her left side in the bed, her knees drawn up in a fetal position. Her eyes were closed, but she was frowning in her sleep. Since both of her hands were clutching her head, it didn't take a medical degree to conclude that she was in pain.

He immediately turned around and headed to the circular desk in the middle of the ER. A dozen nurses and doctors created a chaotic scene buzzing with activity. Some were talking to each other. A handful were on the phone. Several more were sitting at desktop computers or standing at the counter tapping on computer pads. They were all doing their best to ignore him.

He could understand their desire not to be interrupted, especially as overworked as they all appeared to be. But

Raine needed pain medication and he wasn't going to back down until she got it.

The first person who had the misfortune of making eye contact with him became his target. Five minutes later, Raine was sleeping comfortably. Her frown was gone and she was no longer clutching her head.

"As soon as her doctor's release orders come through," another nurse told him, "I'll send someone in with a wheelchair so you can take her home. But don't be surprised if it takes a while. We're slammed around here. I'm not sure when the doctor will input the orders."

"Not my first time in a hospital. I know how slowly the wheels of bureaucracy can turn." He smiled to soften his words and thanked the nurse, who eagerly left, pulling the curtain closed behind him.

Callum settled into one of the ridiculously small chairs built for someone half his size and pulled the duffel bag beside him. After a quick glance at Raine to make sure she was still resting comfortably, he took out one of the thick folders and plopped it on his lap.

"All right, Ms. Quintero, attorney-at-law. Let's see what kind of a mess you've gotten me into."

Chapter Five

The sun was just barely beginning to rise over the mountains and peek into the glass rear wall of Raine's small rental cabin when a loud knock sounded on the front door. She hesitated, even though her spot at the kitchen island put her just a few feet from the entryway. Callum and fellow investigator Faith Lancaster were the only ones she expected to come by. But it seemed far too early in the morning for Callum to show up. Faith had stayed here overnight, checking on her per doctor's orders. But she'd headed down the mountain a few minutes ago to a café she swore had the best breakfast sandwiches for miles around. If she'd come back this quickly, something must have gone wrong—like maybe she forgot her wallet. She'd refused to let Raine pay, no matter how insistent she'd been.

At the hospital last night, after she awoke in the ER to find Callum sitting beside her bed, he too had refused to accept any compensation from her. She'd insisted that she could afford any fee or expenses he'd incur while helping her, and that she owed him a paint job for the scratches his SUV got while heading to the cottage. But he'd informed her that his boss, Grayson Prescott, had approved all expenses related to the work on her brother's case, because of the information she'd provided for their serial killer case. That had her feeling guilty, of course. Once her brother's... situation...was resolved, she'd circle back around to the discussion about reimbursing Unfinished Business, and Callum as well.

Another knock sounded, this one louder, as if her early morning visitor was growing impatient. It must be Callum after all. She couldn't imagine Faith acting impatiently. She'd treated Raine with nothing but understanding and kindness, far more than she deserved given the circumstances.

She scooted her chair back from the kitchen island and looked through the peephole in the door, unsurprised to see Callum staring back at her. She opened the door, and almost forgot how to breathe.

Callum in a suit had been...expected, normal, like most of the people she worked with on a daily basis. Callum in jeans, a snug black T-shirt and a black leather jacket that highlighted his dark hair and midnight blue eyes was anything but expected. Devastatingly handsome was one phrase that came to mind. The light stubble on his chiseled jaw, the golden tan, the...oh my goodness those shoulders, that flat stomach outlined by the formfitting T-shirt. How had she not realized how gorgeous he was until now?

He held up a laptop that she recognized as her own.

"You've been spying on me, Ms. Quintero." He brushed past her, pulling a rolling bag behind him.

Spying? Her stomach sank at the implications of that statement. He must have been exploring more than her brother's files on her computer. She slowly closed the door, mumbling, "Good morning to you too," as she followed him into the kitchen.

"Good morning," he surprised her by replying, his tone amused as he moved her coffee cup from the island to a countertop and sat in the same chair she'd just vacated. Without asking, he shoved the papers she'd been reviewing out of his way and set her laptop in their place.

Faith had better come back soon. Callum on top of a concussion was a combination she wasn't prepared to deal with before finishing her first coffee of the day. She'd like to think that if she hadn't banged her head she wouldn't feel so overwhelmed right now. But he'd been intimidating at the ramshackle cottage even before she'd gotten hurt.

"I need something for this headache." She started past him. His hand shot out and grabbed her arm, stopping her.

"When was your last pain pill? Is your headache worse than it was at the hospital?"

She shook her arm and he let go. But his piercing gaze pinned her in place just as well as his grip had.

Stop it, Raine. There's no reason to be flustered around this man.

Was she off-kilter because this was the first time she'd been *really* alone with him since the cottage? Or because her head was pounding so hard now that she could barely think straight?

"Raine?" His brows drew together in a look of concern that had her more confused than before. "How bad is the headache? Any other neurological symptoms? Dizziness? Fainting? Maybe you should sit."

He started to rise from his chair as if to make her take his place, when her brain finally started working again.

"No, no. I'm fine, or I will be when I take the *prescribed* pain pill I'm *allowed* to take this morning."

His frown told her he wasn't sure he believed her. But he didn't try to stop her again.

She'd swear she felt the heat of his gaze following her as she got the prescription bottle from the cabinet and grabbed a bottled water from the refrigerator. Once she'd downed the pill, knowing relief would soon come for her throbbing head, she sat across from him at the island—with the coffee mug he'd moved earlier. After three deep sips of the caffeine-laden drink of the gods, she finally felt more in control and able to risk looking at him.

He was still staring at her with concern.

Her hand tightened around her coffee mug. "Why act so brusque at the door and then completely switch to being hyperconcerned for my welfare? Even Faith isn't worried anymore. I did fine last night and don't need babysitting at this point."

His eyes widened. "You're upset that I'm worried about you?"

"I'm confused. And aggravated. I don't know how to read you, or..." Her face heated as he continued to stare at her. "Never mind. Like I said, I'm fine, or I will be once that pill and this coffee kick in. And before you ask again, no. I'm not having any other symptoms. Just brain fog and a headache that won't quit." She motioned toward the laptop in front of him. "I think I'd feel better if you confront me with whatever you found on my computer instead of pretending you care. Go on. Interrogate me. You accused me of spying on you."

He closed the laptop and set it aside, his mouth crooking up in a half smile. "Maybe I overreacted. After all, you did admit you'd been watching my routine when you pulled a gun on me. I shouldn't have been so surprised and angry when I saw the mounds of reports you wrote over the past week, cataloging my every move."

She grimaced. "Yes, well. I was prepping for our face-to-face meeting by learning everything I could about you. I wanted to be prepared. Turns out, I wasn't."

He crossed his forearms on top of the island. "Actually, I thought you were rather impressive in how you handled things. If you'd chosen a chair in that cottage that wasn't dry-rotted, I might still be handcuffed to it."

"Really?"

He chuckled. "No, not really. But you seem out of sorts this morning, even more than I'd have expected from your concussion. I was being nice."

She choked, then coughed. "This is you being nice?"

He shrugged, his smile firmly in place. "Let's start over. I'll forget about the stalking and kidnapping—for now—and that you're a lawyer. We've each made a deal with the devil, more or less, and we might as well make the best of it for however long we'll be working together. Or for however long it takes my team to prove, or disprove, your bribe—that research on the serial killer we're after."

His warning about her research had her feeling queasy. But it was the other part of his statement that really caught her attention.

"Deal with the devil? Because I'm a lawyer? Or because I held you at gunpoint?"

"Not sure I could choose one over the other."

She blinked again. "Wow. I don't even... What do you have against lawyers?"

"In the interest of forming a good working relationship and starting over, let's forget I said anything about your chosen profession." He held out his hand. "Hello. I'm Callum Wright, former police detective, currently an investigator for Unfinished Business, specializing in cold cases."

"Really? We're going to do this? Pretend the events of the past day—"

"Or weeks. Of stalking." He winked.

"We're pretending all of that never happened. I'm supposed to, what, ignore that you helped send my brother to death row? And in return you'll ignore that I *researched* you, not stalked, and that I'm a lawyer? So you can stomach being around me?" She arched a brow and crossed her arms.

He pulled his hand back, his smile fading. "New plan. We'll continue to nurse our grudges against each other but do our best to be civil so we can do what needs to be done."

She let out a frustrated breath. "That wasn't what I meant. I just—"

"When you started all of this, what was your goal? What did you hope I could accomplish? As I said, I was basically a gopher for Detective Farley on your brother's case. Before browsing the information last night that you provided, I could barely remember it. So why do you think I can help you? And how? Even if I had exculpatory evidence—which I don't—I have no pull with Georgia's governor to ask him for a pardon."

"It's not the governor we need to influence. In Georgia, he doesn't have that kind of power. The authority to grant pardons or commute death sentences to life in prison is held solely by Georgia's Board of Pardons and Paroles. And even though the governor appoints members to the board, the senate still has to approve them. Plus, they each serve on the board for seven years."

"Meaning the governor can't stack the board during his four-year term to have more sway over their actions."

She nodded. "Exactly. It's difficult, if not impossible, to sway the majority of the board to grant a stay of execution, or clemency. The only hope really is to present some kind of evidence that is so overwhelming that they can't ignore it."

"If you had that kind of evidence already, I imagine you wouldn't have gone to drastic measures to get my attention."

"No. I don't, and I wouldn't have. Obviously, I'm desperate at this point. My brother's set to be executed in a couple of weeks. Earlier you recommended that I hire a lawyer experienced with capital punishment cases. I have two, from two different firms. They've been doing everything they can to work through the appeals process and try to find new evidence that might exonerate Joey. Over the past month, they've been reinterviewing dozens of people the police originally spoke to, trying to find something, anything that would help. A while back, they even managed to get an audience before the board to argue for mercy. Nothing has worked so far and I have little faith that they're going to succeed. That's why I've taken a leave of absence from my job, so I could pursue any avenue I can think of to help him, before it's too late."

"Including risking being disbarred and going to prison yourself by holding someone at gunpoint and kidnapping them?"

Her face heated. "What I did to you isn't something I'm proud of. But my *innocent* brother is the only family I have left and he doesn't deserve to die for something he didn't do. In spite of what you may believe, there are limits to what lines I would cross to help him. With you, for example, the gun wasn't loaded. I was hoping to scare you into doing what I asked. Risking hurting you, or worse, wasn't something I could stomach. Thus, the gun was empty."

His jaw tightened. "Which reminds me, don't ever do that again. Only point a gun at someone if it's loaded and you're prepared to shoot. Otherwise, you're putting your own life at risk by bluffing. Someone calls that bluff and you could be killed."

"Careful, Callum. It almost sounds like you care."

"I do care, as one does for children or fools."

"You think I'm a fool?"

His mouth curved in a sardonic grin. "Well, you're definitely not a child."

She blinked, not sure how to take his comment and smile. On the one hand, he was insulting her by labeling her a fool. On the other, he was giving her a backhanded compliment, seemingly appreciating her as a woman. How could he seem so aggravating in one breath and ridiculously appealing in the next? She needed to get them back to safer ground. Even an argument was better than sitting across from this incredibly handsome man, half wishing she had the courage to bait him with a flirty response.

Clearing her throat, she said, "Regardless, what I'm after is your experience on cold cases in the hopes that you can find evidence to convince the board to at least stay my brother's execution. And the fact that you worked on his case, even in a minor role, would—I believe—have sway over getting the board to listen to you if you requested an audience with them to present new evidence."

He quietly considered that a moment, then shook his head. "You had to be a lawyer, huh?"

She frowned as he pulled out his phone. "I don't see what that has to do with—"

He held up a hand to stop her and pressed the phone to his ear. "Hey, Reid. Yes, it's Callum again. I'm calling about that possible favor we discussed last night. Yeah, looks like I'll be taking you up on it sooner than anticipated."

She crossed her arms and sat back as he spoke with this Reid person. What did Callum have against lawyers? Not that it really mattered. She wasn't going to apologize for her chosen profession. What mattered was helping her brother, Joey. If that meant tolerating a man who made her angry one minute and want to jump him the next, so be it. Her reactions to him made no sense. He confused and frustrated her. But that was something she'd have to deal with, somehow. Focusing on Joey's life being at stake was what she had to do, even if it meant being uncomfortable around Callum Wright for the next few weeks.

He ended the call and slid his phone into his back pants pocket. "How's that headache?"

She frowned, then pressed a hand to her temple. She'd completely forgotten about her headache. A reluctant smile curved her lips. "For the first time since I cracked my head against that hard floor, the pain is gone. Apparently fighting with you is some kind of cure."

"Is that what we're doing? Fighting?"

"What else would you call it?"

That sexy grin curved his lips again, but he simply shook his head. "I'll consider it my sacred duty to pick another fight if your headache returns." He pushed back from the island and stood. "I was going to sit here and discuss the information that I read about your brother's case. But, as you reminded me, the clock is ticking. We can save time by discussing it on the way to the other source I want to talk to. Grab your jacket."

"My jacket? Wait, we're leaving?"

"That's the plan. The sooner the better."

"But Faith, she went to get us breakfast—"

"I'll call her from my car and explain. If you don't mind a drive-through, I can get you something to eat on the way out of town."

"Drive-through is fine, but I don't—"

"Is that the hall closet, I'm guessing?" He motioned toward a door on the wall to the right of the front door.

She nodded.

He yanked open the door and grabbed a waist-length gray jacket. "Is this okay? I don't think it's cold enough today for the heavy coat."

"That's fine, thanks." She took the jacket he held out, then grabbed her purse from the small decorative table a few feet away. "Where are we going?"

After opening the front door, he motioned for her to precede him outside.

She shrugged into her jacket, but instead of doing as he wanted, she stood her ground. "I'm not leaving until you tell me where we're going. I may not agree that the time is well spent driving around in your SUV. I can answer any questions you have, explain the case without us going to some other source to—"

"The man I just spoke to is a friend, someone I used to work with. We trade favors off and on and he currently owes me one, a big one. He's cutting through red tape to make that source I mentioned available. But only if we leave right now so we can arrive in the time frame he specified."

"Where? Who is this source you think can tell you more about my brother's case than I can?"

He arched a brow. "Your brother."

Chapter Six

Raine drew a shaky breath and forced herself to release her death grip on the passenger armrest in Callum's SUV. It had barely taken him four hours to make the drive from Gatlinburg, Tennessee, to the prison off Highway 36 in Jackson, Georgia. That included going through a drive-through for a couple of breakfast sandwiches. It would have taken her at least five, without the sandwiches.

He finally slowed and pulled into line behind a chase car and one of many white-and-red prison buses being escorted toward the gates. His driving had her reliving her childhood fear of roller coasters. At least now he couldn't speed. And they were no longer flying around dangerous curves through the mountains.

"Are you certain your friend has made it possible for us to see my brother? My next allowed visit with Joey isn't until the day of his... The last day of his incarceration. You're not even on his approved visitor list. Only immediate family, his lawyers or select media are normally allowed to see him."

"Reid is high up in the Georgia Department of Corrections. I don't really know what all he does for them, but he assured me he'll get an exception, and that I'll be on the list before we reach the checkpoint."

"He might not have had enough time to make that miracle happen. Does he realize how fast you drive?"

He grinned. "Sorry I made you nervous. I don't normally drive so crazy, but I didn't want us to miss this opportunity."

His easy apology, which seemed legit based on his tone, knocked her off-kilter again. Most men she knew would have been aggravated that she dared criticize their driving, even offhandedly. They certainly wouldn't have been amused, or apologized.

She glanced out the side window, toward the high chain-link fences topped with razor wire that surrounded the prison like a moat around a castle. "The red tape your friend will have to cut for us to see Joey spur of the moment like this is enormous. Visits are supposed to be planned and approved way in advance and they're severely limited or I'd be here much more often. This breaks every policy the prison has, especially for visiting death row inmates. Whatever you did to make him owe you a favor must have been something incredibly significant. Especially to visit on a Tuesday."

His smile faded. "It was. What's special about Tuesday? Reid didn't mention that as a potential problem when I spoke to him."

She wondered about the tension in him in regard to the favor, but didn't feel it was appropriate to pry. "UDS prisoners, Under Death Sentence, are only allowed visitors on Saturdays, Sundays or state holidays. I've never been here on a Tuesday because of that. Tuesdays and Thursdays are intake days at Jackson Prison."

"Jackson Prison? That's not the name of—"

She waved her hand in the air. "That's what the prisoners, and family, call this place. It rolls off the tongue easier than Georgia Diagnostic and Classification Prison."

A hint of his smile returned. "So it does. I'm guessing in-take day, judging by the name and all these buses and chase cars, is when they bring in the new prisoners."

"And ship some out, yes. This is the hub for all the pris-ons in Georgia. You go here first, from all around the state. Buses will be loading and unloading all day. The experts here evaluate each inmate's health, mental status, classify how dangerous they are, whether they need to be in PC, population levels at the other prisons—"

"PC. Protective custody?"

"Yes, to keep them safe from other inmates for various reasons."

"Like if a cop goes to prison?"

"That or, say, someone was convicted of murdering a child. I'm sure you already know that those types of con-victs wouldn't last an hour in the general population. Once the prisoner has been assessed, they're assigned to their camp—their prison—and are shipped back out. It takes two to three weeks for each inmate to be processed and clas-sified. But the bringing in of new men and shipping clas-sified ones out to their new *homes* happens twice a week. Normally, for security reasons, they won't allow visitors to death row inmates on those days. Honestly, I'll be amazed if we reach the checkpoint and they allow us through. It's just not done."

His lack of concern was proven out as soon as the guards outside the crash fence checked both of their IDs. They were immediately waved forward.

When they stopped behind another gate, two men with mirrors extended on long poles checked under the SUV. Whether they were searching for bombs or some kind of contraband, she had no idea. But experience told her they'd do the same thing when she and Callum left, this time to ensure that a prisoner hadn't somehow managed to take a ride to freedom on their undercarriage.

They were directed where to park, in one of the few spots not close to one of the buses. They'd also been instructed not to unlock or open their doors until a guard arrived to escort them, which was the exact opposite of how most of her visits went. She was usually told not to sit in her car for any length of time. She was supposed to immediately exit and head to the building. But today, probably because it was Tuesday and their visit wasn't according to protocol, they had to wait. After setting her ID in the middle console, she stuffed her purse under the front seat.

"You don't want to take your purse inside?"

"Not allowed," she said. "They won't let you bring anything inside except your keys and ID. You should stow your phone, gun, change, whatever you've got in your pockets."

She didn't bother to admit she had her gun in her purse. He'd probably take it from her if he realized she was carrying it around. Faith had given it back to her after she'd promised never to pull it on anyone again unless her life was in danger. How Faith had managed to get it, Raine had no idea. But she was grateful. She might not like guns, or know much about them. But now that she'd bought one, she intended to keep it handy—especially if she had to go into some rough neighborhoods to try to get evidence to help her brother.

After emptying the change from his pockets and locking his wallet and pistol in the glove box, he sat back. There was no smile this time as he studied her. "How many times have you been through this routine?"

"Close to fifty, I'd guess. I visit every time I can get it

approved. Death row inmates don't get the same monthly visits others get. Sometimes I'm allowed in once a quarter, other times only twice a year. It's ridiculous how stingy they are in allowing me to see him."

"I imagine the security is a nightmare for... I think you called them UDS prisoners earlier?"

She nodded.

"Security for them has to be especially rigorous. And the Georgia prison system is grossly understaffed these days. Some stats I've heard is that they have up to seventy percent of their job openings unfilled. There are several lawsuits and federal investigations pending because of it."

"Are you defending them to me? Seriously?" She crossed her arms in agitation.

He slowly shook his head, seeming sincere. "Not at all. What you're going through isn't something I could ever understand. But I can empathize with your frustration. I was making a lame attempt to reduce your frustration by explaining some of the logistical reasons behind those delays."

She lowered her arms. "Thank you, I guess. I mean, I appreciate that you were trying to reason things out. And I do understand the demands on the prison staff to allow the visits. But it seems to me that if someone is at the mercy of the state and is going to be murdered by the state, they should make every attempt at allowing that person's family to see them and try to bring comfort under such horrible circumstances."

"I imagine it's difficult to balance respect for the prisoner's rights and consideration of the victim, and their family. The state doesn't want it to look as if they're coddling prisoners. That would be an insult to the victims."

"Yes, well, I'd agree with that except that my brother is one of the victims. He's innocent."

His jaw tightened, punctuating his feelings on the matter, even after hearing her side of her brother's case during the ride here. But he respected her feelings enough not to argue the point any longer, for which she was grateful.

Although her brain agreed with everything he'd said, her heart rebelled because she didn't feel her brother should be lumped in with other convicts. He was innocent. And although she felt enormous empathy for the victim's family, having met with them herself many times over the years, it was a tight line to walk. The Claremonts deserved justice for their daughter, Alicia. But not at the expense of murdering a man who had nothing to do with her death.

"Looks like the cavalry is here to escort us to safety." Callum motioned toward a group of four burly guards heading toward his SUV.

As he reached for the door handle to get out, she put her hand on his shoulder. "Don't. Wait for them to direct you to open the door. Do one thing wrong, don't follow instructions in even the smallest way, and they'll immediately cancel the visit and send us packing. They run Jackson Prison like a military installation, with zero tolerance for mistakes."

She hated the bitterness in her voice but couldn't quite hide it. She'd been brutally punished by not being able to see her brother on no less than five visits because of some small or imagined infringement of the prison's strict rules. One time she'd forgotten she had cash in her pocket and that was enough to have her turned away when they searched her inside the visitor lobby. Sometimes she wondered if the guards had any feelings at all. Or maybe it was just their stubborn belief in "the system" that made them assume that her brother was truly guilty and therefore his sister must be trash like him.

A guard stopped outside each of their doors and motioned for them to get out. The other two guards stood with their backs to them, watching the "yard" with an intensity that had her beginning to feel something she rarely felt when coming to this place.

Fear.

She glanced around the crowded parking area, at the dozens of shackled prisoners standing in lines outside each bus. Normally when she arrived there weren't any convicts out here. There were so many today that she couldn't count them. And many were looking right at her, as if they'd lunge toward the SUV if given a chance, in a desperate bid for freedom.

"Follow the footprints, go, go, go," the lead guard told them.

She glanced down, a shiver of dread going through her when she realized they were being directed to follow the painted footprints on the asphalt that the prisoners normally walked when entering the prison. Knowing that Joey had once come in on those same buses, shackled head to toe like an animal, and that he'd taken this same path, had her beginning to shake. They were going to kill him, murder him, in less than two weeks. The next time she came here he'd be mere hours from death.

An arm settled around her shoulders. "It's okay," a kind, deep voice whispered. Callum's voice. "Lean on me. You can close your eyes if you want. Just put one foot in front of the other. I've got you."

She selfishly longed to do exactly that, lean on him, close her eyes. She wanted to put her fears, her frustrations, into this strong man's keeping and let him carry her burdens on his broad shoulders. But that wasn't fair to Joey. There was no one for him to lean on, no one to ease *his* burdens. And she wasn't a helpless damsel in distress. She'd been fighting the good fight in every way that she could since the day he'd been arrested, fifteen years ago. Giving up now wasn't an option. She had to be strong, see this through. For Joey.

Smiling her thanks, she gently moved his arm. Then she straightened her shoulders and followed in her condemned brother's footsteps.

Chapter Seven

Callum had half expected Raine to collapse by the car. But she'd surprised him, stiffening her back and marching toward the building as if her near panic attack had never happened.

Once inside, she'd demonstrated her knowledge of the procedures by directing Callum on filling out the visitor log. She'd provided her brother's inmate number from memory, as well as other required information. They both provided their IDs again, and one of the people manning the checkpoint area looked them up online to verify they were who they said they were and that they were preapproved for a visit. Raine explained to Callum that they were also confirming that the prisoner was available, not at court or in medical, that kind of thing. Information on the prisoner was written on a piece of paper and placed in the tray that would go through a metal detector, which was Raine's and his next step in the process.

The invasive procedures after that made TSA security requirements in airports seem pathetically inadequate. They were practically strip-searched, with all metal, shoes, belts, keys and anything else not required for modesty taken away. The metal detector didn't beep on either of them but they were still patted down then taken to separate "privacy rooms" for further searching.

Callum was told to untuck his shirt from his jeans and the male guard ran his hands around inside his waistband and even pulled his jeans away from him and peered down his underwear with a flashlight. Callum wondered what kind of embarrassment they were putting Raine through, but she didn't seem fazed when she met him back in the checkpoint area.

"How friendly did your guard get with you?" he whispered.

She smiled, for the first time in a long time. "I had to untuck, then lift my bra and shake my boobs to prove I didn't have anything tucked beneath them."

He stared at her, truly shocked. "They do that to all the women?"

"I assume so. Can't remember when they haven't done that to me. You get used to it, or as much as you can I guess."

One of the guards must have heard them and stared unflinchingly at Callum, as if to dare him to complain. Remembering Raine's warning about not following procedures to the letter, he didn't. But he sure wanted to. It bothered him to no end that she was treated as if she too was a criminal. He understood that the security measures were intended to keep everyone safe. Still, he didn't like it. Not at all.

The final step in the process was to get their hands stamped. The ink wasn't viewable to the naked eye, but when a guard passed a UV light over them, the stamps glowed. Raine motioned him toward a doorway where yet another guard waited.

In spite of them having just had their hands scanned, he scanned them again and requested the slips of paper they'd been given earlier. The surprise on his face was evident when he read them, and rather than escort them to the visitation area where others had gone, he had them wait while he stepped down the hall and made a call using a landline phone on the wall.

Beside Callum, Raine sighed. Disappointment clouded her expression when she glanced up at him.

"I have a feeling your friend wasn't able to jump through all of those hoops after all," she said. "They aren't going to let us visit a death row inmate since it's not the right visitation day of the week. Joey also may have already used up his hour today, so that would be another reason for them not to let us see him."

"Used up his hour?"

"Death row inmates are locked in their cells twenty-three hours a day. They get one hour for showering or exercise or visitation. Joey didn't know we were coming, so he may have already used his free time."

Callum's respect for what Raine had suffered all these years was expanding exponentially. He honestly didn't think he'd have been able to take all of these onerous rules so well if their roles were reversed. Security was important. Punishment, or justice, made many of the rules necessary. But some of them, like being locked up twenty-three hours a day, seemed cruel. How was someone supposed to stay sane in an environment like that?

He supposed most people didn't care. And he was guilty of never considering the living conditions of death row inmates, until today. But what did treating people like animals say about those in charge of the treatment?

There had to be a better way to keep society safe from those who'd proven they couldn't be allowed to live amongst the public anymore. But Callum didn't have the answers to that quandary. Maybe no one did. The justice system was flawed in many ways. But he'd yet to see a better one anywhere else in the world.

Raine was still watching him, with worry wrinkling her brow.

He cleared his throat and tried to reassure her. "Don't give up yet. Reid's pretty resourceful. He wouldn't have told me he could get us in unless he was sure that he could. One of the things he told me last night was that, contrary to what you'd expect, the closer to the execution date you get the more likely they are to grant extra privileges."

"I've never heard that before. His lawyers didn't tell me that."

"I doubt the prison advertises it. They probably keep it on the hush-hush."

She smiled. It was a small one, but a smile nonetheless. "I can see them doing that, not wanting anyone to know that they don't follow their own authoritarian rules a hundred percent of the time."

The renewed look of hope on her face had him dreading what the guard might say when he returned. If their long drive and ensuing indignities turned out to be for nothing, Reid was going to owe Callum far more than one favor in the future.

A few moments later, the guard returned. Disapproval was heavy on his features as he waved them forward to the next gate. Callum thanked him and got a grunt in reply. He and Raine hurried down the hallway before the guard could change his mind about letting them through.

Another guard took them through another gate, its thick bars painted a cheery yellow in stark contrast to the drab off-white floors and gray cinder-block walls. They headed through a maze of hallways, sometimes coming upon prisoners in those same hallways. The guard with them would bark an order and the inmates immediately moved to the far side and faced the wall. They barely moved as Callum and Raine passed. He could see that military-style discipline she'd spoken about and was grateful for it. No telling what types of crimes those men had committed and the mayhem they'd do to Raine if allowed.

When they finally arrived at the death row portion of the prison, he was struck by how quiet it was. There were no chains rattling or prisoners shouting in the distance. No hum of activity from the sheer number of people in the building. It was as if they'd stepped from the bustling hive of a high school hallway into the tomb-like silence of a library. The only discernible noise was the muted hiss of ventilation equipment and the low tones of their guard's voice as he consulted with another guard who stood on the other side of a closed gate.

"I didn't expect it to be so quiet." Callum kept his voice low, much as he would in the library he'd compared death row to, or maybe a church.

She nodded, her gaze fixed on the guards, no doubt worried once again that they'd turn her and Callum back on the precipice of finally seeing her brother.

"In general, the UDS prisoners are quieter, better behaved than the rest of the population." She kept her voice low as well. "I've been told it's because many of them are still going through the appeals process. They don't want to do anything to jeopardize their chances, however small, of having their sentences overturned or commuted."

He nodded, once again feeling empathy he'd never expected to feel for the nameless, faceless men behind these walls. As a police detective, he'd participated in many cases that had resulted in death penalties for those who were found guilty. But this was his first time actually visiting a maximum security prison, let alone one with a death chamber on the grounds. It was much more difficult to feel satisfaction over a verdict when faced with the reality of that decision. Most, if not all, of the men locked in their cells just past the next gate would only leave this prison one way—in a body bag. It was a sobering reality.

A metallic clanging sounded, followed by the low electronic buzz of the gate rolling back. The earlier gates were opened with keys. This one, Callum realized, must have been unlocked remotely, by a control center that probably had eyes on them right now. There were cameras all over the building. This hallway was no exception. One of them was positioned in the top left corner over the growing opening.

Their guard motioned for them to approach. The second guard stared at them, eyes narrowed as he watched their every move.

"No talking," Raine whispered. "Follow my lead."

She handed the piece of paper she'd been given at check-in to the second guard. Callum did the same. The guard studied it a long moment, then sighed heavily and motioned for them to step through.

The other guard returned back down the hallway as the gate hummed, then began to slowly slide across the opening. As soon as it clanged shut, the three of them headed across a narrow common area devoid of people. There were three tables, and five TVs mounted high up on the walls, but they weren't turned on. Four hallways opened off the common area, presumably leading to the prisoners' cells.

It went against every protective instinct in Callum's body to walk behind Raine through an area designated for the worst of the worst that humanity had to offer. But she'd done this dozens of times before and had taken the lead. She knew the routine. And she'd already warned him not to do anything to break protocol. This close to their goal, he certainly wasn't going to cause any problems that might result in their visit being cut short. Raine would probably never forgive him. And he couldn't stomach the idea of robbing her of what was most likely one of her last chances to see her brother before he died.

At the far end of the room, rather than take them down one of the corridors of cells, the guard stopped them outside a metal door painted the same gray as the rest of the room. Using the radio on his belt, he identified himself and stated that he was escorting two visitors to the visitation area. He announced Callum's and Raine's names, as well as the prisoner's name and ID. Callum expected to hear an electronic buzz like with the gate. Instead, the guard shoved the radio back onto his utility belt and used a key to unlock the door.

A few moments later, Callum and Raine were alone inside the small visitation room with the door locked behind them. Their only instructions were to sit at the third of five windows and that the prisoner would be in shortly. They'd have approximately fifty minutes to talk to him using the old-fashioned telephone attached to the wall. Then the prisoner would be returned to his cell and the guard would escort them back to the general population area.

Raine hesitated in front of the lone metal stool attached to the floor in front of the window. She glanced up at Callum and he shook his head.

"Don't even try to get me to take the only seat," he said. "My mom taught me better manners than that."

She smiled a wobbly smile and sat.

Callum leaned against the partition to her right. "Will we both be able to hear him?"

"It's soundproof, I suppose to give the prisoners some kind of privacy when there are others here. You can only hear using the phone. We'll do our best to share it. If we can't hear well, we'll take turns talking to him."

"Fair enough."

She glanced at the analog clock on the wall above the glass, then watched the empty room beyond, her knuckles whitening where they gripped the laminate countertop in front of her.

Hoping to set her more at ease, Callum relied on the information he'd read last night on her laptop to make small talk. "Joey's older than you, right? Something like ten years?"

Her gaze stayed riveted on the only doorway in the other room as she waited for her brother to emerge.

"Twelve years. I was a senior in high school when he was arrested. Two years later, he was sent to death row."

And several years after that, both of her parents died. She'd had a rough time of it. And yet, from what he'd managed to find out about her through internet and law enforcement types of database searches, she was on track to be named a partner in the law firm where she worked. And she'd already become a wealthy woman in that short amount of time. Against all odds, she'd been hugely successful. Then she'd gambled it all on a foolhardy stunt, willing to give everything up on the slim chance that it would save her brother. Part of him thought she was nuts. But mostly, he was in awe of her family loyalty and the unconditional love that would make her risk it all.

"You do realize the odds of success, of getting his sentence commuted, are almost nonexistent, don't you?"

She finally looked away from the door and met his gaze. The haunted look in her eyes had his heart aching. No matter what she'd done to him on her foolhardy quest, she didn't deserve to suffer that kind of pain. No one did. He had to fist his hands at his sides to keep from reaching out to her and cradling her against his chest.

"I know the odds." Her voice was hollow, incredibly sad. "But until they stick a needle in his arm, I'm not giving up."

Unable to resist the urge to offer comfort in some small way, he took one of her hands in his and gently squeezed. "For your sake, I hope you're right and he's innocent. And that we can get him a stay of execution, if nothing else, then to have more time to fight for his release. But whatever happens, remember it's not your fault. You've done everything you can to help him. Don't blame yourself and wreck the rest of your life with could've, would've, should've."

Her eyes widened as she stared at their joined hands. But before she could say anything, movement on the other side of the glass had both of them turning. She tugged her hand free and pressed it against the glass as a man in a white jumpsuit and shackles on his wrists and ankles shuffled toward the window. A lone guard leaned against the wall about ten feet behind him, watching his every movement.

"What have they done to him?" she whispered brokenly as a tear slid down her cheek. "He looks awful."

The man on the other side of the glass was nothing like Callum had expected and barely resembled the mug shot Callum had viewed last night. He didn't know how much

Joey Quintero had changed since Raine's last visit. But he looked as if he'd aged thirty years since his arrest.

Before entering death row, Joey had been tall and bulky, resembling a football linebacker. Now he was nearly bald, with grayish-white eyebrows and whiskers on his gaunt, lean face. Yellowing skin seemed to sag on his skeleton as he took his seat across from them. But it was the bleakness in his eyes that was the most shocking of all. There was no sign of recognition, no smile of greeting for his sister. And he barely glanced at Callum. This was the face of a man who'd lost everything and had no hope for a future of any kind.

Raine's hand shook as she picked up the phone. She held the receiver next to her ear, tilted away so that Callum could hear as well. He settled on his knees on the floor beside her stool and leaned in close to the phone.

When her brother sat, looking at her with no expression, she managed to muster an encouraging smile and motioned toward the phone on his side of the glass. He seemed to consider it a moment, as if he wasn't going to pick it up. But he finally did.

"Joey, it's so good to see you. Are you feeling okay? You look...tired."

The shackles on his wrists jangled as he rested his elbows on the counter and cradled the phone to his ear. "I live in a six-by-nine box twenty-three hours a day with no TV, no radio, nothing but an uncomfortable bed, a toilet, a sink and those sappy books you send me to pass the time. The guards turn on the lights and wake me up every half hour at night to make sure I haven't managed to escape or steal the executioner's fun by offing myself. What do you expect? Of course I'm tired. I haven't had a good night's sleep in over a decade. Why are you here, Raine? Get on with your life. Forget about me. You've wasted enough time on me as it is."

He raised the phone as if to hang up, but Raine frantically motioned for him to keep talking. His chest lifted in an obvious sigh and he held the phone to his ear again. "What?"

She swallowed, hard, her free hand still pressed against the glass as if she could feel him if she pressed hard enough. "Don't give up, Joey. There's still hope. The man with me is a private investigator and—"

"Another one? How many investigators have you hired over the years? My appeals are exhausted. There's nothing else you can do. Seriously, Raine. Please. Stop this. Let. Me. Go."

"I can't. Don't ask me to do that. We're going to review the case, find some way to prove you're innocent."

He briefly closed his eyes as if in pain, then gave Callum his full attention for the first time. "Put him on the phone."

"He can hear you," she said. "We both can."

His cold gaze flicked to her. "Put him on the phone. Just him."

Callum wanted to slug the other man. His cruel indifference was clearly hurting his sister. He was going through a living hell in here—deserved or not. But that didn't justify him treating Raine this way.

She handed Callum the phone, her face pale and drawn as she clasped her hands in her lap.

Callum drew a bracing breath and focused on not shouting and upsetting Raine any more than she already was. "Mr. Quintero, I'm Callum Wright. I've agreed to take a fresh look at your case and see if we can get a stay of execution, clemency or a conversion of your sentence to life. Your sister has gone to incredible lengths, risked her career, even her own freedom, to convince me to help you. A smile or an I-love-you wouldn't hurt you one bit and it would sure as hell make her feel better."

Raine stared at him, wide-eyed, before quickly looking away.

Joey stared at Callum too. Then he started laughing.

Raine looked absolutely stricken.

Callum motioned to the guard behind Joey, then pointed at Raine. He nodded and spoke into his radio. Moments later, the door in the visitation room opened and another guard stepped in and waved for Raine to follow him.

She blinked and shook her head no.

"Raine." Callum's voice was low, just for her to hear. "Give me five minutes with your brother. Then come back in." When she started shaking her head again, he whispered, "You've trusted me this far. Don't stop now."

She stared at him, then glanced at her brother, obviously torn. Her lips quivered as if she was trying to hold back tears. Then she hurriedly left with the guard.

As soon as the door shut and locked behind them, Callum sat on the stool and faced the amused-looking man across from him.

"Joey. You don't mind if I call you Joey, do you?"

He shrugged, his smug smile still in place.

"Before your sister contacted me, I really hadn't bothered to look into the execution process in detail. Last night I did quite a bit of research on it. Has anyone ever shared with you exactly what's going to happen to you in thirteen days?"

His eyes narrowed and his smile slipped. But he didn't say anything.

"About twenty-four hours before they kill you, they move you to a holding cell called the death watch area. It's not a whole lot different than where you stay right now except it's a little bigger and has a shower. Upgrade. Cool, right?"

His eyelids lowered to half-mast as if he was bored. But he was still holding the phone to his ear, still listening.

"You think you don't have much privacy now, wait until you're in that holding cell. A guard will sit right outside it the whole time monitoring your every move to make sure you don't, as you put it earlier, off yourself and cheat the executioner. Then there's the last meal. In Georgia, it's not some fancy takeout from your favorite restaurant. Other prisoners fix it here in the prison. Don't expect it to taste any better than what you eat every day."

Joey's mouth flattened, his knuckles whitening around the phone.

"If you haven't completely alienated your sister, the one person in this entire world who gives a damn about you, she might be allowed to visit you one last time—from outside of the cell. No touching. No final hug. The only ones who actually get to come into your cell are the warden and chaplain, and the guards of course."

Callum motioned toward Joey's white jumpsuit. "You'll probably wear those same clothes to your final appointment, except for one thing. You'll have to put on an adult diaper. That makes it easier for them to clean up the mess when your bowels empty the moment you die."

Joey swore, a litany of curse words and phrases that questioned Callum's parentage and accused him of several disgusting fetishes.

Callum responded the way Joey had to Raine.

He laughed.

"You don't want to miss this last part," Callum said. "Once they take you to the execution chamber, they strap you to a table, arms spread and tied down, completely vulnerable. That makes it easy for them to shove that needle in your arm. Then they open the curtain. One-way glass. They can see you but you can't see them. And you know who will be out there? Watching? Praying for your soul?"

He leaned up close to the glass. "No one. That is, unless you apologize and fix the hurt you just did to your sister. If you don't, I guarantee she won't be there for you. I'll make sure of it. I refuse to let you hurt her again."

"What the hell do you want from me?" Joey demanded, spittle running down his mouth, his earlier smugness replaced with anger and a flash of fear.

"You want to know how it ends, right? They'll let you say your last words. But, again, no one who cares will be there to hear them. So it really doesn't matter what you say. It's just fodder for the twenty-four-hour news cycle, until the next story comes along and they completely forget you."

Joey's nostrils flared, the whites of his eyes showing as his Adam's apple bobbed in this throat. He was trying to play it cool, pretend nothing Callum was saying mattered. But it clearly did.

Callum continued his attack, firing with both barrels. "They'll pump you full of sodium thiopental to supposedly put you to sleep." He shrugged. "Who really knows what you'll be aware of? What you'll hear. What you'll feel. The second drug is pancuronium bromide. It paralyzes your diaphragm, your lungs, so you can't breathe."

Joey's face turned white. His lips lost their color.

"The last drug they pump into you is potassium chloride. It stops the heart. Assuming everything goes as planned, maybe you won't feel pain. Maybe you will. The only thing for sure is you'll be dead. As dead as Alicia Claremont, the young woman you killed fifteen years ago. Death is never a pretty thing. But imagine dying alone, with only the guards and executioner to keep you company instead of knowing that someone you love, and who loves you, is out there, praying for your soul."

Joey winced and looked away, clearly shaken.

Callum went in for the kill. "If you die with things between you and your sister the way they are now, her last memories of you will erode all the good ones from the past, from when you grew up together and cared about each other. She'll forever resent how you treated her when she's done nothing but sacrifice for you for the past fifteen years. You think you've suffered in here? Think about her, how she's put her hopes and dreams for her life on hold so she can focus on you and trying to get you free. Sure, she made herself a good career, and money. But why do you think she did that? So she could fund your defense. So she could give you the best possible chance at a future, at a life. And you repaid her by being a complete and utter jerk, to put it mildly."

Joey glared at him, red dots of color brightening his pale cheeks. "Don't you get it, dude? I love my sister. I know what she's sacrificed for me. She should be married with babies by now and instead she spends all her free time working on my case." He swore. "I was doing her a favor, trying to make her want to forget me. I don't want her grieving me and ruining even more of her life when I'm gone."

Callum shook his head. "She's going to grieve for you whether you leave bad memories in her heart or good ones. You can't turn off her emotions like a switch. If she didn't care about you, deeply, she wouldn't have stuck with you all these years. One conversation isn't going to somehow keep her from being hurt. The way you spoke to her just piles more hurt on what she's going to feel if we don't succeed in getting your sentence overturned."

"What the hell am I supposed to do then?" Joey demanded.

"Be a decent human being. Apologize, tell her that you're having a bad day and shouldn't have taken it out on her. Do whatever it takes to make her feel better, or I'm off this case. And, believe me, no one else is jumping up and down wanting to help. You want to live? Potentially have a chance at some kind of future, possibly even your freedom? Then you have to do two things. One, convince me you didn't kill Ms. Claremont. Two, grovel to your sister and repair the damage you did earlier."

Joey's eyes widened. "You like her, don't you? That's what this is all about. You're interested in her so you don't want her upset. That's the whole freaking reason you're here, to get into my sister's pants."

"Goodbye, Joey." Callum stood and hung up the phone.

Joey slammed his fist against the glass, gesturing wildly toward the phone and obviously yelling even though Callum couldn't hear him.

The guard behind him pushed away from the wall and said something.

Joey held up his hand, his manner turning placating until the guard positioned himself back against the wall. A look of desperation crossed Joey's face as he urgently motioned toward Callum's phone.

Callum really did want to leave. The clock above the phone showed they had only thirty more minutes for the visit. From what he'd read of this scumbag's case last night, he doubted there was anything Joey could say that could convince him he wasn't the murderer the court believed him to be.

And he really couldn't stomach how Joey had treated Raine.

But as Joey continued to gesture toward the phone, Callum realized he couldn't just walk out and leave it this way. Not for the man on the other side of the glass, but for the woman on the other side of the door. Coming here had given him a new perspective on what she had suffered for years and years. And it had pretty much taken away the sting, and embarrassment, of having been surprised by her at gunpoint. He could understand her desperation now, at how she felt she was without other options. And his respect for her, for the sacrifices she'd made, and had almost made, to help her brother meant Callum couldn't just walk out and crush her hopes at this point. So, for Raine, Callum sat and picked up the phone.

Mimicking Joey's earlier attitude, he demanded, "What?"

"You're cold, dude. Stone-cold."

Callum lifted the phone toward the receiver again.

Joey frantically waved at him.

Callum pressed the phone back to his ear. And waited.

"Okay, okay. I'm sorry, all right? I was out of line when I said that stuff about you. And I don't want to die, not if there's a chance you can stop it and get me off death row."

"And?"

His throat bobbed again as he swallowed. "And I get what you're saying about Raine. I didn't really want to hurt her. I was trying to help, in my own stupid way. I thought it would be easier on her if she was mad at me at the end. She's bull-headed. Anyone else would have given up on me long ago.

But she refuses to stop. I need her to be okay when I'm gone. I just… I don't know how to get her to let go and be okay."

"Did you kill Alicia Claremont?"

He blinked. "No. No, I didn't."

"But you confessed."

He rolled his eyes. "They interrogated me for twenty hours straight. I would have told them I assassinated the pope if it would make them let me lie down and get some sleep. I didn't kill no one, okay?"

Callum stared into the other man's eyes. Usually he could read people pretty well. But he honestly wasn't sure what he saw this time. Joey could be innocent, as Raine believed. Or he could be the savage killer he'd been convicted of being.

"I'll lay it out for you, Joey. I work for a cold case company, Unfinished Business. We have a large team of some of the best investigators in the country, along with our own private lab, just for starters. If anyone can find reasonable doubt this late in the game and convince the board to stay your execution, it's UB. But we're not lifting a single finger on your behalf until you've done one thing."

His fingers curled around the phone. "Anything, man. Name it."

"When your sister comes back in here, you're going to do whatever it takes to make her smile again. Fix the damage you did or you can kiss your last chance at justice, and life, goodbye."

Chapter Eight

Raine glanced back and forth between her brother on the other side of the glass and Callum, who was standing after insisting once again she take the only stool in the little partition. But they weren't sharing the phone this time. Instead, Callum was firing questions at her brother, trying to get as much information as possible before their visit ended. And although her brother had been unbelievably sweet and apologetic to her when she'd returned, his disposition had turned sullen and angry beneath the barrage of questions that Callum was asking.

If it was anyone else, at any other time, she'd have demanded he leave her brother alone. But this was what she'd wanted, what she'd risked everything to get—a top-notch investigator doing everything he could in an extremely limited time frame to try to save her brother's life. For that reason alone, she clasped her hands together and forced herself not to intervene.

"Her name was Alicia Claremont," Callum snapped into the phone. "Quit calling her *that woman*. Have some respect for the victim. If we're able to get you a hearing, you need to adopt a better attitude. Otherwise, you'll alienate the board and they won't bother to help you, regardless of what kind of evidence we're able to assemble."

Joey didn't exactly appear contrite as he responded. But whatever he said seemed to placate Callum, to some extent. He fired off more questions about the case, in rapid succession, barely giving her brother time to respond to each one. It was likely because the clock above the glass kept ticking away their remaining few minutes. But she also suspected it was Callum's interview style, at least in this situation, that catered to her brother's personality. The rapid-fire questions gave Joey no time to be sarcastic or flippant as he often could be. It forced him to let down his guard and say the first thing that came to mind, instead of trying to paint himself a certain way or avoid the uncomfortable questions. She admired Callum's skill and hoped he was getting what he needed in order to make his decision on whether or not to continue trying to help him. If Joey didn't convince Callum that he at least *could* be innocent, then Callum would drop his investigation.

Please, God, she silently prayed. *Help Joey convince Callum that he's not a murderer. If Callum doesn't help him, I don't know what else to do.*

Twenty minutes later, after a tearful goodbye to her brother, she was in Callum's SUV as he drove them outside the last of the prison gates. As always, when leaving her only sibling, there was a mixture of relief and grief inside her. Being inside those gray walls was overwhelmingly stressful. But knowing that her brother, unlike her, couldn't walk out, maybe never would, had her fighting back tears.

As if he understood the turmoil going on inside her, Callum remained silent. Occasionally, he glanced over at her, as if concerned. But he didn't intrude, didn't push. He gave her the space she needed. And for that, she was grateful.

They were well on their way back to Gatlinburg before she finally had her emotions under control enough to say anything.

She cleared her throat, and straightened in her seat. "What did you say to my brother?"

He glanced at her, before putting on his blinker and passing a slow-moving car. "I said a lot of things."

"I mean when you two were alone. After that, when I came back into the visitation room, he'd snapped back to the brother I remember. How did you make that happen?"

He shrugged. "I reasoned with him."

She clenched her hands in her lap. "I love my brother, more than you'll probably ever understand. But I also know him better than anyone. He deals with stress and fear by becoming belligerent and rude. Somehow you managed to make him remember his manners and give me a rare glimpse of the way he used to be, before…before the police pressured him into that false confession and destroyed his life. Whatever you did, thank you. Seriously. That was a rare gift, to see him once more the way he once was. Thank you."

"I'm glad I was able to help."

"You did. You really did. And I'm hopeful that you'll continue helping. Did you get the information that you needed to make your decision?"

"Are you asking if I think he's not guilty of murder?"

"Yes."

He passed another car before answering. "Honestly, he didn't tell me anything that made me think he'd been railroaded into a conviction. He wasn't on drugs or drunk when he confessed. He readily admits that. And he doesn't have an alibi."

"Correction, he has an alibi. Being home alone isn't a crime."

"No. It isn't. But if it can't be corroborated by some other means, it's useless as a defense."

"He'd never even met Alicia. Why would he kill her?"

"One of his friends said he saw Joey and Alicia get into Joey's truck outside a bar the night she was killed."

She rolled her eyes. "Friend? We're talking about Randy Hagen? That guy would do anything for his fifteen minutes of fame. He and Joey weren't friends anymore, hadn't been for a while. Randy had grudges against my brother. I don't believe anything he said on the witness stand. Neither do my brother's lawyers. They talked to him again a few days ago trying to get him to recant. The jerk refuses."

"Maybe because he was telling the truth. His testimony matched your brother's confession."

"I told you—"

"The confession was coerced, says everyone who's ever confessed."

"It was. The detective who interviewed him—your former boss, Farley—had just finished interviewing Randy. Then he took that information into the interview of my brother and lo and behold my brother's so-called confession matched."

He shrugged noncommittally.

She crossed her arms in frustration. "Are you going to help him or not?"

He was silent so long that she was convinced he was trying to figure out how to let her down. No doubt he'd made up his mind about Joey's guilt before they even entered the prison. Her brother's demeanor hadn't helped. And his answers to Callum's questions must not have done him any favors.

What was she going to do now? Tomorrow would mark twelve days until his execution. The two new lawyers Raine had recently hired hadn't made any real progress. Callum was her last resort. Was she really at the point of having to give up? Was there nothing else she could do to save the life of the only family member she had left?

She looked out the window just as they passed a highway sign. She frowned and noted another sign coming up ahead. "We're on Highway 36? That's not the way to Atlanta. You know a faster way to Gatlinburg?"

He surprised her by smiling. "Not hardly. But it's the fastest way to Athens."

She jerked around in her seat, afraid to hope. "Athens? Why?"

"Now who's pretending to be obtuse? It's the scene of the crime, the best way for me to get the lay of the land, to see what the killer saw, make sense of some of the reports I read and compare them to what your brother said today."

"Does that mean you're—"

"I'm going to work your brother's case, at least until I find out he's guilty. The second I'm convinced of his guilt, I'm off the case."

She impulsively took off her seat belt and planted a kiss on his cheek. "Since he's not guilty, that's not a worry. Thank you, Callum. Thank you, thank you, thank you. This means everything to me."

He chuckled and gently pushed her back. "It would mean everything to *me* if you put your seat belt on. Accidents are never planned and I don't want you flying through the windshield. I'm already going to have to get a new paint job. Replacing a broken windshield on top of that would be a major headache."

She laughed and clicked her seat belt into place. "Nice to know you care. About your car, that is."

"I do, you know." He glanced at her, his smile gone, his gaze locked onto her with an intensity that stole her breath. "I care what happens to you. I respect you, admire your courage and willingness to give up everything you've worked for in order to help your family. That kind of loyalty is rare, inspiring."

She blinked, her face growing warm before he finally looked back at the road. "Thank you. I appreciate that. I, ah, admire you as well, to be completely honest here. Even knowing that you worked on my brother's original case, even if it was only running errands for the lead detective, I wouldn't have come to you for help except that I read about your successes as a detective later in your career. And, of course, for Unfinished Business. That was the final factor that made me decide to—"

"Kidnap me at gunpoint?" he teased.

Her face heated even more. "I'm never going to live that down, am I?"

His grin widened. "Probably not."

"Well, I guess it was worth it if it made you decide to work the case. Because I'm so courageous, of course. And loyal."

"There's that, yes. But I'm in this for my own selfish reasons as well. I don't know that I'd have bothered even going to the prison or reading the files if it wasn't for the information you gave us on the serial killer we've been trying to catch. Everyone working that investigation is digging into your research. We're pinning our hopes that it's the key to finally stopping this killer, before he claims another victim."

Her stomach lurched as she forced a smile. Once he focused on the road again, she focused on the scenery passing by her window. What had he said exactly? That everyone was pinning their hopes on the information she'd provided? Were they all working that angle instead of the leads they were following before she came along?

Nausea roiled in her stomach. Her plan had worked, a little too well. She clenched her hands in her lap and drew deep, even breaths to stave off the panic rising inside her.

Sweet Lord. What have I done?

Chapter Nine

The residential neighborhood that Callum pulled into that evening, just outside of Athens, Georgia, was what he supposed would be called transitional, or up-and-coming. Most of the homes appeared to be from a bygone era, built long before Callum was born, maybe even before his parents were born. Largely single-story wooden structures, they were on the small side and boasted cracked and peeling paint, some with their siding sagging or even missing in places. But every fourth or fifth house was completely different, usually two-story, big and modern. People were buying up the older homes and tearing them down, replacing them with the boxy, cookie-cutter look found in so many other subdivisions. And the reason for them buying out here was obvious.

The enormous lots.

This neighborhood was originally built in an era when large lots were the norm. Graceful oak trees and gently rolling yards with occasional flower beds bursting with color gave it a homey feel, a welcoming atmosphere. There was plenty of land on each lot to allow for a much larger home to be built. And it still left room for large backyards with established trees to provide beauty and shade. The newer homes on lots this size didn't exist deeper into the city. Or, if they did, they'd be double the price.

"Nice, isn't it?" Beside him, Raine had a serene smile on her face as she looked out the window, obviously pleased with what she was seeing.

When he realized which homes she was admiring, he couldn't help feeling surprised.

"You like the old ones? Not the new builds?"

"Well, yeah. Don't you? The new ones look like boxes." She motioned toward the window. "These are unique, charming. I mean, sure, they need repairs. But they're different, special, a piece of history to be appreciated."

"And yet you live in a mansion in a development where the houses are so close together that you could jump from roof to roof."

She frowned. "First, it's not a mansion. Second, how would you know about my house?"

"I'm an investigator."

"And you felt you needed to investigate me?"

"Like you did me?"

She grimaced. "Fair enough. I guess." She motioned toward the nearest house again. "If I wasn't bucking for a partnership in a law firm with an image to maintain, I could see myself living here. Absolutely. Then again, my Porsche would be out in the elements with only a carport to protect it. Maybe I couldn't live in one of these after all."

"Porsche. You actually drive one of those things?"

"It's a sweet ride. My gift to myself after a particularly lucrative case. Why do you look so surprised?"

He shrugged. "I guess maybe because all I've seen you in so far is jeans. I'd have guessed you drove a crossover, a small SUV or something like that."

"Maybe I should rethink your abilities as a detective. My other car, the one I drive to the grocery store and things like that, is a truck."

He laughed. "That's a surprise. Regular or four-wheel drive?"

"Four-wheel. Duh."

"Red?"

"Of course."

"Nice. That's what I'd call a sweet ride."

"And yet you drive an SUV."

He grinned. "It's my work car, like your Porsche's yours. My regular ride is a four-by-four. Red."

She laughed and they exchanged a fist bump. "We're more alike than either of us realized."

"I suppose we are. But if I'm going to get anything useful to help me get my bearings on this case before the sun goes down, we need to get busy." He popped his door open.

"Busy doing what?" she asked. "If you wanted to see the crime scene, the Claremonts live one street over."

"Like I said earlier, I want to get the lay of the land." He hopped out and went to the rear of the SUV and opened the hatchback. When Raine joined him, he'd already gotten out his drone and was readying it for takeoff.

"Wow. Way fancier than the one I have," she said.

"You use a drone for work?"

"No. I'm a regular, boring business lawyer. No use for a drone for that. Mine's for weekends to, as you said, get the lay of the land. I scope out places to take pictures, and get some pretty good ones with the drone itself too."

"Pictures."

"Photography. Nature, landscapes, that sort of thing. It's what I wanted to do before my parents talked me into getting a *real* job. I was going to major in photography at college, try to sell pictures to magazines, stuff like that. But I guess it's a good thing that they talked me out of it. Odds are I would have had to work an extra job just to pay the rent. That wouldn't have provided the money I've needed to fund my brother's defense." She cleared her throat, her earlier enthusiasm fading. "Not that it's done him any good."

He stepped back and sent the drone airborne. "We've got thirteen days to find reasonable doubt. Don't give up now."

She nodded but didn't look convinced. He couldn't blame her. Joey's various lawyers had been trying for years to have his conviction overturned, to get him a new trial. Bringing Callum in to save the day was like bringing in a pinch hitter at the bottom of the ninth with two outs in a baseball game. The odds of success were low. But they weren't zero. They had a chance, but only if Joey was truly innocent. And so far, Callum had seen nothing to convince him of that.

"What was your dream, career-wise, when you were younger?" She stood beside him, watching the controller's screen as he directed the drone higher to show him a better view of the neighborhood, including its relation to nearby highways and other local roads.

"My mom told me I've wanted to be a policeman since I was old enough to talk."

"Really? Why? I mean, not that it's a bad thing, of course. It's admirable. Honestly. But what would make a child, a two-or three-year-old, say they wanted to be a cop? And then you being so focused through life that you ended up actually doing it?"

He shrugged, noting how the homes deeper inside the subdivision were on even larger lots, with more trees, overgrown bushes. Lots of places for bad guys to hide. "I suppose because it runs in the family. I grew up around uniforms, guns. My dad was a military policeman. Mom worked the phone lines, a 911 operator. That's how they met. My grandfather on my dad's side was the chief of police in the small town where he grew up, Mayfield, Kentucky."

"No wonder you're inclined to believe in my brother's guilt. I'm surprised you showed mercy and didn't have me arrested after the stunt I pulled."

He smiled. "Yeah, well, like I said. Selfish reasons." What he wouldn't tell her was that in addition to wanting the information she had that might help with UB's current serial killer investigation, he'd also been curious about her.

She was a looker, no denying that. But it was her determination, her willingness to risk it all for her brother that had him wanting to know more about her. In spite of his seemingly illustrious family history in law enforcement, he wasn't close to them. That whole family loyalty thing was nonexistent in the Wright household, particularly with his father. It was the reason he hadn't seen him or the rest of his family since he was eighteen and had left to go to college—on his own dime, working two jobs to pay for it. His parents could have easily footed the bill if they'd wanted. They had for his sister's education.

"There's the Claremont house." She pointed to a white older home on his screen. "That two-story addition on the back is new, built in the last six months."

"How would you know that?"

"Because the last time I visited them, it wasn't there."

He glanced at her, surprised, before he looked back at the screen and sent the drone soaring over the Claremont house. "You've visited the parents of the woman your brother was convicted of murdering?"

She edged away from him, as if suddenly uncomfortable being so close. "It wasn't my idea. It's not like I showed up on their doorstep one day. That would have been wildly inappropriate, given the situation. But I couldn't ignore what had happened. Yes, I believe my brother's innocent. I know he is, with all my heart. But Alicia's parents didn't grow up with Joey. They have no reason not to trust and believe what the police told them. In their hearts, Joey's the enemy, the one who ripped their lives apart. But I'm his sister, his family. It was my responsibility to reach out to them and apologize on my family's behalf. I sent a card, and a letter, through one of Joey's attorneys, expressing my heartfelt condolences on their terrible loss. I told them I sincerely believed the killer was still out there, but that I also wanted them to know I understand why they feel my brother hurt her, and that I'm sorry for the pain they've suffered."

She shrugged. "Lame, I know. But I felt I had to say something."

Raine had surprised him again. She was turning out to be very different from what he'd expected. In spite of her being a lawyer, and the sister of a convicted felon, he was liking her more and more. That was the biggest surprise of all.

"How did they react to the letter?" He finished reviewing the land surrounding the house and sent the drone to explore the neighboring yards, looking for escape routes, ways to sneak onto the property without being seen.

"Instead of sending a reply through the lawyer, or ignoring me altogether, they called me at work."

"You're kidding."

"Nope. I almost had a heart attack, burst into tears when I answered the phone. My assistant thought they were potential clients, didn't recognize the name. When Mr. Claremont introduced himself, it was like being hit by a truck." She shook her head, let out a ragged breath. "He was so sweet, so kind and understanding. They both were, are. They wanted me to come see them at the house."

"When was this?"

"A week after Joey was convicted."

"Amazing. How did that go? I'm guessing pretty well if you see them regularly, enough to know their home renovations hadn't been done six months ago."

"I see them once or twice a year. But the first visit wasn't until several months after they called me. Sending them a letter is one thing. Actually seeing them in person, sitting across from them in the same house where their daughter once lived and knowing that they believed Joey killed her wasn't something I was prepared to do. It took a while to get the courage to see them. When I did, they were incredible. They wanted me to know they didn't hold Joey's actions against me, that they didn't blame me for trying to defend him because he was my brother. They understood me, like no one else ever has. Well, until now, I guess. You seem to have forgiven me for my actions, because you understand family loyalty."

"More like I appreciate the *concept* of family loyalty, not having experienced it myself."

"What do you mean?"

He sighed and steered the drone back toward them. "That's a conversation for another time. Maybe."

She was quiet until he'd stowed the drone in his vehicle and shut the back hatch.

"Now that you've seen where it all happened, what's next?" she asked. "It's a long drive from here to Gatlinburg, and it's already getting dark. We could go into town for dinner and stay at my place tonight, head out in the morning."

"I appreciate the offer. Sounds better than crashing at a hotel tonight. But I'm not finished here. I understand the surroundings better, but not the crime scene itself."

Her gaze shot to his. "You actually want to go inside their home? See where Alicia was…where she was killed?"

"I'd planned on contacting the Claremonts tomorrow, seeing whether they'd let me come to the house, without you, out of respect for them. But now that I know they wouldn't be upset if you came too, we might as well save time by visiting them now. There's a car in their driveway. Someone's home."

Her eyes widened, her expression panicky. Had she made up that story about her letter to them, and their phone call? Maybe she'd fabricated everything to make him feel more empathetic toward her, and vicariously toward Joey. The idea that she'd lie about something like that had him tensing and wondering what else she'd lied about. She was a lawyer, after all. He should have known better than to trust her.

"If you'd rather not go with me—"

"No, no," she interrupted. "I'd love to see them. I'm just—"

"Worried I'll discover you've never really met them?"

Her mouth dropped open, then her face reddened as she snapped her mouth shut. She cleared her throat as if struggling to speak. "You think I lied?"

"Did you?"

She swore beneath her breath. "I guess we'll find out, assuming they'll want to see you. My hesitancy is because I don't want them hurt. I don't want you dredging up awful memories and causing them pain."

"That's for them to decide. Not you."

"Then I guess we should head over there. But I'm going in first, alone, to pave the way and make sure they'll be okay." She marched to the passenger side of the Lexus and hopped in.

"The hell with that," he muttered to himself, as he headed toward the driver's door. "I'll go in first so I can see their reaction to *you*."

Chapter Ten

Raine squeezed Mrs. Claremont's hands in hers, then smiled up at Mr. Claremont just inside their foyer. "Please don't feel you have to leave. I can sit with you while Mr. Wright does a walk-through. We'll be in and out in no time. You won't have to answer any questions."

She ignored Callum behind her. No doubt he was fuming that he wouldn't get a chance to talk to them about Alicia. But these kind people had suffered too much pain already. Raine wasn't going to stand for him interrogating them, even if it was to help Joey.

Mr. Claremont patted her shoulder. "You two take as long as you need. You can call me when we should come back. We understand how important this is to you. And we want you at peace, knowing you explored every option, that you did everything you could for your loved one. We'd do the same if the situation was reversed."

Raine smiled her gratitude through threatening tears. "You've both always been so kind to me, so understanding. I don't know how you do it."

Mrs. Claremont squeezed Raine's hands before letting go. "You act as if we get nothing in return. Talking to you on the phone, seeing you, getting cards, flowers, those things give us something to look forward to in a house that's far too quiet these days. You keep Alicia alive for us. You make us feel alive. As far as we're concerned, you're our second daughter. We love you, Raine."

"I love you too," she whispered brokenly, and hugged them both.

As they stepped out the door, Mrs. Claremont turned back with one last smile. "It will be okay, Raine. You'll get through this. Whatever happens, we're here for you."

She forced a smile and watched them drive away, then slowly shut the door.

"You're shaking." Callum's arm settled around her waist, as if he was afraid she would pass out. "Come on. Sit on the couch."

Being treated as if she was helpless normally would have made her snap back in resentment. She'd worked too long and too hard to make it in a man's world to be treated like a stereotypical weak female. But she did need to sit down. And she was so dang tired of having to be strong all the time. Plus, he was right. She was shaking, and she wasn't sure how much longer her legs were going to hold out.

Her face flaming, she let him lead her to the couch where she gratefully sat. Too embarrassed to look at him, she rested her elbows on her thighs and held her head while she closed her eyes.

"Go ahead," she said. "Look around the house for whatever you think you'll find fifteen years after the murder. I just need a minute."

"The house can wait. Do you want some water? Want to lie down?"

Her cheeks heated even more. "Stop. Just go, do what you

need to do. I'm fine. Or I will be. I just…heck, I don't know what my problem is. But I'll be okay in a few minutes."

Instead of leaving her, he sat beside her and put his ridiculously warm, solid arm around her shoulders. Part of her wanted to push him away for being so nice to her after everything she'd done. The other part wanted to sink against him, maybe even slide her own arm around his waist. Good grief. What was wrong with her tonight?

"I can practically see the wheels spinning in that sharp brain of yours," he teased. "You're not used to feeling vulnerable. But you need to give yourself a break. The stress is getting to you. It would get to anyone in your position. And it's only going to get worse in the next few weeks."

She groaned and sat back, forcing him to move his arm before she embarrassed herself even more and leaned against him.

"As much as I hate to admit it, I think you may be right. It feels as if a giant boulder is crashing down a mountain toward me. I can't seem to get out of the way no matter how fast I run. And yet, I'm not the one in peril. Joey is." She clenched her fists and opened her eyes. "I don't have time to sit here doing nothing while the clock is ticking away the remaining hours of his life."

She started to get up, but he gently pressed her back down.

"You're not going to help your brother like this. You're running on empty. And all that guilt you're carrying around is making you miserable. Those people, the Claremonts, obviously care a great deal about you. And it sounds like you've done a lot more for them over the years besides a few visits here and there. From what I heard, you have nothing to feel guilty about where they're concerned, far from it.

And you've done everything you can to help your brother. You're still doing everything you can. Give yourself permission for some downtime now and then. Otherwise you'll run out of gas and won't be able to do anything for him."

She let out a shaky breath. He was right, about running on empty. She barely slept anymore. And her concentration was shot. But he was wrong that she shouldn't feel guilty. She had far more to feel guilty about than he knew.

He needed to know the truth. She needed to tell him what she'd done. But if she did, would he quit trying to help Joey? If she didn't, would someone else be hurt, because of her lie?

Think, Raine. Figure it out. There has to be a way to fix this without sacrificing Joey in the process.

"You seem better. If you're up for it, we can talk it through," he said.

She looked up, startled. Had she spoken out loud? "Talk it through?"

"The attack, what happened here. I've read the police reports, or as much as I could in only one night, plus yesterday at the hospital. You've probably read them dozens, maybe hundreds of times over the years. I heard Joey's barebones version of events earlier in the limited time that we had with him. But that's still not enough. Let's talk it out, use each other as a sounding board. Then I'll look around, with that in my head, so I can picture what happened and look for holes in the theories the police formed."

Relief had her eagerly grabbing on to the lifeline that he'd given her. She'd avoid confessing her terrible secret for a little while longer. And maybe before that, just maybe, something would click in Callum's investigator mind, something that would be the answer to her, and Joey's, prayers.

"All right." She drew a deep breath, her shakiness easing. "How do we start?"

"For now, let's limit it to the inside of the house. We can discuss the rest after we leave so we're not keeping the Claremonts away longer than necessary. Although I did want to ask about pets. I'm guessing they don't have any now or they'd have said something."

"They don't. And they didn't back then either, if that's your next question. No dog to bark and alert anyone."

"Neighbors? The homes aren't that close together. But if one of them had a dog who tended to alert when someone came around, that would be good to know. Might be indicative of whether the killer was known in the neighborhood or not."

She shook her head. "I've heard dogs in the neighborhood before, but not close by. I don't think any of the houses right around this one had dogs back then."

"All right. We'll move on then. Talk it through."

"We focus on Alicia?"

"For now. We'll talk potential suspects later. Alicia was twenty, a sophomore at Athens Technical College. She still lived with her parents to save money."

She nodded, sitting forward. "She was pursuing a nursing degree. She wanted to help people." Her stomach knotted. Alicia, from all accounts, had been a good student, a good person. She could have made a difference in the world.

"It was a Friday night, Saturday morning, really. She'd been blowing off steam at a local club. Left around two a.m. and drove home."

Raine nodded. "Her parents were out of town for the weekend, visiting a sick friend. They weren't sure they'd be back early enough Monday for Alicia to make it to her first class. So they all agreed she'd stay here."

Callum stood. "If you're better now, I'll walk it through. You can sit and—"

"No. No, I'm good. Really. I want to help."

He held out his hand.

She hesitated, then let him pull her to her feet. Instead of immediately letting go, he smiled and led her toward the foyer. It wasn't as if they were really holding hands. Not as if they were a couple or anything. But it had been so long since she'd touched another person that his hand on hers seemed like a warm hug that went all through her body. And when they reached the foyer, and he pulled his hand free, she suddenly felt bereft, alone, sad.

He frowned. "You sure you're up to this?"

"Yes, yes, of course. Sorry, was just thinking." She smiled, her face heating once again with embarrassment. "Go on. I've never done a walk-through before, or whatever you called it. I'm not sure how this goes."

"There aren't any rules or procedures. It's just the two of us talking it through, walking the scene to the best of our ability." He stood with his back to the front door and waved her over to do the same.

"We're standing where Alicia would have stood that night," he said. "The crime scene photos focused on the bedroom where the police believe everything happened. You've seen the house before, since a few months after the trial. Is it similar to that night or completely different now?"

She scanned the foyer, the arched openings to the left and right, the family room straight ahead. "Huh. I never thought about it before. But I don't think much has changed ever since I started visiting them. It's kind of…frozen in time. How sad."

"It might give them comfort leaving things much as they were when their daughter was around. When I stand here, as if coming through the front door, I see most of the living room. If the furniture is in the same location——"

"It is."

"——then there really aren't any hiding places in there. If the couch had been on the far wall, facing us, I'd say the perpetrator could have hidden behind it. But we're facing the side of the couch, and the mirror above the fireplace mantel shows the other side of it."

"Oh, wow. I didn't think about that."

"If he was in the family room, she'd have seen him as soon as she walked in the door and could have run outside."

"That makes sense." She motioned to her right. "What about the kitchen?"

"Let's check it out." He stepped through the archway into the small, galley-style kitchen, moving all the way to the end. There was a door that led into the carport area. And another one beside it, at the end of the row of cabinets. "The police report said there were no indications anyone came through this door. But there was no sign of forced entry on the front door either."

"Which is why it makes sense that she must have known her attacker. And Joey had never met Alicia."

He opened the door inside the kitchen. "The pantry. It's not a walk-in. No way for someone to hide inside unless they were a small child and could crawl onto one of the shelves." He closed the door. "As for her knowing Joey, that's in dispute, as we already discussed."

"Randy Hagen lied. And him saying he saw the two together just goes to show that he knew her on sight even though he told the police he didn't."

"His testimony was that he saw pictures of her on the news and remembered seeing her with Joey."

"As I said, fabrications."

"How do you know he lied? Because that's what Joey said?"

She lifted her chin. "Yes. And because there weren't any corroborating witnesses. No one else at the bar remembered seeing either of them that night."

"That's not what I remember reading. Others said they thought they saw them, but weren't sure."

She crossed her arms.

"Her credit card statement proves she was there," he continued. "The place was loud, crowded, dark. She didn't do anything to stand out. But she was definitely there. Joey could have been too. If he wasn't, why would Hagen lie about it? What did he have to gain?"

"Revenge. He and Joey both liked the same girl a few years earlier. She dumped Hagen for Joey. That's why they weren't friends anymore."

"Years earlier. And Hagen decides to get back at him by helping send him to death row? Seems extreme." He held up his hands to stop anything she might say in response. "Let's leave that discussion for another time. Back to the question of how the killer got inside the home. The police theorized that Joey rummaged through her purse at the bar and found her spare key. Her parents confirmed she always kept a spare in an inside purse pocket, in case the three of them were heading out of town together. She had a friend who lived on campus who'd watch the place, check it out, make sure a pipe hadn't burst or something like that. The spare key wasn't in her purse when the police found it."

"She could have lost it at any time and just not realized it."

"Maybe," he conceded, not sounding convinced.

"I still think she must have let the killer in," Raine said.

"Or they had a key. All we have is speculation and theories on that right now. The windows were locked. None of the screens were ripped. Neither outside door showed scratches or signs of having been jimmied open. The frames were intact."

"Then the police have to be wrong that he was waiting inside. Maybe she came home with someone she knew and he came inside with her."

"You're thinking Hagen?" he asked.

She shrugged. "Possibly."

"Did she know Hagen?"

"No one's ever proved it. But they haven't proved Joey did either." She arched a brow in challenge.

He smiled and turned around in the kitchen, glancing from the stove to the refrigerator, the countertops. "Normally, in a situation like this, I'd say someone could use a ruse like a pizza delivery to get her to open the door. They could pretend they had accidentally gone to the wrong house. They'd take the box with them when they left so no one would know. Or a package delivery. Any number of things to get someone to open the door for a stranger. But at that time of morning, I just don't see it."

"I don't either, honestly. I sure wouldn't open the door after midnight for anyone I didn't know," she agreed.

"Another possibility is that someone was hiding in the

shrubs by the front door. When she opened it, he stepped in behind her, forced his way inside."

She slowly nodded. "Sounds plausible. But I don't remember the police saying anything about that in their reports."

"They probably didn't find any dirt or leaves inside to support the theory so they didn't mention it."

"It's a window for reasonable doubt, though. A small one, but more than I had before. Thank you."

He smiled. "She may have simply forgotten to lock the door behind herself too, and someone else came in after she did."

She blinked. "That's so obvious, and yet no one—not even me—has brought that up before either."

"I'm sure the police considered all of that. But the detectives would have gone over everything and put the puzzle together the way they think made the most sense."

"That my brother did it."

"Hagen gave them his name. Then Joey confessed. Hard to fault them for believing he was their guy." He held up his hands again. "Let's not talk about false confessions just yet. We'll deal with that later."

She let out a frustrated breath. "What next then?"

"For now, let's assume no one forced their way inside with her. What did she do when she locked the door behind her? Her purse was found on that decorative table beside the front door. Her keys were on top. The kitchen and family room were neat, clean. Nothing to suggest she went into the kitchen for a snack. No pillows out of place or a blanket or throw wrinkled on the back of the couch to suggest she watched TV after coming in."

Raine stood with her back to the door again, an eerie feeling settling over her as she imagined herself in Alicia's position. Coming into the warm, cozy home she'd grown up in, not knowing that her young life was about to come to a horrific end. She went through the motions of putting a purse and keys on the little table, even though her purse was locked in Callum's SUV. Then she looked down. "Shoes. I would have taken off my shoes at my house and put them in the hall closet."

He joined her in the foyer. "There isn't a closet in this little entryway. Bedroom maybe?"

"Maybe." She moved around the corner into the hallway. The first door on the left was more narrow than the others. She pulled it open. Sure enough, it was a closet. Coats and sweaters hung neatly on a pole. And a wooden rack sat beneath them on the floor with several pairs of shoes in it. When she closed the door, it squeaked. "The killer would have heard that."

"If it squeaked back then, and if he was already inside. But I think he would have already known she was inside. He'd hear the front door, or her keys and purse being left on the table. The police theory is that he was waiting in her bedroom. It faces the front yard. They reasoned the perpetrator peeked through the blinds, watching for her arrival."

"All supposition. Guesses. They didn't find any fingerprints to prove it."

He smiled. "That's why they said her murder was premeditated. The killer wore gloves."

"More guesses."

"Educated guesses. It's unlikely that someone could have attacked her and strangled her without leaving DNA or fingerprints unless they wore gloves. And a condom. There was evidence of rape but no semen."

She shivered. "Poor Alicia."

His jaw tightened. "Poor Alicia." He led the way down the hall, looking briefly inside each room they came upon, as if he was creating a map in his mind. In the main bedroom, he studied the pictures on the walls, used his phone camera to capture the images, as well as some of the collections arranged on the top of the dresser.

"You think the killer came into this room too?" Raine asked from the doorway.

"I think if he did, then knowledge of anything in these various rooms is something he'd have, a way to prove his identity if he mentions anything here. There weren't any pictures of these rooms in the police reports, nothing in the press releases. And I remember the responding officer said all of the doors in this hall were closed, except the last one."

"Alicia's room."

He nodded and stepped into the parents' walk-in closet. The back boasted white wallpaper with sprays of purple flowers across it. Again, he took a picture, likely because that was a detail he hadn't known before. Then the two of them headed into the hall. They paused just outside of the door to the room that they'd specifically come here tonight to see.

Alicia's room. The place where she'd been attacked, beaten, sexually assaulted, and then strangled and left for her parents to discover Monday morning when they'd returned from out of town.

She'd suffered a brutal death. Whoever had killed her deserved the worst punishment the courts could offer. And her parents deserved justice, the knowledge that whoever had killed their daughter had paid for their crime. Raine wanted that for them just as badly as they did. But not at the cost of Joey's life. Joey was kind, sweet, or had been as a child, even as a teenager. He'd been bullied, not the kind who'd bullied others. Yes, he'd gotten into trouble, robbing homes, graffiti, property crimes. And he'd done some minor jail time for it. But none of his crimes had ever been against people. He'd never been violent. And he'd pleaded guilty each time he was caught.

Callum put his hand on the knob. "Ready?"

She drew a bracing breath. "Ready."

He pushed the door open.

Raine pressed a hand to her chest. "Oh, dear sweet Lord."

Chapter Eleven

"Not what you expected to see?" Callum asked, not sure why Raine was so shocked.

She slowly shook her head. "It looks...it looks as if Alicia could come home any minute. I thought you'd get an idea of the size of the room, where the closet was, the window, that sort of thing. I had no idea they'd kept it the way it was all those years ago." Her gaze flew to the bed. "Except...that's different. Similar, but not exactly the same as the bedding in the photos."

"The police would have taken the original bedding as evidence. Her parents probably tried to find new bedding like it, but it was discontinued or they couldn't locate the same set. Judging by how everything else looks, her books, her computer—no doubt returned after your brother's case was adjudicated—high school trophies, posters on the wall, they tried to keep it the same. A memorial to their daughter."

"They definitely haven't moved on."

"Many families don't. Alicia may have technically been an adult. But her parents thought of her as their child, their only child. Getting rid of her things must have proved too painful in the beginning. Later, they just closed the door and left it alone. Although, I'd say from the lack of dust in here, it's being cleaned regularly."

"How sad to imagine them doing that." She ran her hands up and down her arms as if chilled. "What did you want to see in here?"

He pulled out his phone and thumbed across the screen, then held it up. "This album contains all of the police photographs taken in the room. Originally, as you said, I wanted to get the feel of the space, the dimensions. But since the original crime scene is so well-preserved, we have a unique opportunity to compare it to the police pictures. If there are any significant details in here not photographed, again, that provides us with information only the true killer would know about."

"Which would help you prove someone else did it if we come up with a suspect."

"It could." Or it could pile on additional proof against Joey Quintero if Callum got another chance to interview him—without Raine present. He'd contact his prison-admin friend tonight and work on getting that set up.

"All right," Raine said, seemingly encouraged. "Let's see what you have there."

He handed her the phone, not feeling that he needed to look at the pictures right now since he'd studied them in-depth last night. Instead, he walked the length and breadth of the room. The closet was small, like everything else in the home. White wooden bifold doors opened accordion style. Not a walk-in, but someone could easily hide inside, behind the hanging clothes, and peer through the slats in the doors. It was typical of many homes built in the same era.

When he swept aside some of the pink hangers, it revealed that the back of the closet was covered with wallpaper. It was white with repeating patterns of pink sprays of flowers clinging to tree branches. His guess was that they were cherry blossoms, but he wasn't sure. He'd have to take a picture before they left since he hadn't seen this in any photos of this room.

To the right of the closet was the wall facing the street, and opposite the full-size bed. Like the wooden bed, the chest of drawers and small desk on the window wall were white. When he pushed down on one of the aluminum blinds to check the window lock, he saw the frame was nailed shut. He'd have to ask the Claremonts about that since he didn't know if that was the way it had been fifteen years ago or a more recent change. Given the current state of everything else in the room, likely it was done way back then and just wasn't noted in a police report.

Which was disappointing and encouraging at the same time.

Disappointing, because he'd expect more of his fellow detectives. Encouraging in that it meant not everything was documented, so he and Raine had a chance of finding something that might steer them in a new direction.

Or confirm Joey's guilt.

"Do you think any of these books in her desk drawers are relevant?" Raine asked.

He glanced over to see what she'd found, a stash of books in the bottom drawer, seven or eight from the looks of it. More books sat on sagging shelves attached to the wall opposite the closet. Apparently, Alicia was a prolific reader. There was a broad range of nonfiction and fiction books in many genres.

"Couldn't hurt. You never know what the killer may have done in here before or after killing Alicia. He may remember some of those books, for whatever reason. If he does, that's great evidence to prove he was in this room. They aren't in plain sight, not in the police photos. Good job, Raine."

She smiled and began snapping pictures of them.

Callum was relieved to see her smile again. She'd seemed so lost earlier, as if the weight of the world—and her brother's alleged crime—was on her shoulders and hers alone. While Callum doubted those books in the drawer would help them, it made her feel as if she was furthering the investigation. And one never knew for sure what small detail might bring an entire puzzle into focus.

They spent a good deal of time in the room, noting every detail. But aside from getting a feel for the layout, and lack of hiding places, about all Callum felt they had as additional potentially significant information to note were the pink hangers in the closet, the wallpaper and those books Raine had found in the desk.

He was just about to suggest they leave the room when he looked in the last place he'd almost forgotten to look. Up. They were faint, hard to see with the light on. But they were there. He crossed to the light switch and flipped it off.

Raine gasped beside him as she too looked up. "Glow-in-the-dark stars. They're all over the ceiling."

Callum snapped a picture. "Definitely not something the average person looking at police photos would know about. But the killer, if he was in this room with the light out, would definitely have noticed them." He flipped the light back on and the stars almost completely disappeared, fading in with the textured ceiling.

"I had those when I was a teenager," Raine said, her voice sad. "It's sweet that she kept them even as a young adult going to college. They were probably sentimental to her."

"I had them too. But mine had planets and spaceships."

She smiled again, but this time it was much more subdued. "Can we get out of here now?"

"After you."

They returned to the foyer.

"Do you want to look in the new part of the home too?" Raine motioned toward the door in the back left side of the family room.

Callum hesitated. "Since it wasn't here during the crime, it's probably not necessary. But now that you've mentioned it, let's take a quick look just in case it makes us think of something else that we need to ask the Claremonts."

He pushed open the door and they stepped into a large room with a soaring ceiling. Where the rest of the house was stuck in time, this addition was the epitome of modern, black-and-white industrial design. A huge TV hung on the far wall. Comfortable-looking white leather couches formed a U-shape facing the TV. To the left and right of the TV were expansive sliding glass doors with black iron grids that led out onto a stone deck with an outdoor kitchen tucked into one side.

"Wow," Raine said. "This is super nice. I'll bet this is where they spend most of their time. I sure would."

He looked up at the black beams on the soaring ceiling. "From the outside you'd think it was two stories. But it's really only one, with high ceilings."

"I'm glad they have this. It's nice to know they don't spend all of their time in the past. This is a happy room." She turned around and the smile died on her face. "Oh no."

Callum turned to see what she'd seen. His heart sank when he saw what could only be described as a shrine to the Claremonts' dead daughter. Row upon row of pictures filled the massive wall, showing Alicia in various phases of her life, from birth, to toddler, to teen and finally a few, though not many, from her college years. It appeared that every picture had been carefully chosen to only show happy times because in every single one, Alicia was smiling at the camera.

Raine rubbed her arms again. "I've never, not my entire adult life, ever doubted my brother. I've never thought he did this. But I've also never realized the full extent of how Alicia's death hurt the Claremonts, until now." She turned to face him. "I don't want this to happen to another family if there's some way for me to prevent it. We need to leave. Right now."

She hurried toward the door.

He raced after her but didn't catch up until she was in the foyer about to open the front door.

"Wait, Raine. Just wait." He grabbed her shoulder and gently turned her around. "What's wrong? I mean besides the obvious, that you're sad about Alicia's family. And worried about Joey."

She shook her head, her hair flying around her shoulders. "It's far worse than any of that." Tears spilled down her cheeks. "We have to go. I need to talk to you, to tell you... I lied, Callum. I kept a terrible secret. I didn't think it would matter, but then you said... And then I saw... I can't—"

"Breathe, Raine. Just breathe. Whatever it is, it can't be that bad."

Her eyes squeezed shut, tears dripping down her cheeks. "I did something awful. And if I don't fix it, if I don't tell you what I did, another woman might die."

Chapter Twelve

After seeing physical proof of the pain the Claremonts had suffered all these years, were still suffering, it was one of the hardest things Raine had ever done to speak to Mrs. Claremont on the phone without breaking down. But Callum had insisted they leave the house and that she tell the Claremonts they could return before she made her confession.

Confession was supposed to be good for the soul. But Raine feared it was going to destroy her. Still, *not* confessing would be even worse, because someone else could be hurt.

She ended the call and slid her phone into her purse on the console between them. "Done," she said. "They finished dinner in town and were driving around the area waiting for my call. They're heading home right now. She was so sweet, so worried about me, about us." She shook her head. "I don't understand how she does it. And I certainly don't deserve it." She clutched her hands together in her lap. "Can we pull over now, so we can talk?"

"Just a few more minutes. I don't want to be sitting on the side of the road and the Claremonts pass by and stop to check on us."

"Oh, gosh, no. Good thinking." She finally focused on their surroundings. "You're going into town. My house isn't far from here. We could go there. Eat later, assuming you still want to be around me."

"I'm sure whatever you want to tell me isn't nearly as bad as you think. And, yes, I was already planning on going to your place first."

"You know my address? Wait, of course you do. You looked me up online, accused me of living in a mansion."

"What's good for the goose—"

"Is good for the gander. I know, I know. I followed you, searched for your information online. It's only fair that you do the same. I get it. Doesn't mean I like it, but I get it."

He turned down the lane that led to only one place, the gated community where she lived.

"Do you have a key fob or something so we can get through the guard gate?"

She smiled, vaguely amused in spite of the stress that was ready to tear her apart. "We won't need a key fob, or a sticker on the windshield, anything like that. Just slow down and use the owner lane when we're at the guard shack. And roll your window down."

He gave her a puzzled look but nodded.

When they arrived at the gate, he stayed to the right, avoiding the few cars lined up in the visitor lane speaking to the guard.

"Excuse me for a sec." She unbuckled her seat belt and leaned over him toward his window. A few seconds later, a beep sounded and the gate began to swing open.

"Well, I'll be damned." Callum glanced at her. "Some kind of facial recognition, right? There was a camera hidden somewhere?"

"In the bushes, so we don't have to look at an ugly pole with a camera on top as we smile and go on through."

"Rich people." He shook his head. "Eccentric and strange. But kind of cool."

"Rich people? If I'm wealthy, what are you? Your salary at UB—"

"Is none of your business."

"And readily available, at least the range, if you search hard enough. Calling me rich like it's a bad thing is pretty lame when you earn close to what I do, maybe more. And neither of us needs to apologize for what we have. We both rose from modest backgrounds and worked our butts off to create opportunities. No one ever handed me anything I didn't earn, that's for darn sure."

He smiled as he made a right turn onto her street. "My apologies for apparently being a snob and not realizing it."

She clasped her hands together again. "You're not the one who owes anyone an apology. And you're never going to forgive me once I tell you what I did. I just pray you'll please, please think about it before you react. My brother shouldn't die because of my mistakes. I need your help, desperately, to help him."

"You honestly think whatever this thing is that you've done, this secret, is going to make me quit the investigation?"

She winced. "If I was in your position, yes. But I'm banking on you being a better person than me."

He chuckled and motioned toward the windshield as he pulled into the circular brick driveway at the front of her house. "Honey, we're home."

Raine led the way up the front walk with a mixture of dread and anticipation. She dreaded their upcoming conversation. But she was looking forward to being home. It had been weeks since she'd last been here and she was tired of living out of a suitcase. Having a hot shower in her own bathroom would be a treat. And getting to sleep in her own bed, heaven.

But first, a little hell. She had to face the consequences of what she'd done.

At the door, he stopped beside her. "Let me guess, facial recognition again?"

"Actually, no. I've never been that great with electronics. And the idea of being locked out of my home because of a power outage or computer issue scares me. I prefer the old-fashioned method." She pulled a key out of her purse.

He grinned. "Good to know that I'm not the only one."

"Who uses a key?"

"Who has trouble with electronics. Don't tell Asher that I admitted it. He teases me enough as it is."

She smiled and pushed open the door, then sucked in a shocked breath at the devastation inside.

Callum swore and pushed her behind him, a gun suddenly in his hand. "Get in the car and lock the doors. Call 911. Do it. Now."

She took off running toward his SUV.

Chapter Thirteen

Callum stepped around an overturned table in the massive, two-story foyer, sweeping his pistol left and right. Gray-and-white marbled floors were probably the fashion star of the entire home. But they were currently littered with broken dishes and glasses, shredded pillows, and decorative tables and chairs either knocked over or splintered into kindling. Whoever had trashed her house wasn't in it for robbery. Or if they were, it was an afterthought. They'd come prepared to do damage. What he needed to find out was whether they were still here, and whether they were armed.

In spite of the cavernous feel of the entryway and main room beyond it, which also sported a two-story ceiling, the first floor didn't boast many rooms, at least, not separate ones. Open concept, he thought he'd heard it called. He could see foyer to main room to the backyard, and kitchen and dining areas by standing in one spot and turning around. No one was there. Which meant they were either in the back hall underneath the curved, sweeping staircase, on the second floor or long gone.

He was hoping they were still here. Because he really wanted to wring their neck. Raine didn't need this kind of stress or fear lumped on top of everything else she was going through right now.

Trying to avoid crunching any of the glass beneath his shoes, he quietly made his way under the stairs. A handful of doors opened off the little hall back there. One by one, he threw them open and aimed his pistol inside. Empty, all of them. These rooms—an office, two guest bedrooms and a bathroom—had been spared the vandalism done to the other areas.

A thump sounded overhead.

Callum smiled. The jerk was still here. He eased back to the foyer, then rushed around the bottom of the stairs, aiming his gun toward the landing at the top. Clear. No one there, or at least, not where he could see them.

Ever so slowly and carefully, he crept up the shiny marble stairs toward the second floor. As soon as he reached the top, another thump sounded, off to his right. There were a ridiculous number of doors off the wide landing. And a skylight overhead allowed the waning sunlight to keep the shadows at bay. Aside from a couple of overstuffed chairs and one low side table, there weren't any hiding places on the landing. The perp had to be in one of the rooms, if they even realized Callum was here.

There were three doors to check close to where he'd heard the last sound. He stood frozen in place, barely breathing as he tried not to make any noise that would alert his prey. When another minute ticked by without anything, he figured the game was up. The person he was after must have realized someone was here and was trying to be quiet now too.

He aimed the pistol in his right hand up toward the ceiling while he grabbed the doorknob for the first door. He quickly swung it open, ducking down as he rushed inside, sweeping his pistol around. A bedroom. He cleared the attached bathroom and closet, then peered out the opening. Clear.

The second door led to another bedroom, also empty. He was just about to open the third door on this side of the landing when he heard the crunching of glass downstairs. He swore. The perp must have gotten past him when he was checking the other two rooms. He whirled around and ran to the top of the stairs and aimed his pistol down them.

Nothing.

Slowly, carefully, he descended the stairs, looking all around. When he reached the bottom, he glanced toward the back wall of the house, which was mostly floor-to-ceiling windows with three sets of double French doors. All were closed. Looking toward the foyer, he saw the front door was closed too. Which meant the bad guy was either in one of the rooms under the stairs now, or outside.

Raine is outside.

Ah, hell.

He took off running toward the front door and threw it open.

A pistol was aimed directly at his chest. It was Raine, pointing her gun at him. He swore and grabbed it, yanking it away from her.

"I'm sorry, I'm sorry," she said. "I thought you were the bad guy."

"And I thought he was outside and you were in danger. Why aren't you in the car, doors locked, like I told you?"

"I was, but you were gone too long. I got worried and— behind you!"

He whirled around.

A figure dressed all in black took off through the family room toward the back doors.

"Halt, or I'll shoot," Callum yelled, sprinting after him.

The perp flipped a dead bolt and flung open a French door.

"Lock yourself in one of the rooms downstairs," Callum yelled back to Raine. Then he ran out the open door toward the fleeing figure.

Ten minutes later, Callum swore a blue streak and headed toward Raine's home. The back of her property faced a wooded area that appeared to be some kind of huge nature preserve. He'd done his best to follow the fleeing man but he'd lost him. If Raine wasn't waiting at her house, he'd have kept searching. But he didn't trust her not to come looking for him again. And he didn't want her in these woods with a potentially armed criminal hiding out here.

By the time he reached the house, the police were there, crawling all over the place. He had to drop his pistol and explain who he was to two uniformed cops. Raine stepped out and told them he wasn't the bad guy, that he was the detective she'd told them about.

"Private investigator," Callum corrected. "Formerly a detective with the Athens-Clarke County Police Department."

"Give him back his weapon. He's one of the good guys," a man in a gray business suit said as he joined Raine on the patio. "It's been a hot minute, Callum. Good to see you again."

"Danny, hey. What's it been, a couple of months?" Callum took his pistol from one of the officers and slid it into the inside pocket of his jacket. "I chased the intruder into the woods but he disappeared. I never saw a weapon, but he could very well be armed."

Danny issued instructions and several police went off in pursuit.

"Let's get back inside." Callum steered Raine toward the open French doors. "If the intruder does have a gun, I don't want to give him a target."

The three of them headed to a grouping of white leather chairs and a couch in front of an equally white fireplace. This furniture had been spared being slashed with a knife, probably because Callum and Raine had interrupted his little vandalism party.

"You two are friends?" Raine glanced back and forth between them.

The detective laughed. "I guess you could say that. I married his sister. And we were partners in homicide for three years."

"More like partners in crime," Callum teased.

Raine frowned. "I don't understand."

Danny waved toward Callum. "In spite of being one of the best detectives we've ever had, Callum decided to take an undercover gig for almost a year to help bring down a crime ring in Athens. He dragged me into it and we were badass fake criminals. Pardon my language, ma'am."

She smiled. "No worries. I've heard far worse, probably said it too."

He laughed, then sobered and motioned toward the destruction around them. "It's a shame someone broke in and did all this damage. Looks like a nice place. I know you told me you didn't get a good look at the perpetrator. What about you, Callum? Can you give me a description? I'll put out a BOLO."

"BOLO?" Raine asked.

"Be on the lookout," Callum explained. "Old cop shows used to say APB, all-points bulletin. Same thing. Just tells law enforcement to keep an eye out for someone. Five-eight, slim build, maybe a hundred seventy pounds. Dressed all in black, including his shoes, gloves and knit hat pulled down low around his neck and over his ears. I only managed a glimpse of his profile, not a straight-on look at him. He's white, dark brown hair sticking out of the bottom of his hat, could be anywhere from midtwenties to late thirties. It's not much, I know."

Raine blinked. "It's a lot more than I got. All I could tell Detective Cooper was that he was dressed like a ninja."

Danny chuckled. "Told you Callum was one of the best. Still is, I imagine. Working for that cold case company now. Ms. Quintero said you're helping with her brother's case."

"Looking into it, yes. Turns out, it's one I gophered on years ago, for Farley."

The detective winced. "I didn't wish the guy dead, but can't say I miss working with him."

"Raine believes he pressured her brother into a false confession."

Danny's brows raised in surprise. "Well, now. He was unorthodox, tough. But I've never heard anyone accuse him of that before. Got any proof?"

Callum intervened. "I've been in touch with a professor in the criminal justice studies program at the University of Georgia, in Athens. She's studying the interview report on Joey so she can offer an opinion on whether it could have been a false confession." Raine looked at him in surprise and he realized he'd never gotten around to telling her about the professor. "She's an expert in the field. When our liaison called for the files on the case, she wasn't able to get any recordings of Mr. Quintero's interviews, said Farley apparently never recorded them. You worked with him more than I did, and more recently. Was that unusual for him?"

"Good question. I know he griped about modern technology because he wasn't good with it." His mouth quirked. "Kind of like someone else I know."

"Whatever. Does that mean he avoided it?"

Danny nodded. "When he could get away with it. Honestly, it wouldn't surprise me if a lot of his interviews were done the old-fashioned way, pen and paper, no audio or video. It doesn't mean anything improper was going on. But I can look into it, let you know what I find, see if there was any kind of suspicious pattern to his interrogations."

"I'd appreciate it. We're in a hurry too."

Danny glanced at Raine, a sympathetic look on his face. "Understood. I'll get back to you as soon as I can. I'll focus on trying to find a pattern in the cases around the same time period as Mr. Quintero's. But I have to work this scene first and file my report."

He picked up a computer tablet he must have left on a side table earlier. "Ms. Quintero gave me her version of what happened while you were chasing the suspect. Let's hear it from your point of view, Callum."

Danny was just as thorough as Callum remembered him being when they'd worked together. While Raine was sent to inventory the home and determine if anything was actually taken, instead of just destroyed, Danny grilled Callum on every detail of Callum's search of the home. By the time he started in on the details of his chase through the woods, Raine had already reported back that nothing was taken and was sitting on the couch with him again.

Danny shifted in his chair across from them. "All right. Let's see if there's anything else I need to add, another wrinkle that might tell me whether this is some nut or a drunk college frat boy out vandalizing homes, or something more."

Raine's eyes widened. "What do you mean, something more?"

"It seems awfully coincidental that you two are in town working on a murder case and your house gets broken into. Maybe the bad guy came here looking for your notes to see what you might have found out, and got mad and tore the place up when he didn't find any."

She went pale and twisted her hands in her lap. "Then it's a good thing my computer isn't here. Or my printed-out files."

"Hold on," Callum said. "Going down that path assumes someone would have a reason to worry about the investigation. It was resolved in the courts and we've yet to find evidence of anyone else being involved in Ms. Claremont's murder."

Raine's eyes flashed with anger. "I told you, Joey's innocent. It makes perfect sense that the real murderer would be worried about me digging into his case."

Danny held up his hands. "Hang on. You two want to argue, do it on your time. I'm just getting the background here so I cover every possibility. Callum, you mentioned earlier that you and Ms. Quintero had just come back from speaking to the Claremonts about what happened when their daughter was killed."

"More like I wanted firsthand knowledge of the crime scene's layout, the neighborhood and geography around it. I wasn't going to bother the parents of the deceased unless or until I felt it was absolutely necessary. However, since Raine has a close friendship with the deceased's parents, we took advantage of that and were able to tour their home. A few hours later, we came back here to review the case and make our plans for what to do tomorrow."

"And once you arrived, you opened the door and found that the home had been ransacked."

"Exactly."

"But nothing was stolen. Seems odd that someone would have done so much damage without stealing anything." He motioned to the broken side table, papers scattered on the floor, the shredded pillows strewed around. "There's emotion here, anger. And it seems to be directed at you, Ms. Quintero. You told me earlier that you don't know anyone who'd want to hurt you. Regardless of whether or not your brother is guilty, is there anything you've done, perhaps before Callum was involved in the case, that could have made someone feel threatened, or angry? Something related to the case you're working?"

She stared at him, her brow furrowed. "I honestly don't know. It's not like we've spoken to anyone today except my brother at the prison, and the Claremonts. No one else knew we were coming to town today. My brother's lawyers have been interviewing people off and on in town recently. And I was asking questions around town too, but that was weeks ago. I suppose Randy Hagen could have heard about all that and wanted to punish me by breaking in and tearing things up. He lied under oath in the trial against my brother. For all I know, he may be the one who killed Alicia Claremont."

Callum exchanged a pained look with Danny. "You can look into him if you want. But he had an alibi during the time when Alicia was attacked. I can't see him having a motive to vandalize Raine's property."

"Maybe you should look into his alibi," Raine insisted.

Danny glanced back and forth between them, looking puzzled. "Alibi for the break-in or the murder fifteen years ago?"

"Break-in," Callum said.

"Murder," Raine said, at the same time. She glanced at Callum, her aggravation dissolving into a look of guilt. "There are other cases I've been looking into. Perhaps this is related to those. We came here tonight so I could tell Callum that—"

Callum stood, interrupting her. "We're wasting Danny's time. He doesn't need all the details about the other cases UB is investigating."

Danny stood, looking relieved. "I'll put out a BOLO specifically for Hagen as well as one on our unknown intruder. They could be one and the same, but if not, we're covered. I'll send a press release to the media too, get an alert out on the news. If Hagen is around, someone should see him and turn him in. And if he's the intruder, we'll kill two birds with one stone. Callum, if something comes up in this other investigation you're working and you think it could shed light on another suspect—"

"I'll absolutely reach out."

"Good enough for me. It's getting late and I have a report to type up."

Raine looked ready to burst with things she wanted to tell the detective. Callum put his arm around her shoulders, pulling her close. Danny's brows raised, no doubt thinking something was going on between them. Callum didn't care. It did the trick. It flustered Raine and made her go silent. She was staring up at him in surprise, no doubt trying to figure out how she'd given him the wrong signal somewhere along the way.

Danny looked around, as if searching for the crime scene tech.

"He's gone," Callum told him. "Took some latent prints from the French doors and the stairs while we were talking and left."

Raine finally looked at Danny again, a new mystery gathering her attention. "Why did he look for fingerprints? Callum said the guy was wearing gloves."

"Standard procedure," Danny explained. "Sometimes a criminal won't put gloves on outside a place. They don't want someone seeing the gloves and becoming suspicious enough to call the police. Once inside, they put gloves on and plan on wiping down the front door on their way out. But Callum sent our guy fleeing, so he might not have had a chance to wipe any prints away. We may luck out and get an ID."

He glanced around, as if looking for the other policemen and women. But he was the only one there now.

"Son of a... They all left me. Again."

Callum laughed. "You always were one of the last at any scene."

Danny grinned. "Guess not much has changed since we worked together. Callum, once your current investigation is wrapped up, maybe you can stop by the house for dinner. I enjoy watching the games with you at your place. But it'd be nice to host you at our house every once in a while. It would be great to have you and Lucy together again. She misses you."

Callum kept smiling, but it wasn't easy. "Lucy doesn't miss me, Danny. Neither does anyone else in my family. They haven't for many, many years. But I appreciate you lying just the same. Don't forget to look into Farley's records when you can."

Danny shook his head, but didn't argue or deny the truth. "Will do. Ms. Quintero, I'm sorry about what happened to your beautiful home. Athens PD will do everything we can to catch the bad guy. And for tonight, at least, my boss has approved having a couple of patrol cars canvassing the neighborhood, for added security."

"Thank you. I appreciate it."

Danny gave Callum a two-fingered salute and headed toward the foyer.

As soon as the door closed behind Danny, Raine threw Callum's arm off her shoulder and turned to face him. "Explain to me why you kept interrupting me when I was trying to tell Detective Cooper about my work on the serial killer investigation, information that could be related to the break-in."

"It's not."

"How would you know?"

"I'll explain, after you explain something to me. Where the hell did you get another gun? And where did you hide it so the police wouldn't find it, since my brother-in-law failed to mention anything about it?"

Chapter Fourteen

Raine poked him in the chest. Callum could tell she wasn't the least bit intimidated. Damn she was sexy when she was angry.

She poked him again to emphasize her words as she spoke. "When were you going to tell me you had a false-confession expert lined up for us to talk to? We're supposed to be partners on this case. I'm the one who hired you, not the other way around."

"Is that what you call it when you kidnap someone? Hiring them?"

"Why throw that in my face again? I thought we were way past that."

He shrugged. "Maybe I enjoy riling you up. Stop trying to distract me. Where'd you get the gun? And where is it now?"

"And here I thought you were an investigator."

"It was Faith, wasn't it? She gave it back to you."

Her eyes widened and her face turned a light pink.

He couldn't help but grin. "I love that you blush so easily. You look good with some color in your cheeks. And it's a dead giveaway, a tell. I always know when you're covering something up."

"So you think," she grumbled.

"What? I'm not sure I heard that."

She cleared her throat. "Don't blame Faith for giving me back my gun. I bought it for protection and wanted it with me in case we have to go into sketchy areas while investigating."

"Don't worry. I won't lambast her for it. She'd just give me a lecture about women's rights until I begged for mercy and forgot why I was mad in the first place."

"I'm liking Faith more and more. As to where I put the gun, I'm not telling. You'll only take it away again."

"Damn straight. I don't want to wake up with it in my face."

"I would never. I mean, not now anyway."

He rolled his eyes. "Good to know."

"You're impossible," she complained. "You never think I can take care of myself. I'll bet the real reason you didn't catch the jerk who broke in is because you were worried about me being here all by my lonesome, unprotected."

"Why would you think that?"

"Look at you. You're in excellent shape. I can't imagine some punk getting away if you were running after him."

"You think I'm in excellent shape, huh?"

"Yeah, well. Don't let it go to your head. It was just a… biological observation. Nothing personal."

He laughed. "Can't say I've heard that one before. I'm going to take it as a compliment." He winked.

She blinked, obviously not sure what to make of that wink. It was so easy to fluster her. He'd probably start doing it more often, just for fun.

She let out a slow deep breath, as if praying for patience. Then she looked up at him, her hands twisting together.

Uh-oh.

"Callum?"

"Raine?"

She sighed. "I told you, when we left the Claremonts, that I had a secret to confess. With everything that happened tonight, I never got the chance. But I can't live with myself if I let one more day go by without telling you the truth."

"Because another woman could die? I think that's what you said earlier."

"Yes. Exactly. And don't take that tone with me."

"What tone?"

"Like you're not taking me seriously. This is important."

"Then I suppose I'd better sit down." He reclined back on the couch. "Nice sofa by the way. This leather is crazy soft."

"Be serious."

"I'm always serious about leather."

She plopped down beside him. "I mean it."

"So do I. Leather is—"

She grabbed his left hand in both of hers. "Pay attention."

The feel of her soft hands holding his had his entire body paying attention. But not in the way she was thinking. As she rattled on about research and files and saving her brother, he pondered when he'd crossed the line from being downright irritated with her and wanting her gone, to being enthralled by the way her hands felt, and how silky her hair looked, and how soft and curvy she was.

Damn. And she was a lawyer to boot.

"Are you listening to me, Callum? Did you hear what I said? Pete Scoggin isn't the serial killer. He's got a criminal record, yes. A friend of mine at the courthouse helped me look up old cases similar to my brother's and his name came up as a suspect in one of them. I included that with the other cases I found and purposely skewed everything to make it look like he could be the real killer. Don't you see? I was desperate, trying to create some kind of carrot to dangle in front of you to convince you to help my brother. I was hoping you'd look into that angle later, after helping me. And by then I could tell you the truth so you didn't waste any time on Scoggin. But you said your team was switching gears, looking at the information I gave you instead of what they were researching before I came along. And that's been scaring me. I'm terrified that looking into the wrong information will allow the real killer time to select another victim. I tried to tell that to Detective Cooper but you stopped me."

Her gaze searched his and she squeezed his hand. "Callum? Why are you looking at me like that?"

"Like what?"

"Like you're…amused. Or something. You should be angry."

"Why would I be angry with you?"

She pulled her hands back and fisted them beside her. "Did you hear anything I just said?"

"Maybe not everything. But I heard most of it."

She stared at him, as if waiting. When he didn't react, she smacked the seat cushion beside her leg. "If that's true, you should be horrified."

He smiled.

Her eyes narrowed. "Why aren't you horrified, Callum? You don't even seem surprised."

"I'm not. You're a lawyer."

She blinked. "And?"

"You're a lawyer who held me at gunpoint and handcuffed me to a chair, not in a good way either."

Her eyes widened.

He decided to take mercy on her. "Look, I wasn't going to take anything you gave me at face value. Asher thought your files seemed golden, that they'd really help. And I'll admit I was hoping they would. But we couldn't risk our entire investigation on your veracity, not until we could prove, or disprove, the information you provided."

"I don't... I don't understand. You told me everyone was focusing on the files that I turned over. I thought you had stopped your original investigation and were relying entirely on my data. That's why I was worried the killer would hurt someone else because you diverted resources."

"We didn't divert resources. I spoke to my boss and he agreed to add additional investigators to the case so we could look into the new info while continuing with our existing info at the same time."

"You mean, so what happened is, I didn't put anyone in danger by sending you off on a wild-goose chase?"

"Nope."

"You lied."

He arched a brow. "So did you."

She pressed a hand to her brow as if she had a headache. "When, exactly, did you discover my secret, that my information was bogus?"

"It wasn't entirely bogus. You did a lot of good research. You just...extrapolated and exaggerated some of it. As to *when* I realized that? It was the first day, when you were in the hospital. I sat in your room in the ER and did some cross-checking on those new murders you told us about. Asher did the same. We have access to a lot of databases that you don't. It wasn't hard to figure out."

"Are you...are you saying you've been leading me along

all this time? I've been dying inside, worried about what I'd done." She stared at him, her green eyes flashing with anger.

"Don't go all sanctimonious on me now. You lied to get what you wanted and I lied because I don't trust lawyers, or criminals, of which you were both. I didn't trust you, don't trust you. And all you've done is proven that I'm right not to do so."

The hurt look in her eyes before she glanced away had him feeling like a heel. He'd answered her questions, but he should have been more delicate in how he'd phrased those answers. Hurting her was never his plan.

"Look, Raine. I didn't mean to—"

"I'll deal with the mess down here later. I'm going upstairs to get a shower. There's a guest room under the stairs that the intruder didn't trash. There are extra linens in the closet, fresh pillows. The kitchen should be well stocked too, except the milk is likely bad now. But the freezer's full. There's also beer, wine, bottled water—"

"Raine. Look at me."

She briefly squeezed her eyes shut, then looked up at him. "Yes?"

"When I said all of that, I was—" His phone buzzed in his pocket. He frowned and pressed the button to silence it without looking at it. "I was answering your questions. But when I did, I should have—" His phone buzzed again. He swore and pulled it out of his pocket to check the screen. It was a text from Asher, with only three characters. 911. He swore again. "I'm sorry, Raine. I have to take this."

"Of course you do. After all, I'm just a lawyer. I'm not even worth your time." She headed toward the stairs.

"Raine, wait."

She jogged up the stairs and disappeared. A moment later, a door slammed overhead.

He started after her, but his phone buzzed again. He stopped and pressed the button to take the call.

"Asher, this had better be a real emergency and not one of your pranks."

"Where are you right now?"

Callum stiffened, his friend's tone telling him this wasn't a joke. "At Raine's house. In Athens. Why?"

"She's there with you?"

"Yes. Her house was broken into. The police just left and she's gone upstairs to take a shower."

"Broken into? Did they catch the guy? I'm assuming you're both okay or you'd have said something."

"We're fine. They haven't caught the guy. Not yet. What's going on? What's the emergency?"

"Remember the name Raine gave us, the guy she said could be the serial killer?"

"Pete Scoggin. But we already determined he had alibis for the killings."

"Most. Not all. There was one we couldn't alibi him out of, so Faith and I did our due diligence just to feel confident that we could mark him off our suspect list. She couldn't prove that he was in that one victim's vicinity during the time of the attack. But she couldn't disprove it either. We've found several links between him and the victim that Raine didn't come close to finding. They were neighbors once, like Raine said. But she didn't know about all of the complaints we found in city hall that the victim made against him. She reported alleged code violations on his property, called animal control because he'd leave his dog chained up without food and water in the backyard, things like that.

There were calls to the police too. Noise complaints, vandalism she believed he'd done to her place, that sort of thing."

"Vandalism?" A chill went up his spine as he glanced up the stairs. He headed to the front door to make sure it was locked. Then he checked the back doors too.

"There was other stuff, problems between him, the victim, and other people too," Asher continued. "Sounds like he was that nightmare neighbor who bullied everyone on the street. But the victim was the only one who ever really stood up to him."

"Did the police list him as a suspect in her murder? Sounds like they at least should have interviewed him."

"Nope. The victim moved months before her death. Supposedly it was for a job opportunity. That's what she told her friends. But Faith and I are thinking—"

"It was to get away from her obnoxious neighbor."

"Bingo. We think maybe he threatened her and she realized she was in trouble. So she made a plan to get out of there. But he wasn't about to let her get away, not after all the fines the city imposed on him, and the police calls. Everything we've found on this guy supports him as a hothead who never let a perceived insult go unanswered. I've asked our law enforcement liaison to work with the police to get a subpoena for cell tower records. We need to prove whether he was near the victim's new home at the time of her murder. That'll take days. But we know for sure he wasn't at his house during that time. His whereabouts were unknown. He called in sick to work but his neighbors never saw him. And it sounds like they all kept tabs on him because they were afraid."

"Bottom line it for me, Asher."

"We believe this murder was the one that Raine used as

her basis to build phony links to the other murders, as we've already figured out. I don't think she realized she may have actually stumbled onto a real killer. And it's sure looking as if she did."

"She performed surveillance on him," Callum said. "I remember reading that in the file."

"She did. Because of that, once Faith found the additional info early this morning, we sent a local PI to keep an eye on Scoggin. We want to make sure we know where he is at all times, just in case he saw Raine at any time and figured out who she was. If he thinks the cops are on to him—"

"He may blame her, or want to eliminate her as a potential witness. You said the PI is watching him?"

"He was. But Scoggin made him. He realized he had a tail and lost our guy. He's in the wind."

Callum's hand tightened around the phone. "What's his last known address?"

"Athens."

Callum drew his gun and sprinted for the stairs.

Chapter Fifteen

Raine shut off the shower and squeezed her hair to wring out the excess water. The bathroom door flew open. She gasped and jerked back as Callum ran inside. Gun in hand, pointed at the floor, he barely glanced at her and ran to the closet at the other end of the bathroom.

She grabbed the towel hanging over the top of the glass door and threw it around her, covering up just as he emerged. He'd put his gun away and was on the phone now.

"What's going on?" She stepped out of the shower onto the bath rug, clutching the towel against her body.

"It's okay," he silently mouthed, still on the phone. A second later, he was gone, the door closing behind him.

She should have been angry at the invasion of her privacy. But it was obvious that something was wrong. He'd come in here to make sure she was okay, and that no one else was with her. That much was obvious. What wasn't obvious was *why*. Why would he think someone else was up here? And who was he speaking to on the phone?

She hurriedly towel-dried her hair, not bothering with makeup. After throwing on a pair of jeans and a dark blue blouse, she stepped into her bedroom.

The first thing she noticed was that Callum was standing by one of the windows, peering through the plantation shutters toward the street out front. The second was that the wooden chair that normally sat at her reading desk was propped under the door handle on her bedroom door. No one was getting in, or out.

"Callum, good grief. What's going on? Why did you barge into the bathroom while I was naked, with your gun out?"

He flipped the shutters closed and walked over to her, his jaw set, worry lines creasing his brow. "To my credit, I did knock before going into the bathroom. And I called out your name, twice. You didn't answer."

"Yes, well, my head was probably under the water at the time. I didn't hear you."

"You've seen Pete Scoggin before. Describe him to me."

"Scoggin? What? Why?"

"Please."

She sighed. "Of course I've seen him. I performed surveillance on him. But I told you he had nothing to do with the murder cases I presented to you. It was all a fabrication to get your help."

"Not entirely." He leaned against the thick cherrywood post of her footboard. "You fabricated the alleged connection between Scoggin and the other murders you had in your files, presenting him as the serial killer we were searching for. But you were more right about him than you realized. It looks like he may very well have killed the first victim you looked into."

She pressed a hand to her chest. "Nancy Piraino? That was a guess more than anything, that he should be a suspect in her death. You really think he could be the one who murdered her?"

"It's looking that way. Faith and Asher dug into his background, and the victim's—"

"Nancy."

"Nancy. No one else in her life even remotely seems to have any reason to want to hurt her. Scoggin is the only one we've been able to find with both motive and opportunity."

She glanced at the chair under the door, her throat tightening. "And you think, what, that he's the one who broke into my home and tore it up? And that he might have gotten back in somehow?"

"The police are the ones who cleared the upstairs after I lost the suspect in the woods. Once I realized that the surveillance on Scoggin lost him, I had to make sure he hadn't managed to double back and sneak into the house again during the chaos."

She shivered and wrapped her arms around her waist. "Why would he come after me? Because he blames me for, what? Telling Unfinished Business about him? How would he even know I did that?"

"Not UB specifically. But you were watching him for a while. He may have noticed, took down your license plate number at some point, figured out who you were. We put out feelers to the police about him the same day we got your files. The police interviewed him that day, but had nothing to hold him on so they didn't arrest him. Now he's gone missing. No one knows where he is. He'd done some vandalism to Nancy's home at one point. I don't like that coincidence considering someone broke into your home and did the same. I haven't seen a picture of him yet. Can you describe him?"

She shrugged. "Nothing that really stands out. Shorter than you by several inches, probably about five-eight, five-nine. He wasn't heavy, average build I guess. Maybe even on the skinny side. Dark hair…" She drew a sharp breath. "I'm describing the same man we saw tonight."

He nodded. "You are." He pulled out his phone again and thumbed through some pictures, then held it up toward her. "Recognize this guy?"

"No, I… Wait. He's older, a little heavier, though not by much. Randy Hagen?"

"That's his most recent mug shot, from his latest drug arrest. Based on what you just said, he could be a double for Scoggin. Which means the guy I chased into the woods could be either one of them. If Hagen knows you've been nosing around and throwing his name into the mix to try to free your brother, he could have decided to try to scare you. I'm sure he wouldn't appreciate being labeled as a potential suspect, or accused of committing perjury at your brother's trial if it means he could get in trouble."

"He wouldn't be wrong. He could definitely get in trouble." She climbed onto the foot of the bed and sat a few feet away from where he was leaning. "If he was proven to have perjured himself at trial, it wouldn't matter that the statute of limitations on perjury is only a few years. Here in Georgia, the clock doesn't start ticking on the limitations until the offense has been discovered. That means he could still be tried. And if convicted, since his false testimony sent someone to death row, he'd receive an automatic life sentence."

He whistled. "That's a hell of an incentive to want to keep you from talking to the police."

A sickening feeling shot through her, as if she'd just plunged down a steep incline. "Is he… Is either Scoggin or Hagen—"

"In the house? I don't believe so. But with you out of

my sight up here, I had to make sure you were okay first. I didn't get a chance to search the whole house yet. We're not staying anyway, not with two men potentially close by with motives to want to hurt you."

"Not staying? You really think I'm in danger?"

"I'd rather overreact than assume you're safe here and be proven wrong. Your address is public knowledge. A simple internet search would find you. Someone already did."

She shivered and rubbed her arms. "Where can we go then? A hotel?"

"I want you somewhere safer than that, somewhere not out in public or easily found through an internet records search."

"Where would that be?"

Red and blue lights flashed across the shutters covering the windows.

He went to the nearest one and peered out. "I called Danny, Detective Cooper. He's going to put out a BOLO on Scoggin too, across Georgia and Tennessee, specifically for being wanted in connection with the murder of Nancy Piraino. It will be broadcast all over the media. We'll find him. I also asked Danny to send over one of the patrol officers he'd asked to watch the neighborhood. They're going to escort us, follow my SUV to make sure no one else follows us. We're going to a house where you'll be safe."

He crossed to the door, then moved the chair out from under the doorknob. "I'll let him know you'll be down in a few minutes. Pack a bag. We'll leave as soon as you're ready."

"Callum, wait. Where are we going? What house are you talking about where you think I'll be safe?"

He paused in the doorway and looked back at her. "Mine."

Chapter Sixteen

They headed east on State Road 78, which Raine knew better as Lexington Road. Behind them, the police car followed, keeping an eye out to ensure that no one else followed them. Not long after passing the airport, Lexington became Athens Road, but still Callum showed no signs of slowing or making any turns.

"You said I should go someplace where no one would know to look," she said. "If someone, say Hagen, hears that we were asking questions around town, he might know to look for your place in case I went there with you."

"Good thinking, counselor. But the property deed, even the utilities, aren't registered under my name. They're under a maze of shell corporations. I did that back when I received some threats as a detective with ACCPD. I didn't want any bad guys I'd put away to find out where I lived. When I moved to Gatlinburg, I did the same there. Neither home will come back to me unless someone does an incredible amount of digging. And even then, when they pull records to figure out who's behind each corporation, I'd find out. I bribed a city clerk to flag my file so that if anyone ever requested the information, I'd be notified."

"That explains why I never could find your address when I was internet stalking you."

He grinned. "Good to know my precautions worked."

"The curiosity is killing me. How much farther is this shell-corporation-owned place?"

"Another ten minutes or so. It was an aggravatingly long drive to and from work back in the day. Now that I live in Gatlinburg, I rarely make it out here. The last time was months ago, when I took a handful of days off between cases."

"Must be an awfully nice place to have made your long commute worth it, and to keep it even after you moved to Tennessee."

He smiled. "Emphasis on *awful*. The house is small and plain, nothing to brag about. It's the property that's nice. A wooded oasis not too far from city amenities but isolated enough so that no one knows your business. It was my grandfather's, on my dad's side of the family. He willed it to me when he passed away. I'd just turned eighteen."

"Eighteen, wow. Young to become a landowner. You keep it for sentimental reasons?"

"More like I keep it to tick off my family. They were furious that Granddad willed it to me instead of my dad. My parents and siblings tried to get me to sell it and split the proceeds. I refused, on principle mostly. My grandfather didn't want it sold. If my dad had planned on keeping it, I'd have signed it right over. But all he wanted to do was sell to a developer to split into parcels and build a subdivision." He glanced at her. "That family tension went on for years, getting worse over time. Family gatherings were a study in walking on eggshells to avoid arguments. After a particularly uncomfortable visit, with everyone again trying to get me to sell and me refusing, my family decided I was being greedy and pretty much shunned me. That was five years ago."

"That's truly awful. Is there a reason they were so pushy about your property? Like maybe they were hurting for money and wanted the proceeds?"

"If that was the case, I'd have sold immediately. No one in my family is wealthy. But we're not hurting by any means. All of us have good-paying jobs. And my parents made enough after selling their small chain of office-supply stores to a big-box retailer to retire early."

"I'm so sorry they treated you like that. Possessions should never come between people who are supposed to love each other."

"Don't be sorry. I get along fine on my own."

"You shouldn't have to though. As your family, they should love you unconditionally."

His Adam's apple bobbed in his throat but he didn't reply.

The flash of pain she'd seen in his eyes told her far more than his flippant words and matter-of-fact demeanor. Unable to resist the impulse, she put her left hand over his right hand that was resting on the console between them.

His gaze shot to hers in surprise. Then he surprised *her* by turning his hand palm up and threading their fingers together.

"Thanks, Raine." His deep voice sent a warm thrill up her spine as his hand tightened on hers. "If anyone knows about loyalty and unconditional love, it's you. That's one of the things I admire about you."

She blinked. "You admire me? The woman who held you at gunpoint?"

He laughed, the stress lines in his brow easing. "Not the

most auspicious of first-meets, for sure. But I get it now. I understand why you did it. And the fact that you did, knowing the gun wasn't loaded and putting your own life at risk to make sure you didn't hurt an innocent person, well, that's far more telling about your character than anything else. You're a good person, Raine Quintero. Even if you are a lawyer."

She rolled her eyes and tugged her hand free, more because she was tempted to scoot closer than because she was upset. "I'm not sure if that was a compliment or an insult."

"A little of both. My apologies." He winked.

Her face warmed and she blew out a shaky breath. Callum was a charmer. If she wasn't careful, she was going to fall for the cop partly responsible for her brother being in prison—on death row, no less. That wasn't family loyalty. That was the complete opposite. Her brother would be ashamed of her, and hurt. Which had a world of guilt crashing down on her. Here he was, counting down the few remaining days of his life in a six-by-nine cell, and she was flirting instead of working to free him. She kind of hated herself in that moment.

"What's the plan now?" she asked. "Once we get to your place."

He gave her a questioning look, no doubt wondering at her sudden mood change. But he took it in stride, casually moving the hand that had held hers onto the steering wheel as he drove them farther away from town.

"First, I'll put in an order to a delivery service to drop off some groceries, come morning. I've got a refrigerator in the carport where they can put it if we're not there when they arrive. For tonight, we'll survive on whatever I've got in the freezer."

"I meant what are we going to do next to help my brother.

It's getting late. I know we can't do much more tonight. But you work cold cases all the time. You must have some kind of game plan for approaching them aside from visiting the crime scene."

He put on his left blinker and slowed to a stop, waiting for the headlights of an oncoming car to pass and rolling down his window. As soon as the car went by, he turned left onto a narrow dirt-and-gravel road surrounded by thick trees illuminated by his headlights. He waved out the window. Raine looked over her shoulder to see the cop car turning around in the middle of the road. Then he headed back toward town.

"The policeman isn't coming with us down this street?" she asked.

"No need. It's my driveway."

She straightened in surprise and looked around—or tried. It was too dark to see much. The tree branches overhead blocked out the moonlight. And there weren't any spotlights anywhere on the property.

Until he made one last turn.

"Oh, wow," she breathed.

He chuckled. "And now you see why my grandfather loved this place so much."

He pulled to a stop about twenty yards from the small white concrete block ranch home that sat off to their right. Raine barely spared it a glance. What had her attention was the play of landscaping lights all across the yard, both front and back. Except that it wasn't so much a yard as manicured land with gorgeous groupings of ornamental trees and plants, illuminated by sparkling white lights.

Woven amongst the plantings was a stone walkway that went all the way to the sparkling water beyond. The pond didn't seem to be very large, although in the daylight it might be bigger than she thought. A fountain splashed in the middle, lit by a ring of floating spotlights. And a short dock that looked more suited to sitting and relaxing than launching any kind of small boat stuck out just a few short yards into the water, with ornamental lamp posts on each end.

"It's incredible. Beautiful. I'll bet you sit on that dock for hours when you come up here. It's a perfect reading spot."

"I hadn't thought of that before. Reading isn't something I get much time to do outside of work. But it's a great place to fish, or just unwind, drink a beer and pretend the rest of the world doesn't exist."

"How does it stay this nice? You said you don't get up here much."

"Not enough to keep up the property, for sure. It costs a small fortune to have a landscaping company maintain it. But every time I think about stopping the expense, letting nature take over, I remember my grandma out here on her hands and knees tending to all the beds. She and Granddad planted almost every plant, every bush, every tree out here. I helped weed and water and clear areas for new beddings more times than I can count. Letting it go feels like, I don't know, like letting *them* go I suppose. Seems silly, but—"

"Not at all. You honor them and their memory by keeping this place up. It's a living memorial to their lives and their love for you. Destroying this, mowing it all down to build cookie-cutter homes, would be a travesty. Your family doesn't deserve this property if they can't appreciate it."

When it finally dawned on her that he'd been silent for some time, she tore her gaze away from the fantasyland outside the windows and found him intently watching her. Under the light of the moon, the dash and the twinkling landscape lights in the distance, everything suddenly seemed...magical, full of possibilities. The stress, the unknowns, her worries about the investigation faded away as he slowly unclipped his seat belt, all while capturing her gaze with his.

Somehow, she managed to unbuckle hers as well, and then they were in each other's arms. Like the magician she now knew him to be, he wrapped her in an achingly sweet embrace and pressed his lips to hers. Briefly, far too briefly. But oh so wonderful. Then his lips moved to the column of her throat, making her gasp from the heat.

He groaned deep in his throat and half turned, pressing her against the back of the seat. This time, when his lips captured hers, there was nothing brief about it. He took his time, making love to her mouth with his, caressing, stroking, giving and taking until she wanted to weep from the beauty of it.

When he finally pulled back, he gently stroked her hair, moving her bangs back from her eyes.

"That was...beautiful," she whispered. "I've never been kissed like that before."

"That's a shame," he whispered back. "You should be kissed like that thoroughly, and often. Treasured and cherished."

"Careful. You may be ruining me for others."

He smiled, his warm hands blazing a trail down the sides of her face to her neck, her shoulders. "Is that what I'm doing? Ruining you for others?" He pressed a tender kiss against her collarbone.

She shivered. "What others?"

He chuckled, his hot breath making her shiver again before he pulled back. "Sadly, we have to stop, or I'm going to make love to you right here in the cab of my SUV. And you deserve much better than that. Let's get inside the house."

He drove into the carport, and just like that, the brain cells that had deserted Raine came rushing back. Make love? What the heck was she thinking to even want him to do that? Because she did. She wanted him, more than she'd ever wanted anyone. And she didn't understand it. Yes, he was handsome, incredibly so. And strong, and gentle, and smart, and...and he was the investigator working her brother's case. No matter how much she longed to be in his arms, that had to take a back seat to what truly mattered.

Saving Joey's life.

Her door opened and Callum was standing there holding the bag she'd packed, his smile fading as he watched her grab her purse.

"The moment's gone, isn't it?" His tone dripped with regret. "I gave you too much time to think."

"It's a good thing you did. We have to stay focused on what matters."

He stared at her a long moment, then nodded as if coming to some kind of understanding. "What matters. Absolutely. I should have known better. It won't happen again."

As he started to turn away, she tossed her purse to the floor and grabbed his hand. "Callum, wait."

He turned around, his brows arched in question. She reached for him and pulled him closer, then framed his face with her hands. She pressed a whisper-soft kiss against his lips, then stared up into his eyes. "I'm sorry. I didn't mean that the way it sounded. What we just did, who you are, matters. But it's so unexpected, surprising, because we barely know each other. And I'm not sure how to even deal with this...thing that's happening between us right now.

I'm struggling just to hold myself together, knowing that my brother is going to die in a matter of days if I don't pull some kind of miracle out of my hat. I need to focus on that right now, instead of losing myself in you, even though I so desperately want to. I'm not making much sense, I know, but can you understand that? A little? You do matter, Callum. You matter a great deal to me. Somehow. Impossibly, in such a short time. But there it is. Truth."

He smiled as he gently pushed her hair back again. "You're full of surprises, Raine Quintero. And I do understand what you're saying. Leave it to the lawyer to make a strong argument. But I don't agree with the premise. I think you can mix business and pleasure. And I've learned that sometimes *not* thinking about a problem a hundred percent of the time helps me focus better when I come back to that problem."

"Are you arguing that making love will help us focus better, Callum?"

His smile broadened. "Would it get you into my bed if I were?"

She laughed. "No. We have work to do. And no time to waste." She held up a hand. "Not waste. Time to spend on other things that are no doubt pleasurable—"

"Hot, wonderful, mind-blowing—"

She laughed. "We need to work on this lack of confidence of yours."

"I'm at your service, whenever you're ready."

"Good grief." She fanned herself. "You're incorrigible."

"And stopping, right now. I'm honestly not trying to change your mind. I respect your decision. Let's get inside and I'll answer your earlier question."

He headed to the side door and fit his key in the lock.

She grabbed her purse and hurried after him as the door swung open. "My earlier question?"

"You wanted to know my plans for solving your brother's cold case."

She blinked. "Right. Your plans. See what I mean? You distracted me."

"The pleasure was all mine, I assure you. But I'll try to be good from here on out."

She shook her head in exasperation. This man was a rascal, irresistible. He kept saying she was a surprise. Well, he was even more of a surprise to her. Not at all what she'd expected. He was rapidly becoming everything she never realized she wanted. But if she gave in to her longings now, and they couldn't save her brother, would she ever be able to forgive herself? Or him? That wasn't the kind of guilt she wanted to contemplate. Which meant any kind of a relationship between her and Callum wasn't possible, not now. And depending on what happened to Joey, maybe not ever.

Chapter Seventeen

Raine's request to know Callum's plans for pursuing her brother's case still had her head spinning the next afternoon as they headed to yet another appointment. What had surprised her the most as he went through the list of things being done in the investigation was that he had several people at his company, Unfinished Business, helping. She hadn't even realized that. She thought everyone was working other cases or the serial killer one. But apparently they approached all of their cases as a team, sharing resources as needed, especially with something as critical as trying to beat the ticking clock of an upcoming execution.

Team members had been validating information from the trial transcripts and police files. They'd been working on that since the moment she'd handed over her printed files and computer, even before she'd been released from the hospital.

UB had its own in-house lab. One of its analysts was reviewing the physical evidence from the case, or at least the inventory list of it in the police files. They were examining the reports on the forensic testing that had been done to see whether they felt other evidence should also be tested. Of course, if they wanted additional tests, there would have to be a strong argument to get the prosecution to even allow them access. And that kind of testing took time, time Joey didn't have. Raine wasn't holding out much hope on the forensics front. But she deeply appreciated them looking, just the same. Miracles happened. She only needed one.

Key witness testimony had been read and was being compared with written reports by the prosecution and defense. Callum had explained that was to ensure all discovery rules had been followed. If any evidence hadn't been properly turned over to the defense before trial, that could be used to argue that the trial was unfair. But, again, Raine doubted that strategy would result in anything. It was an obvious one that should have been found out years ago if discovery rules had been violated.

Her hopes really hinged on the interviews, both with witnesses who'd testified and others who hadn't. If someone recanted their testimony, or substantially changed it from what they'd originally said, that could be used to argue an unfair trial. It would be looked at as new evidence, which was what they desperately needed. She was really hoping that Callum or his peers could come up with new witnesses who could completely call Joey's guilt into doubt. The board couldn't ignore evidence like that. They would have to act, even if only to temporarily put a halt to the execution.

UB's investigators were also conducting searches on various law enforcement databases, looking for similar crimes much as she'd done, but with access to data she couldn't get.

Experts were being consulted on all kinds of things. And UB lawyers were looking into the appeals that had been done on Joey's behalf, searching for loopholes and opportunities that may have been previously overlooked.

And that was just what Raine could remember from last

night's discussion. At one point, she'd begged for mercy. And she'd apologized for even questioning him. Obviously, the UB investigators—especially Callum—knew what they were doing. Her worries that she and Callum weren't working hard enough to make a dent were completely unfounded. People were working the case around the clock. Dozens of avenues were being explored. But of course, even knowing that, she couldn't afford for her or Callum to slow down.

He was the boots on the ground, their expert in Athens. He was the one who could speak to people in person, push for an interview that may have been refused over the phone to someone at UB in Gatlinburg. What she and Callum did could result in the one little piece of information that would tip the board in their favor. They had to keep going. Which was why—after spending hours already today talking to witnesses—they were now on the campus of the University of Georgia.

Over half an hour earlier, an administrator had led them to a criminal justice studies waiting area outside the office of Professor Irena Kassin—expert on the phenomenon of false confessions. They had an appointment but the time had come and gone. Apparently the wheels of justice moved slowly even on a college campus.

Callum had already cautioned Raine not to get her hopes up with any of these interviews. But he'd especially warned her about this upcoming one. The idea that Joey's confession may have been coerced wasn't new. It was the basic argument in many of his lawyer's court proceedings over the years. For it to be argued again, successfully this time, they'd have to come up with some extremely compelling evidence.

So far, in spite of all of their hard work and the full resources of UB at their disposal, they had nothing. That was why, in spite of Callum's warnings, Raine was putting her hopes on this professor. Her credentials were impeccable. She'd not only written several books about false confessions, she'd conducted numerous scientific studies on it. And she'd testified in over fifty cases. What impressed Raine the most about that number was that she'd testified almost equally for the defense and the prosecution. Looking at her record, no one could accuse her of bias one way or the other. If she was convinced that Joey's confession was bogus, that had to carry weight with the prison board. It *had* to.

The door to Professor Kassin's office finally opened. A man in a dark-colored business suit came out, nodded at them and left. The young admin headed into the office. A moment later she emerged and motioned for them to go in.

Raine wasn't sure what she'd expected of a criminal justice professor with several books and nationally acclaimed studies on her résumé. But it certainly wasn't the fashion-forward beautiful brunette who greeted them. She seemed to smile more warmly at Callum, hold his hand perhaps a little longer than necessary as they exchanged pleasantries. It was all Raine could manage not to knock the woman's hand away. And wasn't that ridiculous? One kiss. She and Callum had shared one kiss. She shouldn't be feeling like she wanted to claw another woman's eyes out just because she smiled at him.

But dang it, she did.

Thankfully, her uncharacteristic jealousy quickly faded as the professor began to educate them about the science behind the study of false confessions. Instead, Raine became engrossed in the depth of Kassin's knowledge. And impressed that she'd spent several hours this morning preparing for their interview. She'd studied the police reports on Joey's alleged confession that UB had provided. And she'd also managed to read through parts of the trial transcript, at least the ones relevant to his interrogation. She must have spent half her day preparing to speak to them. That alone had Raine feeling guilty for her silly jealousy, and overwhelmingly grateful.

Kassin smiled from behind her desk. "I know I've thrown a lot at you in a short amount of time. The amount of information out there on the false-confession phenomenon can be overwhelming. I'll summarize some of the main points, and try to relate it back to Mr. Quintero's specific situation."

Behind her desk, she flipped through some notes on a yellow legal pad. She ran a long red fingernail across several items, then nodded as if to assure herself about what she'd written. Smiling again, she tapped the first bullet point and sat back in her chair.

"I'll try to frame things with some statistics. It should help to paint a better picture of what we've been discussing. The statistics come from cases where a conviction was overturned due to new evidence. This gives us a pool of cases to study where we know an innocent person was wrongly convicted. When we examine those wrongful convictions, we find that false confessions—where a suspect says they committed the crime even though they didn't—are the leading cause of those convictions in homicide cases. Shocking, isn't it?"

"Not to me," Raine said. "My brother is walking proof."

"I'll admit it's a surprise on my part," Callum said. "I've never heard it stated that way and honestly didn't expect it."

Kassin nodded. "It gets worse. When examining cases—not just homicides—that were overturned as a result of the work done by various innocence groups, we find that anywhere from twenty-five percent to sixty-six percent of them involved false confessions. Extrapolating that out, one can conclude that fifty thousand or more innocent people are in prison right now, just in this country alone, because they confessed to a crime they didn't commit. That is a staggeringly high amount. And it points to a major flaw in our judicial system."

Raine was stunned at the percentages the professor had just quoted.

Callum seemed equally surprised. He leaned forward in his chair and rested his elbows on his knees. "Assuming all of those figures you quoted are accurate—"

"They are," Kassin assured him.

He smiled. "What I can't understand is how it happens in the first place. No one could make me confess to something I didn't do, especially not murder."

"And that, Mr. Wright, is the problem. People don't understand how it can happen. Therefore, they automatically assume it doesn't. But since we can prove it does happen, with an alarming frequency, we need to understand how and why it occurs. And then we need to retrain law enforcement and prosecutors to recognize it and prevent it. Interrogation techniques at the very least need to change."

Callum sat back and crossed his arms. "If you're going to argue that detectives should follow a whole new set of rules and play nice, you'll never get support for that. You can't tie the hands of the good guys when working with criminals who have no morals and no rules. We'd never convict anyone if that was the case."

"I disagree. But more importantly, your argument nicely

illustrates one of the main issues involved in false confessions. Detectives assume people are guilty when they interview them. The whole no-morals-and-no-rules thing implies they're criminals and that they must have committed the offense about which they are being interviewed. That's a bias going into the interrogation that automatically skews things against the suspect."

Callum shook his head, clearly displeased. "Innocent until proven guilty guides the jury in a court of law. If detectives never believed someone was guilty, they'd never make an arrest or interrogate them in the first place."

Kassin nodded. "I agree with you on that last point. It's a dilemma. As for changing up how interrogations are conducted, that's something that has to be explored or we'll never solve the problem of false confessions. But you're not here to solve that problem. You and Ms. Quintero are here to understand the problem, and how it may or may not relate to her brother's situation."

She sat forward and addressed her next comments to Raine. "There are many factors that can lead to someone saying they committed a crime even when they didn't. Being overly tired, or mentally challenged in some way, or even under the influence of some kind of substance makes the suspect vulnerable to suggestion."

Callum was the focus of her next comments. "Police interrogation techniques have a huge impact, as you might imagine. Law enforcement is trained to use psychology that, unfortunately, can influence anyone—guilty or not. That includes isolating a suspect in an uncomfortable room with few amenities. The environment is unfamiliar and makes the suspect nervous, unsure. Interviewers wield all the power.

They barrage suspects by accusing them of being guilty, over and over."

"Sounds like brainwashing," Raine said.

Callum shot her an aggravated glance.

"That's a good way to describe it," the professor agreed. "Imagine yourself in a room for hours, feeling helpless, powerless. You're tired, confused and being told you're a bad person by the people in charge with all the power. Then one of them may play good cop, commiserate with you, try to give you an out—an excuse for your behavior. If the suspect denies their guilt, the investigator often interrupts them and tells them they're guilty. They'll provide a counterpoint, arguments to discredit any facts the suspect may present. Again, psychology is huge here. The interviewers won't allow the suspect to go quiet. They keep them talking so they can't stop and calm down and think about what they're saying."

"I never conducted my interviews that way," Callum protested.

"That's commendable," she said. "Have you ever lied to a suspect? Acted polite and as if you're their friend? Encouraged them to get it off their chest and everything will be okay?"

He sat back, quiet.

"Your silence tells me you have," she said. "And I'm not saying there's necessarily anything wrong with that, in and of itself. But if you combine that, gaining the suspect's trust, and they are already vulnerable, such as through mental defect, they may tell you what they think you want to hear. And they'll do that thinking they're pleasing you, and that once they make you happy you'll let them go home."

He shook his head. "No one is going to confess to murder and think they're going to get to go home afterward."

"I can show you files from dozens of cases that prove otherwise."

The look on Callum's face had Raine worried that this was going to devolve into a heated debate. That wasn't going to help Joey.

"Hold it," Raine said. "Can we please get back on track? Let's not argue about this. We're here to learn, to see whether Professor Kassin thinks Joey's confession was coerced."

Callum blew out a deep breath. "My apologies to both of you. I was a junior detective when I worked on Joey's case and this is hitting a little close to home."

Kassin's eyes widened. "I don't recall seeing your name in the file as one of the interrogators."

"Perhaps junior detective is too generous." A wry grin twisted his lips. "Detective Farley was the lead on the case. He interviewed Joey. I was his gopher. But the idea that something untoward could have gone on while I was working there bugs me. If I believed Farley was coercing any innocent people into lying, I assure you I'd have put a stop to it somehow."

Raine touched his shoulder to get his attention. "I've learned enough about you to know, one hundred percent, that you would never knowingly do anything to impinge on a suspect's rights or try to get a confession at all costs."

His look of surprise had her feeling even worse about how she'd first met him. He was a man of character and she never should have taken his choice away from him about helping her. Instead, she should have tried harder to get an audience with him and let him choose whether or not he wanted to help.

The professor flipped a page on her legal pad, no doubt her unsubtle way of regaining their attention. "The last part I'll add is that length of time of an interrogation comes into play. The longer it goes on, the more a suspect is likely to lie just to make it end. The younger a suspect is, as well, the more vulnerable he or she is." She flipped another page. "Regarding Joey's interviews, there were several things that concerned me."

One by one, she listed potential problems with his interviews, especially the last one, where he supposedly confessed.

"The interviews were long. Joey expressed he was suffering from insomnia, so he was already tired. There was no recording, either audio or visual, of the interviews. The printed confession that Joey signed has phrasing and word choices that never appear in other samples of his writing that his lawyer included in his file. In short, when I review everything in its entirety, there are some red flags. I have concerns about whether he was unduly influenced or coerced to sign a write-up of the confession that didn't accurately reflect what he said."

Raine stared at her, frozen, afraid to hope, afraid to even breathe. "I don't... I'm not sure what to do with that. Are you saying...are you saying in your expert opinion that—"

The look of empathy on the professor's face had Raine clutching a hand to her chest.

Don't say it. Don't say it. Don't—

"Ms. Quintero, there are definitely parts of your brother's interrogations that concern me. But looking at everything in total, at all of his interviews and how they were handled, there's nothing there that I can absolutely point to and say his confession was coerced."

Barely aware that Callum had placed a supportive hand on her shoulder, she stared in shock at the other woman. "I don't understand. You said there are red flags. You have concerns. You can speak to the board and—"

"What I can do, and will do, is offer a critique and recommendations to ACCPD for future interrogations. As for speaking to the prison board on Mr. Quintero's behalf, I can't in good conscience do that. I'm sorry, Ms. Quintero. But there's nothing I can do to help your brother."

Chapter Eighteen

Once Raine had recovered from Professor Kassin's devastating conclusions—or lack of conclusions—she'd put her brave face back on and accompanied Callum on dozens of other interviews. But here it was, more than a week later, and in spite of how incredibly hard he was working, the lack of sleep, the endless hours he spent poring over files in his home office, they weren't any closer to saving Joey.

And time was their enemy.

It hit her hard, during breakfast on Callum's back patio earlier this morning, that the next handful of days could very well be her brother's last. And here she was, in Callum's SUV now, watching the landscape roll past the window while he drove them to yet another interview.

She'd spent this precious time talking to strangers, driving countless miles, with nothing to show for it. Was there some point at which she should stop, give up? Should she instead go see her brother, take advantage of the lax visiting rules as his execution date drew near? Did it make more sense to talk to him through a thick pane of glass and an old-fashioned phone, with nothing new to share, no hope to give him? Or was her time better spent in the seemingly endless conference calls with his lawyers? And brainstorming with Callum. No matter what she did, it didn't seem as if it even mattered anymore.

A single tear spilled over her lashes and ran down her cheek. She quickly wiped it away and drew a ragged breath.

Callum's warm, strong hand was suddenly on top of hers. She automatically threaded her fingers with his and took the comfort he offered. They'd become so used to each other's moods that they often didn't even have to say anything to understand what the other was thinking, feeling. It was a closeness she treasured and relied on so much now that she didn't know how she'd survive without his support going forward. Here she was, the hardened lawyer who'd spent most of her adult life fighting for justice in one way or another. And yet, when it really mattered, she was losing the battle and thinking about giving up.

"Don't give up yet, Raine. We're not done. Not even close." He squeezed her hand.

Her throat tightened. It was as if he'd read her thoughts. Again. Somehow, when she was at her lowest, he always knew what to say, and how to make her feel better. Just knowing he hadn't given up gave her the strength to straighten in her seat and sniff back the tears.

When she trusted her voice again to be able to speak, she asked, "How is the serial killer investigation going? You haven't given me any updates lately, except to say no new victims have been discovered. Maybe the killer died. Or he was sent to prison on some other charge. Wouldn't that be a blessing?"

"If it meant he'd never be out on the streets again, hurting anyone else, it sure would be. But the families of his victims need closure, if that even exists. At the very least, they need to *know* the man who hurt their loved ones is locked away for good. I did speak to Asher this morning, when you were taking your shower. The team has zeroed in on a suspect. Ever hear of a guy named Drake Knox when you were looking into the case?"

"Drake Knox." She thought a moment, then shook her head. "Doesn't ring a bell. Who is he?"

"Someone who would never appear on the police radar. He's a trust fund baby, living off his inherited wealth. Never worked a day in his life, doesn't have to. No criminal record. No history, that we know of, of animal abuse or other warning signs typical of someone who goes on to become a serial killer. Then again, he was an only child, raised in the family mansion on property up in the Smoky Mountains, somewhat isolated. He was homeschooled, not that it's a precursor or cause of psychopathic tendencies. But it paints a picture of him growing up pretty much alone, with only his parents or nannies to socialize him."

"If he's so antitypical and isn't on police radar, why does UB think he's the killer you've been looking for?"

"Asher isn't sure he's the killer, not yet. He's just the only viable suspect they've come up with, so they're looking deeply into his past and trying to form timelines for where he might have been during the killings. His name originally came up as someone in the area during the same time frame as two of the murders. There have been few links between any of the victims. They've been pretty random. So to find someone who was in the social circle, for a brief time at least, of two victims got Asher and Faith curious about him. So far, they've linked him to an additional victim as far as timelines go and being in the area when the murder happened. That's a total of three, and they're still looking for more links."

"Sounds promising. I hope they're onto something."

"There is one more thing that makes Knox look promising. Four of the victims' cars were found to have illegal GPS trackers on them, attached to the frame. Knox was pulled over in a traffic stop once, years ago, and one of the things the cop noted on the ticket was that Knox had GPS tracking equipment sitting on the seat beside him. He thought it was odd enough to put it in his write-up."

"That's really odd. How did he explain it? Knox?"

"He didn't. He told the cop it was none of his business what he had in his car. And since it was a simple traffic stop, he's right. The officer didn't have any just cause to do a search. But obviously it raises flags. A theory we've always had about the victims is that they were stalked for some time before being killed. That's based on the fact that these women had busy lives and he always managed to get to them when they were alone, like when their boyfriends in two of those cases were gone on business trips. A GPS tracker would make following them easy."

He squeezed her hand again. "Enough about that. Let's focus on Joey's case. You don't have to go on all of these interviews with me. If you don't feel up to it today, I can—"

"Don't tell me to go home now. I'd never forgive myself if we can't... If we're unable to stop... If I didn't do everything I could for my brother. You never know. I could think of the one question in an interview that might shake some new information loose. Or I could connect the dots in a different way than you and come up with a new avenue to explore. I want to be there."

"Fair enough. I spoke to Danny, Detective Cooper, this morning too. The BOLOs are still out on Scoggin and Hagen. No sightings of either of them. UB is actively researching Scoggin to try to find him, see if he's a one-off killer or whether Knox could be responsible for that one too. Danny did finally finish evaluating the cases that Farley worked."

As he passed a slow-moving car, she said, "I'm guessing from your tone this is going to be another disappointment."

He nodded. "There aren't any patterns to show that Farley purposely chose to not record confessions and recorded other, non-confession interviews. Danny even reviewed the data with Internal Affairs to make sure he wasn't missing anything. They agreed with him. There's no basis to think Farley was anything other than lazy or inept about being consistent with recording interviews. And like Professor Kassin, IA doesn't feel there's enough evidence in the written transcripts of Joey's confession to argue it was coerced. I'm sorry, Raine. I wish I had better news."

She tugged her hand free and wrapped her arms around her middle as she looked out the window. "Not your fault. You're doing everything humanly possible, as well as half the team at UB."

"Half is stretching it. They've had to move resources to dig into the Knox angle and follow up on Scoggin too. But if we have anything we need help with, we can get some local PIs in on it."

"I understand." And she did. UB had many cases to focus on. Expending most of their resources to help her with a closed case, when they were working on a cold case that had heated up, didn't make sense. If she was the owner of UB, she'd have reallocated resources too. But that didn't mean it didn't sink her hopes even lower.

"Four days," she whispered brokenly. "They're going to kill him in four days."

"Not if we can stop it. I told you, don't give up yet. I made an appointment with Joey's lawyers and the prison board for the morning of his scheduled execution date. We'll present whatever we've found. They'll rule on it right after the meeting, granting a stay if they feel they need more time."

"Well, that's something. That's a good thing."

"It is," he agreed as he slowed and turned into an apartment complex.

"Thank you, Callum. For everything. I don't know how I would have gotten through all of this without you. Truly."

"My pleasure. Now, stop moping around and engage that amazing brain of yours. We're about to conduct another interview."

He parked in front of the first apartment building on the left. Then he leaned over and pressed a whisper-soft kiss against her lips, then quickly pulled back. "Oops. Couldn't help it." He winked, making a lie out of his apology.

She laughed, unable to resist his charm, as always. "I'll forgive you this once."

He grinned and they both got out of the SUV.

Regret gnawed at Raine once they were sitting on a couch across from the woman who lived in apartment 1101. Her name was Rose Garcia and she'd dated Joey for two years. And yet, Raine had only met her a few times. Rose had testified as a character witness at Joey's trial, on behalf of the defense. But Raine barely knew her. She and Joey had been like ships passing in the night, partly because he was so much older than her. It was only after his arrest, and conviction, that she'd made the efforts she should have made earlier. Their age gap should never have been an excuse to not be involved in her brother's life. It was one of many regrets she had to live with.

"Rose, we appreciate your time," Callum said. "And you've been very helpful in telling us Joey's usual routines, where he liked to go, people he considered his friends. Now, I'd like you to focus on the day that Alicia Claremont was murdered. The prosecution's timeline indicated that there was a three-hour window in which Joey could have killed her. Is there any additional information about that day that you've remembered that can help us flesh out the timeline, narrow that window of opportunity? Perhaps you have something written down that might jog your memory, a diary, or journal? Maybe an old calendar you saved that has appointments and notes on it about Joey? Documents with dates in particular could really help. Lawyers love those as evidence."

Rose twisted her hands in her lap, her gaze darting around the worn, beige-colored room. "I testified at his trial. I told them he was a good person."

Callum glanced at Raine before continuing. "Are you worried about telling us something different than what you said under oath?"

She twisted her hands even harder, her knuckles whitening.

Raine scooted forward on the couch. "Rose? Can you look at me, please?" She kept her voice soft, as unthreatening and nonjudgmental as possible.

Finally Rose met her gaze. "You're Joey's sister."

She smiled sadly, her stomach dropping at the implications in Rose's hesitation, her demeanor and her worry over Raine being his sister. "It's okay to tell the truth, whatever it is. That's exactly what we want, no matter what. No one's going to get upset at you."

Rose chewed her bottom lip and looked down at her hands.

Callum gave Rose a sympathetic look. "Would it be easier to talk if Raine leaves the room?"

Still, Rose remained silent.

Raine stood. "I'll wait in the car."

"No." Rose sighed heavily and stood. "Have a seat. Please. If you really want the truth, then you deserve to hear it. Give me a minute." She headed down the short hallway and disappeared into what Raine assumed was her bedroom.

Callum's hand covered hers. "Are you sure you want to be here for whatever she's going to say?"

"Yes. As she said, I want the truth."

He studied her for a long moment, then nodded and pulled his hand back.

Rose emerged from her room and returned to her spot in the recliner across from them. In her hands was a blue spiral-bound notebook, the kind you could get for a few dollars at a convenience store. But from the worn look of it and dog-eared pages, she'd had it a long time.

As she placed it on the glass coffee table between them and flipped it open, Raine couldn't help but tense. The word *DIARY* was spelled out in block letters across the top, along with a date—two months prior to Alicia's murder.

The woman's hands shook as she flipped through the pages, stopping at the first one written in red ink instead of the blue that had been used on other pages. The date, again, was at the top—six weeks before Joey's trial. A legal-sized envelope was nestled against the opposite page. Rose took it out and set it on the coffee table. But instead of opening it, she flipped to the end of the journal.

Another envelope lay there, this one much thicker than the first. Written in blue ink across it was one word—*trial*. She handed the envelope to Callum.

"You want me to open this?" he asked.

She nodded. "Please. You can show Raine too. I think she's seen most of them before."

And she had. As Callum thumbed through them, leaning close to Raine so she could see them too, she recognized them as having been entered into evidence at trial. Or, at least, copies of these photos. She didn't think very much of the evidence had been released, not while there was still a chance of another trial, no matter how remote.

"We were happy then," Rose said. "Good times."

Callum stopped thumbing through the pictures. "Not all the times were good?"

Rose's cheeks turned a light pink as she glanced at Raine. She cleared her throat. "No. They weren't." She picked up the first envelope that obviously contained more photos and handed it to him.

As soon as he pulled out the first picture, Raine gasped and pressed a hand to her throat. It was a selfie of Rose, standing in front of a bathroom mirror. Her throat had purplish bruises on it. Even without being a forensic expert, Raine could easily tell what had made those bruises. Hands.

"Rose?" Callum asked, his voice soft. "Who did this to you?"

Her eyes brightened with unshed tears. "My sweet Joey. I don't even remember what I did to make him mad." She twisted her hands and looking imploringly at Raine. "I didn't lie about him being sweet at the trial. I wanted people to know he was a good person. He was sweet, kind, smart. He took good care of me...when he was sober. I just...didn't tell them about when he wasn't sober."

Raine fought back her own tears as Callum flipped

through the other pictures. When he was through, he put them in the envelope and slid them across the table.

"Those are some awful injuries," he said, his voice still kind, gentle. "Are you saying Joey was responsible for all of them?"

She nodded. "But only because he was drunk, or sometimes high. I loved him. Still do. But that last time, the throat, he choked me. I passed out. When I woke up, he went white as a sheet, as if he'd seen a ghost. I'm pretty sure he thought he'd killed me." She wiped her eyes, refusing to let the tears fall. "I don't know why I took those pictures, or why I kept them. I guess it was my subconscious, wanting proof for later, when I was in denial. Countless nights, after he'd been out drinking, I'd sit in my room, waiting for him to come home. Wondering if tonight would be one of those nights. I think…those pictures, seeing how many there were, are what finally gave me the courage to leave him."

"I'm so sorry," Raine whispered. "So sorry."

Rose shook her head. "Don't be. It's not your fault. It wasn't Joey's either, not really. Alcohol released a monster inside him. He never would have done it if he was in his right mind. He loved me."

Raine exchanged an agonized glance with Callum. They didn't have to speak for her to know that he was remembering the same thing she was—the police report for when Joey was arrested. Although sober by the time they found him, he reeked of alcohol and had bloodshot eyes, indicating a recent binge.

"I don't doubt you, Rose. But for this to be evidence, we need proof. Do you have anything to show that Joey is the one who did these things to you? Maybe you told a friend, your mom, a sister?"

She motioned toward the diary. "It's all there, in writing. With dates. You said dates are good to have written down, right?"

He nodded and thumbed through the diary.

"The red ink," Rose said. "I wrote the entries that go along with the pictures in red ink."

As Raine watched Callum turn the pages, skimming entries, the amount of red ink had her stomach roiling with nausea.

Callum closed the diary and set it beside the envelopes. "One more question, Rose. In spite of Joey's abuse of you, you still testified to help him. The prosecutor even asked whether you felt Joey could have killed Alicia. You said no. Was that the truth?"

Her chin trembled, and the tears she'd been trying to hold back slid down her cheeks. "You have to understand. I loved Joey, but I was scared of him too. If I'd said anything bad on the stand, and he got out, came home…" She held her hands up in a helpless gesture. "I had to protect myself."

"Understood," Callum said. "But you have to say it. We need to hear it from you, in your own words. Do you think Joey Quintero had the opportunity, and could have killed Alicia Claremont?"

Rose picked up the smaller envelope and thumbed through the pictures. She paused, staring at one as she answered Callum.

"I went to bed before Joey came home the night Alicia was murdered. So I wasn't able to say whether he was with me at the time of her death. All I could say on the stand was that he was in bed when I woke up the next morning. I was honest about that, and everything else I testified about— except one thing. Do I think that Joey could have strangled and killed Alicia Claremont?" She set the picture down on the coffee table, faceup, the picture that showed the bruises around her throat. "Absolutely."

Chapter Nineteen

Callum stood beside the couch in his main room, his heart aching as Raine paced back and forth in front of him, venting about the case. At least she'd stopped crying. She'd cried most of the way to his house after Rose Garcia—the best character witness they had for her brother—declared in no uncertain terms that she believed he could have killed Alicia Claremont.

So far, Raine had refused to let him try to comfort her, not that he even knew how to do that. How could he make her feel better when everyone they'd spoken to either had nothing good to say about her brother, or something damning. She'd lost her parents and was about to lose her brother unless he figured out how to stop it.

But damned if he knew how at this point.

Raine stopped in front of him, her eyes red, dried tears forming tracks through her makeup. And she'd never looked more beautiful. He wanted to hold her, help her, somehow. But he'd learned in the past hour that she didn't want to be touched. Not now. Maybe not ever again if this week ended in the tragic way it appeared it was going to end.

"You heard what she said." Raine gestured helplessly. "Rose defended Joey, said he would only hurt someone if he was drunk, or on drugs. But you and I have both read the police reports. No trace evidence. No DNA. And she was raped. A man out of his mind drunk doesn't put a condom on before he rapes someone. If Joey did it, he did it because he wanted to, not because he blacked out or was out of his mind with alcohol. He would have gotten drunk *after* he killed her. Not before."

"Raine—"

"Don't. Don't tell me it will all be okay. My God. Is he a killer? Is my brother a murderer after all? Have I been fooling myself this whole time?"

She started pacing back and forth again, so he didn't even try to answer what were likely rhetorical questions anyway. He didn't believe for a minute that she was ready to truly believe in Joey's guilt. She'd been supporting him and fighting for him for too long to cross that line right now. But she was struggling, because she was smart, and logical. Even a sister who desperately loved her brother couldn't deny the facts in front of her forever.

What they needed were more facts, something to turn the investigation completely around. The main problem he was encountering, of course, was that he wasn't convinced that her brother was innocent. Just the opposite. Even with Professor Kassin's doubts about the confession, every bit of circumstantial evidence pointed to Joey being the one who'd killed Alicia. And no evidence pointed to anyone else.

Or did it? Raine herself had said the police had zeroed in on Joey from the start—because he lived close by, had a rocky past and had allegedly been seen with Alicia in a bar.

By Randy Hagen.

"We've exhausted all avenues of trying to rehabilitate

Joey as being innocent. The evidence just isn't there to sway anyone into changing their minds."

She stopped in front of him again, her gaze searching his. The look on her face was nothing short of devastation. "I never thought I'd hear you say that. I'm in the middle of a freak-out and you're giving up too?"

Unable to stop himself, he reached for her. When she didn't pull back this time, he cradled her against his chest and rested the top of his chin on her head.

"I'm not giving up. I'm accepting the facts we have right now, and switching gears. We need new facts. Instead of trying to prove that Joey could be innocent, we need to prove that someone else could have killed Alicia. We need to look at any viable suspects and try to create reasonable doubt. Right now, the only other person who seems a likely candidate to have killed her is Randy Hagen."

"Okay. Good, that's good. I've always said I didn't trust him, that he could have killed Alicia. But no one believed me."

"No one had any evidence to support that theory. We need to look for it. Sit down for a moment. Let's talk this through." He gently pushed her onto the couch facing him.

"Let's assume for a moment that he's the one who killed Alicia, that he lied when he testified, trying to frame Joey. You were investigating him on your own before you got my help. What did you do? Where did you go? Bars, right? That's why we theorized he might be the one who broke into your house, because he was mad that you and Joey's lawyers were asking questions about him in his hangout spots."

She nodded. "I visited every bar in town asking about him. It certainly wasn't a secret that I believed he'd lied on the stand about Joey."

"And then, when time was running out on Joey, you went to Gatlinburg looking for my help. Randy could have been forced to stay home to avoid questions by his friends in the bars. He didn't want this whole thing dragged up again. Maybe he drank himself into a rage and headed to your place, watched it off and on to see whether or not you were home. When he worked up enough courage, he broke in and tried to find your notes and files about him. When that didn't work out, because you'd taken everything with you to Gatlinburg, he trashed the place. He didn't expect us to pull up when he was still there, so he ran."

"You really think that's what happened?"

He shrugged. "It's a guess, an educated guess, but still just conjecture. It would make sense, though, if he was guilty, that he'd be worried about you digging up the case again. Now let's turn it around and assume he's not guilty."

"We're back to saying Joey killed Alicia?"

"No, not at all. We're brainstorming different angles to see what shakes loose. If we assume Hagen's not guilty, what's his motive for trashing your place, if he's the one who did it?" He already had an answer ready. But he wanted to shake her out of her feelings of helplessness. If he could get her reengaged with the case, she'd at least feel that she was contributing, and still cling to hope. Plus, she really was smart, a quick thinker. Maybe she *would* come up with something he hadn't thought of that could help.

"The perjury angle," she finally said. "Even if he's innocent of murder, if he lied on the stand about seeing Joey with Alicia at the bar, he committed perjury. If I had evidence of that, it could send him to prison. He'd be worried about me, innocent or guilty."

"Agreed," he said. "We need to look at him more in-depth. But we need to be careful. He could react like a cornered animal if he thinks we're onto him about the breaking and entering and he feels he has a lot to lose."

She shivered. "Okay. How do we, as you said, look into him? I got nothing from my inquiries."

"Let me guess. No one in the bars would talk to you?"

"Pretty much. Why would you assume that?"

He grinned. "Because you're a lawyer. No one in a bar wants to talk to a lawyer. They've all got their own sins to hide."

She rolled her eyes. "I'm a business lawyer. I don't handle criminal cases."

"The barflies don't understand the difference." He chuckled, then turned serious. "We need to look into Randy's alibi during the time that Alicia was killed. Do you remember his alibi? I don't remember reading about that in the police files. But I was focused more on Joey."

"So were the police. They barely looked at Randy after latching on to Joey as a suspect. Supposedly Randy was home. To his credit, Joey's trial defense attorney tried to explore Randy's alibi. But basically his story was that he was watching TV. His proof was that he gave the plot of the show he was watching. But everything is on demand these days, even back then. He could have watched it another time so he could speak to the plot."

"Excellent point. We can look into that. I wonder why the police accepted it so readily?"

"I guess because there wasn't any evidence pointing to him," she grudgingly admitted.

"Maybe. But given Farley's less-than-stellar reputation, there could be something more. Not that I think Farley would cover for someone he thought was guilty. I really don't see him doing that. But if he needed Randy's testimony to get who Farley thought was the bad guy, he may have done everything he could to ensure that Randy seemed like a credible witness. That includes propping up a weak alibi. We need to find out if there was another reason for them to put forth that alibi. Maybe they couldn't prove where Randy was at the time and came up with that story, again, so he could testify and be believable."

"That would be an awful thing to do."

"Hopefully that's not what happened. But we're exploring theoretical possibilities. Let me get Asher on it, have him run a criminal background report on Randy around the time of the murder. I'll have him run more than just local stuff, just to be extra thorough."

After giving Asher the assignment, Callum grabbed a quick snack of cheese and crackers for Raine and himself. Neither of them had felt like having lunch earlier. But now his stomach was starting to poke his ribs. Thankfully, he was able to coax her into eating some too. Emotions and stress would only get a person so far. He didn't want her getting sick and run-down because of this roller-coaster couple of weeks.

They'd just finished their snack when Asher called back. Callum was stacking their plates in the dishwasher and glanced across the kitchen island at Raine as he answered his phone.

"Hey, Asher. I've got you on speaker so Raine can hear. You have something for us already?"

"Thanks to our boss's amazing network of database access he's set up, I do. You're not going to believe this. Hagen's alibi is bogus. Completely made up. He wasn't home during the time of the murder."

Raine fist-pumped the air, but Callum shook his head in warning as he pushed for more information.

"Since the databases are law enforcement ones, and you're saying he wasn't home, I'm guessing he was in police custody at the time?"

Raine's eyes widened in dismay.

"Bingo," Asher said. "The Atlanta Police Department, over an hour away, had him locked up for public intoxication."

Raine slid onto a bar stool in front of the kitchen island. "He was in jail?"

"All night. He didn't kill Alicia, couldn't have."

She shook her head. "I don't understand. The police knew he was in jail, but they allowed him to use another alibi on the stand?"

"Not the Athens police," Asher said. "Atlanta police. It would depend on what type of search they did, how far they dug, as to whether they knew about his arrest."

"ACCPD knew," Callum said. "Randy wouldn't have risked being accused of murder. He'd have told them he had an airtight alibi. That means Farley, or the prosecutor, or both, covered for him. They knew that admitting he was in jail at the time made him a much less credible witness. They didn't want that coming out at trial. The jurors might not believe his testimony about seeing Joey with Alicia if they thought he wasn't credible."

Raine crossed her arms on top of the island. "So our hope that we might find another suspect we could argue had opportunity to kill Alicia is out. Hagen didn't kill her."

"No," Callum said. "He didn't. But we can prove he lied on the stand about his alibi. If he lied about one thing, he may have lied about another—like whether he saw your brother with Alicia. He's not the only bar patron who thought they might have seen them together, or at least Joey trying to talk to her. But he's the only one who swore at trial that it was definitely Joey. That's a piece of new, provable evidence—the first we've found. It's finally a start in the right direction. Thanks, Asher. Appreciate you jumping on that for us."

"You bet. If you need anything else, just call."

"I don't want to get too excited about this," Raine said. "It doesn't seem like enough to change the board's mind. Or am I not looking at it right?"

"I agree it probably wouldn't sway the board enough to grant a stay. But it might sway Randy. If we can find him, we may be able to convince him to admit he lied—assuming that he did—about Joey."

"Why would he agree to that?"

He smiled. "He wouldn't. Not on purpose, or at least not where someone in law enforcement would hear him. I'm thinking we try to interview him in a setting where he feels comfortable, and he's willing to brag about the truth, thinking we can't do anything about it. Maybe after a few beers."

"A bar. You want to interview him in a bar, and get him drunk."

"Loose, not drunk. What's that saying? Loose lips sink ships? We need to confirm whether his testimony about your brother is true or not. We've got nothing to lose, everything to gain."

She stood. "Okay, so we hit all the bars in town again. I know the ones that were his favorites back then. Those should be the first ones we try."

"You're not coming with me."

"What? Why not?"

"You already tried to find him earlier at the bars. Either he was there and snuck out the back when his friends saw you, or he heard you were looking for him and stayed away. I might have better luck on my own. He won't recognize me."

"He might if he's the one you chased in the woods behind my house."

He nodded. "There is that. But he was so busy trying to get away, I don't think he was trying to get a good look at my face. I'm the better choice for this particular task."

"Great. And what am I supposed to do while you go bar-hopping?"

He laughed. "I won't drink and have fun. Promise." He stepped around to the other side of the island and gently grasped her shoulders. "You've had a really rough day, Raine. Take this as a welcome break. Maybe try to have a nap, or eat something more than crackers. You haven't been eating well at all."

"Careful, Callum. You're sounding awfully concerned about a lawyer."

His smile broadened. "I'm currently rethinking my animosity toward lawyers, or at least one in particular." When she didn't smile, he sighed heavily. "My charm isn't working today."

"What charm?" She arched a brow.

"Ouch. I'll have to work on that. In the meantime, like I said, take a break. And keep trusting me. You chose the right man for the job. Let me do what I do. And let me do it without distractions, without worrying about your safety."

He gave her a quick kiss, then hurried toward the carport entry before he did something stupid, like *really* kiss her. Now wasn't the time. She was vulnerable, not necessarily thinking clearly after the stress of today. And they'd agreed to keep it professional between them, to focus on the case.

But dang it was hard. What he really wanted to do, more than anything right now, was hold her and somehow chase away all the hurts and fears. But he wasn't strong enough to do that without wanting more. Much more.

A few minutes down the road, his phone pinged. He expected to see Asher's number on the screen again, perhaps giving him another update. Instead, he was surprised to see his friend Noah Reid's number.

"Hey, Noah. It's great to hear from you again. But I'm kind of busy right now, working the Quintero case. Can we catch up later?"

"Absolutely. I want to try the fishing out there in your pond again. But that's not why I called."

As Callum listened, he stiffened in surprise. "You're kidding. Okay, yes." He checked the time on his watch. "I can make it. Might be a couple of minutes late, but I'll be there."

Callum hung up and immediately called Asher. "Hey, man. I need your help. Can you get some local PIs on the search for Hagen? He's more at home in a bar than his place. Shouldn't be too hard to find him if someone he's not familiar with subtly puts out feelers. I don't think he's high on ACCPD's priority list or they'd have located him by now. I was going to look for him, but something else has come up."

"Sure, okay. I know a few guys I can call. Maybe a gal too, someone pretty who might have better luck getting his attention. What do you want done once they locate him?"

Callum quickly explained his goal of getting Randy to admit he lied—if he lied. "And make sure when he leaves that someone tails him. I don't want him going anywhere near my place in Athens while Raine's there alone."

"You're not with her? Where are you?"

"On my way to Jackson Prison."

Chapter Twenty

Raine finished straightening up the kitchen, not that there was a lot to clean. Callum kept everything neat and orderly, a man after her own heart. But she washed down the countertops, making sure to get any crumbs.

The sound of the carport door to the house opening surprised her. Callum had only been gone a few minutes. He must have forgotten something. The door clicked closed behind her as she tossed a paper towel into the garbage.

"I thought he'd never leave."

She whirled around at the sound of the unfamiliar voice. A man stood about ten feet away, dressed all in black. He was tall and muscular, like Callum. But unlike Callum, he was blond and pale, as if he spent most of his time indoors.

Dark eyes stared back at her with a disturbing, feral intensity. Then he smiled, a cold, cruel smile. And she started to shake.

"Who are you? What do you want?"

"Ah, that's right. You haven't met me yet, have you, dear? Maybe you haven't even heard about me. You and that investigator you hired have been focused on the Scoggin fellow." His lip curled in a sneer. "Trying to give him credit for one of my kills. You got him in a tizzy by performing surveillance on him. He wrote down your license plate number, figured out who you were. When more investigators showed up, watching him, he knew you must have been behind it."

She grasped the edge of the kitchen island, her whole body shaking now. "Credit for your kills? You mean Nancy? You killed her?"

"I killed them all, darlin'. Including Nancy. And I didn't appreciate hearing on the news that Scoggin was wanted for her death. I work hard on my projects. I may not want anyone knowing they were mine. You know, the whole prison thing. But someone else taking credit, well, I can't have that. But I'm getting ahead of myself. Raine Quintero, I'm Drake Knox. And the pleasure, I assure you, is about to be all mine."

His smile widened, showing perfect white teeth that reminded her more of a badger's than a human being's. "And I must say, I'm flattered by how white your face just turned. You must have heard of me after all."

Her gun. She had to get her gun. It was in the guest bedroom, in the side table drawer. Could she reach it before he reached her?

She inched her way around the island, toward the family room. He arched a brow as he watched, not the least bit concerned, which made her even more terrified. Images of his victims, the police photos she'd bribed a clerk to give her, appeared in her mind's eye. All had been strangled to death. But before that, their killer had tortured them. The coroners in each case had theorized the victims had been bound, cut, beaten and raped. For hours.

She had to get her gun. Distraction. She needed a distraction.

"Are you saying Scoggin trashed my house?"

He cocked his head like a bird watching a worm wriggling on the ground, just before he snatched it up. And killed it.

"Let me guess," he said. "You thought it was that silly Hagen fellow. Low-life little criminal whose entire résumé consists of petty theft and drunk driving. That sort of thing. I can see him trashing your place, I suppose. But once your shenanigans got Scoggin in the limelight, well, he just couldn't control his temper."

She reached the end of the island. She was about fifteen feet away from him now. He still hadn't moved.

"How...how do you know all of this?" One step away from the island, toward the family room part of the open concept room. Could she get the couch in between them before she took off running for the bedroom?

He smiled, seemingly amused as she dared to take another step toward the couch. "My apologies for the confusion, Raine. Can I call you Raine?" He waved a hand, as if waving away his question. "Of course I'll call you Raine. After all, we're about to become great...friends."

Oh, God. Please help me. Another step. Why wasn't he moving? Why did he seem so confident that she wasn't going to get away? It didn't matter. She had to get that gun. Another step.

His only reaction to her movements was to continue watching her, and to put his hands in the pockets of his black jacket. "I should clarify, instead of starting in the middle of the story. Scoggin went on the run, that whole BOLO thing—after trashing your place. As luck would have it, the minute I heard on the news that he was wanted for my work, I looked into his past and figured out he had a cabin up in the mountains. Or, to be more accurate, his ex-wife did. She got it in the divorce. I figured he'd head there if he wanted to hide, rather than to his own home or places he was known to frequent. So I went there first, and waited. Let's just say he was quite forthcoming in answering all of my questions."

She took another step, and swallowed, hard. "You killed him?"

"Of course."

Her stomach dropped at how casually he spoke about murdering someone. "And Hagen too I'm guessing."

He rolled his eyes. "Hagen isn't worth a thought in my head. Scoggin, on the other hand, as I already explained, had to be taken care of."

"What does this have to do with me? I've never done anything to you."

He frowned, looking aggravated. "You're not listening. Scoggin. You're the reason I was forced to stray from my plans for UB to take care of Scoggin."

She blinked. "Your plans for UB? I don't understand."

He watched her take another step. Twenty feet away now. She'd reached the opposite end of the couch. Did she dare try to gain the last few feet to the entrance of the hallway before she took off running?

"I've been keeping an eye on the Unfinished Business team for months, ever since the local police announced that UB was going to take on my cold cases, investigate my kills. And I've been tracking them the same way I track my victims. I have GPS locators on some of their vehicles. Including your boyfriend, Mr. Wright's. Have for a while now, even before he came to Athens."

He laughed. "Isn't that funny? You finally find your Mr. Right, pun intended, and you'll never be able to have that bright shiny future you've probably fantasized about since you were a little girl. It's how I knew he was staying here. I've been watching you, and was delighted that you were both together. First, I'll take care of you, for causing me such trouble. Then, when your prince charming arrives, I'll take care of him."

She took off running.

A crackling, sizzling sound filled the air. Something hit her between the shoulder blades. Blinding hot pain shot through every nerve in her body, dropping her gasping and writhing to the floor.

Chapter Twenty-One

It was well past dark by the time Callum started up the long driveway to his Athens home. He was worried about Raine. He'd tried calling her several times on his way here but she hadn't answered. Likely it was nothing. She could be taking that nap he'd recommended, or a long, hot bath. Or maybe she was out fiddling with the plants in the backyard as she often liked to do to de-stress, and had left her phone inside. She'd done it before, which was the only reason he hadn't called his brother-in-law to drive the half hour from town to check on her.

But now that he was almost there, an itchy feeling started in his shoulder blades. She'd never not answered his calls this long before.

Short of the last turn, he parked beneath some trees and killed the lights. When he got out of the SUV, he quietly pushed the door closed rather than let it slam shut. Crouching down, he made his way to the last group of trees before the clearing around the house.

As usual, the lights shone from the backyard. And landscape lighting lit up the beddings and ornamental trees in the front. But the house itself was dark.

Forgoing another call, he sent her a text this time.

Sweetheart, I'm on the way home. Should be there in about an hour. Will you wait up for me?

A minute later, a reply popped onto his screen.

I'm up. See you soon.

He swore and punched the speed dial for his brother-in-law. "Danny, hey, it's Callum. Something's wrong at my house. I think Raine may be in trouble."

"You think? What's going on?"

He explained about the text. "I've never called her sweetheart. And she didn't say a thing about it. Someone else must have her phone."

"That's weak, Callum. You're a half hour out of town and—"

"Asking my brother-in-law and former partner to trust me on this. Something's wrong. Send help. No lights. No sirens. Use the element of surprise. You know someone recently broke into her home. I think they're here right now, with her."

"Hagen?"

"No. The guy we sent looking for him found him and is tailing him. It's not Hagen. Could be Scoggin." Or worse. He prayed it wasn't worse. "Just get someone out here. Hurry. And bring an ambulance too. Just in case."

"Okay, okay. I'm on it. Wait for backup. Keep an eye on the place and call me if the situation changes before we get there."

Callum hung up without answering. Waiting for backup wasn't an option. He silenced the phone, then drew his gun.

He'd keep an eye on the situation, from the inside. No way in hell was he waiting out here if Raine was in trouble.

RAINE'S RESPECT FOR police officers who voluntarily got tased as part of their training had gone up a thousand percent. Being tased hurt beyond anything she'd ever experienced. And it wasn't the five-second ride she heard cops talk about. Knox had pressed the trigger over and over until she'd screamed and begged for mercy, or tried to through clenched teeth.

His version of mercy was to rip the Taser darts out of her back and handcuff her to a bar stool in the middle of the living room. Naked. And bleeding. Because the sicko had a love for knives as well.

Funny how after the first few cuts, the others didn't hurt as much. And too bad Callum's bar stools weren't the kind with arms and backs. She could have tried that neat trick of his, holding up the arms of the bar stool and smashing it on the floor to break free. Except that her ankles were cuffed to the legs of the stool too. That wouldn't work. Why was she so warm? Naked and warm was weird, wasn't it? Unless you were in a shower. Shouldn't she be cold? Maybe it was the blood, smeared on her skin, warming her.

Hot shooting pain snapped her head back. She whimpered and forced her eyes open.

"Welcome back." Knox grinned and lowered his hand. "Had to slap you pretty hard that time. Stop going to la-la land. We've barely started our fun."

"What did your mother ever do to you to make you such a sicko?"

He growled like a feral animal and slapped her again. She cried out in pain and the world suddenly tilted.

Knox swore and grabbed her, setting the stool back on all four legs and straightening her on it. "This may not be my best idea," he admitted, sounding disgusted. "What idiot uses bar stools and doesn't have a table and chairs?"

"This idiot."

Knox whirled around, but he wasn't fast enough. Callum slammed into him, knocking him to the floor.

Raine cried out as the stool tilted again. It fell over against the couch, knocking her head on the arm, hard. The scuffling and grunting on the floor close by told her Knox and Callum were in an all-out brawl—one fighting to save her, one fighting to kill her.

She blinked through the dark fog trying to pull her under. *Stay conscious. You have to help Callum.* She dragged in a ragged breath and slapped her cheeks, hoping the pain would clear her head. Slapped her cheeks? She stared in wonder at her hands, the handcuffs dangling from both wrists. They weren't cuffed to the bar stool anymore. When she pushed against the couch, she realized why. The stool had broken during her fall.

Her ankles were still cuffed to what remained of the legs of the stool, but she could move around.

Gun. Hadn't she been getting her gun when Knox stunned her? If she could get it, she could help Callum and—

"Raine, look out!"

She jerked around just as a knife came slashing down at her. It missed her by mere inches and the momentum sent Knox crashing to the floor again.

"Move, move," Callum yelled, as he lunged toward Knox.

She grasped the back of the couch and used all her strength to pull herself over it, dragging the broken stool with her. When she hit the floor on the other side, the rest of the stool shattered like kindling, bits of it scraping against her. It didn't even hurt. And she wasn't warm anymore. She was cold, her teeth chattering together.

"Well, shoot," she mumbled, her tongue feeling oddly thick. "Wait. *Shoot.* I need my gun." She pushed herself up on her hands and knees, pieces of wood clinging like a spider to her left calf. She swore and kicked at it, then fell again. Her arms and legs weren't working right.

So cold.

A deafening scream sounded from the other side of the couch. Then everything went quiet.

Raine lay there, not sure what to do.

Her teeth chattered again. "C-C-Callum?"

He was suddenly there beside her, looking down at her with such fear in his eyes that she wondered if Knox was behind her. She tried to look over her shoulder.

"Where is he?"

"Dead. Oh, honey. What did he do to you?" His hands shook as he searched for injuries.

Suddenly the front door and carport door burst open at the same time. "Police, don't move!"

She strained to see Callum in the chaos as people raced inside. One minute he was there, the next he wasn't. "Callum? Where did you go?"

She heard swearing and cursing, a scuffle.

"Let him go. He's my brother-in-law, the guy who called me for help."

Was that Detective Cooper's voice? Danny?

Callum's face appeared over hers again. A blanket seemed to magically be in his hands and he covered her with it, pressing down on her belly.

"Don't, that hurts," she cried out, pushing at his hands.

"I'm so sorry, sweetheart. I have to stop the bleeding. You've got a really bad cut on your belly."

"Don't call me sweetheart."

"There's my girl. Okay, honey. I won't call you sweetheart."

She laughed, then clutched his hands over her middle. "Ouch."

"Get that ambulance here, now!" Callum yelled.

"Two minutes out," Danny told him.

"You'll be okay, Raine. Just hold on. Hold on."

She clutched his jacket. "I'm holding on. You hold on too. Don't let me go." She coughed, then gasped, her face white with pain.

"Easy, Raine. I've got you. I won't let go."

She smiled, then closed her eyes and went limp.

Chapter Twenty-Two

The doorbell chime had Raine glancing up from her computer. Callum was early. They weren't due to leave for another forty-five minutes. Maybe he wanted to arrive even earlier than they'd planned. Could he be as nervous as she was about speaking to the prison board?

No. She smiled at that ridiculous thought. Callum wouldn't be nervous. He was always confident and capable, even when facing certain death. He'd saved her from Knox a few days ago. And she had faith that if anyone could save her brother today, it was Callum. This was Joey's last chance. His only chance. If this didn't work, he'd be executed this evening.

Tears started in her eyes. She brushed them away and drew a shaky breath. *Good thoughts. Think good thoughts. We're going to save him. We have to.*

As she pushed up from her chair in her home office, she sucked in a sharp breath. Her injuries made her stiff and sore. But she was grateful and thankful to be alive. The wounds would heal. Again, thanks to Callum.

She shuffled down the hallway beneath the stairs toward the foyer. Just before she reached the door, the doorbell chimed again.

"Just a second," she called out, flipping the top dead bolt, then a second one, thanks to his thoughtfulness. She still couldn't believe that he'd hired someone to clean her house, replace all of the destroyed items and reinforce every door and window with new locks right after her home had been broken into. He'd had all of that done while the two of them were running all over the place interviewing witnesses, and she hadn't even known about it.

"Did you check the peephole before unlocking the door?" Callum called out.

She smiled and looked through the peephole, even though she didn't need to. Then she opened the door. Callum in a business suit was devastating, even more so than Callum in jeans. How had she not been this affected seeing him in a suit before? He was gorgeous, in anything.

She let out a shaky breath, and tried hard not to stare. Now wasn't the time. Maybe later, hopefully, they could talk, see where this…thing between them was going. But first, Joey. They had to be successful today. She couldn't even consider the alternative.

"You're early," she said. "The appointment isn't until two o'clock."

His smile didn't quite reach his eyes. "I wanted to check on you. It's only been a couple of days since…since what happened. Are you feeling okay? You really should have stayed in the hospital more than one day."

"I'm fine. I fainted from blood loss. You keep acting like I almost died."

"You *did* almost die."

"No. I was almost murdered, but you prevented Knox from doing that. Big difference. Stop worrying about me. Is that why you came early? To mother hen me?"

He smiled again, barely. "That, and to make sure that everything was fixed the way you wanted it."

"My house? Are you kidding? It's better than new. I still can't believe you won't let me reimburse you. But I sincerely appreciate what you did. After Knox…well, it was wonderful being able to come home from the hospital and not have to worry about the repairs. Thank you."

"Of course. What about you, though? Are you sure you're okay? Feeling good enough to make the trip to Jackson Prison? After everything you've been through—"

She put her hand on his arm. "Nothing will keep me from being there today. Stop worrying about me. I'm alive and perfectly fine. Bruised, with a few minor cuts here and there, but—"

"Minor?" He swore. "You had thirty-seven stitches. That's not minor."

"I can't believe you kept track of the total. But the worst cut only needed twelve."

He blanched. "Good grief. If I hadn't already killed the bastard I'd kill him again."

"He'd have done far worse than some punches and cuts if you hadn't saved me. That's exactly what you did, you know. You saved me, and the lives of other women he'd have gone on to torture and murder if you and your team hadn't figured out he was the serial killer. It's over. Let it go. I have."

His jaw tightened, but he gave her a curt nod. "I wanted to update you about Hagen too."

She motioned toward the family room. "We don't have to stand. There's still plenty of time before we have to leave. Come sit on the couch with me."

He hesitated, as if he was going to tell her no. But then he nodded again and followed her across the room. She made a concerted effort to move as normally as possible so he wouldn't start fussing about her injuries again. Getting up and sitting were the hardest parts. But she forced a smile through the pain as she lowered herself to the couch.

When he chose a wing chair instead of sitting beside her, she couldn't help the twinge of disappointment. But it was the new worry lines on his forehead that had her attention.

"Callum, if you're still concerned about me, don't be. I'm really okay. Promise."

"I'll always be concerned about you, Raine. But there are a few more updates that I need to give you." He ran a hand through his short hair, a gesture she'd never seen him do before.

"What's going on, Callum? You're making me nervous, even more than I already was with today being Joey's board review." She refused to mention the elephant in the room, that it was also the day that Joey was scheduled to die.

He winced. "That's what I wanted to update you about. The board review. Even though the investigator Asher hired got Hagen to swear out an affidavit that he'd lied about seeing Joey with Alicia, the prosecutor is refusing to pursue perjury charges against him. His reasoning is that other witnesses said they thought they saw Joey with Alicia too. Even though they didn't swear they were positive about that under oath, the sheer number of witnesses who gave statements that they thought they saw him is overwhelming, again in the prosecutor's opinion. He doesn't feel it would have made a difference in Joey's ultimate conviction, even if Hagen hadn't lied."

Her stomach knotted. "If the prosecutor doesn't think Hagen's retraction would make a difference, what are our chances that the board will?"

He cleared his throat. "About that. I'm not going to try to talk you out of meeting with the board—"

"I should hope not. Wait, talk *me* out of meeting with them? We're *both* going before them." She searched his eyes, her stomach twisting even more. "Aren't we?"

"In good conscience, no. I can't speak to them on your brother's behalf."

She stared at him in shock. "I don't... I don't understand. Why not?"

His tortured gaze met hers. "Because I believe that your brother killed Alicia Claremont."

Before she could catch her breath over that statement, he continued.

"I agree with the prosecutor. Hagen's retraction isn't strong enough to convince me that a jury wouldn't have convicted him, even without Hagen's testimony. No other viable suspects are on anyone's radar. Joey's the only one who could have killed her. He had motive, and opportunity."

"What about an as-yet-unknown stranger as the perpetrator? Strangers do home invasions and kill people they don't know. Look at Knox, for goodness' sake. He didn't know any of the women he murdered. It does happen. The police just haven't found the right suspect yet."

"There's no forensic evidence that a stranger was involved—"

"And there's no forensic evidence that Joey was involved," she countered, hating the desperation in her voice.

He sighed. "Alicia wouldn't have opened her door to someone she didn't know that late at night. And there was no sign of a break-in. She'd met Joey in the bar—"

"No. She didn't." She clutched her hands together again. "Hagen retracted."

"Other people saw them, as we've discussed. And you

saw Rose's diary, those pictures. You saw what he did to her. You heard her say that even though she deeply loved Joey, she was convinced he could kill. We spoke to other witnesses from the trial, including experts, and no one has changed their opinions or their stories since their very first statements years ago. Your biggest argument for him is that his confession was coerced. The leading expert on false confessions said she couldn't conclude that it had been."

"She couldn't conclude that it hadn't been either."

"Raine—"

"Stop. Stop trying to convince me that my brother is a killer." She wrapped her arms around her middle.

"I don't mean to try to convince you of that. It was never my intention to take your belief in his innocence away from you."

"Then what *is* your intention?"

"I want you to understand my beliefs, that I have a different view of what happened than you do. And I want you to understand why I can't go against those beliefs. More than anything, I'd hoped I could find proof of his innocence. I wanted to give you that gift, to make you happy. But I can't."

"I gambled everything, I gambled my brother's life, on you helping me save him. And now you're refusing to do the one thing I absolutely needed you to do—talk to the prison board and tell them he's innocent."

"From the very beginning, our agreement was that I would investigate, that I would search for the truth. And if I didn't find anything to point to his innocence, I was done. I never lied about that."

She squeezed her hands together so hard they ached. "If you do this, Callum, if you refuse to go with me and speak to them about the outstanding questions, the doubts, Hagen's retraction, then it's just me. His sister. Pleading for his life. What kind of chance would I have? A family member doesn't have the credibility that you would. I need you. I need your expertise, your reputation in law enforcement. Callum, I'm begging you. Please. Just talk to them."

"I already have."

Her world tilted on its axis as terror flooded through her veins. "What are you saying?"

"I met with them early this morning and gave my full report."

"I don't… Full report? Why didn't you wait and go with me? What report are you talking about? You're not making sense. My God, Callum. What did you tell them?"

His pain-filled gaze searched hers. "The truth. I told them the truth, that I investigated his case and found nothing to justify me arguing on his behalf. I'm still taking you to your appointment. I don't want you going through all of this alone at the prison, especially if, well. I'll drive you there, go with you inside, be there for you afterward. But I won't go before the board and try to convince them of his innocence. I'm sorry. I can't."

"Get out," she rasped, her voice breaking. "Get out of my house. I never want to see you again. Ever."

"Raine, don't do this. We—"

"Get out!"

He stared at her a long moment, then stood. "I'm sorry. I truly am. If you need anything—"

"What I need, you refuse to give. Go."

He sighed, then headed toward the door. "Goodbye, Raine."

She ignored him, refusing to look his way.

The door opened, then shut with a firm click.

She crumpled into a ball and gave in to the sobs she'd been fighting to hold back.

Chapter Twenty-Three

Raine stood at her back doors, looking out at the view of the preservation area that once had given her peace. Now nothing gave her peace.

Three months ago, her world had been filled with new hope and possibilities. But a lot had happened in those three months.

Callum had betrayed her.

The board denied her appeal.

Her brother was murdered by the state.

She drew a ragged breath, the pain still so fresh it was as if it had all happened yesterday. Not the physical pain, the wounds that Knox had inflicted. Those were mostly healed. It was the anguish, the heartache that she doubted would ever heal.

So much had been left unsaid. Her brother had refused to even talk to her the day of his execution. Instead, he'd sent a brief note saying he loved her and to please remember him kindly. That was it. How was she supposed to heal the hole in her heart with a stupid note?

And how was she supposed to move forward when there was another hole to fill, the one left by Callum?

She blew out a long breath, then turned to study the progress she'd made in the past week. Most everything was packed into boxes and labeled either to be given to charity or to go into storage. The few things she was keeping would go with her. There was nothing left for her here. Her parents were gone. Her brother was gone. The long hours she'd dedicated to work and to the fight to save Joey had deprived her of any close friends. And the fulfillment she used to get from her job had evaporated. She'd resigned, cutting the last link she had with Athens.

Well, except for the Claremonts.

They'd always been so kind to her. Even when she'd told them that she'd finally accepted her brother's guilt, and apologized for the pain her ignorance and Joey's horrible actions had caused them, they only offered love and support in return. Never any judgment or condemnation. But even though they'd no doubt welcome her if she went to see them in the future, she didn't plan to ever darken their doorstep again. It was time to let the past go. It was time to move on, literally.

If she was going to live again, to find joy again, somehow she had to find a new purpose in her life. Saving Joey had been the impetus behind almost every adult decision she'd made. Without that need, that drive, she was floundering. Lost. And ashamed.

Because she missed Callum far more than she did her brother.

She'd loved Joey, still did. But time had a way of clearing the veils she'd had over her eyes for so long. Had they ever really been close? No. He was dating and partying when she was still in elementary school. They hadn't seen each other much growing up because he moved out on his own while she was still living with their parents. But he was all she had. And when that was threatened, she'd dedicated her life to fixing the wrong, to getting justice. But she was no longer sure what justice meant in Joey's case.

Everything Callum and the other investigators at Unfinished Business had found only supported her brother's guilt and reinforced what was said in the trial. And her brother had confessed. Was she too blinded by her own determination to see the truth? Her heart said no. But her mind, her logic, that supposed intelligence Callum had admired, all said something completely different.

That Joey had murdered Alicia Claremont.

She scanned the boxes piled high in her family room again. What was she going to do next? Where was she going to go? How would she ever find peace and happiness in the wreckage that her life had become?

The doorbell chimed, startling her. She certainly wasn't expecting anyone. It was probably a salesman who'd managed to sneak past the guard at the gate. It wouldn't be the first time.

She headed to the front door and looked through the peephole. A trim dark-skinned man in a light gray business suit stood there, a black leather satchel in his hand.

"Yes?" she called out.

"Ma'am, Ms. Quintero, my name is Noah Reid. Callum Wright may have mentioned me?"

She blinked, then slowly opened the door. "Mr. Reid. You're the one who helped Callum and me get to see my brother without having to wade through red tape. Thank you."

He smiled. "It's always my pleasure to help Callum. I'm forever in his debt. He saved my life once, nearly died himself doing it. Did he tell you about that?"

She shook her head. "No. He didn't."

"Well, that's a story for another day." His smile faded. "My condolences about your brother. I'm so sorry for your loss."

"I appreciate that."

He held up the satchel. "If you have a few minutes, there are some things that I feel you should know."

"Oh, of course. Where are my manners? Come in, please."

RAINE STOOD ON the unfamiliar porch checking the address on her phone one more time. This was the right place. But no one had answered her repeated knocks and ringing of the doorbell. She was sure she'd heard voices at some point. Maybe they were in the backyard? She'd come too far not to at least check.

She followed the stone pathway that led around the side of the garage toward the back of the property. There wasn't a fence, which was common in Gatlinburg. No one wanted to block their gorgeous views of the mountains. And as she rounded the garage, she could certainly appreciate the one here. The snow-covered mountaintops towered in the distance, and yet they felt close enough to touch. Beautiful.

"Raine?"

She turned with a smile to face Callum.

And the blonde woman beside him, holding his hand.

Her smile faltered. "I, ah, I'm sorry. I was trying to surprise you, but, ah, you've got company. I'll go." She turned and hurried down the side of the garage, humiliation scorching her cheeks. He'd moved on, and she was an idiot.

"Raine, wait." Strong hands grabbed her shoulders, then gently turned her around. Callum stared down at her, his gaze searching hers as he cupped her face. "Is it really you, or am I dreaming?"

"More like a nightmare." She pushed his hands away. "My fault. I shouldn't have shown up like this. I'll leave you to your...whatever she is." She turned around again.

"You mean my sister? Lucy?"

She stopped, then slowly turned to face him. "That woman? She's—"

"Lucy Cooper, Danny's wife. My sister. She and Danny came for a visit."

"And we were just leaving," a feminine voice said behind him. Lucy stepped around Callum and smiled. "My husband's pulling up right now out front. He just filled the tank for our trip back to Athens." She held out her hand. "You must be Raine. Callum has told me a lot about you."

"Lucy, don't," he warned.

"Don't what, brother? Tell her you can't stop talking about her?"

Raine glanced at him in surprise as she shook Lucy's hand. "You've been talking about me?"

"All good things," Lucy assured her. "Nice meeting you. Hope to see you again." She stood on tiptoe and kissed Callum's cheek. "Don't be a stranger. I mean it. We expect a visit this summer, if not before."

"We'll see." He was talking to his sister, but watching Raine the whole time.

Lucy chuckled. "Well, I can tell I'll be missed." She was still laughing as she moved past them and disappeared around the corner.

A moment later, the fading sound of a car engine indicated she and Danny had left and were heading down the mountain.

"How did you find where I live?" Callum asked.

"Asher."

"He never could keep a secret."

She shifted on her feet and tugged her jacket closer. "Could we go inside, where it's warm? It's much colder here in the mountains than in Athens."

"Oh, of course. Sorry. I'm just...surprised to see you." He led the way around the back and opened the sliding glass door for her to enter.

She stepped inside, barely registering the interior other than to take the nearest seat—which happened to be his couch. As he sat beside her, she turned to face him.

"It's nice to see that you're back in touch with your sister. How did that happen?"

"She contacted me a month ago to let me know my father was dying."

"Oh no. I'm so sorry."

"If I hadn't had you as an example of how to be supportive of family, no matter what, I'd have hung up on her. Instead, I bit the bullet and went and saw him. It's because of you that I was able to look past my stubborn pride and reconnect with him, with my family. We made our peace before Dad passed away. And I'm trying to rebuild the bridges with my relatives. Again, thanks to you." He stared intently at her. "Are you okay? I heard...about your brother, that your appeal with the board was unsuccessful. I really am sorry."

She swallowed and forced a smile.

"Is that why you're here? Your brother?"

"What do you... Oh, you mean to berate you or something? Blame you for him being executed?"

He winced. "It would be your right."

"No, Callum. It wouldn't be my right. You did everything you could to try to find something to show he was innocent. You did that for me, and I appreciate it, in spite of how poorly I behaved the last time I saw you."

His brow wrinkled in confusion. "Raine, I'm a bit lost. Why, exactly, are you here if not to curse me for betraying you?"

She sighed and reached into her purse, then pulled out a sheaf of papers. "I'm here about these."

He took them and scanned the first page, then the next, then shuffled through the rest before tossing them onto the coffee table. "How did you get those?"

"Your friend. Noah Reid."

He swore. "You were never supposed to see them."

"Why? Why would you not want me to see the documentation that absolutely one hundred percent proves my brother did kill Alicia Claremont?"

His jaw tightened but he didn't say anything.

"That day that Knox came after me, you went to the prison. Reid said he'd called you with information he'd been working to gather on my brother's case. And you went to look into that information and even spoke to my brother. No less than a dozen former cellmates of his, along with some prison guards, gave affidavits saying Joey confessed several times to them over the years that he killed Alicia. The kicker is that you spoke to Joey that day, and he…" A sob caught in her throat.

Callum's gaze filled with anguish. "Don't. Don't do this to yourself. I never wanted you to experience this pain."

"Joey confessed to you that day. He bragged about the kill, described the flowers on the back of Mrs. Claremont's closet, those books we found in Alicia's drawer, those glow-in-the-dark stars on her bedroom ceiling, other things not in police reports or in crime scene photos. The guard over-heard him. That's what one of those papers says. My brother couldn't have known those details unless he was the killer. That's why you told the prison board you weren't convinced of his innocence. That's why you wouldn't stand with me before them to plead for his life. What I don't understand is why you didn't show me the affidavits. Why not tell me the truth? If I'd known he was truly guilty, beyond a doubt, I wouldn't have gone to the board to argue for a stay."

He took her hands in his, his thumbs rubbing slow, gentle circles across the backs. "Because you were in denial. It was too much to deal with at the time. And I didn't want to destroy your last moments with your brother. I wanted you to have good memories of him. But I couldn't lie to the board either, and be the one responsible for him perhaps one day going back into society. It was a fine line to walk. I did what my conscience dictated. But I wanted to protect you too. Or, at least, I tried."

"Don't you see, Callum? You did protect me. Over and over again. From Knox, from things too painful for me to bear at the time. But I know the truth now, and I'm at peace with it. And I thank God that you followed your conscience. Because the real tragedy would have been if I'd managed to get Joey eventually released and he killed again. That's something I don't think I could have lived with. So, you see, once again you saved me. I was just too blind to see it at the time. But I see it now. And I'm here to beg for your forgiveness."

He stared at her in wonder. "You don't hate me?"

Tears dripped down her cheeks as she tightened her hands on his. "Maybe I did, or thought I did, at first. But even be-fore Reid came to my house to give me those papers, I'd let go of the hate, the anger. And I was desperately lonely for you. I was on my way back to you without even realizing it. All Reid did was give me an excuse. I love you, Callum Wright. I love you with all my heart. I just hope I haven't destroyed any chance that you might one day grow to love me too."

A beautiful smile bloomed on his face, lightening his expression and filling his eyes with happiness. And hope. And something else she was too afraid to name in case she was wrong.

"I love you too, Raine Quintero. I think I've loved you since the moment I found out you pointed an unloaded gun at me." He grinned.

"I wasn't wrong about what I saw in your eyes," she whispered through her tears.

"What?"

"Just kiss me, sweetheart. Kiss me and never let me go."

He laughed. "Okay, honey. For better or worse."

Her eyes widened as she stared up at him. "Better or worse?"

He winked. "Until death do us part. If you'll have me."

"If that's a proposal, it's the worst one ever."

"Marry me anyway?"

"Yes, yes, yes." She threw her arms around him and he kissed her.

And never let her go.

* * * * *

COMING SOON!

We really hope you enjoyed reading this book. If you're looking for more romance be sure to head to the shops when new books are available on

Thursday 9th November

To see which titles are coming soon, please visit
millsandboon.co.uk/nextmonth

MILLS & BOON